A LOVE STORY FOR MY SISTER

Jaishree Misra

HarperCollins *Publishers* India

First published in India in 2015 by
HarperCollins *Publishers* India

P-ISBN: 978-93-5177-017-6
E-ISBN: 978-93-5177-018-3

2 4 6 8 10 9 7 5 3 1

HarperCollins *Publishers*

A-75, Sector 57, Noida, Uttar Pradesh 201301, India
1 London Bridge Street, London SE1 9GF, United Kingdom
Hazelton Lanes, 55 Avenue Road, Suite 2900, Toronto, Ontario M5R 3L2
and 1995 Markham Road, Scarborough, Ontario M1B 5M8, Canada
25 Ryde Road, Pymble, Sydney, NSW 2073, Australia
195 Broadway, New York, NY 10007, USA

Typeset in 10.5/13 Adobe Jenson, Rockwell and Lucida Calligraphy at

'...displace, transmute, dissemble. Bring down the fogs of the imagination! What are novelists for?'

—Ian McEwan, *Atonement*

'You owe reality nothing. And the truth of your feelings everything.'

—Richard Hugo, *The Triggering Town*

Pia, 1997

I first read about Margaret Wheeler the week my elder sister was murdered. According to that newspaper they were alike. Which, in my opinion, was not correct at all. *Some* things were similar – like they were both girls and they were both eighteen years old but, apart from that, it was what Mum would call 'just bizaaah'. Well, for one, I sat and calculated in the back of my social studies notebook that they were separated by a full one-hundred-and-forty years. How can anything or anyone be alike after such a long time?

Actually, when I think about it now, many things felt just bizaaah in those first few days or maybe they only seemed like that because I wasn't getting enough oxygen or something. You see, the world had gone so totally still after Tara died, it hurt to breathe. It was as if the air had suddenly grown thin, like on a mountain top. I was dizzy for days, my lungs and chest just hurting and hurting all the time. But I couldn't tell Mum and Dad because they weren't doing so good themselves.

Now that five months have passed and everything is slowly cooling down (the temperatures too), I can see that it was only the inside of our house that had gone totally still actually. Not the city of Delhi out there which through our closed and curtained windows seemed clearly off its head with what Dad kept describing as 'media-madness', even though some of the craziness was just normal traffic and noise and stuff. Mum said – a bit sarkily – that Dad should have realized a long time ago he'd grown up in a pretty mad business, his father being a career journalist and all. It wasn't very nice of her to say that, seeing that poor old Dadu had passed away and couldn't defend his career choice. But that week Mum had been going at everyone like a Hollywood baddie with an Uzi, whether they were living persons or dead. All except Tara, that is. Dad obviously didn't like Mum having a go at Dadu like that but he didn't say anything to her. He just left the room and I think I heard him opening the drinks cabinet even though it was not six o'clock yet.

That whole week after Tara died, our house was really dark and silent, the only noises coming from the air cooler, humming and rattling in the back veranda and the sound of Mum's sobs starting up again when someone came on a condolence visit. But the minute the front door was opened, we could hear total jhamela outside, caused mostly by red-faced, sweating journalists clutching cameras and recording equipment, trying to barge into the house. Usha Aunty (our neighbour and closest family friend) once shouted, 'Those bastards will pierce our fortifications over my dead body.' Then, because she had said 'dead body' in front of Dad, which made him wince because of what had happened to Tara, Usha Aunty started jabbering non-stop. 'It's like they're in competition with Delhi's dust and heat in trying to creep into the house, these journos. But we're well prepared, aren't we, Nev? I'm sure we've thought of everything…' She tapped her right forefinger one by one against the tips of her fingers as she counted. 'Peephole for the front door, double padlocks on the back door, window latches, cotton-lined bamboo chiks which won't let even one sunray in, let alone a paparazzo's lens. Good thing I finally found a decent carpenter, hain na? Like gold dust they are these days, carpenters who even turn up for such small-small jobs. Gurgaon's high-rises are the new Mecca, na?' Here, Usha Aunty ran out of breath, so she stopped suddenly, peering at Dad through the half-dark of the evening. 'Is there anything else I should organize, Nev? Some food or chai or something?'

Of all the journos making attempts to get through to us, the scariest were those we couldn't see actually, the ones sitting inside a brand-new satellite broadcast van with a huge dish on top. This van had taken up a permanent position just beyond the wall of our otherwise boring colony where – as my now dead sister often moaned – nothing ever *happened*. Tara should have known that nothing ever happened because our colony (Press Enclave, Saket, New Delhi, India) had been built for retired journalists, although some who had passed away, like my Dadu, had handed down their houses to their children who were also mostly journalists. Or lawyers and teachers and other such high-blow jobs, which is why it was all so boring in the first place.

Only our family was a little different actually, what with Dad being a dentist and Mum an Englishwoman who had spent her whole time in India, trying not to behave like an Englishwoman, or 'a bloody pampered ex-pat', as she put it. I suppose Usha Aunty was also not the Press Enclave type either, since she was a five-star hotel manager who had never married (at the age of forty-two, imagine!) and who had moved from Mumbai to the house next door only five years ago. This was when her mother, the oldest resident of our block, developed an illness called demensha which made her sing old Hindi film songs loudly from her balcony, annoying the Khannas who lived on that side. Usha Aunty's father had been a film critic for the *Statesman* newspaper when he had been alive so maybe the songs came from there but the Khannas never got that. Mum said Usha Aunty was supposed to have moved from Mumbai to make peace with the Khannas but from what I could see she didn't waste too much time over this. In fact, she was grinning madly just yesterday when she commented that it must please her mother no end to finally have a proper audience which was now not just the Khannas but also all those journos standing outside. Usha Aunty also had what she'd once called 'a colourful past'.

She said this to Mum with a sort of cat-like smile and Tara later told me that it meant she probably had loads of affairs which I just could *not* imagine because Usha Aunty was really fat and comfy and not the sort of glam-sham filmy-heroine type who went around having affairs.

I don't know if those satellite vans managed to film any videos of my family because our TV, which – thanks to my brother, Neel – usually had a cricket game on at full volume all the time, sat silent through those weeks after Tara had gone, gleaming in the dim living room like a beast waiting to spring the minute our backs were turned. Newspapers were also banned – a most unusual thing, seeing that Dadu used to have three syndicated columns that went out in at least a dozen papers, all of which he subscribed to and chuckled over on Sunday mornings. After Dadi (or Granny Regina, as she preferred to be called) died, and we moved into their home to take care of Dadu who was just hopeless at that sort of thing, we grew used to having newspapers heaped high on every single flat surface. Stacks of magazines even became side-tables and shelves in our crazy old Dadu's house. But now that it was Tara's photos splashed all over the front pages of magazines and newspapers, and because it wasn't due to anything fantastic like any of us winning a Pulitzer or Booker (Dadu's *big* dream for his grandchildren), it was I suppose natural that all such publications should be banned from the house.

My mother, however, was evidently keeping track of the news, probably via Usha Aunty. On one of those nights when Mum had gone to bed early, I heard her telling Dad in a cloggy, teary voice that she had never even seen some of those newspaper pictures of Tara before. He replied in his usual soft-spoken way that they must have been taken at last year's Diwali party at the community centre or on one of our school trips. So that was *another* weird thing – that our teachers and neighbours were busy giving out my sister's photos to the media! It made me wonder whether newspapers paid for things like old photographs when a murdered person happened to be in them, but there was no one I could ask. When Tara was around, she was the person I turned to when I had questions that might shock people because she only laughed and pinched my cheeks. But before the thought of her not being around started to make my throat and chest start to ache again, I reminded myself of how bad Tara was at saying 'I don't know'. Most probably she'd have given me what the boys at school called a 'goli', i.e., totally wrong information, and I would be no wiser about the price of dead people's photographs. Then I scolded myself for thinking so disrespectfully about my sister when she had just been killed.

Dad said that it was precisely because we lived in Press Enclave that the journalists were so 'obsessed' with Tara's case. But Mum said that she'd have thought the media would want to protect one of their own, close ranks around the grandchild of a distinguished old journalist and all that. I was confused, because my parents were screaming at each other when this discussion was going on, when they really should have been screaming at the journalists, and I ended up hiding in my room and did not hear how the argument ended.

Sitting there in the dark by myself, and seeing the blurred flashing yellow lights on the satellite van beyond my window, I felt that I sort of agreed with Dad. It must have been because Tara was like those female journos you saw on TV every night – same kind of pretty face, same nice way of speaking English etc. – that they had all become so fixated on her. 'You see, Ellie,' Dad had tried to explain to Mum in that trying-to-be-calm voice of his that never, ever calmed her, 'there's a kind of fascination that arises from fear. You know the feeling of dread when you read a story about something that could happen to *you,* like a plane crash or a car accident. Unlike floods and droughts and things that only seem to happen to poor people. *That's* where this interest in Tara comes from, if you ask me. All parents of young girls in Delhi must know this could just as easily have happened to *them*. That, sadly, is the fascination.'

But Dad's theory was, as usual, not doing too great a job of calming Mum as she started to wail at this point, blubbing loudly, looking almost like a cartoon character with big fat tears spouting right out of her eyes. 'Oh stop *analysing*, Neville! I can't bear it, I can't bloody bear it! *Do* something! Get them all out of here. Please! Oh, I just want my daughter back, please, please…'

When my mother was crying for Tara like that, it sometimes felt like she had forgotten all about me but maybe I only imagined this bit. I tried not to mind that Mum spoke about Tara as though she was the only daughter she had when, in fact, Tara had gone and I was the only daughter Mum had. But more than once that week I saw my mother looking at me with a semi-puzzled expression on her face, as though trying to figure out who I was. It was really, really scary.

Well, thank God for Usha Aunty in those days. Not only did she visit us daily, before work and after work, and helped with my homework, she also did all our shopping and kitchen supervising and sometimes even some cooking. Everyone was making so much effort to protect Neel and me from the media buzz around Tara, but Usha Aunty made a mistake when she brought around some household supplies from Saket market one evening. She was only being her usual helpful self during, what she called, 'The Siege'. So, it was on one of those evenings, when she had just come in through the back door with a couple of cloth bags full of food, that I saw that newspaper piece about Tara and Margaret.

It was exactly six days after they had found Tara's body, a typical hot mid-summer evening. The small backyard was hot and brown at any rate, and lifeless too except for the dust that moved from one part of the compound to the other as though it too was trapped like us. It was a complete contrast to the view from the front windows that was busy with crazy traffic and all kinds of comings and goings and, of course, the flashing lights and blinding silver gleam of the TV vans just beyond the colony walls.

Usha Aunty dumped the bags on the kitchen table and went straight inside to check on Mum. To see what she had bought, because I was both hungry and bored of re-reading all my books and looking out of the windows, I opened the bags and started taking the fruit and things out. That month (May 1997) had been the hottest on record since the 1960s, I heard someone on All India Radio say. So, maybe to keep the mangoes from getting pulpy, the fruit-wallah had wrapped them up in newspaper. Of course, I immediately scanned that scrap of paper for news of Tara and at first saw nothing. I think Usha Aunty was giving strict warnings to the fruit and vegetable-wallahs to avoid using the front pages which, I heard her tell Mum, were all continuing to carry 'big-big pictures' of my sister. But then I suddenly saw it – a narrow column right along the edge of a page with a small photo of Tara halfway up. Wrapped around four plump yellow safedas, it was page six from *Delhi Today* – a paper we never normally read – and the article was written by someone called Dr Ornob Ghosh. The title was 'Stockholm Syndrome' and the words were followed by two big question marks. The picture was the same one we had in the hallway, alongside Neel's and mine, when Tara's braces had just come off and the photographer at our cousin Nina's wedding had told her she looked like a Bollywood film star, though he couldn't figure out which one. Tara told us that many times over dinner that night, the bit about the Bollywood film star, wondering which film star the photographer might have meant, until Mum finally asked her to shut up. We all knew what a big-head Tara could be sometimes.

My whole body started to tremble when I saw my sister's face, now small and crumpled on the dining table, beaming and grinning with all her straightened new teeth on display. No one in my family had ever done anything at that point, good or bad, to have earned a photo in the papers and, unlike my friend Gayatri at school, whose mother was in the Congress party, I wasn't used to seeing familiar faces in the papers at all. Maybe that's when it really sank in, the full and total terribleness of what was happening. So I quickly stuffed the page into the front of my shirt where my heart was really thudding. I could feel it scratching against my chest as Dad came into the kitchen and got himself a glass of water from the Aquaguard tap. He didn't add the whisky he'd recently taken to quickly sloshing in but stood holding the glass and gazing out at the dry, dusty yard outside. He seemed to have forgotten that he had poured out water to drink as he stood there gazing. While gazing, he also must have seen that the laundry-airer Mummy had brought back from England on one of her trips had gone wonky again but he just stood there and didn't go out to do anything about it. He totally hated wonky things – it was a family joke that they reminded him of all those teeth that needed straightening – but I didn't really expect that he would step out and sort out the airer. Not just because it was so hot but also because he'd pretty much stopped doing jobs around the house for a while now. Mostly he just did a lot of gazing out of the back window like now. I guess he'd have gazed out of the bigger window out front too if the street hadn't been crawling with all those photographers, one of whom had even managed on the first day to get a picture of Mum weeping on Usha Aunty's shoulder, using some kind of special lens.

So, with the living room curtained-up and TV-less, we were holed up in the kitchen and dining at the back and ended up spending a lot of time in our own bedrooms instead. Of course the dining chairs weren't the comfiest but really it was just all too grim, sitting around a family table that had a great big hole where Tara was meant to be.

Even after ten minutes of hanging around, Dad was *still* looking at the empty backyard as though there was a great big circus going on out there, so I decided to escape to my bedroom before he noticed my puffed-up-with-paper chest. I didn't want the same trouble Tara had got into a few years ago for stuffing two tennis balls down the front of a tight tee-shirt to create two round little boobies because she wanted to look 'sexy'.

I slipped quietly out of the kitchen and pulled out the newspaper only once I was in my room and had the door firmly shut. Despite the fan going full blast, I felt like a cake slowly swelling up in an oven, it was that hot. But I kept the window closed because mine was a front-facing room, very near the colony gate. The journos outside were making a right royal racket and even through the closed windows, I could hear them yelling things like, 'Ready, one, two … behenchod ready ho ki nahin?' and 'Live, arrey bhai, going live now!'

Maybe taking a tip from the journos (and the heat and the dust), a bumblebee who had been busy with Mum's marigolds in the window-box was now trying to pierce one of Usha Aunty's fortifications, head-butting the glass pane madly, but its zzz-thud-zzz-thud and all else faded away as I smoothed out the paper and tried to ignore Tara's happy smile while I read.

Pia, 2013

Not that I understood very much at the time of what Dr Ghosh had written about my sister; I'd only just turned eleven that summer after all. But I've wished many times since then that I'd had the nous to keep that bit of newspaper. I didn't, probably for fear that Mum would find it in my room, and I remember stuffing it into my knapsack and throwing it into the garbage heap outside my school the following morning. Pity, because not only would it have made a useful addition to my research folder, it would have also acted as a kind of keepsake, ghoulish as that sounds.

The thing is, if I ever looked for a starting point for many things, I would say it was that article. It really did kick off a series of events that shaped the rest of my life, without a doubt. At the time, I merely worked out that Dr Ghosh was not a medical doctor because 'Professor of Clinical Psychology, All India Institute of Medical Sciences' was printed in small italics next to his name. I could also tell that he was somehow blaming Tara for what had happened to her, though in a very roundabout way.

It was much, much later that I even began to understand what Stockholm Syndrome was. Not that I ever fully bought into the idea, of course, remaining ambivalent about that aspect of Tara's death for a long time afterwards. To be honest, in some respects I haven't gone past much of what I felt as an eleven-year-old; I'm still confused by the idea that Tara could possibly have caused her own death. She may have acted stupidly but when had eighteen-year-olds not done the odd stupid thing? But it occurred to me some years after Tara's death that if, in fact, she had continued to behave selfishly, she would probably still be alive. It was, ironically, what I feel sure was a generous act – the decision to come home, I mean – that might have cost Tara her life. And that, to me, was the saddest thing of all.

There were so many theories around what Tara did, many offered up by the Delhi Police who seemed more confounded about it than anyone else. From what I recall, however, Dr Ghosh's article was quite certain that Tara's was 'an extreme and tragic case of Stockholm Syndrome'. He had identified a woman called Margaret Wheeler as being one of the more positive outcomes of the syndrome, describing her also as one of the earliest recorded cases. 1857. I had no concept, aged eleven, of all the other events of 1857 – clearly Horrible Histories hadn't covered the subject – but what I did lodge in my head somewhere was the term 'Stockholm Syndrome', never mentioning it to anyone, as something told me that it did not make Tara look good. When, much later, I was able to research it a bit more, I found that none of the other victims of the syndrome mentioned by Dr Ghosh – Margaret Wheeler and Patty Hearst and Mary McElroy – had been murdered. But this was kind of glossed over.

Actually, I wasn't quite eleven that summer my sister died, but I was 'an uncommonly intelligent ten-year-old', to quote one school report. Despite the uncommon intelligence, however, many events of that year went over my head. And obviously I had no idea at the time of the part Margaret would subsequently play in my life. It may sound fanciful but there was certainly some kind of mystical connection, perhaps initially sparked by the fact that, like Tara and me, Margaret too was of mixed race. She was only one-fourth Indian, though, her father being British and mother Anglo-Indian. 'Half-caste' was the term used in many of the primary sources I had found in my research on her, which did not shock me particularly, given that the term was still used with little embarrassment in India, sometimes even to my face.

Anyway, it was my 'Margaret connection' and my early findings on her that, without a doubt, led later to my broader interest in nineteenth-century British-Indian history. That, subsequently, became my subject in college and took me back to England more often than those childhood holidays with my mother did. Margaret also kick-started my dream of becoming a novelist, so that was yet another somewhat fortuitous link.

At first, however, my focus had been only on that whole Stockholm Syndrome thing which apparently linked my sister to Margaret. Many years later, when I first looked up the syndrome on the internet, the same names popped up that Dr Ghosh had mentioned except, this time, Tara's had been added to the list. I remember staring in disbelief at the screen the first time I saw my sister's name there, and I remember too trying to rub it away with my forefinger but, by then, there were numerous sites that mentioned Tara Fernandez anyway. 127,230 search results, the last time I looked. Finding out more became a sort of thing with me after that. Mum wasn't happy. 'Couldn't you find something else to write about?' she asked once, adding, 'Don't waste your not inconsiderable talents on the past, darling, it's all too ghoulish.'

But I knew that I was onto something with Margaret's story. A sort of comfort, maybe, or understanding ... and answers to all those questions I'd been storing in my head since I was eleven. I'm still not sure about it but it was as if I would somehow be less angry with Tara if I could understand what had happened to Margaret. After all, hers was supposedly a *positive* outcome of Stockholm Syndrome, which Tara's certainly wasn't. Besides, I'd read in the *Hindu Literary Supplement* that novelists tended to write about things that puzzled them as a way of understanding them. So I told myself that that was what I was doing. I was setting out to be a novelist, after all, and Margaret represented so many things that puzzled me, especially that whole Stockholm Syndrome business.

How on earth could one fall in love with someone who had abducted and kept one captive? I'd read the narratives of women kidnapped during India's partition who may have exhibited the same syndrome; women who refused to go back to their villages when the two new governments tried to help families recover their daughters who had been kidnapped or raped. But those women, like Margaret, belonged to another era. They were victims to a whole set of restrictions that didn't apply today. It simply did not explain why my beautiful and bolshie sister had done that same senseless thing in 1997.

Tara's smiling picture still hung in the hallway of our house, frozen at eighteen, while I had long since guiltily slipped past that milestone. Eighteen. That was my sister's age when she was taken away from us, the exact same age that Margaret had been when she'd been captured too.

The Story of Margaret Wheeler

A Novel by Pia Fernandez

Chapter One

Cawnpore, 1857

Margaret stepped out of the barracks, blinking as she followed her mother into the searing yellow afternoon. The guns were finally stilled for the temporary truce that had been called and – like the curtains of smoke that had no breeze to blow them away – silence too hung heavy in the air.

What a contrast to that noisy first night of firing when the whining sound of grape-shot and brisk rat-a-tat of musket fire had been drowned out by the terrified screams of women and children who had never experienced anything like it before. There had been close to a thousand people in the camp on that long-ago day, far too many for the pitifully inadequate housing arrangements that had been hastily put together. It was easiest to maintain long-held hierarchies and so the Indian servants, who had loyally accompanied their masters, had to sleep in tents and mud outhouses while the Eurasians were consigned to exposed verandas.

Margaret, being General Wheeler's daughter, was

ensconced with her family in an inner room of the tiled building but that did not prevent the noise from penetrating through to them. Through the thick brick walls, she could even hear the keening of women who, on those first few days, had already lost husbands and children to rebel fire that just kept coming and coming. One major impact every eight minutes, she heard someone say. Some of the wounds had been frightful – in the makeshift hospital was a man with a ragged, massive shrapnel wound in his groin and a woman still alive but with her entire face blown off. Worse, though, than the twenty-day siege was the steady, unrelenting march of those dreaded diseases of cholera and typhoid that had the power more merciful bullets didn't of reducing their victims to sacks of skin and bone within days.

The advance of diseases was helped along by the unbearable heat – what else could one expect of Cawnpore in mid-summer? Like the other women, Margaret had been forced to stay indoors these twenty days to save herself from the gunfire. Now the June sun fell on her face and arms as though greedily seeking out pale, forbidden skin. She squeezed her eyelids together again, adjusting them to the brightness, and the camp slowly materialized, shimmering translucent in the heat. Her gaze went first to the dry well that sat in the shade of the spreading jamun tree in the eastern corner. So many people had been hastily buried in it under cover of night, but it was the thought of her own beloved elder brother, Wyatt, that wrenched grievously at her heart; especially that dreadful evening, two days ago, when his head had been shot completely off with a musket ball. He had been sitting and talking to Mamma on the veranda when the shot had found its target so cruelly, the impact spattering their stunned mother's clothes with his blood and hair and brains. Margaret had caught only a glimpse of her brother's disembodied head before someone had swiftly bundled her away but the image of a swollen ball with purple lips had burnt itself in her mind. The skin had already turned stark white, the face staring with glassy eyes, nothing like the laughing, charming expression her brother always wore. That evening they threw Wyatt's body into the well and then, with additional prayers, threw his head, wrapped now in an old shirt as though the careful packaging could confer a modicum of respect, in after. And Mamma, poor Mamma, standing some distance away, had not shed a tear. Margaret had watched her grow increasingly stony-faced these past three weeks, going about her tasks in the camp with a stoic air that seemed so wrong, so abnormal.

Finding the stillness unreal and curiously unsettling, Margaret's eyes flicked across to the distant barren dunes to where the rebels had set up their camp. But all was silent during the ceasefire, as had been promised. It was a rare chance to survey the scene and, almost unable to bear it, she now looked tentatively across to the other side of the compound, the corner housing the working water-well. The earth around it was still stained purple from the blood of those brave souls who had lost their lives trying to draw water for the children; those children, that is, who hadn't already succumbed to disease.

Oh, what a terrible June it had been – hell come to earth. And how odd that they had all been at church, Father Symonds droning on about hell fires, just as the trouble had started. The world, such a jolly, peaceful place, had taken only a few minutes to turn on its head...

Margaret had got ready that morning – what she now thought of as 'the last morning' – and worn her bright yellow grenadine dress before running out to join Mamma in the carriage. They had been driven to the church, even though it was but a short stroll away, the family having been delayed at breakfast by the late arrival of the man from whom Mamma bought her victuals. Bread and eggs and butter that came every Sunday from the dairy farm in the next village. Who could have imagined, as Margaret and Godfrey bantered at the table, that it was to be the final breakfast they would eat at the family table and that, within just a few hours, life was never going to be the same again?

On the way to church, they passed a small battalion of soldiers, probably on their way to the parade ground, and, even as some of them had touched their turbans in deference to her father, Margaret had seen the look thrown at her by one of them – partly admiring and partly insolent. He was that dark-eyed man she had noticed around the camp a few times before who wore his cavalryman's uniform with a certain carelessness and swagger, the small brass button at his throat invariably left unbuttoned. She'd thought nothing of his look then, of course (it wasn't the first time, after all), but she had subsequently agonized many times in the following few days when cannon fire from the rebel forces rang incessantly around them in the swirling, stinking dark. Why had she not told Papa about the audacious way in which that sowar had looked at her? Why had she not made more of it? Seen it as the signal it was of what was to come. But how had men like that come to hate them so? That was the really puzzling bit.

The church's congregation had first heard the cries while opening their hymn books with the customary rustling and clearing of throats. At first, Margaret had thought the distant shouting merely some commotion among the syces, perhaps caused by a brawl between them or a troublesome horse. But a sudden spate of what were either firecrackers or gunshots startled her. She saw that many of the others too were looking up in surprise from their hymn books. It was very unlikely that anyone would have the audacity to set off firecrackers when the British officers were at church and Margaret felt Emma's arm, linked with hers, grip her hand in frightened recognition that those were, indeed, gunshots. Despite Father Symond's call for calm, everyone except for poor deaf old Clara Partridge got up and rushed for the windows, Margaret and Emma among them. To her utter stupefaction, Margaret saw a small group of sowars on their horses, all of them holding rifles in their free hands, one of them shooting in the air. The man with the insolent gaze was amongst them, riding like the devil on a strong black steed and shouting instructions to the others. Once again, even from that distance, he caught Margaret's gaze as she stood at the church window, locking his eyes with hers as though to deliberately mock her. And, just as suddenly, the group of horsemen had all ridden off towards the Civil Lines, leaving only a cloud of dust in their wake.

Margaret, gripping the window frame, had found herself shivering in the heat of that hot May morning as the tumult that followed in the church was unprecedented – women and children screaming and everyone shoving everyone else in their haste to get out. Emma and Margaret, clinging to each other, managed to duck outside and, spotting the faithful Gobind Das bringing their carriage to the steps of the church, had run pell-mell for it. Lifting their skirts, they tumbled in and, looking frantically out of the window, Margaret saw her Pa running along, pulling Mamma after him. But where was Godfrey?

'Godfrey, Godfrey's still in the church, helping old

Mrs Partridge,' Mamma wheezed while hauling herself into the carriage and, on hearing that, Pa had turned back in search of his son.

The wait for them had seemed interminable as Margaret stared anxiously out of the carriage, searching for her father and brother, and scanning the horizon lest the horsemen should return. Other people had also boarded their landaus and gigs and some were already driving away from the church, returning to the safety of their houses. Others were running down the road on foot while some of the men on horseback were rounding up the stragglers. The poor servants looked terrified as well, running helter-skelter, yelling guttural cries, terrified eyes rolling. Some were shouting incoherently about the 'dushman-log', as though unsure of whether safety lay with their sahibs or as far from them as they could get.

Of course, everyone had heard of the troubles at Berhampore and Meerut last month, those incredible mass killings of Europeans, and Cawnpore – safe so far – had recently even sent reinforcements to Sir Henry Havelock in Lucknow's cantonment. But did today's gunshots mean that Cawnpore too was now going the way of the other stations? It simply could not be, given how popular General Wheeler was amongst his troops. They adored him, especially as he had married a woman who was half-Hindu and always made it a point to speak to his troops in their mother-tongue.

Finally, when Margaret thought her heart would burst out of its ribcage from the way it thumped, her father and brother appeared at the church door. Her mother let off a small moan of relief. Dear kind Godfrey had one hand around Mrs Partridge who looked ready to faint right away. Together with his father, Godfrey lifted the elderly verger bodily and carried her down the church steps. The women in the carriage shuffled up to make room for them as the door was opened and Margaret saw her father almost push Mrs Partridge through it in his haste. Patience had never been a virtue of Pa's and today he looked as though he was about to have a coronary, pink in the face and panting for breath. Ma, relieved to see her favourite son again, covered his face in tears and kisses, all of which Godfrey accepted in his customary calm manner.

Luckily, no Britisher had been killed in Cawnpore that morning, despite reports coming in from towns as near as Gajner of disturbances and mutinying by the troops, alongside more strange talk about Indian soldiers fearing forced conversions and gun cartridges being greased with the fat of pigs. Mindful of stories of unrest in the city and a recent mysterious outbreak of fire in the infantry lines, Hugh Wheeler had already started blockading an entrenchment on the plains to the east of the city. Now, after the morning's disturbance outside the church, he was taking no chances and insisted, via an urgent notice flashed around the cantonment, that all the Europeans and their domestic staff should move into those makeshift barracks with immediate effect.

Margaret and her mother were given less than two hours to return to the house from church and collect a few belongings together for the family. They had run from room to room, picking up shoes and bonnets and thrown them all higgledy-piggledy into a pair of gunnysacks. Margaret's mouth was dry from the fear but she was unable even to stop for a drink of water when they got to the kitchen and started to chuck fruit and food into baskets. Luckily, the bag of victuals bought in the morning had not been unpacked and so that was thrown into the carriage as it was.

It was in the midst of that upheaval that Emma had

come flying into the Wheeler house, her gown streaked with dirt, her hair undone and hanging in wild curls around her face. 'Oh Margaret, you're packing too. Please say you're coming with us...' she said, panting, when she saw her friend standing surrounded by baskets of food and supplies.

'We're going to the entrenchment that Papa and some of his sepoys are getting ready on the eastern side of the camp. Aren't you coming? I thought there were orders...'

Emma shook her head, her lip starting to tremble. 'My father insists on staying back in Cawnpore but he wants us to go to Allahabad. Mamma's brother, my Uncle Steve, is a vicar at St Mary's and he'll take care of us. Papa thinks we'll be safer there...' Emma started to weep at the horrified look on Margaret's face.

'But Allahabad's so far...' Margaret breathed, her voice choking in fear. 'And those rebels we saw, heaven knows in which direction they were headed. They could already be on the Allahabad road.'

'We're taking Babu's boat and going downriver. He's got Indian clothes for us to wear but luckily the boat has a thatch so we'll be able to stay hidden for the most part. Babu's been given Papa's old matchlock and swears he'll be able to protect us. He's going on about how I was a mere babe-in-arms when he came to work for us and how it's his dying duty to look after me as though I were his own daughter. Oh Margaret, please come with us...'

Margaret stepped forward and folded her friend's trembling figure in her arms, holding her tight. 'Darling Emma. I would have asked Papa at the very least. But I couldn't possibly leave Mamma on her own to look after Papa and the boys. Charles is still only a baby, don't forget.'

The two girls stood clutching each other for a few seconds before drawing apart. Both their faces were tearstained but Margaret's voice was calm as she wiped her friend's face with the palm of her hand and said, 'Godspeed, my darling Emma. Stay safe. We'll meet again when this madness has blown over.'

Emma nodded, unable to control her sobs. 'Right here in Cawnpore, where we've seen such happy times. We'll meet again, Margaret, right here, in beautiful Cawnpore, where we shall surely be happy once more.'

Pia, 2013

I lowered myself from the train at Kanpur station, clutching my backpack before me. Once steady on my feet, I hoisted it over one shoulder, shaking my head firmly at the eager throng of porters. Not that I relished doing the poor fellows out of business but I'd travelled around often enough to know that carrying one's own luggage is the fastest and cheapest route out of a railway station. I thrust my way through the disembarking crowds, noticing that Kanpur's station made for an especially grim specimen of rail travel. Nothing like the romanticized version of the Indian railway system I'd recently seen on a BBC travel show. To be fair to Michael Palin – that nice presenter Mum mooned so excessively over – it was the smell that was the really distressing part here, that sickly stench of urine and sweat, mixed in with the food frying at snack counters. Stink was not a feature that lent itself to a visual medium like TV, and Mr Palin was clearly just too polite to mention it. What had interested me more, however, was how he pronounced 'Kanpur' in the way all the old British texts spelt it ... Cawnpore. The accent hadn't changed much with the passage of the years then.

Unwilling to clutch a scarf over my nose, as I had seen many cityfied people do, I held my breath and picked my way past chattering family groups and mounds of mismatched luggage and lumpy hessian sacks of mail. I ignored the many curious looks received by foolhardy 'firangees' who braved the railway system, my half 'n' half racial mix inevitably leading to my being regarded as a foreigner. I minded it only sometimes because being mistaken for a firangee generally worked in my favour, Indians continuing to be annoyingly awed by white skin. Even worse were folks like my dad's extended family in Goa who refused to acknowledge they were a part of India at all. My granny Regina – when she had still been alive – had been one of the chief offenders, keeping the ancient Portuguese ancestry determinedly alive, underlining not just the 'good fortune' of being born toffee-brown rather than chocolate-brown, but never allowing anyone in the family to fall prey to the fashion many modern Goans were following of giving their children traditional Indian names. Curiously, it had been my English mum who had rebelled against that, insisting on us having Hindi names and telling us to address our grandfather as Dadu, rather than Grandpa Claude, seeing that we lived in Delhi 'and not bloody Manchester'. But she did draw the line at getting us to call Granny Regina 'Dadi' as Granny was way too feisty to take on. I now know that Mum had also copped out a bit on our names anyway, choosing easy to pronounce, semi-western names for us that no one in England could possibly struggle with whenever we were taken there as children. What had been a real source of irritation to me, however, was that both Tara and Neel had inherited Dad's dark hair and eyes and, most enviably, that mixed-race type of skin tone that turned a gorgeous golden every summer, while I'd got stuck with Mum's pallid colouring that was prone to the most dreadful attacks of prickly heat.

I abruptly halted my march down the platform, remembering the solemn promise Mum had extracted from me to prevent prickly heat attacks while travelling. Fishing out a pack of wet-wipes from the side pocket of my backpack, I wiped my face and the back of my neck which were, mere minutes after getting out of the air-conditioned compartment, already sticky with sweat.

I'd been to Kanpur once before but had travelled then in the winter months and in relative comfort, ensconced in one of a pair of Tata Safari vans along with an entire television crew. As a twenty-two-year-old rookie producer, it had been the most thrilling start to my career when I'd been asked to join a BBC team who were filming the story of the Ganges, charting the course of India's holy river from its source up in the Himalayas all the way across to the eastern coast where it emptied itself into the Bay of Bengal. The team had traversed the Gangetic plains, briefly stopping off at Kanpur to shoot a few sequences of the old leather factories on the riverside that went back to British times. The fact that I was half-English might have helped but, overtly anyway, it was the fact that I had done my MPhil dissertation at Delhi University on British-Indian history in the nineteenth century that had got me the job. Pure luck that I'd seen the advert in *India Today* and, obviously, I'd applied for it without a second's delay. It had been terrifically exhilarating to not just be offered the assignment but also to find that I actually knew more about the history of some of the places we stopped at than even the senior-most producer who was travelling with us. But the six-month contract came to an abrupt end when the filming was over and the crew returned to London to do their editing and scripting. I'd spent the subsequent two years scrubbing around the edges of Delhi's journo set, picking up the odd freelance assignment for *Outlook* and the *Hindustan Times*, thanks mostly to my journalistic lineage as Dadu had left a host of old friends behind in top editorial posts.

I dodged past an ancient cow that was sashaying down the platform as though firmly intending to board the train to Delhi. With a grin, I remembered how admiring the BBC crew had been of my insouciance with the variety of animal life that drifted in and out of that trip of ours. Once, in Allahabad, everyone had fallen about in amusement when we came across a monkey performing a consummate breast stroke up and down the swimming pool while hotel staff ran around the perimeter, unsuccessfully shouting and waving sticks. That story had tickled Mum on the phone but she had got cross when I went on to tell her of how I had gone on to befriend the monkey with bread rolls sneaked out of the embarrassingly extensive buffet breakfast served at the hotel. He was especially keen on the granary ones, I recall, grabbing them greedily off my palm. Poor Mum. What if she'd known that urban monkeys were in fact only one of the many dangers I courted on that trip? Passionate and often unprotected sex with a dark-eyed young BBC runner called Shiv had been another but that I certainly wasn't going to tell her about.

The funny thing was how Mum had weirdly gone all ex-pat and somehow 'firang' in her sensibilities after what had happened to Tara, almost as though she blamed the Indian half of her daughter for all that had happened. There were times when she seemed to have completely forgotten the ardour with which she herself had married Dad in the first place: the bundles of letters and faded photographs we had marvelled at as children that showed a hopeful young couple, he a dark-skinned Indian with Brylcreemed hair and she a chubby, rosy-cheeked English girl, both smiling sunnily into the camera as they stood on the windswept deck of the ship that had brought Mum to this country all those years ago. It was strange and sad how she had turned against that choice after Tara died, seeming to will herself to forget that wonderfully romantic adventure she herself had undertaken when she'd chosen to marry across continents and cultures, even making a conscious and deliberate decision to live in the country of her husband's birth. Mum, who had taken to Indian life as though born to it, wearing salwaar kameezes and learning to cook daal-sabzi, had, after Tara's death, done a tragic turnaround, using expressions like 'these bloody Indians!' whenever something exasperated her. Had she actually forgotten that she was surrounded by Indians, not least her own husband and children? Worse, there were days after my sister died when Mum could barely bring herself to speak with civility to poor old Dad, and some of their arguments when I was entering my teens had been pretty damned painful. Enough to put me off marriage for life. I'd go as far as to say that their arguments had probably even contributed to my becoming a travel journalist, providing me with a legitimate reason to escape home as often as possible.

I looked around me now, savouring that familiar old pleasure in seeing things that could not be further removed from my usual life. The magazine stall was fluttering with covers showing Hindi lettering and buxom women wearing great quantities of eyeliner – a far cry from the slick, size-zero nymphettes who stood with bony arms and legs akimbo on the covers of all those new glossy mags that were thrust at our car windows when we stopped at Delhi's traffic lights. It was oddly reassuring to know that small-town India still appreciated that curvy Indian look. The front of Kanpur station's main tea stall was lined with thick glass bottles holding syrupy neon-coloured liquids, behind which were cans that bore the more familiar logos of Pepsi and Coke. A sadhu in filthy saffron robes was leaning against a pillar, not begging like they did in Delhi but just sitting, waiting perhaps for a train that would take him to a big city where he'd probably start hustling the minute he arrived. All so fabulously chalk-'n'-cheese, despite being less than 500 kilometres from home.

I thrust the used wet-wipe into my pocket and adjusted the straps of my backpack that were digging into my shoulders. Then I trudged on, grimacing while remembering how different my last trip out of Delhi had been – an easy 2,000-word assignment for *Vogue* to accompany a glossy photo-shoot featuring sari-clad women carrying Hermes bags in a Rajasthani village. Except for a couple of daytrips out to the shoot, the 'work' had involved an unusually high-end stay alongside three top-class models at Udaipur's plush Lake Palace hotel and, whenever we had stepped out of our uber-luxurious environs, we were transported around in an air-conditioned Fortuner that had a boot stacked high with chilled mineral water bottles.

The reason I was now striding down a stinky station platform all by myself, however, was because I was on a completely private endeavour to finally try and finish the Margaret Wheeler story I'd started writing way back in college. As befitted the lot of a novelist, no five-star hotel suite awaited me, no crew banter and camaraderie and certainly no chance of an expense account. It was enough to even miss those willowy models with their sucked-in cheeks. In truth, I was content to be by myself. It was, as a matter of fact, totally appropriate to be alone for this particular project as I was going to need my full quota of emotional balance and fortitude to deal with my subject matter and even a friend or a boyfriend (not that I had one at the moment anyway) would have been unnecessary distractions to the whole enterprise. Besides, the chance of being able to scrimp and live cheaply was much so easier when I was travelling on my own.

A couple of literary agents I'd contacted by email had shown some interest in my growing manuscript but they had both said I ought to finish it before expecting publishers to take time out to read it. I touched the little flash-drive that always hung around my neck, my crucifix-substitute, precious back-up to the nine chapters already written. Forty-thousand words bashed out at varying speeds and levels of enthusiasm, whenever I had managed the time and energy ... it was, all said and done, progressing reasonably quickly. But, while browsing through my laptop on the train to Kanpur, I'd come to the gloomy conclusion that something crucial was wrong with the manuscript. I probably didn't need to anguish over what that was as I knew it was something to do with Tara and the shadow she continued to cast over my life. My beautiful, dead sister, whose absence affected my life so much more than if she had still been around. Sometimes I wondered if Neel felt the same way. Me, his pesky kid sister, he could safely ignore from where he now lived, halfway across the world, but Tara … Tara was the sibling who would haunt both of us for all time to come.

My walk down the interminable platform ended as I entered the station forecourt, a massive high-ceilinged space that was being cooled very ineffectually by a dozen rattling ceiling fans. There would have been no station when Margaret Wheeler first fled Kanpur but she would almost certainly have seen the rise of the railways towards the latter half of her life when she had come back to live here. It would have made it way easier for her to go to a British camp and contact the surviving members of her family but that she never did. Not that I was life's best advocate for strong family links but, whichever way I looked at it, Margaret's deliberate decision to run away forever from those who loved her seemed curious and unforgiveable.

With a feeling not dissimilar to emerging from a dream, I now looked around me at the seething mass of humanity outside Kanpur station, listening to the relentless, ceaseless cacophony of a crowd and feeling the heat of the June sun burn every bit of exposed skin it could find. For the first time since setting off from Delhi, I felt a terrible sinking feeling in my stomach. Where on earth was I going to start looking for Margaret in this unholy mess?

I headed towards the auto-rickshaws outside the station, having to physically shove past eager taxi drivers who were clamouring for my custom. The scootie-wallah I stumbled towards looked startled; of course he too thought I was a foreigner and most foreigners would opt for a taxi, especially in this heat. In fact, most foreigners would have had the good sense to not be cavorting about north India at all in the month of June. But, in my bid to fully understand the events of that summer 156 years ago, I'd purposely chosen to arrive in Kanpur at exactly the same time as the uprising had taken place. It was, as Mum had said, 'a form of madness', adding quite unnecessarily, 'Madness inherited, of course, from your father's Portuguese clan and their antic disposition.' She had at that point remembered one of her beloved Shakespeare quotes and raised her voice in that la-di-da manner she had when she was feeling British – 'Oh that way madness lies, daughter! Shun that, no more of that!' And, having delivered this shot, she had swiftly retreated behind her newspaper to close off all argument. Either that, or she knew it was no use trying to taunt me out of any chosen line of action. I'd proven over the years to be at least as strong-willed as my sister had been, though in a less dramatic way.

'Cantonment Road, Bhaiyya,' I said, clambering into the scootie.

I was pleased to note the driver zeroing his meter with a noisy clang before starting up the engine and taking off. This would never happen in Delhi. We bounced over the uneven car park of the station and, after exiting it, wove our way down the narrow, choked streets of the bazaar that I remembered from my previous visit to Kanpur. I peered out at the sari shops trailing their colourful wares like garish nylon bunting. Little headless mannequins were propped up on the pavement, dressed in children's party clothes; tiny faux bridal lehengas for girls and shiny polyester pyjama-tunics for boys. I had attended a Sikh wedding recently – that of an ex-colleague at the *Hindustan Times* – and had observed that even the tiniest of children were dressed to the nines in what may even have been miniature designer garb, the boys with slicked-back gelled hair and little girls wearing maroon lipstick and paraandis in their braids, looking for all the world like miniature practising brides and grooms.

It was only as my scootie left the crowded part of town and

bounced speedily into the army area that the scenery started looking less familiar. The BBC team had evidently missed the nicer part of Kanpur on that visit. Here the roads were wider, lined by large trees, and I could see generous-sized bungalows set back amidst shrubbery. Everything looked clean and well-maintained, dry leaves brushed into neat little piles every few yards. Cantonments were always well maintained but the contrast with the town centre we'd left behind was nonetheless remarkable. Not only were the pavements edged with white paint, the paint had also been run around the bottom halves of all the tree trunks that stood on the roadside, making them look like obedient schoolgirls in white skirts. I remembered from my research that Kanpur's was one of the few cantonments that had been left in virtually the same state it had been in under the British but that was only because the fighting had taken place elsewhere. In many other towns, it was the cantonments that had taken the brunt of mob fury during the Mutiny, their buildings destroyed, burnt and razed to the ground. Human capacity for inflicting cruelties on fellow humans was at one of its nadirs in that time, right down there with Nazism and apartheid, and Kanpur had seen some of the worst.

I took my diary out of a side pocket of my backpack in order to locate the full address of the place to which I was headed. All Soul's Church, Cambridge Road. I leaned forward to ask the driver if he knew where it was. He nodded, 'Kanpur Club backside.' He was obviously a man of few words, so I sat back to examine this place that, despite its history, still seemed curiously fond of its old British names. Looking out at a series of nondescript, boxy, concrete buildings, I wondered where all the historic buildings were, and if Kanpur's Treasury was still in the cantonment area too. From my research dates, I knew that it was at midnight on 5th June that the mutinying sowars of the 2nd Cavalry had broken into the Treasury before making off on horseback for the garrison's magazine, also manned by Indian troops. They had failed to report for duty after the initial disturbances and, after quietly regrouping under cover of night, they armed themselves and then stole towards General Wheeler's entrenchment in the darkness. It had been prearranged that Nana Sahib's troops would be awaiting them and, together, the allies silently surrounded the British camp on the entrenchment. After last-minute negotiations, the rebels had been joined by the sepoys of the 1st and 56th Regiments too, so by this time, it was a largeish army that had assembled to fight the British. Only the 53rd still stood by Wheeler at that point, although even he wouldn't have known for how long that would be.

I looked at the quiet road and the baking dun fields beyond and felt a sudden frisson to think that all those dramatic events had unfolded right here on this unremarkable soil, at exactly this time of year in 1857...

We arrived at the church and I searched in my purse for the right amount to pay. Handing it over, I added a little extra for what in Delhi would have been an unusually correct and legal use of the meter, and was rewarded with a sudden gummy smile. 'If you are wanting auto-rickshaw for sight-seeing, you call me,' the driver said, still insisting on speaking in English. 'I know all the sights for seeing and all the shops. My name is Abdul.'

He whipped out a small scrap of paper before scribbling a mobile number down on it. I pocketed it with a smile, not telling him just yet that I could speak Hindi perfectly fluently. It wouldn't have been much use anyway for, increasingly, many younger people seemed to be using every opportunity to brush up their English language skills, bumbling along even though Hindi would have been far less painful all round. Of course Mum would scoff: 'Aspirational India's zillion hopefuls. Where on earth do they all think they're going? Buckinghamshire?' Weary of battling the bitterness my caustic mother wore around her like a protective sheath, I'd long stopped trying to tell her that a typical twenty-year-old could more than quadruple his income by being fluent in English. Anyway, as scooties were going to be my main mode of travel around Kanpur, it was more than likely I would be meeting Abdul again before too long, so there was time yet for lots of free English tuition. I certainly didn't mind.

A plump man wearing a white cassock was now walking swiftly down the drive in my direction and so, climbing out of the scootie, I turned my attention to him. 'Father Kuriakose?' I queried as he approached the wicket gate to open it for me.

'Yes, yes, I am indeed Father Kuriakose. And you must be Pia Fernandez. I am so happy to meet you.' The accent was strongly south Indian and I found my outstretched hand gripped in a warm double handshake.

'I can't tell you how pleased I am to finally meet you, Father.' Despite not being either particularly good or godly, I genuinely shared the priest's delight at finally meeting each other after what must have been an exchange of at least thirty emails thanks to Yuni-net. 'What a massive help you've been with my research so far.'

'Oh it is nothing, nothing. I am happy always to assist a scholar. Now come inside quickly, quickly. It is too hot here.'

I picked up my backpack again, waving aside the priest's offer to help, and followed his frocked figure down the path as he continued talking. 'There is plenty of time later to see the church and Mutiny memorial. I have made all the arrangements. Let us go into the house now so that you can have something to eat and drink. They served you breakfast on the train?'

'Breakfast and lunch!' I replied. 'The food just kept coming.'

'Oh yes, service on the Shatabdi is most generous. Good good. Come, please come inside and meet my wife.'

I wondered if Father Kuriakose's house was a kind of vicarage or maybe a parsonage, these being mere words to me, the child of confirmed atheists. I had found the website of the Church of Northern India from a kindly soul who'd seen my repeated queries on Yuni-net and further research had led me to the fortuitously net-savvy Father Kuriakose.

The house that I was escorted into was a modern building, sprawling but sparsely furnished. I could hear the distant throb of a desert cooler and a damp breeze was blowing pleasantly down the hallway. A lady clad in a crisp embroidered sari materialized out of the murk.

'This is my wife. Elsamma. Elsie,' Father Kuriakose said.

She smiled warmly, although her welcome was quieter than her husband's. Her hair was pulled into in a small bun at the back of her head but her face was framed by escaping grey curls that jiggled pleasantly when she nodded. I was ushered into a living room and, parked on a sofa, took a long grateful swig from the glass of water that had been brought in by a maid.

'I knew Kanpur would be hotter than Delhi but this is something else.' I leaned forward to put the glass down on a lace coaster. 'What is the temperature here these days?'

'Forty-four degrees today, can you believe it?' Elsie replied. 'Very hot but by end June–July it will start getting sultry also. Then it is even more difficult to cope up.'

'You said in your email that you *wanted* to travel around here in the summer. Which is why I did not try to dissuade you,' Father Kuriakose said, adding, 'Elsie kept telling me to write and ask you to come in the winter when Kanpur is more bearable. It gets quite pleasant then, actually, and our trees are all flowering, rather than bare like now.'

I laughed. 'My mother was equally worried about my crazy summer holiday plans. But, honestly, I'm made of sterner stuff than you would think.' I cast a rueful glance down at my thin frame, clad today in loose cargoes and a linen kurti that was already clammy with sweat and sticking to my back like wet paper. I looked at Elsie as I wasn't sure how much she knew of my plans. 'It's not a pleasure trip, you see, but meant for researching this book I'm working on. June must be the worst time to come here but I really did need to see Kanpur as near to what it would have been like when the Uprising took place.'

'But it must have been such a different place in 1857!' Elsie exclaimed.

'Too right.' I laughed. 'It's a researcher's nightmare when you expect to see an old church or bungalow and find a mechanic's market instead. Luckily, though, some things don't change with the passage of the years. The seasons, for one, and the general landscape...'

'So it was in the height of summer that the 1857 war of independence happened?'

'Pretty much all of it,' I replied, 'although the last battle was at Kalpi in 1858, you know when the Rani of Jhansi died...' I trailed off, uncertain of how much detail Elsie wanted to hear of my research. But her next remark indicated that her husband had already told her something of my plans.

'I have been asking my husband and I must say it's all quite interesting,' Elsie said. 'But much more than Margaret Wheeler, I find the story of her friend, Amelia Horne, more moving. Poor thing, what she must have gone through, being kidnapped like that by a Muslim soldier.'

I nodded, remembering the harrowing first-person account I'd read in the British Library of Amelia's abduction and rape. 'That's so true but then Amelia did come back after the rebellion was crushed, which Margaret never did. That's what really fascinates me, actually ... the *reason* for which Margaret spurned her heritage, refusing to return to Kanpur even when the British Army was out searching for her. That's the bit that never made sense to me. After all, Margaret had been kidnapped as brutally too.'

Margaret's decision had certainly been more puzzling than anything my elder sister had done but I didn't tell Elsie that, of course. I hardly ever talked about Tara if I could help it. It was much easier to stick to the safety of Margaret's story.

'And she went on to marry her kidnapper, no?' Elsie remarked.

Stupidly, I was momentarily confused by whether she was referring to Margaret or my sister but I recovered myself swiftly. 'I'm impressed by how much you know about Margaret,' I said. Few people in Delhi seemed to have heard about Margaret Wheeler but perhaps Kanpur remembered its daughter better. Elsie was still looking enquiring so I addressed her earlier question. 'Yes, Margaret did go on to marry her kidnapper, even though it was very likely that the man was probably among those that had killed her family. Pretty baffling, really.'

Father Kuriakose chipped in here. 'I believe that poor girl was even forced to convert to Islam by her kidnappers. And yet she was subsequently seen willingly going to the North West frontier dressed in the clothes of a Muslim woman.'

I nodded. 'There have been eyewitness reports about that. And, even when the British, post-victory, sent out search parties for Margaret and promised her kidnapper amnesty in public announcements if he brought her back, she – unlike her friend, Amelia – never returned.'

'So strange and so sad…' Elsie remarked with a sigh. Then she smiled encouragingly at me. 'Maybe your research here will answer all those questions.'

'I certainly hope so!'

Father Kuriakose cleared his throat. 'So, in all your research so far you never found any letters or explanations from Margaret herself? Did she really just vanish after that?'

'Not vanish exactly because she did eventually surface, seemingly willingly living the life of a Muslim wife and mother in what's now Pakistan.'

'Maybe she was being kept captive,' Elsa offered.

I shook my head. 'Not for that number of years. And it's unlikely that an Englishwoman could be kept hidden anywhere in British India for that length of time anyway.'

'You told me in one of your emails that there may have been some letters written between Margaret and a friend of hers?' Father Kuriakose asked.

'Yes, Emma Clarke. But these are reported letters, only referred to in some of Emma's writings. I've never actually seen any. Anyway, it was a long time before Margaret made proper contact with anyone from her old world. In fact, over sixty years after she'd disappeared, a Catholic priest was summoned to an old haveli in the Muslim quarter of Kanpur to perform benediction on a dying eighty-year-old. That woman turned out to be Margaret, the daughter of General Wheeler and, when the priest had asked her if she had suffered in the years she had gone "missing", she reportedly smiled and said, "He was kind to me!"'

Elsie shook her head, sharing my disbelief. Margaret's was a story that always elicited feelings of shock whenever I narrated it to women. Sometimes I wondered how much of our reaction arose from a shared twenty-first-century sensibility. And then, of course, I thought of Tara again.

'Ah, before I forget…' Father Kuriakose got up to walk across to a cabinet. He opened it and took a small package out which he handed to me. 'The book and DVD I mentioned.'

I tried not to yelp in excitement. '*The Flight of the Pigeons*! Yes?'

'Yes, and *Junoon,* the Shyam Benegal movie I wrote to you about that was based on Ruskin Bond's story of the Uprising. And there's a similar storyline about a girl who gets captured in a Hindi film called *Pinjra,* I believe. I have asked the person in my congregation who mentioned it to try and get a copy of that for you too.'

'You're very sweet, Father, to use your entire congregation as researchers for my project,' I said, unembarrassed to praise this kind pastor whom I had so fortuitously stumbled upon and whose emails had been nothing but interested and helpful. Looking down, I examined the cover of the Ruskin Bond book. 'I read a review of this a long time ago, actually, but just didn't get around to looking for it in the Delhi bookshops. I shall be immersed in it tonight, I assure you. Thanks ever so much. How much do I owe you for these?'

'Ah, it is hardly anything,' Father Kuriakose replied, waving his hand.

'No, no, I can't have that!' I responded, thinking of a way to counter this. 'You will make it very difficult for me to ask your help with anything else, you know.'

'Okay, okay, we will add it to your bill when you leave Kanpur.' He laughed. 'But first Elsie will show you your room. You may want to freshen up and get some rest before doing anything else.'

'That's very sweet of you but I must say I feel far too excited to be resting actually…'

'Oh, no, no. It is much too hot to be going out just now,' Elsie protested. 'I think you should take some lunch and rest in the afternoon and, when the sun starts cooling down at four or five, you can go out.'

I had grown unused to taking such stern instructions, even from Mum, but I recognized the good sense in Elise Kuriakose's advice. It was not worth arguing with my hostess even though I was keen to get going straight away on my perambulations around Kanpur. 'I think you're probably right,' I relented, relaxing back into the cushions. 'Maybe I should go and get showered to cool off a bit. It was a rather early start this morning too.'

I bent to pick up my backpack when Father Kuriakose spoke again. 'Oh I nearly forgot to mention something that someone else in my congregation was talking about the other day. As you know, I have been telling everyone I meet about your research project because you never know where the next bit of information will come from. But this lady said that a neighbour of hers knows a Muslim family in whose possession there may be some Englishwoman's papers. She didn't recognize the name of Margaret Wheeler when I asked her, however.'

I shot a hopeful look up at the priest. This would be an amazing breakthrough if it was indeed something to do with Margaret. 'An Englishwoman's personal papers?' I asked, aware that my voice betrayed my sudden pulsing excitement.

'She was not sure they were personal papers, maybe some letters or diaries.'

I nodded my head vigorously, sitting up. 'Dare I hope they may be Margaret's diaries, or be those letters exchanged with Emma. Or perhaps even Amelia Horne's letters.' I turned to Elsie to explain. 'Amy, the Anglo-Indian girl we were talking about, wrote a detailed account of her kidnapping after she came back and, in one of those journals, she mentions a correspondence with Margaret. Margaret's other friend, Emma Clarke, escaped the Kanpur slaughter by going to Allahabad and both she and Amelia would surely have done their best to persuade Margaret to return to the British camp too once the trouble had blown over. Perhaps these are their letters. God, I'd be thrilled, obviously, if they were! You have no idea how much they would help in revealing what actually happened to her. Besides, if there are letters with this ... you did say Muslim family, did you not? Well, I may even find some of Margaret's living descendants. That would be beyond my wildest dreams!'

Father Kuriakose smiled at my animated gabbling. 'Well, we will find out soon. I have asked Mrs Masih to find out more ... the woman in my congregation who mentioned it.'

'Oh thank you, thank you, Father Kuriakose. How long do

you think she'll need to enquire about the papers, this Mrs Masih…' Then I laughed. 'Forgive me, you must think I'm so impatient but I warn you, once I get going, I'm unstoppable!'

Elsie got up with a smile. 'It will happen,' she said reassuringly. 'You will get all the information you need if the Lord has His way. Now come with me and let me show you your room.'

The Lord had been of very little help in my life so far but I reckoned it would not be clever to say this while staying in a vicarage/parsonage. Instead, I got up and obediently followed Elsie back into the hallway and up a set of stairs. Mum would have been astonished at my meekness. A landing at the top of the stairs led off into a couple of rooms but Elsie was now leading the way up another, narrower flight of stairs which opened up into a roof terrace. At the far end of the terrace was a small barsaati, covered cap-like with a dense green creeper. I saw that the plant was a madhu-malati as we neared and caught a whiff of heavy, cloying fragrance, ducking under tendrils laden with pink flowers.

'Oh this is charming,' I cried as Elsie opened wooden double-doors to reveal a small bedsit with a kitchenette visible at one end. '*Exactly* what I need.'

She looked pleased at my reaction. 'We got this barsaati made for our daughter when she was still living at home but it has been locked up since she got married. Now, when she comes with the baby, she prefers to sleep downstairs in the room next to ours.'

'It's just perfect,' I said, looking around at the single bed that was covered with a cotton bedcover. There was a small table, just the right size for my laptop, although the old-fashioned wooden chair did not look geared for long hours of use. It was all clean and thoughtfully put together, with even a two-seater sofa tucked under the single window and a small portable cooler.

Elsie walked across to push open a door that revealed a

bathroom. I peered in – it was basic, windowless and decorated in swathes of painted concrete that was peeling slightly. But I was not about to complain. For the pittance the Kuriakoses were charging for my two-week stay, this could not have been better. I turned to my hostess, 'Thank you,' I said. 'You and Father Kuriakose have been absolutely wonderful so far. You'll have to tell me if you'd mind being mentioned in my list of acknowledgements when the book is published!'

Elsie shrugged, embarrassed, and left soon after ordering me to unpack and unwind. I looked around once more, suppressing the happy squeal that was rising within me. When I had written to Father Kuriakose asking for help with finding a decent place to stay, and he had offered his own guestroom, it had been difficult to know what to expect, but this … this little barsaati surpassed all expectations. Not least because it was so near where so much of the action had taken place, all of which would hopefully soon go into my book. I was dead pleased the God connection hadn't put me off during my early communication with Father Kuriakose. I recalled how tickled Neel had been when he'd heard from Mum of my plans to stay with a priest in Kanpur, WhatsApping some joke about born-again Christians.

I pushed open the window to examine the view. A gust of warm wind blew into the room but, with eyes screwed up and squinting against the midday sun, I looked out at the Kanpur landscape. From here, I could see the front of the church and a stretch of open land beyond. The earth looked cracked and parched, with barely any green to break the monotony. A stray dust-devil was the only thing moving in that shimmering hot landscape. The few trees that stood in the church compound were denuded down to half their leaf cover and even these poor leaves were covered in a fine coating of dust. Just one tree stood in glorious yellow bloom – some kind of laburnum, I guessed. Trees were Dad's thing really, not mine, and I was usually only half-listening when he pointed out the different varieties on our morning walks around the deer park near our house.

I closed the window, conscious of needing to keep the blazing midday heat at bay. The single ceiling fan that Elsie had switched on as soon as we had entered the room was circling in desultory fashion, chucking down gusts of unpleasantly hot air. I examined the new-fangled cooler to figure out its workings. There was a small hole with a plastic plug that said 'water', so I went into the bathroom, emerging with a mugful from the tap. Once I had poured the contents into the hole and re-plugged it, I switched the contraption on and was pleased to feel a blast of cool air swirl around my legs. Without further delay, I yanked off my clothes and walked in my bra and panties towards the bathroom. Standing under a rather weak jet of lukewarm water a few minutes later, I squeezed a generous blob of shower-gel into my palm, trying to think of what it would have been like for poor Margaret and the others holed up in General Wheeler's entrenchment just up the road from here to have been stuck without water in the heat of that terrible siege...

The Story of Margaret Wheeler

Chapter Two

Margaret held the damp cloth against Godfrey's burning forehead. It was filthy and stained with someone's blood but there wasn't enough water to wash the bandages out properly. And it was far more important to somehow bring her poor brother's raging fever down than worry about the state of the bandages. All normal standards of hygiene had been suspended for weeks anyway.

It was abundantly clear by now that her father would never forgive himself for his grievous error of judgement regarding the camp's water supply. The solitary well on the entrenchment lay exposed on the western flank and was, as a consequence, in full view and firing range of the enemy forces. In the early days, there were casualties every time some brave soul ventured out to haul up a bucket and so a policy had been made to pull water up only under cover of night. On hot days like this, though, when children lay on their sickbeds, pleading in small cracked voices for water, it was only understandable that the precious stocks would have dwindled by afternoon. Yesterday a frightful row had broken out between Eileen Frazier and Charlotte Primm, both of whose babies were suffering from typhoid and in grave need of medical help. The poor women knew that there was little point squabbling with each other over water and what little was left of the medicines but Margaret could not imagine what it must be like for such young mothers to be faced with the sure knowledge that their children were dying before their eyes. The only doctor on the camp – Dr Aitken – was running a fever himself but, sternly refusing to lie down, he continued to do his rounds, stopping once in a while only to sip on a cup of water. Both chaplains had lost their lives in the first two weeks so now there was no one left to pray properly for the dead.

Margaret felt Godfrey's head stir in her lap. He groaned, his lips chapped so badly they were cracked and bleeding. Margaret bent down to whisper into his ear, 'What is it, darling? Is it water you want?'

Godfrey's soft grey eyes, now rheumy like an old man's, stared up at her as though trying to remember who she was. 'Water?' she asked again.

He moved his head slightly, trying to nod. She dipped one end of the bandage into the cup by her side before squeezing out a couple of drops into the side of his mouth. His tongue flickered out, greedily searching for the precious liquid, before he closed his eyes again. Margaret cast a glance down at her brother's thigh, still suppurating from the shrapnel wound he had taken a week ago. With no disinfectant left in the medical supplies, it was refusing to heal and was now turning gangrenous. That, Dr Aitken had said, was the cause of Godfrey's fever. Poor, kind Godfrey, who had insisted on fetching water from the well when it wasn't dark enough … Margaret swallowed back angry tears. Sitting around and crying, like Amy had spent most of the week doing, was not going to achieve anything, was it? It certainly wouldn't help Godfrey, nor bring Wyatt back.

Margaret eased her brother's head off her lap and

placed it gently on a makeshift pillow fashioned out of her spare gown. She had not changed out of the yellow grenadine one she had been wearing when they came to the camp, except that it was by now dark brown from the grime and blood of those she had been tending to these past few days. If she stopped to reflect on the number of people she had seen die these past three weeks, she would go mad. Worse, once they had died, there was no way of giving them a proper burial and so these days bodies were merely dragged across to the disused well before being thrown in with a swiftly muttered prayer.

After Godfrey had settled back into an uneasy sleep with a small frown creasing his forehead, Margaret got up to go and help her mother in the kitchen. The camp's kitchen had been set up in a small outhouse that was, fortunately, shielded from the enemy's view by a couple of the stables and privies. Margaret ducked from one building to another, as was her habit, using Godfrey's damp handkerchief to wipe her hands as clean as they could get. Mamma was supervising one of the khansaamas who was stirring a watery gruel of flour and water in a pot while, in a far corner of the kitchen, Amy sat snivelling as she made a hash of kneading a ball of dough. Margaret tried to contain her irritation. She and Amy had never been close back in their days in the camp but, since moving to the entrenchment, they had made a sincere effort to befriend each other. Margaret missed Emma dreadfully and Amy was the only other girl here who was her age. But Amy was such a terrible cry-baby and, more than once, Margaret had had to give her a stern talking-to because her rather overdramatic manner and uncontrolled tears often set the children off until the whole roomful was left wailing.

Now she contained her annoyance and walked up to

Amy to sit down next to her and put an arm around her shoulders. After all, both Amy's mother and stepfather had died only a few days ago, buried under falling masonry when the building in which they had taken refuge was hit. This had left poor Amy orphaned as she had lost her father many years ago when she was only a little girl. Margaret was suddenly painfully conscious that, despite Wyatt's shocking death, she still had both parents and two of her younger brothers alive and near her. Her two older brothers were stationed in Bombay and no one knew yet if they were alive or dead. She knew her mother worried about them all the time, even though she said nothing. There had been no news from anywhere for days now and, who knew, they might be the last surviving Europeans left after the carnage.

'Here, take this and wipe your hands, Amy. I'll finish off the dough for you, if you like.' Margaret handed Amy the damp rag she had been carrying.

Amy threw her a grateful look as Margaret pulled the platter of dough towards herself. 'Thanks, Margaret,' she whispered, adding, 'I just can't stop thinking of my poor mamma being dead and how alone I am in the world now.' Her pointed chin crumpled briefly and Margaret felt another wave of sympathy.

'Come, Amy, you're not alone. Not when you have all of us,' Margaret said as evenly as she could. Then she added more emphatically, 'Look, you'll never be on your own as long as the rest of us are alive. You know that.'

Amy started to sniffle again but was stopped by a sudden flurry at the door. It was General Wheeler coming in, accompanied by an elderly Englishwoman. Everyone in the kitchen paused to take in this unusual occurrence as the general had far too much on his hands to ever stop by the kitchen. The elderly lady was an unfamiliar figure too and Margaret quickly guessed that she was another emissary being sent with a message from Nana Sahib's army outside. He had, this past week, twice sent elderly Englishwomen who were in his captivity with messages to General Wheeler's forces to surrender. On the last occasion, her father had sent the envoy back with a terse refusal but Nana Sahib was obviously keeping the pressure up. Margaret could not help wondering if her father would crack this time; they were so very close to the edge.

'Frances,' Hugh Wheeler said to his wife, 'This is Mrs Jacobi. Like Mrs Greenway last week, she too brings a message from Nana Sahib. Do we have a cup of tea to give her?'

Margaret knew the tea stocks were nearly finished but she saw her mother nod before carefully pouring out a cup of water into a saucepan.

'Oh that's kind,' Mrs Jacobi said, looking around the blackened kitchen with barely masked horror. Margaret could see her thinking that she was probably better off in Nana's captivity than here at the British camp. 'You poor people have suffered untold miseries here, I can see,' she blurted, adding hastily, 'How brave you have been, how brave.'

The Wheelers ignored the compliment, both of them too exhausted by their three-week siege to respond in a positive fashion. The number of deaths – first to the firing and disease and now to drought and starvation – had recently become too many to even keep track of.

'What is Nana Sahib offering?' Frances Wheeler asked.

'Oh it's a remarkable offer,' Mrs Jacobi said, with a slightly dramatic air, as she sat down with a flourish of her skirts. Margaret could tell that the old woman was curiously relishing her role of mediator. 'You see, the

Nana can't advance any closer because of your gunpowder-filled trenches. Besides, his own troops are tiring in this heat. An everlasting stand-off like this isn't going to do anyone any good, is it?' She was taking her role with great earnestness indeed. Margaret noted, too, that her parents continued to remain discreet about the rumoured gunpowder trenches that Mrs Greenway had also alluded to. They certainly weren't going to disabuse anyone from Nana's camp about a falsehood that was providing them with such fortuitous protection.

Hugh Wheeler was speaking now and Margaret noticed that a small crowd had formed outside the kitchen door – British and Indian jostled together, the remaining survivors of the siege, all desperate to know if salvation was finally on its way. Her father was probably at least partially addressing them as he said, 'Well, Nana Sahib is apparently offering safe passage to Allahabad. He wants done with this siege, according to Mrs Jacobi. Just wants us out of Cawnpore so that he can expand his territory beyond Bithur. Typically opportunistic, so I don't suppose he wants trouble.'

'What sort of passage?' Frances asked.

Mrs Jacobi was quick to respond this time. 'River boats,' she said. 'Sixty of them ... more even ... depending on how many of you decide to go. I would recommend you all do, of course. Safety in numbers. Of course, I too have asked for an official reprieve so that I can travel with you to a British camp in Allahabad.'

There were murmurs around the kitchen and from the growing crowd at the door. This was what everyone had been waiting to hear. But could one trust Nana? Margaret decided to ask the question that was probably on everyone's lips. 'Do you think his offer is a ploy, Papa?' she asked.

Hugh Wheeler, not normally a waverer, looked

uncertain. Before the siege, he had had a few dealings with Nana Sahib, the Maharaja of Bithur, who had always come across as pleasant and affable even in the months he had spent bargaining with the British to be allowed to keep the pension that his father, the Peshwa, had been awarded. But it was worth remembering that Nana's many petitions had been rejected and that was probably why he had been so quick to lead the renegades against them as soon as the uprising had started. Who knows, he might even have instigated the mutiny here in Cawnpore. Certainly, his right-hand man, a Muslim called Azimullah, who had gone as far as the Parliament in London with the Nana's petitions, absolutely hated the British. There had never been anything secret about that. But, if all that the Nana now wanted was for them to leave Cawnpore, it might work in their favour too. Once the British forces had had a chance to recoup their energies and gather further resources together, they could plan a return to the city in order to recapture it. That would be the sensible way forward. But there was still much to worry about, given the reports trickling in from Meerut of a large-scale massacre of Europeans. It was hard to know if those stories were true or merely part of Nana's propaganda.

'Well, Nana Sahib has no reason to want us captured,' Hugh Wheeler said finally, although his tone was not as confident as it should have been.

'Nothing at all to gain by keeping you here at Cawnpore,' Mrs Jacobi chipped in. 'You'd be less of a bother to him downriver at Allahabad. He grumbles sometimes at how much it costs him to keep Mrs Greenway and me in the manner we are accustomed to. And we don't make it easy for him either, no siree!'

While Hugh Wheeler hesitated, looking at his wife's face for some hint of her own feelings, there was a commotion at the door. One of the children came barging in. He was babbling so loudly he was almost incoherent. 'Margaret, quick! It's Godfrey!' he shouted. 'He's choking, gone all blue in the face … come quick!'

Margaret dropped the ball of dough onto the table and ran out of the kitchen. Suddenly uncaring for all else, she pushed past the people who were in her way, shouting for Dr Aitken. Her heart was thumping like a cannon gone mad as she ran into what had become the makeshift hospital, terrified of what she would find. There had been so many deaths these past three weeks, she was almost inured to them now. But not Godfrey, please God, not Godfrey! Margaret forced the rising tears back down in her throat … she had to be strong … but, more than any of her other siblings, it was Godfrey's loss she simply would not be able to bear. They had grown up together, being so close in age. 'Two brown peas in a pod,' Mamma had often said when they turned up all dusty and hungry at the kitchen door after play.

Dr Aitken was already at Godfrey's bedside but one look at the doctor's slumped shoulders as he dropped his stethoscope and turned away from the boy told Margaret all she needed to know. She fell to her knees and frantically shook her brother's prone body but his head lolled lifelessly on the pillow. How cruel, how cruel was this fate to rob her of two siblings in the space of a few days! First Wyatt and now Godfrey, her inseparable childhood companion.

'Godfrey, please! Wake up!' Margaret screamed before she repeated the words in a whisper, pressing her face hard against her brother's, as though hoping to give him her own breath. She could feel people gathering behind her in sympathy. A few of the women had started to whimper and cry; Godfrey had always been popular for his kindness, especially to the elderly and the children. From somewhere in the crowd a low moan emerged that grew into a loud heartrending wail. Margaret did not need to turn around to see that it was her mother finally breaking down. She had been a rock of support to so many of the other mothers who had lost their children, seeming to cope with Wyatt's terrible death by cloaking herself in silence but now Godfrey … Margaret wondered, with a sudden clutch of terror, how many more losses lay ahead.

Pia, 2013

I woke from a restive afternoon nap, sweating behind my neck. I must have been dreaming … Mum's face was floating before my eyes, wearing that reproachful look she usually put on whenever I announced solo trips out of Delhi. I'd grown inured to her many objections to my travels over the years, learning to deftly sidestep them. It was strange that, while Tara's death all those years ago had reduced Mum to a state of permanent nervous apprehension, it had made me more belligerent than I might otherwise have been. I had always refused to be cowed or frightened by that horrible early experience, going out and taking on life with a kind of pugnacious stubbornness and sometimes doing things that were – even I had to admit – downright risky.

I lay blinking for a few moments, disoriented by the extreme heat, gradually remembering that I was not in Delhi but in Kanpur. It was so hot, even the back of my knees were damp with sweat. The cooler was whirring with a dry rasping sound; it had obviously run out of water hours ago and was now pumping hot air. After my shower, I had fallen asleep still clad in my bath towel but I could not tell now if its dampness was from the bath or my perspiration. Getting up, I stumbled to my backpack and pulled out a modest, knee-length cotton dress. Buttoning it up, I hurriedly pushed my feet into a pair of stout walking sandals and ran a brush through my tangled hair before tying it back with a band. It would be well past five and I was conscious that there would only be another couple of hours of light left. Because of where I was stuck in my manuscript, it was important to get to Satichaura Ghat, the spot where Margaret had last seen her parents. Hopefully being there, at that very site on the river where the carnage had taken place, would help jog the narrative along again. In one of his emails, Father Kuriakose had told me that the locals still called it 'Mashkar Ghat', an odd word, he had said, that meant nothing in Hindi until he had worked out that it was a mangled version of the English word 'massacre'.

The first floor of the house was quiet, not a soul in sight, and so I went further down the stairs to the ground floor. Here, there were sounds of pots and pans coming from behind a pair of double doors and so I skirted past the dining table, decorated with greying lace doilies, and tentatively pushed open the door to what turned out to be the kitchen. Elsie Kuriakose was standing by a large hob, frying something in a large kadhai. Her face was flushed from the heat but she smiled when she saw me.

'You've woken up,' she said. 'Good, so you can have a cup of tea with something to eat. My husband has gone out with some church visitors from Delhi but he will join us for dinner later.'

'Are those pakoras? They smell delicious,' I said. 'Actually, would you mind very much if I skipped tea? I have a couple of places I want to see before it gets too late.'

'But how will you go? Father Kuriakose is not here to take you.'

'Oh I'll manage, don't worry. I certainly don't expect Father Kuriakose to traipse around everywhere with me. In fact, the scootie wallah who brought me here has given me his number so shall I just try calling him?'

Elsie looked relieved. 'That is a very good idea. So you won't have to go off in search of an auto by yourself. Cantonment area is not good for getting auto-rickshaws and, sometimes, Kanpur itself is not so safe for young girls like you, you know.'

I took it that Elsie was referring to my pale skin and cotton dress when she said 'young girls like you'. She was absolutely right that Indians didn't usually look at me and feel a huge kinship and I could hardly hold it against her for expressing exactly the kind of concerns my mum did when I was out and about in Delhi. But, despite everything, I had remained stubbornly determined to think of men as, by and large, a harmless species. Of course, those who had come out from the numerous small towns and villages surrounding Delhi tended to stare, both out of curiosity and perhaps admiration ... well, that was the most positive angle I could come up with. But I'd found on my many travels that all it usually took was a little effort to engage gawping men in a bit of Hindi chit-chat and they soon turned all matey and helpful. There was no convincing Mum, however, who only shuddered expressively when I offered her my strategy.

I opened the small purse I had slung around my neck to search for the scrap of paper on which I'd written the scootie man's phone number. Fishing it out along with my phone, I keyed in the digits and decided to open up in Hindi. 'Hello? Abdul? I am the person you picked up this morning. We went from the station to the cantonment church, remember?'

The man recognized me but was clearly puzzled. 'Yes I remember you. But how you are speaking Hindi and also English?' His tone was approving as well as semi-accusing.

I laughed. 'Bhaiyya, I *am* Indian. Not firang, although I know I look like one.'

This was accepted with a small laugh. There were, after all, a number of Indians with fair skin and light eyes so I didn't need to go into that whole incredulous 'you are half-caste' thing. 'Achha, I need to go out now,' I continued. 'From the church where you dropped me. To Satichaura Ghat this time. Are you nearby by any chance? Near the cantonment? Can you come soon? ... Oh that's good!'

I hung up as all Abdul's replies had been unhesitatingly in the affirmative and turned again to Elsie, sounding a bit surprised myself. 'That's sorted, I think! Well, he says he'll be here in ten minutes.'

Elsie swiftly bagged up what turned out to be banana fritters and not pakoras, handing an oil-stained paper package to me. 'When you travel you always get hungry, no? Satichaura Ghat is not that far but you may want to go walking up along the river. The government is trying to build a few walkways here and there. This is if you get hungry.'

I took the bag gratefully. 'Thank you ... these will be delicious when I'm sitting by the riverside. Well, I'll go wait for the scootie in the front room, shall I? He said he wasn't far.'

'Sure there's no time for a cup of tea?'

I nodded. 'Perhaps I can take a bottle of water for when I eat these. I'll go and fetch mine from upstairs.'

'No, no, don't go all the way up the stairs again. Here, just take this.' Elsie handed me an empty mineral water bottle and added, 'You'll find filtered water in that small tap by the side of the sink over there. Or just take some from the fridge.'

I filled the bottle up, listening to the language passing between Elsie and her maid. I discerned the lilt of Malayalam. Screwing the cap back onto the bottle, I smiled at Elsie. 'You're from Kerala. I recognized the language.'

Elsie nodded. 'You know Malayalam?'

I hastily shook my head. 'I spent two weeks down in Kerala once – Trivandrum, Kovalam, went as far up as Alleppey and Cochin – but the only words I learnt to say were "meen", because I adored the fish curries there, and, of course, "vellum",' I said, waving my bottle of water in the air.

'Oho, that is very good!' Elsie cried, turning to her maid to explain what I had just said. They chattered between them some more in Malayalam while the maid looked curiously at me but my attention was now on the sound of a scootie coming down the road. 'Ah, yes, that must be your auto fellow,' Elsie said as we heard the gate latch being opened and an auto come spluttering down the drive. 'Good, so now you will be able to go for your trip up to the river and come back here before it is too dark. You *must* come back before it is dark, okay?'

I grinned and nodded. Elsie's bossiness was too kindly to be offensive; I would have to get used to it if I was going to stay in her house for a few weeks. I picked up my things again. 'Well, I'm off then. And, don't worry, I don't plan to be out too late. See you later!'

I ran down the corridor that joined the kitchen to the living room and let myself out of the front door. The day was still surprisingly hot, despite the sun now hanging low and deep orange in the dusty sky. The scootie-wallah had been as good as his word and seemed just as pleased to see that I had kept mine in summoning him again so soon. 'Hello, Abdul, you came quick,' I said in cheery Hindi.

'Hello, good evening, Madam,' the man replied, insisting on sticking with English in that 'aspirational' way which so irritates Mum.

I saw no harm in helping his language skills along and responded this time in English while getting into the back seat. Speaking slowly so as not to lose him, I introduced myself. 'Well, I am Pia. And you may be seeing me a lot, Abdul. I'm in Kanpur to ... how do you say it ... research for a book I'm writing, you know, so I'll need to be going here and there a bit. It could be that your auto-rickshaw is going to be my main mode of transport.'

'No problem. I am always near with my auto-rickshaw,' Abdul said. 'Where you are going today, Madam?'

'Ah, right now, I need to go to Satichaura Ghat. Do you know where that it?' Abdul looked uncertain and so I decided to elaborate. Perhaps the name of the ghat had indeed changed over the years. 'It's the ghat on the river where a group of English people were killed long ago. You know, in 1857? By Nana Sahib's troops, they say. Satichaura? ... No? ... Perhaps the name Mashkar Ghat means something then?'

'Ah, Mashkar Ghat! Yes, yes, I know Mashkar Ghat,' Abdul said, starting up his scootie and taking off down the road without further delay. I settled back on my seat, thinking it strange that the people of Kanpur had come to associate the ghat so firmly with that long-ago massacre of the British. A bit like I did Jahanpanah forest with Tara's death, even though its popularity with walkers and illicit lovers was clear indication that no one else remembered what had happened there fifteen years ago. As we raced through the quiet streets of the cantonment, I looked out at the sleeping bungalows and decided that it was definitely a bit far-fetched to imagine that the bloody incident that had so transformed Margaret's life had left Kanpur labouring with guilt over what had been done to those hapless English folk on that terrible June day.

I observed the neat stretch of tarred road we were travelling, making a mental note to ask Father Kuriakose if this would have been the route Hugh Wheeler had led his party down on the day they were massacred. The camp that had come to be called 'Wheeler's Entrenchment' was, I knew, in the present cantonment area and it would only be logical to assume that the party would have taken the shortest possible route to the river. Nana Sahib had apparently even sent a few carriages and dolies to carry the old and the injured but the rest of them would have walked. How pleased they would have been to leave that wretched camp behind and make for the river where the promised boats to Allahabad awaited them.

The Story of Margaret Wheeler

Chapter Three

Margaret glared at her father, her face incredulous. 'Pa, please, the little children couldn't possibly walk. Not Nell and Louisa-May. Both so ill they can barely stand!'

Hugh Wheeler's response was uncharacteristically gruff. 'It'll have to do, Margaret,' he said. 'I'm not about to grovel before that Nana Sahib to ask for more.'

'But we need at least fifty doolies and hackeries. So many invalids, and the wounded sepoys too. And all our sick women and children. Oh, what do we do, Pa? The river's at least two miles away!' Margaret was aware that her voice was beginning to tremble with unshed tears. She had remained strong so far for her poor parents' sake and really did not want to crumble now. Everyone knew that it was at least partially her father's stubbornness that had led to this situation and she now felt a wave of uncustomary anger with his stubborn refusal to bend.

Havildar-Major Gobind Ram, who was standing nearby, cleared his throat before breaking into the conversation in his soothing Awadhi Hindi. 'General Sahib, you do not need to ask. We can send a message through one of the sipahis and explain the situation to Nana Sahib. He is, by all accounts, a reasonable man.

And, after all, he will not want trouble either.' The havildar paused, assessing the general's mood before continuing. 'It will not take very much for the feelings of the local people to change. Who knows what grudges they bear against the Angrez-log? Some old trumped-up excuse will be enough to get somebody going against their old masters. Nana Sahib should be persuaded that it is in everyone's interests for our party to make its way as quickly as possible down to the boats. We will also request for an early morning passage so that the day is not too hot. Once we are on the river, we will be safe, General Sahib.'

Margaret watched her father listen carefully to his deputy. He was one of the few native officers who had stayed loyal and she knew that Hugh Wheeler set great store by his opinion. Suddenly Hugh Wheeler's shoulders slumped and Margaret felt both relief and sorrow flood through her. She did so hate to see her father look defeated by this awful situation they were all trapped in.

'Get Delafosse to compose a letter from me, Havildar-Sahib,' General Wheeler said presently. 'He has called a meeting with Nana Sahib. Moore, Whiting and Roche will attend so we can send it through them.'

Feeling less anxious, Margaret hurried back into the hospital quarter to help pack away the few remaining supplies. The boat journey to Allahabad could take all day, depending on the currents, so they would need food and water, medicines and bandages. She looked down at her tattered old dress; there was still the spare one that had been used as a pillow on Godfrey's sickbed. She had promised herself she would wear it only when this ghastly siege was over and they were out of the entrenchment so perhaps the time had come to finally discard this dress she had worn for three whole weeks.

Pulling her spare frock out from the bedclothes, Margaret shook it out. It had been a pretty green once, the colour of fresh grass, but, having absorbed the blood and sweat of so many who had used it as a pillow, it had acquired numerous streaks of brown running its entire length. Still, it was a far sight better than the wretched thing she had been wearing for so long. She would probably have forgotten the colour it had once been if her father had not said 'Buttercups' so appreciatively at breakfast that morning.

Taking the dress in her arms, Margaret ran for the ladies' bath-hut. There was barely any water left in the cauldron but it would have to do. Tearing her old gown into little strips – the battered grenadine coming apart easily with the force of her fingers – Margaret used the bits that were relatively less filthy like a flannel, rubbing her limbs and body till they were red and sore. Then she pulled her gown over her head, heaving a sigh of relief at having something marginally cleaner than before finally lie against her skin. There had been nights when she had lain sleepless, feeling the lice and bedbugs crawl all over her body. Margaret ran the comb that had been shared by virtually everyone who used this bath-hut through her dark, luxuriant hair, now damp with the cupful of water she had thought it fair to use. It had not been washed in days and lay matted against her scalp but she pulled its length up into a tight chignon at the top of her head, fastening it in place with an ivory clip shaped like a daisy. When she found a pair of scissors, she would happily chop all her hair off. But there wasn't time for anything like that now as she was needed to help with getting the invalids and children ready for the journey. It was heartbreaking to think that some were too sick to be moved at all but Margaret shoved away the unbearable thought of what could happen to those poor souls whom they might end up having to leave behind.

Back in the main barracks, pandemonium reigned. But Margaret could tell at one glance that there was an unusual air of excitement. Children – those who were not too unwell to do anything but lie on their beds, staring unseeingly at the ceiling – ran about, shoving and screaming while the women tried to pack a few things together.

Hugh Wheeler's instructions when they had moved to the camp had been clear: 'No pictures and gee-gaws, no sentimental knick-knacks, no ornaments, no furniture.' Only the essentials, in addition to money and jewellery, had been allowed, the latter to be used for the purpose of barter for food and medical supplies. But, despite that, people had brought all kinds of things to the camp in their carriages and there was now a lot of hand-wringing about the items that would need to be left behind because, if they carried anything too large, they would need to walk to the river. That was the general's rule. But everyone looked happy today, Margaret thought. And who wouldn't be ecstatic at finally being able to leave behind the hellish existence of the past three weeks? In Allahabad, they would hopefully return to cantonment life – or some sort of semblance of it – until these winds of madness had been stilled. Already there was talk of reinforcements being sent from the Punjab and possibly even from abroad. A shipload of troops was on its way from Burma, according to some reports.

It was late in the evening when word came that Nana Sahib had acquiesced to their request for transport. Sixteen elephants, fifty palanquins and a large number of bullock carts were going to be sent! Nana's armed guards would arrive at the crack of dawn and the

European party was expected to be ready to leave forthwith. A great cheer went up in the kitchen where everyone had gathered to eat their supper together. Margaret cast a happy glance at the clusters of tables around which people were settling for their evening meal. Despite the tattered clothing and meagre portions, there was an air of great celebration in the room, akin almost to those grand parties that had been served in the officers' mess, back when the world had still been normal. And, just as if he was ordering the finest roast, General Wheeler was shouting out instructions for double servings of chapatis to be given out tonight. Margaret knew that it would accompany the standard fare of watery dal alongside chunks of grilled horse meat, those poor beasts that had been shot down in the relentless rebel fire. But, on this lovely night, everyone was already setting upon this offering as though they were being served the most lavish banquet, toasting each other with draughts of cloudy water drawn from the camp's nearly dry well.

Pia, 2013

Abdul's scootie turned off the main road onto a mud track which started to narrow as the river approached. I stuck my entire torso out of the back portion to get a better view but, apart from giant trees and a small stone temple, I could see little else. It was important to get a better sense of the road that Margaret and the British party would have taken that fateful day and so I tapped his shoulder. 'Abdul, do you think we could stop here, please? I think I'd like to walk the rest of the way.'

Abdul obliged, pulling up his vehicle under a peepul tree that stood at the rear entrance of the temple. A woman was scurrying in with a steel plate full of flowers. She pulled her sari over her head as she cast a curious glance in our direction. Abdul locked his vehicle, presumably to accompany me to the river. I was glad for the company and did not demur. He seemed to know when to stop talking and was a quiet and undistracting sort of presence. Besides, because of the way that Tara's and Margaret's stories had got intertwined in my head, it was at moments like this that the memory of what had happened to my sister invariably threatened to engulf me and I was glad for the man's company. My feelings were, however, well under control this evening as we started to walk down the lane, Abdul following a few respectful paces behind. The tree cover overhead was luxuriant enough to keep the fierceness of the sun at bay and only a few dappled coins of light played around on the dust track before me.

It felt strange to imagine that this was probably the same

road Margaret would have taken with the British party, unaware that – in less than an hour – her whole world was going to be torn asunder. Given the age of the trees and the neglected state of the track, it was unlikely that much had changed since the day she had been kidnapped. I looked up at the gnarled old branches and, just as I used to do back at Jahanpanah as a teenager, I willed them with all my heart to give up the terrible secrets they had witnessed and held on to all these years. I had read one account which suggested that Margaret had not been kidnapped at all but that she had gone willingly with the handsome Pathan cavalryman she had secretly loved for a while. That certainly made for a more plausible story since she had never come back, but the more common contemporary reports – later proven untrue of course – were that she had courageously fought off her captor before killing herself and jumping down a well. This was clearly not the case, given the evidence that she had lived to a ripe old age but how hard it must have been for the Victorians to accept that one of their girls had, for reasons unknown, willingly married a native. Worse, a Muslim, and one who had mutinied against them too.

The book by Saul David that I had read so avidly during my early research had described some of those events in fascinating detail. It was where I had also first read about the sorry procession of British officers, women and children who had made their way out of Wheeler's war-torn entrenchment to board the boats that had been promised by Nana Sahib. Unwashed, flea-ridden, some of them wounded and ill and stick-thin, they had left their camp at dawn on the morning of 27 June. At first, trying to cling on to what was left of their pride and with immense trepidation, they filed down a road that was already flanked by crowds of onlookers, some of whom were hissing and jeering as they climbed on to the carts that had been sent for them. Most of the local population had turned up, compelled by curiosity at the sight of their erstwhile masters reduced to such a sorry spectacle in their torn and filthy clothes. It must have been hard for those townsfolk to imagine that these were the same seemingly blessed creatures who, before the Uprising, were to be seen in town or in the cantonment wearing gowns and hats in bright silk and chiffons as they floated down the road in gleaming carriages, sometimes followed by syces trotting behind them on foot.

There were eyewitness reports in some books of how a handful of the local people had barely waited for the British to depart before rushing, minutes later, into the abandoned barracks to scavenge for treasure. They had been largely disappointed, finding only a stinking heap of corpses covered in flies and a few people who were still alive but too ill to be moved. The image that had stuck in my mind was that of another sort of scavenger, though – vultures and other carrion birds that had been seen circling over the entrenchment after the British party had left. But that was because of one of my starker childhood memories about Tara.

We turned a bend and saw the Ganga, brown and muddy and flowing sluggishly along. The banks were wide and dry, perhaps due to the summer heat, and dotted with sodden paper bags and empty plastic bottles. But the middle section of the river was a surprising contrast, moving along swiftly as though trying to make up for its lateral somnolence. These were the currents that had carried to safety those few British soldiers who had escaped the massacre. It was their reports that had filtered into all those books that had chronicled the events of Satichaura Ghat and it now felt completely incredible to think that, even though Kanpur would have changed beyond recognition since Margaret's time, I was seeing the same river and the same trees and the same sunshine glinting on the water that she would have witnessed all those years ago.

I stopped at the top of a set of worn and crumbling steps. A couple of elderly men sat under a nearby tree, observing me without embarrassment or restraint. I smiled at them and asked, 'Satichaura Ghat?', pointing at the steps leading to the river below. They continued to gaze blankly at me, chewing on what was probably tobacco, and so I was relieved when Abdul came to my rescue, repeating my question in local Hindi and throwing in the name Mashkar Ghat as well. One of the men shook his head as he replied in a dialect that I couldn't completely understand. Abdul turned to me. 'He does not know Satichaura. But he knows Mashkar Ghat when I asked him.'

I nodded. Clearly then the old name had completely passed out of use, giving way to that bloody incident by which it would be remembered locally forevermore. I looked around. There was nothing to mark the spot, no plaques or stone tablets. As anticipated, I felt a prickle behind my eyes as I thought of that small clearing in Jahanpanah, similarly unmarked, that was now indistinct from any other part of the forest, with its dense tree cover and the weeds growing underfoot. For days after Tara's body had been found, the place had been cordoned off by plastic police tape, guarded night and day from even the most curious and determined trespassers. No one knew but, once the initial investigations were over, I made a few excursions of my own – ghoulish little solitary excursions that I never dared tell my parents about. On one such trip, I had found a few stray bouquets of drying flowers tied to a nearby tree. There were no cards or tags on them and I wondered – because I wasn't a hard-boiled cynic back then – if Tara had perhaps had a lovelorn admirer at her school; a smooth-faced schoolboy of the sort that Mum sometimes lamented Tara had not chosen to be her boyfriend.

'If she'd had a nice boyfriend … like that tall head boy in her school, what's his name? Dilip Soman? Or even Dr Pandit's son in B-block … none of this would have happened you know.' Such had been Mum's helpless refrain for some time after Tara had died. It seemed to bring her some comfort to imagine Tara alive and going steady with a nice boy so no one ever disputed it. However, very soon, whoever it was bringing those flowers to Jahanpanah (even if it was, indeed, Tara's potential *nice* boyfriend), seemed to lose interest like everyone else and the green of the forest took over once again.

As I stood wondering if it was worth making my way down to the river bank which was covered in what looked like thickets of prickly pear, a boat came into view, bobbing its way around the tree-lined bank. Spotting me, the oarsman swiftly made his way across to the ghat. He called out to Abdul to ask if I was interested in a cruise down the river, using his oars to slow the boat down as he neared us. I was thrilled, of course, at this stroke of luck for what better way to try and replicate the experience Margaret and the others would have had as they boarded their vessels.

'How much?' I asked, trying not to look too eager.

'Three hundred rupees, one hour,' was the reply.

I laughed. 'Two hundred.'

'Okay, two-fifty.'

I would have jumped in even if he had said five hundred and so I nodded before eagerly making my way down to the boat. The bottom few steps were slimy with moss and so I took the boatman's hand to haul myself aboard. Abdul followed and, once again, I was grateful for his presence. Despite my devil-may-care attitude to personal safety, even I knew where to draw the line in being totally foolhardy. With a shove of the oars on the muddy shallows, we were off, the two old men who were still squatting and chewing meditatively, continuing to gaze silently at us as though watching a movie.

I quelled momentary irritation as the boatman struck up conversation with me, because I really did want to concentrate on the scenery unfolding around us. With my trusty little notepad ready in my pocket, I was keen to observe and note everything that I could possibly use so that I could write up a couple of chapters when I returned to my room.

'You are English? American?' the boatman asked.

I hesitated before deciding to be honest. 'My mother's English.'

'Ah, Shakespeare, Queen Elizabeth, Dickens,' he said cheerily.

I couldn't help smiling. Not merely aspirational but a student of literature and history too. Casting a glance about me, I changed the subject. 'Is the river sometimes wider than this? There doesn't seem to be much water.' It seemed the man had not understood my question and so I repeated it in Hindi.

'Arrey, your Hindi is very good! Ah, yes, yes, river very big there,' he said, pointing downriver in the direction we were headed. 'I show you just now.'

He was right for, in a few minutes, the river had widened to nearly a kilometre between banks. On one side, fat old trees hung over its edges and on my left was a largeish island of sorts. I spotted a pack of dogs on the island who, on spotting us, ran for the nearer shore to set off a chorus of barks and howls.

'We no go there. Very dangerous,' Abdul said under his breath.

I was aware that many Muslims disliked dogs and tried to laugh away his fear. But the boatman seemed equally keen to push his vessel away from the island, paddling energetically to fight the currents that were likely to take us too close. 'They are very dangerous,' he agreed. 'They kill and eat man.'

I stopped smiling and looked out at the pack more closely. They looked like feral dogs did everywhere else in India – and you did see them everywhere, even in Delhi's most affluent residential areas – but I suppressed a shiver as I thought of those dead Englishmen and women back in June 1857. Some of the eyewitness reports had mentioned that their remains had been consumed by wild dogs. I rubbed my arms, suppressing a sudden shiver.

As the boatman's efforts took us back to the middle of the river, I looked at the southern banks again, at the stone steps and the low-hanging tree branches, seemingly designed for boats to be tethered. This was where the vessels promised by Nana Sahib had been moored that June morning. It had never been properly established if the Nana was directly responsible for the massacre but he was later roundly blamed by the British authorities for murderous treachery. For his part, he later denied all knowledge of the conspiracy, claiming that a nefarious plot had been hatched by some of his soldiers who hated the British enough to not only want all of them dead but also land him with the blame for having helped them. According to the sources I had read, some English officers had been despatched to the riverside the previous evening to check on Nana's promised arrangements and they had returned satisfied. There were at least fifty thatched boats moored on the mud banks, according to them, and the riverside was a hive of activity as plentiful rations were seen being loaded on board ... there seemed no reason to believe that Nana would deceive them or that anything would go wrong.

Nevertheless, it must have been with a mixture of hope and dread that the English party had set off that morning and I thought of the four hundred–odd men, women and children who had been so unexpectedly set upon as they were boarding the boats right here where I sat. Among the dead that day were Margaret's father and her two youngest brothers, Robert and Charles, aged just nine and six.

The Story of Margaret Wheeler

Chapter Four

The cool of the morning was giving way to simmering heat by the time General Wheeler's party arrived at the river. The beginning of the journey had been far from propitious; Nana Sahib's soldiers had insisted on confiscating all the jewellery and money that the Europeans had tried secreting about their persons. When doughty old Mrs Somerville objected, a sepoy had clubbed her arm with his lathi, causing her to drop her precious jewellery box in the dust. Some of the British officers objected to this but one of Nana Sahib's older havildars rushed to reassure them that the belongings were only being taken off them temporarily as the road to the river was allegedly crawling with gangs of brigands. Nevertheless, mutual suspicion hung heavy in the air as the caravan of bullock carts and elephants gradually wound its way down to the riverside.

On arriving at their destination, some of the children, unable to contain their excitement, broke free from their mothers' grasps and, leaping out of carts and palanquins, ran towards the river. They had been so starved of water during the days of the siege that most had been reduced to chewing on bits of leather to keep their salivary glands going. Was it any wonder that they now leapt into the water, splashing with wild joy in the muddy shallows and yelling with glee. Gun-toting sepoys stood guard on the banks, watching impassively. A few labourers were still loading the boats with provisions as the British men and women started disembarking from their doolies and elephant howdahs. The wounded and invalids were helped by the few remaining native staff and there was all the expected commotion of four hundred people trying to board their vessels.

Margaret smiled at the sight of little Charles who usually hated baths and was now seen sitting half-submerged in the shallows, giggling with merriment and spattering anyone who came near with muddy water. She lifted the hem of her green dress and stepped into the water herself, feeling the delicious cool of it wrap itself around her feet and ankles. Water, precious water ... how precious she had not known until robbed of it during the siege. With a small prayer of thanks, Margaret remembered the number of times she had looked out from a tiny window of the barracks and imagined she could see a lake shimmering in the distance only to realize with a sinking feeling that it was merely a mirage in the heat.

Her father was doing his duty diligently and noisily, as he was wont to, wading through the sandbars and shouting instructions to pull the boats off the mud and into the water. It was true, the boats had been perched so high up on the banks, they would be difficult to drag down once everyone was on board. But, in their rush to get aboard, a number of the women had already started clambering onto the vessels, helping each other and their children behind them. In the midst of the confusion, Margaret's heart skipped a beat momentarily as she sensed someone staring at her. On turning her head, she spotted him – the same tall, dark-eyed man who had ridden through the churchyard that morning and who always looked at her as though filled with contempt. His face was inscrutable today but Margaret saw that he was on horseback and carried a musket in his arms. Quickly looking away, she lifted her now soaking skirt and followed Amy Horne who was wading across to the nearest boat.

Before they had reached the vessel, however, there was a crack of what sounded like gunfire and, with astonished eyes, Margaret saw her father fall. At first unsure if he had merely slipped, she tried to run to his side, hampered by the weight of the water in her petticoats. 'Papa!' she screamed as she saw him surface briefly, his face twisted with pain, before he fell again, flailing in water that was already turning pink with his blood.

When Margaret reached his side, she became vaguely aware that the crack of gunfire had taken on a staccato sound as dozens of muskets and rifles opened fire. 'They're firing at us,' she thought distractedly as she heard people around her start to scream. Women and children were jumping off boats and trying to take cover by diving into the shallows or running for the cover of the trees. Unmindful of her own safety, Margaret tried to haul her father out of the river, holding him by his armpits. He was a deadweight, his tattered old uniform heavy with water and blood, and Margaret could only budge him a few inches. As she was struggling, she became aware that Amy was screaming and clinging to her skirts. Looking over her shoulder, Margaret saw that a soldier had grabbed Amy's hand and was trying to pull her towards him. Margaret held tightly on to Amy's free arm, pulling as hard as she could in the opposite direction but she stopped when she saw the soldier lift his gun and bring the butt down on Amy's head with a horrible crack. Amy fell but, before she hit the water, her assailant had gathered her up in his arms and carried her across to the bank. Horrified, Margaret could neither follow nor help. One hand still clutching her father's uniform while he lay half-submerged in the mud, she looked frantically around for her mother and brothers but could not see any of them in the disarray. Smoke was now drifting above the water, turning mid-morning to dusk and adding to the terrible confusion on the river banks. Margaret looked down at her father's face again but it was now still and sunk just below the water. Letting go of his uniform with an anguished cry, she stumbled through the swirling darkness in desperate search for her mother. All around her were chopping sounds of swords going through flesh and the most horrendous gargling cries of those who were being murdered. At her feet, Margaret could see the wide-eyed faces of those who had fallen and she scanned them, terrified she would spot her mother's beloved face. As she stumbled over a corpse, nearly falling to her knees, a figure on a horse loomed before her half-shrouded in the smoke. Just as Margaret recognized the man, she found herself being scooped out of the water to be thrown across the saddle. Her head hit something hard and, half in a faint, she was barely aware of horse's hooves ringing in her head and juddering through every sinew in her body as she was carried away up the riverbank and into the forests...

When Margaret came to, she was in a clearing, lying on her side. From somewhere deep inside arose a submerged memory of killing and screaming and an angry red river swallowing up her beloved father. Was it a mere nightmare? Was she still asleep? Here, there was only blissful silence, the sounds of birds and other small scurrying forest creatures. Then the knowledge of all that had happened rose terrifyingly up, travelling like a slow pain through Margaret's body. She wanted to throw up. Where was she? She had obviously been brought far from the scenes of mayhem at the ghats and was now in some unrecognizable forest. Hearing men's voices nearby, speaking in Hindi, Margaret swiftly closed her eyes and tried to remain as still as possible so that no one would know she had regained consciousness. Straining to hear the words, she thought she heard the word 'qatl' a few times ... murder. Another wave of fear and sorrow welled up in her throat as she remembered the awful sight of her father being shot before her eyes. Poor Pa ... his worst fears come true ... those men he had loved and trusted ... dear God, why? Papa had not deserved what had come to him. And where was Mamma? Had she died too? Worst of all, what terrible fate awaited her now, alone in this forest with a group of murderous men...

Margaret stiffened as she heard a woman's voice. Amy! It was clearly Amy's voice, pleading for her life. Margaret listened carefully, the tears in Amy's voice making her shake with fright. She instructed herself to stay calm. It was really important not to panic at this stage as that would only make her and Amy more vulnerable to these rapacious men. Biting down hard on her bottom lip to stop it from trembling, Margaret weighed the consequences of getting up to help her poor friend. But it seemed wiser to remain still and take stock of this perilous situation. It sounded as though the men were arguing among themselves but Margaret could only catch the odd word or two over Amy's hysterical and heartrending cries. Margaret squeezed her eyes tight as a man's voice raised itself sharply and demanded that Amy be quiet with a harsh, 'Chup, randi!'

Margaret had only heard the word 'randi' once before, when a fight had broken out in the servants' quarters behind their house in the cantonment and two women had started screaming at each other. Godfrey had told her, it was one of the rudest words in the Hindi language. And here was this man – a soldier in her father's regiment – using it to silence Amy!

'Please, please, Amy,' Margaret thought in desperation, 'stay calm and silent, you'll only make it worse by pleading like this!' But Amy continued to cry and beg, her moans getting gradually louder again as her entreaties fell on deaf ears. Suddenly there was the sound of a ringing slap, loud as the crack of a whip. The shock of it silenced Amy momentarily but Margaret could not pretend to be asleep any more. Getting up swiftly, she lunged at the startled group with an angry cry but nearly fell over as she did so. She found to her horror that her feet were tied together. Steadying herself with difficulty, she saw that there were three men sitting in a circle, while Amy was hunched nearby, leaning against a tree. One of the men – the same abhorrent man with the kohl-lined eyes who had captured her – got up and came across to where Margaret stood trembling with one arm still raised. 'Shhh...' he said, forcing her arm down and then pushing her down to a seated position like Amy.

Margaret could not believe his insolence, him a lowly sepoy, touching her, the daughter of a general! She was further enraged to see a glint of amusement in his eyes as he offered her his flask of water. She shook her head and turned her face away. When the man returned to talk to his two conspirators in whispered tones, Margaret tried to catch Amy's eye. Seeing that there were two of them, there was a faint chance they could escape together into the forests and hide until nightfall. But

Amy was still weeping and whimpering, her face slumped on her knees and hidden from view by the folds of her skirt.

Margaret knew that if anyone was capable of making a plan of escape, it was her. Poor Amy had never been of a strong disposition and who knew what awful things might already have been done to her by those animals while Margaret had been unconscious! Margaret's mind raced, searching for ways in which they could get away. She could ask for a privy or to be allowed to go in the forests but, if she did manage to run away, she would be leaving Amy at the mercy of these men. They would never allow the pair of them to go off together – that much was sure. Before she could think of another plan, however, the men appeared to have come to a decision. While one of them got up to see to their horses that were tethered nearby, the other two approached the women. One was the man who had captured her and Margaret recognized the other as the man who had so mercilessly clubbed Amy on her head before carrying her away. Both men had scarves and ropes in their hands and, before Margaret could demur, she felt her hands being swiftly tied together behind her back. Just as quickly, the man who was standing behind her proceeded to gag and blindfold her too. Despite writhing and struggling, Margaret felt herself being picked up and thrown once again atop a horse. The man mounted the beast behind her and, as it bucked slightly in protest at the additional weight, he made soft clicking sounds with his throat. Margaret felt her abductor use his knees to apply pressure on the horse's flanks and, once the animal had been controlled, they started to ride though the forest, at first cautiously but soon picking up great speed. Over the sound of the thundering hooves, Margaret desperately tried to discern if the other two horses were also accompanying them but this was difficult to tell. All she knew with a terrifying awareness, as her bound body was jolted and wracked by the ride, was that she was being taken somewhere far away from the world she knew. Where was her family ... her mother and brothers ... would she never see them again? This seemed impossible to accept. All Margaret knew with any certainty, even through her confusion and terror, was that her life had changed irrevocably and that there would very likely be no return.

Pia, 2013

I sat quietly as the boat completed a full circle and returned to Satichaura Ghat. Luckily, the boatman and Abdul had struck up conversation and so I was left to mull over my thoughts. It was true that Margaret, plucked away from this riverside, had little chance of returning once she had been taken away by Nizam Ali Khan. The old world had been torn asunder anyway. Poor Margaret had seen her father cut down before her eyes and, within a few weeks, she would find out that her mother's fate had not been much better as the womenfolk had been taken from Satichaura to the Bibigarh only to be put to death. From Wikipedia I'd learnt that Margaret did have two older brothers who survived the Mutiny but what would life in a British cantonment have been like if she had come back after being 'contaminated' by her capture? Not much better than poor Amy's who had made that very choice but found herself becoming a social pariah, surrounded by sternly prudish Victorian morals that squarely blamed her for the tragic events she'd had no control over at all.

I recalled the journals I'd seen in the British Library, written by Amy, which recorded the harrowing details of her abduction and subsequent forced conversion. She had not specifically mentioned rape but that was surely what she had been subjected to by Ismail Khan, the sowar who had captured and laid claim to her after Satichaura. When, ten months after the Kanpur uprising, the British had swept back to power and carried out the most horrific revenge and reprisals, Amy had made a deal with her captor, agreeing to plead for amnesty on his behalf if he would only let her go back to her people. Perhaps it was the risk of keeping a white girl hidden once British power had been restored, but Ismail had agreed and, one April morning in 1858, Amy turned up at the house of her great-uncle in Allahabad, shattered and exhausted but free. That choice, surely available to Margaret too, was not the one she had taken. It looked like I was going to have to write my novel to figure out why.

Jolted back to the present by the soft thudding of the boat's prow against the ghat, I realized that my hour was up and we were back on shore. I got up and leapt onto the steps of the ghat before unzipping my purse to pay the boatman the agreed amount. Once he had rowed away, I climbed a few steps to sit down and look again at the river that had swallowed up and carried away so many of the dead on that horrific day.

The old men who had been chewing tobacco had gone and even Abdul, bored perhaps by my introspection, wandered off to inspect his auto-rickshaw. Now completely alone, I stared at the drifting brown water, plunged into a somewhat disturbed state by my wanderings up the river. In order to distract myself, I tried to recall the names of the people who had escaped the massacre and lived to tell the tale but could not remember even one now. Fishing out my notebook, I riffled through its pages until I found the page marked 'Satichaura'. I had been conscientious back at the National Archives and the names were duly listed there: Thomson, Delafosse, Private Murphy (against whose name I had scribbled 84th) and Private Sullivan (1st Madras Fusiliers) – these were the only known British male survivors at Satichaura. Margaret and Amy were the sole female survivors. The men, saved downstream by a minor raja who was a British loyalist, eventually joined a rescue force that was already on its way up the river. They had given evidence and left papers that were the stuff of a researcher's dreams and without which I would never have been able to piece together the early part of Margaret's story. What I would do to find the latter part of her story was still a complete blank – unless Father Kuriakose's contact did indeed come up with Margaret's letters. What a discovery that would be!

I was aware, of course, that when I got around to writing the relevant chapter, I would have to balance the cruelty displayed by Nana Sahib's men at Satichaura and Bibigarh with the merciless British reprisals that followed when they swept back to power. Hindus had been force-fed beef and Muslims pork before they were smeared with animal juices, tied to the mouths of cannons and shot to smithereens. According to Hibbert's account, General Neill, intent on finding rebels to punish, had pulled men and women out at random from their huts and houses and marched some of them across to the Bibigarh to make them lick the floor clean of the dried blood of its victims. The astonishing brutalities displayed by both sides were, perhaps, in keeping with those less civilized times but human behaviour had not changed that much really. My sister's case was proof of that.

The Story of Margaret Wheeler

Chapter Five

At the end of what must have been a three- or four-mile journey, Margaret, still blindfolded, felt the horse she was being carried on come to an abrupt halt. It whinnied softly as the rider dismounted and tethered it to a tree. Margaret was pulled off the animal and she felt a man's arms and body support her as she lost her balance and swayed on her bound feet. Trying unsuccessfully to rescue what was left of her dignity, Margaret attempted to pull away but she stopped as she felt the man kneel to untie the bonds that were holding her ankles together. Then, just as abruptly, she was being propelled again and she took a few stumbling steps forward. There were sounds of a door being unlocked before she was shoved inside a space that smelt of damp hay and sawdust. Once again, Margaret felt revulsion rise within her, forced into unseemly proximity with her captor as he stood behind her to untie the scarves that had bound her eyes and her mouth. He was so close, she could smell his perspiration and feel his breath on the back of her neck. Blinking as the cloths came off, Margaret saw that they were in a small dark shed with a string bed in one corner. The only other piece of furniture was a wooden table with an unlit kerosene lantern on it.

Locking the door behind them, and carefully pocketing the key, the man made his way across to the lantern and, using a piece of flint, he lit the wick. Ghostly silhouettes formed on the brick walls as the flame took. Turning from it to face Margaret, the man spoke for the first time. His voice was low and not as rough as she would have expected but his face was in the shadows so she could not see the expression on it.

'It is safe here,' the man said in Hindi, 'so do not try to run away. I will go and get some food for you.'

Taking courage from his low tone, Margaret responded sharply. 'I do not want your food,' she said. 'I want to go back to my people. You have no right to bring me here.'

He hesitated for a moment before replying. 'Your people are all dead. Your houses burnt. You have nowhere to go.'

For the first time since seeing her father fall, Margaret felt close to breaking down. But determined not to weep before this man, she took a step forward and, summoning all her courage, she spat squarely in his face. 'It is you who have killed my people. You killed my father. I saw it for myself.'

The man froze as the spittle landed on his face and, for an instant, Margaret thought he was going to strike her or worse. Then, slowly wiping his face with the scarf that had bound her eyes, he replied, his voice calm but shaking slightly. 'You have no idea who is on your side and who isn't. Not your fault. These times are such. But one thing I will tell you – if you attempt escaping from here, you will be robbed of your honour and quite likely be mutilated and killed in a most horrible fashion. There are some very angry men out there. But, if you stay here for a few days, you will be away from the trouble and, when it is all over, you can decide where you want to go.'

And, saying this, the man turned on his heel and strode across the room. Margaret watched, silent and confused, as he unlocked the door and closed it sharply behind him. She heard the key turn in the lock outside and, in another few minutes, the sound of horse's hooves told her that her captor had ridden away, leaving her all alone.

Pia, 2013

By the time I returned to Father Kuriakose's house that evening, I was tired from my riverside exploration and all the images and thoughts it had set off. I was, in fact, quite ready to go straight to bed so I could wake up early and work on my manuscript. But Elsie would naturally not hear of this. Perhaps it was just as well because after I'd been fortified by a generous dinner of meat curry and rice I found myself wide awake again and, armed with a mug of coffee, I went up to my room to switch my laptop on and make a few notes of the day's observations.

Unsure of whether Father Kuriakose's internet connection would have Wi-Fi, I'd invested in a data-card back in Delhi. At dinner I had forgotten to ask and so I plugged the device in now. Wearily, I watched the yellow ball bounce on the screen, fully expecting that it would throw me out but I was dead pleased to see the blue light come on, indicating that I was connected to the web. And the speed wasn't bad either!

My Facebook page was full of unread messages, although it had only been a couple of days since I had last checked in Delhi. I devoured the page now, looking for news from home to lift my spirits a bit. There was one message from Neel with a few photographs of him and his girlfriend holidaying in a really lovely place called Sedona, three plaintive messages from Ritwik (the poor guy clearly wanted to get back together with me), one each from Esha and Sheels, both with pictures of Esha's birthday party that I had missed. Because my parents weren't on Facebook,

I checked my gmail account too and found, as expected, one mail from Mum, a couple from Dad, one from Neel's office email address titled 'Forgot earlier – kurkure'. There was also an email from Max Dominic Darwin, that rather dishy-looking and helpful research assistant I'd met at the British Library, titled 'Thomson, The Story of Cawnpore' and a couple of spam messages that had escaped the filter.

Mum sounded anxious and lonely in her rather short mail and I felt that old familiar pang of guilt. 'I hope you're taking good care of yourself, darling. Small-town India can offer strange and disturbing experiences (only connect to good old Forster!) and you know I couldn't bear it if anything bad happened to you.' Just as quickly, she had veered off into one of her customary tangents, though: 'Aunty Vee called today. It's typically kind, isn't it, that she should remember Tara's anniversary coming up? She called just to check that we're all right and I told her naturally that we were. Thought it best not to mention that you were gadding about the country by yourself for that would only have distressed her terribly.'

I leaned back on my propped-up pillow and looked at the ceiling, counting in my head. Of course ... fifteen years! It was almost exactly fifteen years since my elder sister had been killed. Incredibly, I'd kind of forgotten. But only because travelling inevitably resulted in days and dates getting stupidly jumbled up in my head. Yes, we were all right, as Mum had said – fifteen years is a long time even when the most horrific stuff happened – but I knew that all it would take was for a journalist to remember the date of Tara's anniversary and dash off an article on a quiet news day and the whole damn thing would be raked up all over again.

As a family, we had coped admirably at the time, all things considered, and many press reports had referred to 'the dignified Fernandez family'. It was the title, in fact, of a picture I'd spotted on the second page of the *Times of India* that I found in the school library which showed Mum and Dad flanked by Neel and me at Tara's funeral. Mum was wearing a black cocktail sheath with a white dupatta and salwaar but I don't think anyone noticed the weird combination. Aunty Vee had rooted around forever in Mum's cupboard before she could find anything in black at all as there was a time when Mum had declared black to be 'too bloody British', spurning it in favour of a wardrobe full of vibrant Indian colours. Poor Aunty Vee had insisted on coming out from England to be with us for a week, despite Dad's insistence that Uncle Jeff needed her more due to his Parkinson's. But stubborn old Aunty Vee had come and she was right behind Mum in that photograph, both of them hiding their swollen eyes behind enormous sunglasses. Dad was in that shiny grey suit we all hated, his face ashen and drawn. And Neel, then a sulky fourteen-year-old, was wearing a suit too but with trainers and the Phillies cap he had worn all of that summer as though it would protect him not just from the sun but from the media crowding around Tara's death too. He had coped far less well than the rest of us with those paps and cameramen lurking just outside our door – probably something to do with being photographed all spotty and gangly and being remembered like that for posterity. In the picture, only I looked properly dressed, wearing the frock that had been bought for my tenth birthday party that had, appropriately, black stripes running lengthwise down pale grey silk. Also appropriate to the funeral was the fact that Tara had chosen it for my party, helping me as I had tried on a whole plethora of dresses and tops in the minuscule changing booth at Tiddlywinks in GK market, six months before she had died. It had been really quite thrilling going shopping for the first time with her rather than Mum, especially as I had just started developing an interest in clothes and shoes. Curiously, this was another thing that simply got shelved after that as I subsequently grew up as one of those rare girls who gave little consideration to what I threw on by way of clothes.

I clicked open Neel's mail next and found a typical one-liner, sent hastily from his office in Phoenix, asking me to send six packs of spicy masala kurkure through a colleague who was visiting Delhi this week. Clearly, he'd completely forgotten about my Kanpur trip despite it being plastered all over my Facebook page. Brothers!

I then looked at Max Darwin's email again, and couldn't help wondering for the hundredth time if my fevered imagination had conjured up the little frisson that had passed between us in the British Library that winter morning. Then I swiftly clicked his mail shut and marked it as 'unread' so I could reply to him when I was feeling less vulnerable, my head less mussed up.

Two out of Dad's three mails were jokes, forwarded from one of his tennis buddies but the third, with the subject line 'Mum', was sobering. 'She's missing you dreadfully, Pia. I hate to make you guilty but maybe the timing of this Kanpur trip was a bit unfortunate. I suppose we're all thinking about Tara in one way or another as her anniversary looms but your mother ... she's in mortal dread of some journalist turning up at our door to ask questions about all that old stuff and nothing I say will convince her that journalists have far more pressing issues to cover these days, what with the upcoming elections and this never-ending IPL thing.'

'You're wrong, Dad,' I thought, concerned suddenly for my mother whose suspicions about journalists were always far more accurate than Dad's. The pushy door-stepping that had gone on at the time of Tara's death had given me an early lesson in media hunger for salacious stories. The IPL betting story was already starting to look like tired old news whereas Tara's murder, when it had happened, had all the essential ingredients required to fill page after page for days on end. After all, it offered everything –

love and sex, rivalry and jealousy, not to mention young photogenic faces. One thing I'd found was that if anything could make a senseless and tragic young death any worse, it was the world 'unsolved'.

Something inside me had shifted while I'd been checking my mails and I now no longer had the heart to either send out replies or work on my manuscript. I shut the computer down and, as it whined softly to a close, the night sounds outside became more audible through the open window – crickets and bullfrogs and, in the distance, the howl of what was probably a jackal. I thought about those wild dogs I'd seen on that island while cruising the river, the first time ever I'd felt fear rather than fondness for dogs. Getting up, I turned the cooler on, having checked that its water tank was full, and lay down on my bed to try and get some sleep. But despite the comforting throb of the pumping water, sleep would not come for a long time as I tossed and turned, the sheet on my bed getting gradually crumpled and damp with sweat.

The Story of Margaret Wheeler

Chapter Six

Margaret sprang awake with a jolt. She lay listening for footsteps outside the cabin but all was silent, save for the sounds of jackals howling in the distance and an owl hooting from a nearby tree. The man, her captor, had returned once but barely made any conversation on that occasion, merely placing a parcel of food on the table along with an urn of water. Margaret stayed where she was, huddled on a corner of the string bed and turning her face away when he pointed at the parcel and said, 'Eat'.

He left soon after, without attempting any more conversation, and, as before, Margaret had tried the door following his departure, rattling it on its hinges but it was clearly stronger than it looked. There was a solitary window at the back of the hut and Margaret had flown to that as well, battering it with her fists, shouting at the top of her voice and pushing with all her might at its barred shutters but it was so firmly shut, she guessed that it had probably been reinforced from the outside. There was a small area that had been curtained off, containing a copper basin of water and a small privy. Had her captor prearranged all this, Margaret wondered. Imagining him carefully planning and preparing this remote little prison in readiness for her capture, she felt another wave of revulsion at such beastly behaviour. What made him think he could treat her as though she were no better than those bedraggled little parrots she had seen stuck in cages waiting to be sold in Cawnpore's bazaars?

What was her fate? Would she be raped by her captor? Would she be sold as a white slave to some wealthy, cruel man? Back at the cantonment, Margaret had overheard some of the whisperings that took place among the Englishwomen who were convinced that native men had always nursed rapacious intent against them. 'It's the heat, my dear. Does dreadful things to the native mind,' old Mrs Sykes had said sagely through a mouthful of bread at a tea party once. Margaret recalled the noticeable collective frisson that went around the room at the thought, with the delicate Miss Simmons visibly shrinking in her chair as a bearer loomed rapaciously over her with a plate of chicken sandwiches.

Margaret felt thankful that she had been spared that horror so far but surely the man would come back for her at some point and then there would be no mercy. And where had poor Amy been taken? It was unimaginable that they had been separated and carted off by these men to suit some nefarious purposes of their own. Like inanimate spoils of war, there to be snatched and used and discarded.

Margaret picked up the flickering kerosene lamp, careful not to touch the hot glass shade, trying to assess if there was enough kerosene in the bottom to set fire to the door. Perhaps she could make a hole big enough to squeeze herself out from. But, from the weight she could tell that there was barely an inch of fuel in the lamp. Not enough for more than a very small fire. Besides, she might get horribly burnt if the room caught fire with her trapped inside.

Margaret slumped back on the bed and eyed the parcel of food in the far corner. It was at least a day since she had last eaten. She recalled that last banquet at the camp ... the stacks of chapattis and horse meat sizzling in the great frying pan ... she heard her stomach now rumbling furiously. But she was damned if she would touch the food brought by that animal. Who knew, it might even be poisoned or, worse, spiked with some drug that would make her lose control of her senses. No, it was important to stay alert and ready for the first opportunity that might come her way to escape her incarceration.

Margaret looked around her at the smoke-blackened walls, wondering what other despicable deeds they had been witness to, trying not to give way to tears. Under her breath, she whispered words of a poem that she and Godfrey had been taught by the nuns down at the cantonment's missionary school they had both attended as children. 'Stone walls do not a prison make, nor iron bars a cage...' but she could not remember the rest, nor who the poet was. Godfrey would have known. He was much cleverer than her. But now he was dead too. Him and Wyatt and Papa ... gone, all gone...

Margaret sank her face into the pillow so that it would absorb the sudden rush of tears that was threatening to overwhelm her. She started to hum an old Irish lullaby, willing herself to go back to sleep. It was one that Mamma had sung to all of them when they were small and that Charles insisted on her singing every night:

> I see the moon, the moon sees me,
> Shining through the leaves of the old oak tree
> Oh, let the light that shines on me
> Shine on the one I love

Over the mountain, over the sea,
Back where my heart is longing to be
Oh, let the light that shines on me
Shine on the one I love.

Finally, unable to bear it any more, Margaret started to weep; large lonely tears coursing down her face and soaking the pillow to which she so helplessly clung.

Pia, 2013

I dreamt of Tara again. Tara in a locked room with walls of blackened bricks. She was weeping and it was so heartbreaking a sight, I woke up with a heavy tugging feeling in my chest. It was a blistering, bright morning, however, and, as my head cleared, I determined to do a full day's work, my spirits gradually restored by the sounds of the household in action downstairs. Fearing I might be late for breakfast, I had a hasty shower and made my way quickly down the stairs. Both the Kuriakoses were at the table, reading the papers alongside mugs of tea.

'Aha, good morning! Bright and early,' Father K said, folding up his paper and putting it away.

'Oh, am I really? Bright and early, I mean,' I replied. 'I thought I was really late.'

'No, no, not late. Except for Sunday, we don't get up too early,' Elsie said, 'and there will always be the maid around to serve you breakfast even if you oversleep so it's no problem.'

'That's really so sweet of you,' I muttered, once again overwhelmed by the sheer niceness of my hosts, being more used to the help-yourself chaos of the kitchen back at home and the anonymous bland service offered by hotel staff on my trips. I took the paper that Father Kuriakose was holding in my direction and glanced at the front page. 'Opposition Challenges Food Safety Bill' … 'Calls for Dhoni to retire' … I had more important things on my mind, however, and launched into my pet subject straightaway. 'Father Kuriakose, I know you emailed me to say that there is nothing left to see at the site of General Wheeler's entrenchment...'

'Yes, it is right here, the entrenchment site. Very near the church ... I can show it to you. But the buildings are long gone and all you will see are the mud flats stretching out for miles.'

'What about the Bibigarh?'

'Ah, better luck there maybe. The old house no longer exists but, when the British regained power, they built a memorial to their women and children who died in the Bibigarh massacre. There was a figure of an angel built over the well into which the bodies were thrown. But that statue was also moved, ninety years later, this time by the Indians when the British left India. After that the angel was replaced by the bust of Tatya Tope who was Nana Sahib's general.' He laughed. 'Yes, complicated, isn't it, when we constantly change the way we remember our histories. But the angel's statue is right here in fact – near the church – in the memorial garden that our church helps to maintain.'

'Would this morning be a good time to explore? Like now?'

'Yes, yes, why not? It is so near, I can take you there myself before my morning meetings.'

I wolfed down my breakfast of toast and dalia porridge, presided over by the redoubtable Elsie Kuriakose, thinking how fond of her my mother would get if she saw how easily she could get me to eat. When we were finally done and Father K had finished what was surely his fifth cup of tea, I fetched my little satchel again and set off with him down the road, both of us shaded from the sun by the huge black umbrella he was wielding. He was recognized by almost everyone we passed along the way, cyclists and walkers saluting and hailing him – he was clearly a popular man in this part of town.

As we went past the tall red-brick church, Father Kuriakose chucked his chin towards it. 'You can come in and look around the church when we get back. The original one that was here before was called St John's, but this building, as you must be knowing, was built in 1875 by the railway architect Walter Granville. He wanted to honour those Christians who died in 1857. Inside, there are several monuments and memorial tablets for you to look at. I will have some work to do in my office anyway, so you will be free to walk around later.' Then, remembering my earlier question, he added, 'You asked about the entrenchment – it was somewhere over there...' He waved his free hand towards the open ground to our right before pointing in the direction of a small hillock. 'You see there, where the ground rises up in a little hill? According to a British historian who came visiting many years ago, that was where General Wheeler's barracks were in 1857. No buildings are left now, of course.'

I squinted through the heat to where he pointed – apart from stretches of dry, sandy soil and a few scrubby plants, there was nothing to see. Nevertheless, I could tell how badly planned Wheeler's endeavour had been. If the topography then was anything like it was now, he could not have chosen a spot more exposed and vulnerable to enemy fire. 'Definitely *not* the best place to mount a siege from!' I laughed.

Father Kuriakose nodded in agreement. 'I also thought it was very strange that Wheeler should have come here, when the entire cantonment would have been at his disposal.'

I knew the reason for this, thanks to my previous research, and was pleased to be able to explain it now. 'Actually, Father, some of Wheeler's men had suggested that they use the garrison's magazine as a refuge for all the Europeans who needed protection at the time. But, apparently, that was already being guarded by a native battalion and, in a time of such mutual suspicion, Wheeler probably thought it wise to leave them well alone rather than provoke a problem.'

'Aha, that makes sense. I often say, complicated things can

have simple explanations when they are viewed with the benefit of hindsight.' Father Kuriakose lifted the edge of his habit off the dusty road and started walking again. 'Through this way now,' he said, pointing with the handle of his umbrella to a small wicket gate. I went in through the gate and held it open for him. We followed a small paved path and I found myself in the midst of a semi-circular lawn formed by a high gothic style wall in the centre of which was a painted white statue of an angel, holding a symbol of peace under a cross. Although some of the paint was mossy and peeling, the garden housing the memorial was immaculately maintained and the bougainvillea creepers were in abundant crimson bloom.

Father Kuriakose went off to talk to the gardener while I wandered around, stopping to read a plaque that had been put up by the Archaeological Survey of India. The information on it was much the same as that Father Kuriakose had just given me. It had no detail at all of the Bibigarh massacre, in which Margaret's mother and younger siblings had been brutally killed alongside two hundred other women and children. Perhaps it had been wise to dismantle the building and obliterate the ghastliness of that memory as much as possible. But what was that saying – about people who forgot their histories being condemned to repeat it? What I did not know, until Father Kuriakose had mentioned it today, was that the well into which the bodies of women and children had been thrown – some purportedly while still alive – had later been cemented over with this angel placed above. That well still lay beneath the ground, now beneath Tatya's statue. I looked up at the serene stone features of the angel, grey and crumbling around the nose and chin, thinking of how she stood guarding the memory of what had been one of the worst atrocities of that uprising. And how sad that, when India had gained independence ninety years later, this hapless angel was seen, rightly or wrongly, as a symbol of British victory and moved to this remote site behind the church. One of the historians I had met at SOAS while doing my initial research back in England told me that many Indian churches had rather magnanimously taken on the responsibility of caring for the graves of the thousands of Britishers who had died in those battles. There were lots of Father Kuriakoses in India then. I looked across the memorial garden in his direction and saw that the priest was now waving at me and pointing to his watch to indicate that he needed to be off.

'Okay bye, Father,' I called out, 'I'll just hang around here for a bit, if it's okay.'

He nodded, raising one hand as though giving benediction and I watched him leave the garden through the small gate. His earlier remark about man's propensity to rewrite history had been interesting, especially given that I was doing something similar through the genre of historical fiction. Me, supposedly a serious history student and university gold medallist! I thought briefly of how pained Professor Sharma of Delhi University – a severe academic purist – would have been to know that one of his best students was writing historical fiction. But there seemed no choice, given how scarce the primary sources on Margaret were. Surely it should suffice merely to tell her story, and tell it well enough to attract people to learning more about her history? I looked up again at the angel with her bowed head. As all students of history become aware, I knew that the greatest value offered by our subject lay in preventing the human race from repeating the same mistakes over and over again but I also knew that history was merely interpretation. So the same set of facts had been presented in one way by the British and in a completely different way by the Indians and, of course, the truth lay somewhere in-between. If, indeed, there was ever such a thing as a single 'truth' that had not shifted and transmuted over the years.

Walking back into the shade offered by a nearby tree, I pondered my task of bringing all these disparate elements of my research together into a cohesive whole. Had I been writing non-fiction, I could have laid bare all the facts and let my readers come to their own conclusions. But, as a novelist, was it not my job to use the fogs of imagination (now, where had I recently read that line?) in order to recreate Margaret's distant, shadowy world. How else could I hope to bring her to life before my readers? No recorded source existed, for instance, to tell me of how she would have received the news of the ghastly Bibigarh massacre in which she had lost her mother and siblings. I had read plenty of eyewitness reports about those poor Englishwomen being chased around the Bibigarh compound, hacked to death by butchers who had been called in when Nana Sahib's sepoys balked at such a grisly task. That nice Max Darwin at the British Library had brought out an entire file full of reports by General Neill's men who had arrived, too late, to find only a well overflowing with hacked body parts. Max had even told me that one soldier's account had described seeing the eyeball of a child stuck to a tree that had been used to bash the smaller children dead and, despite the winter sunshine pouring in through the windows of the British Library and the radiator generously pumping out heat right next to me, I had felt my whole body shiver uncontrollably at that point.

Surely Margaret too would have heard all these stories at the time? Would she have figured out that her mother and little sisters were among the dead? Who would have broken the news to her? And what terrible torments would she have suffered as a consequence?

The Story of Margaret Wheeler

Chapter Seven

Margaret gradually lost count of the passage of days. In the dark confines of her hut in the forest, it was difficult to know when one day ended and the other began. There were times when the brick walls closed in on her, suffocating her and robbing her of sanity, and yet there were other times when her imprisonment seemed not to matter at all. During periods like that, when her mind soared free, travelling up through the trees and into the open blue skies, Margaret walked the streets of the Cawnpore cantonment again, chattering with Emma as they bought hairclips and talcum powder from the local shop before going back home to their families where they would all sit around the table and talk and laugh with no knowledge of what was to come. In those blissful moments of forgetfulness, Margaret could almost convince herself that she was back in the fold of her family but then, just as swiftly and with no warning, the dream would have fled, leaving her worse off for being so alone and so far from home. The forest would close in on her then, its noises rising to a terrible crescendo around the hut, the humid air lifting from the summer earth threatening to engulf and suffocate her. At least two weeks had passed since she had been brought to this prison in the forest, although it felt like two years. And, in that time, Margaret had not seen another soul except for her captor.

She now knew that his name was Nizam Ali Khan and that he was not a local man but a Pathan from the far-off mountains. He had arrived in Cawnpore when soldiers were being recruited for the 2nd Bengal Cavalry as he was an expert horseman and thought it a good way to earn money to help support his widowed mother and two sisters back in Peshawar.

He had told Margaret all this during his periodic visits with food and water when he would let her out of the hut and allow her to walk among the trees for a while. Curiously, except for the fact of her imprisonment, the man's attitude had been kindly on the whole, with him even offering on one occasion to take her to a nearby stream so she could wash her clothes and bathe. But Margaret had greeted all attempts at solicitousness and conversation with stony silence. How could she bring herself to converse with a man who had abducted her and been on the side of those rebels who had killed her father? The only concession she had made was to give up her hunger strike when, weak with starvation and almost unable to walk, she had finally relented and eaten a small portion of rice, nearly bringing it up because her stomach could not recognize food any more. That day, Nizam was almost gentle, stroking her back as she squatted under a tree and retched. He had even fetched water in a lota so that she could wash her face after she had brought up some watery rice and bile. But Margaret still told herself that she was eating his food only so that she would have the strength to escape at the first opportunity. She had simply not been able to understand why the man had incarcerated her, unable to believe that it was for her own protection as he insisted.

'I saw you in the camp and I knew that there would be ruthless men who would try to rob you of your honour when the rebellion happened. There are more and more dakoos and thugs about ... they are coming from everywhere in search of fortune. Much murder and looting is going on. You are safe here.' But all that sounded to Margaret like poppycock. There was definitely some wicked intention that was either being covered up or postponed. It was true that she had grown less fearful of her captor with the passage of time but, nevertheless, she remained watchful and suspicious.

What Margaret had to accept, however, was that Nizam had not defiled her yet, nor even made any indecent advances, despite her total dependence on him. So, even though she could not forgive what he had done to her and still could not bring herself to speak to him, she had stopped treating Nizam like an enemy. As a prisoner gradually comes to regard a guard, Margaret thought of the man like a mere obstacle in her path to freedom, akin to the heavy wooden door of the hut and the metal bars on the window. He was frustrating and annoying but not worth her fear any more. And, somehow, she felt sure of being able to escape him someday when his guard was down.

And then came that night. She had been alone all day and it was late in the evening when she heard the thudding of a horse's hooves coming through the forest – it was a sound she had now grown accustomed to and it did not fill her with trepidation any more. But she was nevertheless startled when Nizam burst in, wild-eyed and trembling. Before Margaret's astonished gaze, he went straight to the corner where the table was, leant his hands on it and, looking down, burst into loud, racking sobs. For a few seconds, she continued to sit on the bed, watching him convulsed in some strange sorrow, and though Margaret felt no particular sympathy, such an unusual situation forced her to finally break her silence with him. She did this as undramatically as possible, asking quietly, 'What has happened? Please tell me.'

There was no reply at first but, gradually, Nizam collected himself and Margaret saw him go into the bath area. She could hear him splash water on his face and when he emerged, he looked calmer, even though his hands were still shaking as he poured water into a glass and drank deeply from it. Feeling a distant flutter of dread, Margaret repeated her question. This time, the man met her gaze briefly, saying merely, 'The barbarity of man is endless.'

Margaret could not help a hollow laugh on hearing these words. 'Strange that you should say that to me,' she said, her voice filling with sarcasm.

Nizam's response was sharp. 'If you think this is barbarous…' He stopped to wave his arm in a gesture that took in the hut and all its belongings before saying, 'You have no idea, no idea at all.'

'Come now. Keeping a woman locked up against her will is not an act of barbarity? Why don't you just admit you're my jailer? Why can't you set me free?'

Nizam strode up to her and grabbed her arm. 'You want to be set free?' he asked, his voice harsh and rasping. Just as suddenly, he released her arm to walk across to the door and fling it open. Margaret had not noticed that, due to the state he was in when he entered, Nizam had forgotten to lock the door. She now looked at the wide open and swinging door, her mind racing. Should she make a break for it? Would he chase after her? The forest was dark but that would give her a better chance of hiding and, in the morning, she could make her way back to a British camp. But, as she hesitated, Nizam slammed the door shut again and, leaning on the door, he started to weep. His face was twisted in some kind of inexplicable agony as he said, 'Out there, it is madness ... such things as no man should ever behold, I have seen today ... women and children ... they have...' His voice broke and fell to a whisper.

As Margaret saw her one chance for escape slip away, she ran to the door and tried to push him aside. He grabbed her arms. 'What are you doing? Where will you go?' he asked.

'Get out of my way, you brute,' Margaret cried, trying to batter his chest with her fists. 'I want to go to my mother ... let me go to my mother.'

Nizam held her wrists and looked into her eyes. She felt a sudden stabbing agony in her chest at the expression on his face. Such a strange mix of anger and compassion she had seen only once before and that had been on the face of Dr Aitken back at the camp when he had to tell one poor mother that her child had died. Margaret knew immediately that Nizam was about to reveal the most appalling news to her. And then it came, each word falling on her heart like a hammer blow.

'Your mother, too, is gone,' the man said roughly. 'Gone. Do you hear? Your mother is gone! And your brothers and sisters. All the women, all the little children ... I saw it all with my own eyes today at the Bibigarh. Butchers from the bazaar, called in to do what no other man would agree to. Cleavers used to kill goats and bulls ... limbs everywhere ... arms and legs and blood, blood, blood ... a whole well overflowing with blood, do you hear me?'

But Margaret did not hear for she had fallen, fainting from the shock of this unbearable news. She did not see her captor lifting her from the floor and placing her on the bed. He covered her up so that she could sleep – the only possible salve for such terrible wounds to the heart.

Pia, 2013

For a few moments, the memorial garden that lay around me was frozen in a blur of green, the butterflies and flowers all suspended unmoving in the hot air. Despite the escalating temperature of the day and the rivulets of sweat that were already finding their way down my neck and legs, I felt cold and shivery. I thought of the Bibigarh and I thought of Margaret. Had she felt relieved to escape that carnage? Or maybe it was guilt that overwhelmed her at having been the one that got away. I was familiar with that feeling; as a child I had wondered, on many occasions, if it would have been better, perhaps, for me to have died rather than Tara. After all, she was always the prettier one, the livelier one, the one who made people laugh. But this old thought resurfacing so suddenly made me nauseous. I squeezed my eyes shut and opened them again, stupidly willing the stone angel beyond the flowerbeds to help steady my thoughts. Maybe it was a touch of heatstroke that was making me giddy. I wondered if I should leave further exploration of the Bibigarh memorial to another day. Perhaps I should go in the evening when it was cooler. I got to my feet and made for the picket gate, heading back to the church.

The interior of the building was agreeably cool despite a faint musty smell. I felt instantly better, knowing people were about. There was no sign of Father Kuriakose but I could hear the hum of voices from behind closed doors. In that peculiarly north Indian way, someone materialized magically with a glass of cold water. I drew deeply on it but was reluctant to relinquish the glass, clinking the rapidly melting ice cubes around it before emptying the pieces of ice into my mouth. Crunching on the minuscule bits, I went to examine the contents of a few glass boxes marked 'Mutiny Memorial' but the musty smell seemed to have gotten worse. Despite my recent escape from the outdoors, I felt a curious need for more fresh air. There wasn't anything in this collection that was likely to throw new light on my research anyway. What might have been more useful was a search through the church's death records to see if I could find details of the visit made by the priest to Margaret's deathbed – it may help me to find the Muslim name she had used, for one. But Father Kuriakose was clearly busy in his office and there was no one else to ask. I decided, instead, to leave the church and head off into town. Leaving word for Father Kuriakose that I would not be home for lunch, I let myself out of the gloomy old building and took a few deep breaths to steady my thoughts.

It was only when I was hit by a blast of heat that I remembered Kanpur's summer temperatures of forty degrees! Nevertheless, there was no point cowering indoors if I wanted to search for the site of the old Bibigarh. Even if there was no building left, surely some trace would remain of the innocents who had lost their lives there. I pulled my sunhat low over my eyes while walking down Cantonment Road, keeping my eyes peeled for an auto-rickshaw. There was little point trying to call Abdul when I was already out here in the sun.

The cantonment was, as my first observations from Abdul's vehicle had indicated, immaculately clean and tidy. There were hardly any people about, which made it easier for me to imagine life as it would have been before the Uprising. Descriptions of British cantonments usually contained those archetypal images of pretty churches and missionary schools and chemists shops with names like 'Dr Campbell's' but the only shop I could spot here was called 'Gulati Foods', selling what looked like the usual range of Indian spices and condiments, lined up in neatly filled hessian sacks.

The heat beat relentlessly down through my feeble straw hat and I could soon feel those familiar rivers of sweat course down my back and legs. Feeling not just hot but also daft for so brainlessly marching around in the heat, I started mentally preparing myself for the possibility of seeing nothing at the site of the Bibigarh. It would no doubt be replaced by a car mechanics market or worse. Kanpur had done little to maximize its history for tourists so was it any wonder that the locals had such trouble trying to understand why I was here at all.

Just when I was debating making a phone call to Abdul, a beat-up little auto-rickshaw came trundling and I flagged it down with immense relief. I asked for Nana Rao Park and climbed in when the driver nodded. It was clearly better known than Satichaura Ghat. He turned his vehicle around and took off at great speed and, within seconds, I could feel Kanpur's dusty air fan the perspiration away from my face.

Before too long, we had reached my destination. At first, all I could see was an open field with a few boys playing a desultory game of cricket. Hopping out of the scootie, I wandered up to the nearest fielder who looked about ten. His attention didn't appear to be on the efforts of his bowling colleague and so I smiled and asked in Hindi if he knew anything about a house called the Bibigarh and the well that was turned into a memorial. He shook his head, dark brown eyes inspecting me solemnly. But my subtle intervention had, it would appear, already disrupted the game. A few of the other fielders and, soon enough, the batsman and bowler came running across to see what I was looking for. Amused that someone who looked like me could speak fluent Hindi, a spate of chatter broke out as the entire cricket team (Sarvodaya Vidyalaya's upper school team, I found out) transformed into a group of amateur historians. Most of the boys instantly knew something about a massacre of 'Angrez-log' and a number of disparate theories were offered regarding the site of the massacre, including that the entire house had been taken apart and moved to a churchyard somewhere. Another of the boys countered this by saying that the Bibigarh had been burnt down, although the well and the people who had been buried there were still lying just a few feet below ground.

'Where?' I persisted.

'Right here,' the boy said with great conviction, stamping one tattered sneaker on the ground.

There was immediate disagreement. 'No, not *here*. Over there,' another boy said. I looked at where he pointed and saw, way beyond the outfield, what looked like a small, raised cemented patch surrounded by a few trees. 'There is also a statue there behind that tree. Of Tatya Tope,' he added.

I gave him a grateful smile. 'I think that's exactly what I'm looking for,' I said. 'I was told that the well had Tatya Tope's statue on it. Thank you, I can find the rest on my own. Sorry to interrupt your game!'

I turned to go, but my presence was obviously offering far greater entertainment than their game and, despite my efforts to dispel them, I found the entire team trooping after me. As we walked along, I got talking to one of the older lads, curious to know how much these young people knew of their local history.

'1857?' he said, wrinkling his brow. 'That is the first war of independence.'

Aware that many people had come to regard the Uprising in that way, I nodded. 'And do you know who Tatya Tope was?'

The boy looked less sure, although another one piped up in Hindi, 'He was a great general. He led the Indian army to fight against the British. And the Indians won.' He stopped short, reddening slightly, and I guessed he was considering the possibility of my being a foreigner and maybe even a member of the erroneously vanquished British army. 'Why do you want to know all this anyway?' he asked, suddenly suspicious.

'I'm writing a book,' I replied.

The boy looked impressed. We had now arrived at Tatya's statue and I gazed at it. The bust was of a man with a small pinched face, wearing a three-cornered Maratha-style turban and a scowling expression. His features were sharp and pointed and, probably quite unintentionally, he wore a nasty expression. Who had Tatya been, I wondered, and due to what painful experiences of his own had he come to wreak such a vengeance on a bunch of hapless prisoners? I guessed that the cemented ground on which we stood was where the well and its terrible store of human remains lay. This, then, was the site of the Bibigarh with nothing to mark its shameful memory but this bust of Tatya's. I tried not to think of the gory details I had read in the ancient papers Max Darwin had so helpfully unearthed for me from the British Library's extensive India catalogues – the infant held by his legs so his head could be bashed on a tree, the screaming women who were dragged by their hair before their limbs were hacked off so that they would fit more easily into the already overflowing well...

I preferred to carry away with me the images I had seen of Kanpur: a dusty game of cricket, a pint-sized wicketkeeper and the friendly faces of these lads, full of curiosity and so eager to help.

The Story of Margaret Wheeler

Chapter Eight

For two weeks, Margaret was unable to eat or sleep, the thought of her mother and younger siblings also dead plunging her spirits so low, all she could do was weep and doze and wake up only to weep some more.

In all that time, Nizam seemed to be trying, in as many ways as he could, to make amends. He brought different kinds of fruits and sweetmeats for Margaret, milk and cheese and once even a coconut but any sort of kindness only served to make her cry even harder.

He did not seem to be leaving the hut as much as before and had taken to sleeping nearby at night too. Sometimes, when it was very hot, just outside the door and once – on the day she was running a fever – on the floor near her bed. His motives were still an enigma but, through the miasma of her grief, Margaret could not help starting to feel less fear of him, and less abhorrence. Even through her anguish, she recognized that Nizam's traumatized reaction to the massacre of the captive Englishwomen indicated that he had not been involved. He could not have been dissembling while so grievously lamenting the killing of innocents by those butchers. This was surely not the behaviour of a cruel man.

Then, one evening, with a huge crack of lightning,

the monsoons broke and, while Nizam sat at the open door, watching the rain pour through the trees, Margaret came and stood near him. He swung around, startled, when she touched her fingertips on his shoulder to get his attention and looked enquiringly up at her.

She took a moment to speak, her words, clogged up in silence all these days, finally emerging from her throat. 'Will you ... will you help look for my older brothers please?'

Nizam was clearly taken aback by this sudden request but did not mock its presumption. After a short silence, he asked, 'You have older brothers?'

Margaret nodded. 'I have two more brothers ... if they ... if they are not also...' she trailed off and he nodded. By now even she knew that very few Europeans could have survived such a bloody uprising.

'Do you know where they are? Which regiment?' Nizam asked.

Margaret cleared her throat. 'Bombay Presidency. George Wheeler and Patrick Wheeler.' The names seemed to be emerging from a world far away, one long vanished into the past.

Nizam nodded presently before looking away. 'I will do my best to find them,' he said. 'And, if they are alive, I will endeavour to get word to them that you are alive. When it is safer, you may be able to go to them and they will look after you. It is time for me too to go back to my land.'

Having said this, he got up and walked into the rain. Margaret watched him disappear behind the trees. She knew she did not need to contemplate escape any more, for something about the sadness with which he spoke made her believe him entirely.

~

Margaret lay for a long time that night, listening to the drumbeat of the rain on the tiled roof of the hut. She only had childhood memories of George and Patrick, her two oldest brothers who had both left home at sixteen to join the East India Company's army. If they had survived this war, they were all she had left. She wondered, too, if Emma had made it to safety. If so, it had been the best decision Emma's father had made on that far-off day to send her and her mother downriver to Allahabad rather than to the ill-fated camp at Cawnpore. Perhaps, if indeed the dak system was still operating, she could try writing a letter and address it to the vicar of St Mary's in Allahabad, for was that not where Emma had said they were going? Nizam might be persuaded to post a letter for her while starting his search for her brothers.

She gazed into the dark, wondering at her willingness to lodge so much faith in this man, her captor, but the growing infrequence of Nizam's outings from the hut had made it clear that he was now disillusioned with the rebellion. Perhaps he was also tiring of having to play jailer to her. It was not easy to ensure that there was always fresh water and food available in the hut especially as she had not been particularly appreciative. But how could she have been, given the way in which she had been brought here? It was still puzzling why he had done that although Margaret was now more willing to believe his earlier protestations that it had been for her own safety.

Margaret's thoughts turned to her older brothers. Did they know of what had happened to Papa and Mama? Would they be astonished to see her, having naturally assumed that the entire family had met its end in the bloody uprising of Cawnpore? Surely they would exult in seeing her alive and well. One of them, probably George, would take her in and she could try to pick up the pieces of her life within the fold of the families her brothers would hopefully go on to have.

A fresh breeze blew in through the door of the hut that was slightly ajar. It held the smell of distant rain and Margaret could see dark clouds pass over a fragile, wafer-thin moon. The frogs and crickets in the undergrowth outside were in noisy anticipation of a downpour and, as Margaret lay wide awake, unable to sleep for the din, it occurred to her that she would need to convince her brothers that all things considered, Nizam had been kind and fair. If they believed that he had forced himself on her during her imprisonment, they would surely cut him down in their rage. Despite all that had happened, Margaret did not want that at all.

She looked at the shadow formed by Nizam's body where he lay on the floor near the door. His vigil had intensified after the Bibigarh massacre. He was around the hut a lot more than before, night and day, but Margaret felt sure that, somewhere along the way, his role had shifted from captor to protector. Clearly, he was now protecting her from the savages who had killed the Englishwomen back in Cawnpore. Nizam was a strange man, no doubt, but all Margaret knew was that he had been good to her and she could not bring herself to hate him any more.

~

She woke the next morning, blinking in the light. The rains had cleared overnight, leaving the sun glinting sharply off all the wet surfaces, the leaves on the trees, the grass beneath. Sitting up in consternation, Margaret realized that the door of the hut was wide open and swinging in the breeze. Where was Nizam, she wondered, scrambling out of bed and running to look outside. But there was no sign of either him or his horse.

She wondered why he had left the door open. Was it an invitation for her to flee, given what she had said about finding her brothers last night? What was she to do? Her every instinct, honed over the days of her incarceration, were to make a run for it.

Leaving the confines of the hut, she started off into the forest, holding her skirt up to wade through sodden leaves and leap over fat tree roots. But, half a mile up, she stopped, out of breath and with the frightening realization of how easily she could get lost and not be able to find her way back if she had to. What if she did come across one of those gangs of brigands that Nizam had warned her of? They certainly would not be as kind to her as Nizam had been, those butchers who had killed her mother and all the other women! What would they do if they found her wandering around here on her own?

Margaret returned slowly to the hut, tears rolling down her face at the thought that her imprisonment was so complete, she did not even know what to do with freedom. Was the world outside really a more frightening one than the one inside this little prison hut? Or, Margaret wondered, had she already lost her confidence to face the world in these few weeks of incarceration? She closed the door behind her and sat on the bed, awaiting Nizam.

Finally, towards nightfall, she heard the familiar sound of his horse's hooves. Looking up when he came in, she saw that his face looked drawn, his clothes covered in dust as though he had been riding for miles. He did not say anything at first, merely placing the customary leaf-covered parcel of food on the table before going into the privy to wash his face and hands from the water in the wooden pail.

When he emerged, Margaret spoke. 'You did not lock the door today,' she said.

Nizam shot her a look, probably guessing that she was trying to assess his motives. He did not reply at first, but turned his attention to the food parcel and cut open the bamboo string with which it had been packed using a small pen-knife. Inside was mutton biriyani, a dish that Margaret used to love when it was made in the kitchens back at home. She watched Nizam divide the rice up into two equal portions before removing half onto a steel plate. He brought this across to her and when she took the plate off him, he spoke. 'The door was unlocked because it is now safe for you.' Then he added with a hollow laugh, 'It is, however, not safe for me any more.' In response to her enquiring look, he continued, 'The British have sent reinforcements to Kanpur. Too late to rescue your people, but the relief force – under the charge of a General Neill – is busy rounding up as many of the rebels as they can to get their revenge. There are bodies of sipahis hanging everywhere, from every tree.'

Margaret sat in silence, the food on her plate uneaten as she digested this information. The uprising was over. The British had come. It was safe. She could go.

As though sensing her confusion, Nizam spoke again, 'I was not able to get any information about your brothers because of the turmoil out there. But, from what I hear, the rebellion did not touch the Bombay Presidency. So both your brothers are probably alive. Tomorrow, I could take you near a British camp, although you will understand when I say that I cannot come in with you.'

Margaret nodded. Then she asked, 'Where will you go?'

'Back to my home in Peshawar,' Nizam replied. 'It is all finished for me over here anyway.'

The silence in the small hut hung heavy between them before Margaret asked, 'Will it be safe for you to travel all the way to the frontier? You said the British will kill you in revenge. What if they catch you?'

Nizam shrugged. 'I will use the forests and the streams to make my journey. First to Nepal and then, from there, I will go west across the mountains.' After a pause, he said, 'We will leave early tomorrow so I can take you to a camp first. Now, eat.'

Through the whole night, Margaret lay awake, looking up at the shadowed ceiling, remembering the life she had had and thinking of the one that now lay ahead. She imagined walking into a British camp and telling them of the horrors she had seen – the disease and deaths during the siege, the killings on the riverbank, her father cut down before her eyes and how Amy and she had been carted away. They would want to know if she had been harmed by the Muslim soldiers, they would want to know if she had been shamed and raped. If she denied this, would they believe her at all? They would go after Nizam and hang him if they caught him. Would she exult then to know that her abductor had been finally punished, or would she grieve to learn of the death of a man who had rescued her from far worse barbarities?

Yes, her fellow Britons would be pleased that she had been returned but Margaret knew that in her rescue lay lifelong imprisonment to the fate that had already befallen her and could never be erased. Margaret had no illusions. She was aware of how people talked and behaved in British cantonments and, after so many days in the captivity of a native sowar, she would be considered soiled goods, to be pitied and reviled, a social pariah. No one would willingly be her friend, no one would ever want to marry her. She would be condemned to a joyless spinsterhood. That, Margaret knew without a shadow of doubt, was the fate that awaited her if Nizam took her to a British camp tomorrow. Which prison was better ... this one or that?

And so it was, early next morning, when Nizam began preparing the horse for the long ride ahead, that Margaret went up to him and asked him simply, 'When you go to Peshawar, will you take me with you please?'

Pia, 2013

I clicked my laptop shut when Elsie's maid came upstairs to summon me for dinner. During a delicious meal of chapatis and meat curry, I reminded Father Kuriakose of the person in his congregation who could lead me to Margaret's letters.

'Ah yes. Mrs Ruby Masih,' he said. 'She will be in church for the service tomorrow so I will definitely ask her then. Perhaps you could come along and speak to her directly?'

Thrilled to be given the chance to do so, I swiftly agreed, wisely refraining from telling Father Kuriakose that I had not attended a Sunday service in years. In fact, the last time I had been in a church was at Tara's funeral fifteen years ago and that wasn't exactly out of choice.

This was entirely different, however, and I was up early the next morning, hurtling down the stairs to be in time for the service. Relieved that Elsie wasn't around to see me skipping breakfast, I stuffed a banana into my bag and left the house to cut across the compound to the church. A few cars were pulling into the church compound that had become a makeshift car park but most people were coming in on foot. The church hall was cool and had the same musty smell I'd noticed yesterday, of old incense and damp books. Sitting in one of the pews at the back, I watched people file in, most of them wearing starched cotton saris and salwaar suits, all carrying Bibles and hymn books. The service itself was quite unremarkable, even though I had little to compare it with. Mum generally referred to churchgoers in scornful tones as 'The God Squad' while Dad – some of whose extended family were quite religious – had found his own favourite expression when he had been doing his postgraduate studies in England, which was 'Church of the Latter Day Morons', always accompanied by an amused snort. I sat, trying not to entertain such sacrilegious thoughts as I listened to Father Kuriakose's sermon and attempted joining in with some of the hymns by mouthing lamely along.

Relieved when it was finally over, I pushed my way through the chattering congregation to reach Father Kuriakose's side, hoping that he had remembered to prime Ruby Masih for my request. He was as good as his word and turned to me as I showed up before him. 'Ah, here she is. Mrs Masih, this is the writer I was telling you about. Pia, this is Ruby Masih.'

I smiled enthusiastically at a small, energetic-looking woman of about thirty, hoping I did not look like a maniac. She nodded at me and spoke in a brisk no-nonsense voice. 'Father Kuriakose is saying that you are seeking some old papers and letters for some historical research you are doing. A book you are writing, yes?'

I mumbled something apologetic about historical fiction being not the kind of research she probably thought I was doing but I seemed to confuse her so I shut up. 'Anyway these papers are not with me but may be in my neighbour's house,' she said. 'I remember Fatima, my neighbour, once saying that one woman in their family, many years ago, was an English lady who had converted to Islam. Her husband's great-great grandmother, I think. Some of them in her husband's family are very white-skinned so she was saying this to us one time. When nobody believed her, she said she has seen papers.'

Excited beyond belief to hear this, I had to stop myself from grabbing this serious-looking woman and lifting her up in my arms to hop all over the place. This ancestor had to be Margaret!

There were surely not many other people who fitted that description; an Englishwoman from long ago who married a Muslim and lived in Kanpur. What a treasure trove those papers could turn out to be! My eyes must have been shining but I kept my voice as calm as possible and tried to sound as much like a serious academic as I could. 'I would be very interested in having a look at those papers, actually. They might indeed have some bearing on my book.'

'That is no problem,' Ruby replied. 'If you're free, you can come with me after church today. I have to go somewhere in town for some work but I will go home first so I can take you to Fatima.'

I nodded, waiting impatiently while Ruby Masih went around chatting with a few others in the congregation. Although I was hanging around the fringes of the crowd, I kept an eagle eye fixed on Ruby's small, busy figure all the while. Finally, a long half-hour later, we were departing the church. I accompanied Ruby a little way down the road where she had parked her car, a small battered Maruti 800. As we approached the vehicle, Ruby told me that she worked selling advertising space for the *Times of India* and I waited while she moved a whole clutch of newspapers aside to make room for me on the passenger seat. Then we took off and I found myself clinging to a small leather loop designed for this purpose as Ruby Masih turned out to be a Formula One driver in disguise. Speeding down the cantonment roads, the passing trees were all a terrifying blur. I thought briefly of what a crying shame it would be if I died in a road accident minutes before finding Margaret's journals. Fortunately, we started to slow down as we reached a more crowded part of town, although we were still weaving past vegetable trollies and vendors selling street food as though taking part in a James Bond car chase. Ruby kept up a steady patter of conversation throughout, showing me the famous Kanpur landmarks – a kulfi shop here, a statue of

Nana Sahib there – using one hand to point at things while the other twisted the steering wheel frantically. I should have appreciated the thoughtful local information but kept my gaze fixed determinedly on the three-foot stretch ahead of us, catching my breath every so often and clinging gamely to my trusty leather loop.

Arrival at our destination could not have been sweeter and, after we had screeched to a halt, I tottered out of Ruby's car, feeling a bit sick at the gills. Recovery was swift, however, as I examined my surroundings with a new surge of excitement. We were on a side road that led away from the bazaar and I saw that the houses on the street were old. Probably quite handsome in their time, they now looked rundown and dilapidated with moss and entire plants growing out of exposed brickwork where chunks of plaster had long fallen out. Tangled electric wires hung low enough to be touched by someone leaning out of the upper balconies. These terraces were made of beautifully filigreed stone and wood but some had fallen away altogether, quite probably eaten by termites.

I followed Ruby to the third house on the lane and we turned into a broken-down pathway. Two rickety wooden steps led to a small veranda. 'You wait here,' she said, before disappearing briefly into the dark of the house. I perched on a half-wall, fanning myself with a newspaper as the temperature had already risen to what was surely at least forty-five degrees. A small statue of Christ on the cross hung over the front doorway, so I knew we weren't yet at the Muslim house I had been promised. Ruby emerged soon enough, this time with a large bag slung over one shoulder and a bottle of cold water for me. 'Come,' she said, 'let's go to Fatima's house. It is the one next door.'

I looked at the house she was waving at, wondering with a surge of anticipation if this was where Nizam Khan had brought

Margaret to finally live. I knew that they had fled at first to the North-West Frontier but, going by the possibly apocryphal story of the Catholic priest at her deathbed, Margaret had almost certainly come back to Kanpur at some point. Not to the British camp where she had spent the early part of her life but, here, to the Muslim quarters behind the bazaar. What had brought them back to this city, I wondered, once the trouble had blown over? Had the mountains seemed too far away and too alien for Margaret and had Nizam wanted her to yearn less for the old life she knew? And that was the other thing – did she yearn at all? Did she watch Englishwomen, restored to their former positions and haughty in their beautiful silk gowns, wafting through Kanpur's streets in gleaming hansom carriages while she respectfully stood aside in her Indian clothes, making room for them to pass?

Hardly able to breathe now out of excitement, I followed Ruby into her neighbour's house and stepped into the main room as she went in, calling out Fatima's name. I had to blink to get my bearings in the darkened interior of the house and was startled to find an old man lying on a string bed in one corner. 'Oh, I'm so sorry to disturb you,' I muttered in Hindi as he looked blearily in our direction but Ruby seemed oblivious, continuing to holler for Fatima.

Fatima finally appeared; a cheerful young woman, plump and fair-skinned, wiping her hands on the end of her dupatta. She was followed by a thin girl of about six who sidled up behind her to peer at us from behind her mother's kameez. My heart did a small flip because she too was fair-skinned but, unlike Fatima, had blue-grey eyes. In another setting and, given another set of clothes, she may well – like me – have been mistaken for an English child. Did she carry Margaret's genes?

Ruby explained my mission in swift Urdu and I waited anxiously as I could not completely understand Fatima's soft-voiced reply. She appeared to be suggesting that we wait for her husband to get home but, when Ruby patted her watch to indicate that she had somewhere to go to, Fatima suddenly smiled and relented. Disappearing for a few minutes, she returned, again with the small girl in tow, this time carrying a small leather-bound folder in a cloth bag. She passed it directly to me. With trembling fingers, I opened the fabric wrapping and slipped a couple of letters out. With just a couple of quick glances, I knew that I had found exactly what I was looking for. In fact, the very first letter that tumbled out started with the words 'Dear Margaret' written in ink that, over the years, had tuned a soft sepia brown. It was amazing – just two days in Kanpur and I had found her!

I looked up at Ruby and Fatima and knew that my face was alight with exhilaration. I was so ecstatic, I wanted to kiss both their baffled faces but, composing myself, I thanked Ruby for having brought me here. Still looking mildly puzzled at my reaction to a tattered piece of paper, she asked if I would like to sit down and look through the contents a bit more. But I wanted more than that, of course.

'Oh please, please, could I take this folder back to Father Kuriakose's house with me? Would you tell Fatima she can trust me please, Ruby? I promise to bring the entire collection back as soon as I've looked at all of it and made my notes. I think this is going to hold a lot of useful information and I will need to make copious notes, you see...'

But, when Ruby relayed my request, Fatima looked worried. She clearly wanted her husband's permission before letting the journal out of her sight and so I decided not to push my luck. Quickly relenting, I said, 'Okay, perhaps I can take a look at it here for now and come back another time to speak to your husband?'

Fatima nodded, pleased to have found a compromise, and so,

clutching my treasure to my chest, I went back into the veranda. The heat of the afternoon was still hanging heavy outside, but under the old, tiled roof, it was relatively cool. I was too excited to care anyway. I could barely contain myself but waited until Ruby left to kick off my sandals, enjoying the cool of the stone slabs beneath my feet. Choosing a corner that was furthest from the entrance, I settled down and, leaning my back against wall, started to read Margaret's letters. It might have been fanciful but, quite miraculously, I could feel her gentle presence floating around me, benevolent and sort of amused by my interest. She was so close, her spirit so palpable, it was as if she had been sitting right here next to me, here on this veranda where she had probably spent many hours when she lived here all those years ago. I wondered whether, if I listened hard enough, I would actually hear her voice attempting to tell me her own extraordinary story.

The Story of Margaret Wheeler

Chapter Nine

Once Margaret had expressed her desire to travel with him, Nizam delayed their departure from their hut in the forest by another day in order to prepare more extensively for the journey. At first he brought her two sets of Indian clothes: loose salwaar kameezes with large dupattas that Margaret could swathe around her head and person. He had also thought of footwear – embroidered leather shoes of the sort worn by peasant women – and kohl to line her eyes with.

'It will make you look like an Indian woman,' he said, holding the small pot out on the palm of his hand. When she fumbled, trying to open it, he took it off her and, smearing a bit on the tip of his forefinger, held the back of her head in order to deftly line one eye with it. Margaret stepped back, startled, blinking her eyes from the stinging pain. But, undaunted, Nizam repeated the exercise, this time reaching for her other eye. On this occasion, Margaret stood still in the crook of his arm, conscious of his proximity and feeling his breath on her face.

He stepped back to inspect his handiwork and smiled. 'Just like one of our girls,' he said.

'How can that be?' Margaret asked, still blinking

with her smarting eyes. 'My eyes are grey, sometimes blue.'

'You wait till you see our girls in Peshawar,' Nizam replied. 'Both my sisters have eyes like yours.'

Margaret watched him prepare the horse for the journey, wondering if perhaps he had been kind to her because she resembled his sisters. But it was best not to question it. She had made her decision now and felt instinctively that it was the right one. Better to be in the protection of a man who had proven himself to be kindly, rather than become a sorry figure of pity and ridicule in a British camp. Yes, surely this was the sensible thing to do.

As the time came to depart the hut, Nizam mounted his horse and then helped Margaret up to sit in front of him. 'When I can, I will get another horse but, for now, we have to go like this. It is quicker and less dangerous too.'

They made their way through the forest, scattering squirrels along the way and, at one point, frightening a deer that swiftly disappeared between the tree trunks with a couple of flashes of its white tail. Soft birdsong from the trees above made everything seem so peaceful, it was impossible to imagine that there was still trouble beyond. They rode in silence and, within an hour, they arrived at a raised macadamized road. Nizam looked both ways, carefully scanning the horizon for British uniforms, before allowing the horse to scramble up. The road stretched empty before them for a while and Margaret held her breath as they passed the first group of people she was seeing in the past few weeks. They were a gang of matchlock men, talking loudly amongst themselves, and she was relieved when they went past without sparing her as much as a second glance, leave alone recognizing her as European. Along the way, there were others, merchants and water bearers and cowherds. Luckily there was no sign of the British army that Nizam had mentioned and Margaret couldn't help wondering if she would feel a change of heart if they happened to pass by. What would it be like to see white men who wore the same uniforms as her brothers and father going past? And how strange that all of them would pass her by, assuming she was just another poor native woman.

She felt another surge of mixed feelings for the man who was sitting behind her on the horse, riding it expertly as he led her to another world. Was it good fortune or bad that had made him carry her away from the riverside that day? From what he had told her, she too would have been massacred along with all those other women at the Bibigarh. Even worse, perhaps, had been Amy's fate. Margaret remembered the poor girl and the ruthless manner in which she had been clubbed on the head before being carted off. Later, there had been those tears and that terrifying slap Amy had received in the forest clearing for crying too much. It did not bode well at all for what may have happened to her since. Margaret felt momentarily ashamed that she had not stopped to ask Nizam what had happened to Amy. She ought to plead for her to be given the same choice that Margaret had of going back to their people. And, given that choice, which one would Amy take, she wondered…

When they stopped near a well that afternoon to give the horse some water and eat some of the fruit and nuts they were carrying, Margaret put her question regarding Amy to Nizam. He looked out into the middle distance as he chewed on a piece of sugar cane, his eyes pensive. 'Is she very dear to you?' he asked.

Margaret was honest. 'She was not my best friend.

That was Emma, who fled to Allahabad and is, I hope, safe. But I used to feel sorry for Amy because she lost her mother in the siege and took her death really badly.'

'I have not seen her after that day myself,' Nizam said, 'but I know that the man who took her, Ismail Ali, is of a ruthless disposition. He was talking about converting her to Islam before making her his concubine. He already has two wives. But I know not where they went. All the rebels have had to scatter for safety's sake.'

Margaret's heart quailed at the thought of poor Amy's suffering at the hands of an unscrupulous man. She finished what was left of her frugal meal in silence before getting up to draw some water from the well. When she took the pail across to offer Nizam a drink, instead of taking it off her, he put his hand over hers on the handle and, with a strange look in his eyes, asked abruptly, 'Will you marry me?'

Still thinking of Amy, Margaret could not help a note of bitterness creep into her voice as she replied, 'Why? Are you looking for a concubine or a third wife too?'

Nizam sprang up in fury, knocking the pail from her hands. 'If I had wanted you to be my concubine, would I have waited all these days?' he demanded. Seeing her fall silent and look down in shame, he softened his voice. 'See,' he said, 'I had noticed you in the camp many months before the revolt. And to me you were the most beautiful girl in the world. Which is why, when the uprising hit Kanpur, I vowed to remove you from the trouble and guard you with my life. I thought you understood that when you asked to come along with me rather than go back to your people. You are going with me willingly to Peshawar and, if you go as my wife, my mother and my sisters will take you in as their own. That is what I want from you. Not a concubine but a wife.'

Margaret heard Nizam out but she had another

question for him which, despite her fear, she knew she had to ask. She looked him straight in the eye and queried, 'Do you already have a wife ... or wives?'

Nizam shook his head. 'I may be Muslim and some of our practices may seem peculiar to you Christians but, for me, one man and one woman have been made for each other. And when you find that person, by Allah's blessings, you love and cherish them with all your heart.'

Hearing a ring of truth in his words, Margaret put her hand on Nizam's arm. She could not bring herself to speak the words but, from her expression and gesture, Nizam understood that she had agreed to become his wife.

He found a maulvi at a small roadside mosque, who conducted the ceremony with no questions asked. Perhaps he too did not recognize her for being English, Margaret thought, seeing her clothes and her dark hair. She did not have to say a word during the ceremony, only sit with her head bent, and so there was nothing at all to give her identity away.

Then they travelled on. Sometimes they went in stealth, especially when they passed British conclaves, but at other times they had to take to open roads because the jungles and rivers were too dangerous, hiding not only hungry hyenas and crocodiles but also more vicious predators like greedy and rapacious bandits. Some of the horrors that Margaret saw on that long journey were worse than those she had experienced in the siege. While the uprising had sparked off so much cruelty, the reprisals being sought by the victorious British were as merciless if not worse. Almost the entire length of road from Cawnpore to Allahabad had gibbets lining it and from them hung the bodies of those who may or may not have been mutineers. When they stopped to refresh themselves and their horse, local villagers told Nizam of how the British army had swept in and taken all their men, young and old, intent on wreaking revenge even when families pleaded generations of loyalty. Margaret wept to hear of such cruelties, wondering whether the two sides would ever reconcile and how someone like her, who belonged to both, would ever live with this terrible divide.

As the road progressed, and there were no more gibbets, Margaret saw trees with the strangest of fruit hanging from their branches. At first she thought they were jackfruit trees with their enormous sack-like produce hanging low onto the road and then she cringed as she saw they were bodies. Dozens and dozens of bodies dangling serenely from branches and swinging in the summer breeze. One sturdy old tree with low-hanging branches had not been able to sustain the bodies high enough and wild pigs were feasting on the legs of a corpse.

Nizam rode on but, when he knew Margaret was weeping, he would place his chin on her head and tighten his arms on the horse's reins, holding her close so that she would know that he shared her anguish. But, much of the time, she slept, too exhausted from all her privations to stay alert on such a long journey. When she woke, she would find her new husband still riding hard to get them away from the troubled areas, and would feel sad that his torso had supported the weight of both their bodies while she had been asleep.

At night, if they had not been able to find a hospitable hearth, they slept under the stars, finding woods that offered shelter and water and a hiding place for the night. On those summer nights, as the heat of the day dissipated away, Nizam would cover them both with his shawl and they would lie together, limbs entwined like lovers anywhere else in the world.

Sometimes kindly villagers took them in and gave them room to stay. It was still too dangerous to reveal Margaret's identity when the British were so intent on revenge and so Nizam would tell them that his wife, Mehrunissa, had been mute from birth. The womenfolk would be fascinated by this and crowd around Margaret, touching her cheeks and exclaiming over her beauty, before they would insist on bathing her and feeding her themselves because God's blessings lay in caring for the voiceless. Even if they guessed that Margaret was not Indian, and held more secrets than they would ever know, they saw the glow on her face when her eyes alighted on her husband and they knew that she was happy.

Pia, 2013

What I found that day in Fatima's house was certainly a treasure, bringing Margaret and her growing feelings for Nizam to glorious life for me. There were diary entries and letters and papers, even clippings from ancient, yellowing newspapers, some in Hindi and Urdu and others in English. Everything was haphazardly thrown together, the whole bundle tied with a bit of grubby twine and shoved into a leather folder. It took me a long time, sitting on the floor of the veranda with all the papers scattered around me, before I could bring some order to it all. Fatima emerged from indoors with a glass of chilled, sweet lassi while I worked and I took it with gratitude. The little 'English' girl, whom I was already mentally calling 'Little Margaret', made periodic visits to the doorway to examine my enterprise but, every time I beckoned her to come nearer, she would dart backwards with a little squeal and disappear into the gloom of the house.

In an hour or so, I had many of the papers sorted and arranged in chronological order but, by now unable to contain my impatience any more, I settled back to read the first.

> *'Dear Margaret,'* the earliest letter I could find, dated November 1857, started, *'my dear, darling Margaret. How overjoyed I am to hear from you! To think that we imagined you were all dead when we heard of the appalling massacres at Cawnpore. It was both overwhelming relief and overweening joy that*

I felt on seeing your handwriting on the envelope that was delivered to me at the vicarage. But from the North-West Frontier! How on earth, my dear sweet friend, did you get all the way there? And in a time of so much strife! But now is not the time to quiz you on that for today I write in haste merely to tell you how comforted I am to know that you escaped the barbarous killings and that you are safe and well. From the reports that are still coming in, we now know that Cawnpore was one of the worst hit stations and my heart aches to think of the horrors that befell your dear papa and mamma, your baby brothers and all those among whom we spent such a happy girlhood.

Although our own journey downriver was fraught with all sorts of anxieties, Mamma and I finally got to Allahabad, which fared considerably better than both Cawnpore and Meerut. Some of the sepoys of the 6th Native Infantry did rise up in arms and kill a group of ensigns fresh out from England but almost all other Europeans had already been moved into the fort which stands at the confluence of the two rivers. It was exactly as your poor papa had tried to do by moving everyone to the barracks but the fort at Allahabad is not only huge, it contains a large magazine and controls the traffic on both the Ganges and Yamuna, as well as the Grand Trunk Road. The safety of our people was thus achieved and, although an evil man, a maulvi called Liaquat Ali, did declare himself ruler of the city, he was soon unseated by the arrival of General Neill and his reinforcements. So, my dear Margaret, with trouble contained within the period of a few days, we were all quite safe. How it breaks my heart to see from your letter that this was not the case for those we left behind in Cawnpore.

In your next letter, you must tell me about life in the North-West Frontier and how you reached the mountains. Are you at a British camp, and is it anything like our cantonment in Cawnpore? Will you celebrate Christmas like we used to, with songs and a tree and wine? Do you have a church nearby? And have you made many new friends?

I will fill you in on all the details of my new life here in Allahabad when I write next but I close this letter in haste as I do not wish to miss the day's dak. It comes laden with kisses for you, my sweet friend, and all those happy days we spent together in such carefree joy.

I remain your dearest friend,

Emma

I leaned back on the half-wall of the veranda, my head spinning. So the two friends had managed to make contact over the miles after all. And it sounded like Margaret had initiated it, after reaching Peshawar. Which meant that the poor girl would have got Emma's reply once she had already started living the life of a Muslim wife. What would it have been like for her to hear news of the kind of British life she could no longer be a part of? Surely, she must have yearned for it? Christmas would have been nearing as she read Emma's letter and it must have been the first time in her life that she would not have celebrated the festival. How strange, though, that – despite writing to Emma to tell her she was safe – she had not felt able to tell her friend that she had married her captor and become a Muslim. Maybe she wanted to ensure the letter would get to Emma first. Or perhaps she felt she needed to test the waters in some way before confessing the full truth.

I looked around at the grimy walls of the old haveli I was sitting in, trying to picture what Margaret's life in this house would have been like. I still could not imagine what could have brought her back here to Kanpur, away from the clean air and sparkling rivers of Nizam's mountain homeland, unless it was indeed to be nearer Emma and all the other things she had grown up with during her girlhood in Kanpur. Had she still held on to some hope of being able to go back to her British life at that point?

Spotting another letter marked 'Allahabad' that was written in a different hand, I picked it up and turned it around. It was signed 'Amy' and, heart quickening again with the thrill of discovery, I read it in great haste.

Allahabad
June 1858

My dear Margaret,

I took your address from Emma, having heard that she has been corresponding with you for a while now. She was understandably reluctant but finally gave it to me on the promise that I would add my own entreaties to hers to come back and live amongst us again. You can imagine how upset all of us in the English camp are at your decision to live among the natives and with the man you call your 'noble rescuer'.

I would have added my entreaties to Emma's and everyone else's, my dear Margaret, if I felt certain that this was the best path for you to take but, having made the decision myself to return to camp life, I feel less sure than ever of its wisdom.

You and I are like sisters in our sorrow. Our destiny, at being plucked away from the horrors of the riverside to a fate much worse, is one that no one else will ever comprehend and one that we will forever have to bear the burden of.

If you return, I will look after you as you did me back at the entrenchment in those dark days. But I wonder if you ever will, dear Margaret. You were always more astute at understanding things than I was and perhaps, from so far away, you were able to anticipate the scorn and prejudice that I am now forced to live with on a daily basis.

I have heard that search parties are being sent out for you and I do not know whether or not to pray that they find you. If they do, there will be comfort in confirming that you are well and living life of your own free choice. I myself will draw more solace from that than in having you return to us forcibly.

But, for now, I am, yours, in grief and love,

Amy

Struck by the controlled pain of Amy's letter, I had to momentarily stop my reading to look away. That same plight continued to be cast by war on women in different parts of the world who were raped before being killed, or picked up and carried off as chattel and, often, like Amy, discarded when it was all over. Discarded first by the enemy and then by their own people to whom they had, by then, become a liability and an embarrassment.

I recalled the harrowing story I had read on the *Guardian* website about the trafficking of women from East European villages to brothels in German and British cities. No matter who won these wars between criminal syndicates and governments, those women were damned forever. Girls lost to drug abuse or death, merely because they were pretty enough to catch some man's eye and wanted a better life for themselves. So it simply went on and on, all over the world and into our own times, despite the many struggles to achieve parity. Would things never change?

'Little Margaret' had appeared again at the door and I looked at her, hoping that her fate in modern-day India would be better than that of the English ancestor she had never even heard of. She had taken to flashing tiny smiles at me but even now, when I called her nearer, she gave a small delighted cry and scampered off again.

I returned to Margaret's papers and was absorbed in a newspaper article from an ancient issue of the *Times* that suggested that the missing Margaret Wheeler had courageously killed her captor before taking her own life. Had that report amused Margaret? Was that why she had kept the clipping? Or had it made her feel angry at the suggestion that suicide was the only honourable course open to her?

Totally engrossed, I looked up with a start when I heard the clang of the gate beyond the veranda. A bearded man wearing a kurta-pyjama was approaching hurriedly down the path and, from Fatima's sudden appearance at the door, I gathered that he was her husband. He greeted me with a cursory adaab and bade me sit down as I scrambled up to my feet. I settled myself on the half-wall, although I noticed he did not sit next to me. His tone was a bit brisk, though not unfriendly.

'My name is Faisal. Fatima, my wife, called me on mobile phone to say visitor is come. So I locked up my shop and came away as quickly as I could.'

'Oh, that's nice of you,' I said, 'but you really shouldn't have taken the trouble. I was perfectly happy to sit here and read these papers all day if required.'

He glanced at the little piles of paper I had formed along the side of the parapet, all carefully weighted down with stuff I had managed to produce from the depths of my bag: a torch, a set of keys, pens, my hairbrush, the banana I still hadn't eaten.

'You are writing some book?' he queried.

I nodded. 'About Margaret Wheeler,' I said, looking at him to see if he recognized the name. He looked blank, which perturbed me slightly as he had clearly not even glanced at these letters that had been in his family's possession for so long. I started to explain. 'Margaret was an Englishwoman who got caught up in the uprising of 1857 and went on to marry the Muslim soldier who had rescued her. I think she may be an ancestor of yours, or related to you in some way,'

Careful to say 'rescued' rather than 'captured', I waited again to see if there would be a glimmer of recognition. However, the man still looked uncertain, saying only, 'That was first war of independence. Many English peoples killed here in Kanpur but also many Indian peoples. Your book is about that?'

'Well that's the backdrop but it's really the story of Margaret herself that I'm pursuing. You have some letters here that would have been hers so you must be related to Margaret in some way. Are you aware of a connection? Or do you have any idea how these letters came to be in your possession?'

At this point, there was a shout from indoors and Faisal walked through the doors, frowning. A rather loud and one-sided conversation in Urdu broke out between Faisal and, I presumed, the old man I had seen earlier lying on a string bed. Faisal signalled that I was to come indoors and, as I stepped in, I saw that the old man was trying to drag himself up into a sitting position without much success. I waited while Faisal and Fatima helped him up and he leaned against a bolster, wheezing with all the effort. He finally spoke, in the loud staccato tones of someone stone deaf and toothless, which explained why his words were completely unintelligible to me. Faisal seemed to understand, however, and translated then for me. 'My father saw Fatima taking out the letters from the almirah for you and wants to know why you are reading them.'

'Will you tell him about my book on Margaret Wheeler, please?'

Faisal raised his voice to explain this in Urdu to the old man while I turned to Fatima. She mouthed 'Abba', pointing at

Faisal, explaining in case I was unfamiliar with the Muslim word for 'father'.

I could not tell how much Faisal's father had understood of his son's shouted efforts but, soon, he was saying something in that same raised voice that could have been mistaken for aggression. Faisal turned to me once again and said, 'He is saying that he does not know of any Margaret but that these letters belong to Mehrunissa begum, his father's grandmother. She was Englishwoman but left her people and converted to Islam to marry his great-grandfather.'

'Mehrunissa,' I breathed, savouring the name in my mouth. So Margaret had become Mehrunissa in order to fully integrate into Muslim life. 'Had your father ever seen Mehrunissa?' I asked and waited again for Faisal to translate.

Faisal turned to me again. 'She lived a long time, my father says. Eighty. Which is abnormal for the women in my family. But not as old as he is now.' Faisal laughed.

'How old is he?' I asked.

'Over ninety.'

I tried doing the sums in my head but found myself getting lost, maths never having been my strong point. It was easier to ask. 'Does that mean he might have seen his father's grandmother when he was a child?'

Following a bit more shouting, Faisal shook his head. 'He is saying that she died the same year that he was born. 1920. So he does not remember her but there was a portrait of hers on the wall in the house where he grew up.'

'Here?' I asked quickly. 'Is the portrait here?'

Faisal looked enquiringly at Fatima but she shook her head, saying that it had got destroyed by 'deemak'; I recognized the word for termites. Though deeply sorry to know that I would never know what Margaret looked like, I knew I was still very lucky to get as far as I had.

'Will you thank your father please, Faisal? I fear I might have tired him out with all my questions. But, if he does remember anything more about Mehrunissa, would you let me know please?'

I smiled at the old man, Margaret's great-grandson, but he was now slumped on his pillows, far away in his thoughts again, chewing meditatively on his lower lip and dribbling onto the front of his kurta. Although keen to wander around the house to get a feel for the way in which Margaret may have lived, I hesitated, conscious that this was a conservative Muslim family and that I might inadvertently tread on delicate sensibilities. I was, however, determined to finish reading Margaret's letters and so, with some trepidation, I put my request to Faisal.

'The papers and letters in this folder…' I said diffidently, '…would you mind if I took them back to where I am staying? I will record or scan anything I need and bring it right back, of course. Maybe in a day or two?'

I waited while Faisal and Fatima conferred quietly in Urdu. When he turned to me again, the question came that I had been fearing all along. 'Money? You will pay money for these papers?' Faisal asked.

I had to think swiftly on my feet. 'Well, I was only thinking of borrowing the folder from you. And I'm happy to give you something by way of surety but I am only a penniless writer. No money,' I said, trying to make light of the conversation by pulling out the empty pocket of my trousers. I was, however, conscious of the fact that something which belonged to these people, who were clearly far from well off, had helped me immeasurably in my understanding of Margaret. I wanted to be able to assist them if I could and so I said, 'There is something I could try to do for you, though. I could sign a surety of some sort with you … you know, give you a token sum of money … and then offer the papers to an English museum or archive to buy them from me. I know some people in the British Library and they might consider these papers quite valuable. That money would be yours, of course, and I will make sure it gets safely across to you.'

I waited, looking at Faisal's face, hoping he had understood what I was trying to say and hoping too that he believed me. Something about the desperation on my face must have made the sincerity of my intentions come across. The small frown with which he had been regarding me disappeared and he nodded. 'Okay,' he agreed, 'you takes the papers and tries to sell them in England. I will use the money for her education,' he said, looking at his little daughter who was now playing a solitary but energetic game of hopscotch on the uneven path outside the house.

'I can't think of a better use for the papers than that. Thank you,' I responded, suddenly feeling very moved.

Faisal nodded and waited while I knelt on the floor, gathering Margaret's precious collection of papers together. He helped to pick up a couple, glancing only briefly at them with a faintly puzzled expression before passing them on to me. How odd he must think my behaviour as I took them carefully off him, bowing as though he were conferring a much-sought diploma or prize on me.

Leaving the house a few minutes later, I lightly stroked the cheek of the little girl who had stopped her manic hopping to make room for me to walk down the path. As I closed the gate behind me, with Margaret's letters safely stashed in my sling-bag, my heart sang at the thought that I might be able to use them to contribute to the education of her great-great-granddaughter, a pretty little girl who may well have inherited her blue-grey eyes.

The muezzin was calling the faithful to prayer from minarets towering over the grimy rooftops and scraggly electricity lines but, unusually for me, I had no desire to stop and savour the atmosphere today. The precious booty I was carrying in my shoulder bag was way more compelling. I found my way to the main road by following the sound of traffic and, on turning a corner, found myself assailed by the screech of horns and tyres. Luckily, there were plenty of auto-rickshaws plying, so I hailed one and made my way back to the cantonment. I wondered if Elsie was likely to have some leftovers for me as, in all my excitement, I had completely forgotten about both breakfast and lunch!

The house was quiet when I got in, without a soul in sight, but the main door was unlocked. I made my way to the dining room. On the table were two small bowls of meat curry and rice covered with steel plates. I had a quick solitary lunch and then spent all afternoon and evening up in my room, trying to decipher Margaret's handwriting which, though large and flowery, was smudged in places and faded to near invisibility in others. She had maintained a scanty diary of sorts in an old notebook, of the sort schoolchildren would use and I had to handle it very carefully as the thin cardboard covers started coming apart in my hands even as I opened it.

Her entries were brief and concentrated entirely on her early days in Peshawar. There was also a mix of factual material, sketchy notes of family events and birthdays, even shopping lists, although every so often she appeared to have employed her 'diary' in the traditional manner, using it to record confidences and private thoughts. It was those entries that gripped me but, eventually, I persuaded myself to stop reading and take notes instead. With no access to scanners or photocopiers, I had to do this laboriously, using longhand and pausing in my endeavours only when Elsie returned to the house and summoned me down for dinner.

Father Kuriakose was dining at a parishioner's house but Elsie and I ate together and she seemed pleased, if not a little mystified, at my overwhelming exultation at the day's events. Allowing me to bolt down my meal, she did not demur when I returned as quickly as I could to my room.

I opened Margaret's old notebook and this time used my laptop to make transcripts of her jottings. From what I could tell, Margaret had been understandably more diligent with her diary entries and letters in the early days of her marriage and this enthusiasm slowly dwindled over time, only the odd newspaper cutting marking the latter part of her life. Perhaps becoming a mother had occupied her energies, subsequently bringing her diary writing to an end.

It was very late at night when I put the last of Margaret's papers down, this being a small paper clipping about George Wheeler having been made a general in the British army ... I knew the name from the very first Wikipedia search I had done on Hugh Wheeler. George was Hugh Wheeler's oldest son, Margaret's long-lost brother who had escaped the 1857 killings. I looked at the tiny, yellowed scrap of paper between my fingers, imagining the care with which Margaret would have scoured the English papers for news of people she knew, cutting out and putting away every single report that still connected her in some way to her old life.

I smoothed a finger over the crumbly, yellow shred. How would Margaret, by then not so young herself, have felt to hear so distantly of her brother's successful career? Did it bring back the choices she had once had, and make her regret the one she had taken perhaps? Surely finding a piece of news like that would have acted as a strong reminder of the family she had lost. What indeed was the life she'd have had if she had made the decision to go and live with her brothers rather than choose a life with Nizam?

And what of him? Nizam? Had he observed his wife pore over this little collection of papers and would he have realized that it was no affront to him that she needed that comfort? Or, given that he probably knew no English, would he have felt threatened and distanced every time he saw her scribbling page after page in her journal, private thoughts that he would never know of unless she told him?

To my surprise, I found that my cheeks were wet with sudden tears. I had not realized how moving it would be to have Margaret come to life in my mind like this. Without warning, she had morphed from being a name on my computer screen into a living, breathing woman who had lived and loved and lost, just like me. Faintly embarrassed by such uncharacteristic sentiment over a manuscript, I got up and made my way to the bathroom to sluice some cold water over my face and blow my nose.

It was only when I returned to my desk, and saw the icon on my laptop screen reminding me that I had Facebook messages and unread emails waiting, that I acknowledged the real reason for my sudden tears. I did not dare look at my Gmail account now; without a doubt, Mum and Dad's messages would be full of the pain of Tara's approaching anniversary and I didn't think I could cope with all that at this moment. Margaret and Tara had always been linked together in my head but, as I'd gradually come to understand Margaret's decisions, I was starting to see that there was no shame if indeed Tara too had stayed away from home quite willingly. Quite simply because it had been better for her in some manner that would always remain inexplicable to us, and possibly even to her. And was she not entitled to that choice? Wasn't this theory much better than assuming – as my poor parents had done all these years – that Tara had left home quite simply because she had somehow grown to hate being with us? This, even in the face of the police trying to convince my parents at the time that Tara had got caught up in a gang and been – as that newspaper article from long ago had revealed – a victim of Stockholm Syndrome, just like Margaret. Such a strange name for a process by which people develop sympathetic feelings for their abductors, taken from an incident in a Swedish bank, of all places, when a bunch of bank employees sympathized with a group of robbers during a heist!

I brushed away these thoughts. I had work to do, and painstaking work too, transcribing all of Margaret's diary entries into a notebook. I tried to focus my mind on my immediate tasks. I considered taking the bundle of Margaret's journal and papers across to a scanning shop in town the next day, but this would almost certainly damage the crumbling parchment-like pages. Having promised to sell the papers in England to help with 'Little Margaret's' education, this little collection of papers was now obviously doubly valuable. No, I would much rather transcribe everything I needed by hand.

I dragged myself out of bed and sat down to work. Hours passed unnoticed while I bent over the desk. It was only when my fingers started cramping that I looked up and saw it was nearing three in the morning. I had not even realized it!

If Margaret really did have the choice, what would she have done? I wondered. Flown away from Peshawar to return to her old life? Her journal entry offered such an intriguing glimpse into her mind but had left that question frustratingly unanswered, trailing off in what was probably her own indecision. Or perhaps she had left the question hanging because she had been called away from her desk to attend to some domestic chore. Maybe her husband had come into the room and she had hastily shoved her diary aside to greet him with a loving smile. I could have sat imagining the pair of them in their mountain home for a long time but dragged myself back to logging my research. Perhaps another diary entry would indicate better if she had been genuinely happy with the choice she had made.

I carefully put away all my papers and got into bed but it was a long time before sleep came, various memories of my sister slipping in and out of my head. When I did finally fall into an uneasy slumber, it was Tara's face I saw, half-hidden by a shawl, as she was taken on horseback across miles of Indian desert by a man she barely knew. She looked back at me, fear filling her eyes, mouthing something I could not make out. What was she trying to tell me? I had never seen such a beseeching expression on her face before. In the distance was a stretch of dark, craggy mountains and I called out to her, frantic, because I knew that, once she got to them, she would never be able to come back. But my cries were lost in the hot desert air even as Tara rode on and on, until she was a mere speck on the horizon and then, like a shimmering mirage, she was gone.

Tara, 1997

Tara stretched herself in bed, reluctant to remove her feet from the warm burrow they had found in the depths of her blanket. The floor would be freezing cold on a day as wintry as this. Even when the bar-heater was on at full tilt, the bathroom was like an icebox from December to February. She could surely have another few minutes in her warm bed. What was the difference between being really late and really, *really* late for school anyway?

The bedroom curtains were not fully drawn and, from where she lay, Tara could see nothing but a rectangle of damp grey sky outside. The faint spattering on the windowpane was starting to sound suspiciously like Delhi's unerring winter rain too. What Mum called a peeving morning, Tara thought, shortly to be made infinitely worse by the ceaseless drone of Samuel, the history teacher who awaited her at 'eight a.m. on the dot, no coming late, is that understood, Tara Fernandez?'

'Damn, damn, bloody, bloody,' Tara muttered, flashing an aggrieved look at the bedside clock before finally hauling herself out of bed. She scampered to the toilet down the corridor with teeth chattering, arms wrapped around her body. The tiled floor was freezing – freezing *and* wet, thanks to Pia having had first go at the bath today. Aha, Chhoti Sibling had left her rubber chappals by the bathtub! Tara promptly slipped her feet into them. Although they were damp – and three sizes too small – it was better than being barefoot and having one's feet turning into twin lumps of ice.

Bathroom routine done, Tara limped back to her room, still wearing Pia's chappals. If Chhoti Sibling saw Tara's size-six feet stretching her favourite slippers completely out of shape, she would, no doubt, holler very loudly, making full use of her screechy voice box, but it was safe right now as Tara could hear Pia bantering in the kitchen with their father in her high-pitched tone.

Tara stood before her mirror; it was no-uniform day at school so she had to decide between skinny jeans with a checked flannel shirt and hooded jacket (complete with suede boots and the totally necessary overdose of eye make-up) or that black tube skirt with leggings and the deep purple v-neck Aunty Vee had sent from England for Christmas. Tara decided swiftly on the latter, thinking roguishly about the effect a skirt would have on her numbed-by-winter male classmates. First major decision of the day successfully executed, Tara kicked off Pia's chappals and yanked off her nightshirt, getting changed as close to the heater as she could get.

Once she was ready, Tara executed her customary dozen or so twirls and pouts before the mirror, examining her face with the hollow-cheeks expression that suited her so well but which she hadn't tried out on the wider world yet. She knew her mother despaired at this kind of behaviour and, of course, she was vain but then so were all the other girls at school. And probably all self-respecting seventeen-year-olds across the world. Tara, in fact, felt particularly entitled to a tiny bit of vanity seeing that she was 'so uniquely pretty', as Rajan Mathai in the science section had said shyly the other day, plucking up every ounce of his limited courage.

Tara walked to the kitchen with reluctance, taking a deep breath. Breakfast with the family was way too convivial an activity for her and she really did hate having to digest soggy toast when she'd be perfectly happy to eat nothing till midday by which time she'd have worked up a real appetite for a bottle of Sprite and a pack of Uncle's masala chips. She walked through the door, bag already slung across chest in order to signal that she really had no time to waste. But skipping breakfast was impossible when both Mum and Dad were at the table. Mum was already pointing to the pan of oats on the stove and Dad was waving a horrid, spotty banana at her as Tara tried to slink past them to the back door.

'I'll take this with me,' Tara said, trying not to grimace as she accepted the banana that she really, really did not want. 'No time, honestly. Gotta go. Late for Samuel already!'

'D'you want a lift?' Mum asked, getting up and looking out of the window. 'I'm running Pia down today, seeing how wet and cold it is. Four degrees on the thermostat. You think we'll get hail? I think we might get hail, you know.'

Tara hesitated. She usually hated anything that curtailed her freedom but the offer of a lift, in what were near sub-zero conditions outside, was too tempting. 'Ya 'kay fine,' she said in habitual monosyllabic mode as she sat down without too much enthusiasm.

'Time for a lovely bowl of creamy oats then,' Mum said cheerily, passing her the pan and a jug of milk. Tara did not object but ladled out a minuscule portion onto a cereal bowl, knowing there was little point in arguing. There had been one positive effect of exam stress and that was her fantastic weight drop from a positively chunky fifty-eight kilos to fifty-four. Most of her classmates were complaining about the reverse problem because of the increased amounts of inactivity so Tara felt very lucky to have gone the other way. Her weight loss had, however, been the subject of much drama and discussion at this very table and, rather than rail against it, she'd learnt that it was a lot easier to duck and weave around the compulsory regimen her father had put in place. Having a medic of sorts for a dad was a cruel trick of fate, dissent being so much harder when up against the logic of biology and science.

Tara got up to fetch a carton of juice from the fridge and saw her father eyeing her skirt quizzically. '*What?*' she asked in semi-aggressive tone, sensing his disapproval. Before he could say anything, however, she added sourly, 'It's no-uniform day, in case you'd forgotten.'

'No, I hadn't forgotten. Couldn't help noticing the length of your skirt, that's all. Or lack thereof.'

'Lack? It's only like an inch above my knee!'

'Okay, maybe it isn't the length then but something's not quite right ... it's just a bit ... sort of *tight*, isn't it? Isn't it, Ellie?'

Tara got in swiftly before her mother responded. 'It's *meant* to be a fitted skirt, Dad!' She paused as though needing extra time to deal with the stupidity of grown men. Then, for effect, she shook her head and cried, 'God!' very loudly.

Predictably, her mother sided instantly with her father, although her voice was mild. 'You know, I think Dad might have a point, Tara. It's a bit ... figure-hugging, shall we say.'

'I *knew* you'd side with him!' Tara yelled, barely able to contain her exasperation. 'In case you'd forgotten, this was given to me by Aunty Vee, okay?' This was her trump card but Mum looked unmoved.

'Aunty Vee would have intended it for parties and outings, I think, not school. Even on a no-uniform day, I think you're expected to at least vaguely resemble a schoolgirl, you know.'

Emboldened by his wife's support, Neville Fernandez piped up again. 'Yes, and also that's rather a lot of make-up on your face too, young lady.' He was trying to sound like he was joking around rather than telling her off.

But a telling-off this was, without doubt. Aggression was usually the best form of defence at times like this, Tara had found. She got up and raised herself to full height and spoke in a voice dripping with the sarcasm she normally reserved for the very dull and stupid. 'In case you didn't know, Dad,' she said, 'every *street* in my life is a catwalk.'

She had read that very impressive line in a magazine article but, rather than achieving the desired effect, Tara noticed her parents exchange an amused glance as she sat down again with an angry thump. To add insult to injury, Mum pushed the box of tissues in her direction. 'Well, regardless of how you look on your private little catwalk, Ms Tara Fernandez, I can't see Mrs Luthra being best pleased with all that bronze glitter. You're going to school, remember, not a nightclub.' Eleanor cast another worried glance at the kitchen clock. 'No time to change your clothes now but you may as well wipe some of that make-up off while you're still here.'

Tara tore out a tissue from the box on the sideboard with the kind of ferocity that she hoped would indicate just how much her parents were annoying her. After lightly wafting it around her face, she hid her face in her cereal bowl, pushing the glutinous mess around in her bowl with her spoon and only occasionally taking a portion to her mouth. Then, partially to distract her mother away from her, Tara turned to her sister. Pia was, as usual, lost in her own world and had not heard a word of the conversation going on around her. Chewing on a piece of toast heaped with its traditional load of marmalade, Chhoti Sibling was avidly engrossed in her latest Horrible Histories acquisition, her little nose almost touching the page as she read. Tara grinned inwardly at the title – *The Groovy Greeks*. Her sister, often an inconvenience, did have some endearing qualities, she had to admit. In fact, Pia's fascination with Horrible Histories was so intense that she often knew more than Tara did about some topics that were part of the ICSE syllabus. But this information was never, ever to be disclosed to her; as it is, she thought no end of her superior brain power with all those first ranks and gold stars she kept getting. 'Come on, eat up, Pia!' Tara commanded instead in a bossy, big-sister voice, 'I can't sit here forever, waiting for you to finish your chapter, you know.'

Pia put her book down with a big sigh and an angry frown before carefully pushing her spectacles back up her nose with a jammy finger. She spoke in her usual deliberate and precise way, 'It's the *second* time I'm reading it actually.' Looking at the clock, she added pertly, 'And, you might be late, Tara, but *I* don't have to go for another ten minutes.'

'Stop being cheeky,' Tara replied. 'You'll leave when I tell you to.'

It wasn't like Pia to give over. 'You can harangue me all you like but Neel – over whom you have *zero* control – isn't even here yet, ha.'

'Har-rang, Pia,' their mother corrected, 'not har-rang-you.'

'You never said we were taking Neel too,' Tara wailed, turning to her mother. 'Now I'll definitely be late!'

'That's rich!' her mother responded. 'You didn't expect I'd drive all the way to your school without offering to take Neel too?'

'You could still go on the bus, Tara,' Dad offered unhelpfully, putting his newspaper away. 'That was the original plan, wasn't it? Won't take you longer than fifteen minutes to get to your bus stop.'

'Of course it will! Especially when the wind's blowing like that. And now it's raining too,' Tara said. She could hear her voice rising in that plaintive whine she knew her father hated.

Eleanor Fernandez picked up the keys and went to the door of the kitchen. 'NEEL!' she yelled in a stentorian voice developed over her years as a mother of three. 'Come on, you're getting us all late!' As she returned to the kitchen, there was the slamming of a door followed by the thundering of footsteps charging down the corridor.

Neel made his customary dramatic entrance, sweeping in with blazer flying and tie loosely looped around his neck. He dumped his satchel unceremoniously on top of the TV, causing its strap to dangle over the screen, cutting right through the face of the NDTV news presenter. Then he proceeded to drop his cap on his sister's head in order to distract her so that he could steal her marmalade toast. Though secretly pleased at any attention received from her adored older brother, Pia tried to sound cross with a faux-irritated nasal 'Stoppit, Neel!'

This was all about as much family interaction as Tara could stand and so she got up to take charge, scraping her chair on the floor with a fractious screech. 'Ooof, Pia, you've been chewing that piece of toast through three chapters. I don't think you really want it. You can eat it in the car, Neel. C'mon, let's *go*!'

In the car-porch, Tara brushed away what Mum referred to as 'crisp shrapnel' from the passenger seat before climbing in. That was the main problem with adopting a hip Goth style; black was a damn magnet for all manner of crumb and fluff. After everyone had climbed in with their schoolbags and the doors had slammed shut, their mother reversed their Esteem out of the drive and drove down to the colony gate. She cursed softly under her breath because her view was blocked by a van parked right alongside the wall.

'Why have the guards allowed a van to be parked there? No one should ever park there. Bloody stupid place to choose, completely blocking my view of on-coming traffic,' Eleanor exclaimed in annoyance.

'Not that there aren't already two million cars coming down Press Enclave Road, Ma. This is the megalopolis of Delhi. Not an English village, remember?' Neel drawled from the back seat.

Eleanor ignored him while Tara swung around to have a look at the offending van. It wasn't one of the Press Enclave regulars. Of late, parking had become such a major issue in the colony, everyone had taken to monitoring everyone else's movements (or those of their cars, more specifically). Noisy arguments that included wild profanity sometimes broke out over even a few inches of parking space. Usha Aunty was responsible for some of the most vociferous of these spats, her red Zen being parked as far back in its slot as possible, lest anyone exploit its minuscule size to use up some of the allocated parking space she had paid good money to get. Mr Sikhri, who had the flat on the other side of hers, was always trying to manoeuvre his son's motorcycle in between the flower pots, which meant that its front wheel was sticking right over the painted white line right into Usha Aunty's territory.

'There's no driver in the van so you can't even go aggro,' Tara said in a disappointed voice to her mother. 'Must belong to workmen visiting one of the houses.'

'Well, if they're not gone by the time I get back from my shopping, I'm going to have words!' Eleanor muttered, using what she imagined was her dark and threatening voice.

'Oooh, aggro, makes me nervous, all this female aggro,' Neel piped up in a falsetto from the back seat, adding in his more normal drawl, 'So that's where you get it from, Tara.' He grinned and returned his attention to the Game Boy, thumbs flying over its keys while his utterances earned a simultaneous 'Shut up!' from both mother and sister.

They drove on, joining the traffic on Hauz Rani Road as they made their way to Delhi High School where both Tara and Neel bailed out, leaving their mother to drive Pia to the junior school which had a later start. Losing Neel as fast as she could, Tara ran up the stairs to the Arts block and sashayed down the corridor past Rajan Mathai's class, aware that he and his pimply young friend whose name she could never remember would be slavering in anticipation of that daily treat as usual, this time packaged beautifully in a short skirt and the bronzer she had managed to salvage on her face despite Mum's best efforts. Arriving in class a few minutes late, Tara saw to her relief that Samuel had only just come in and everyone was still talking and shuffling about. She made her way past chairs and schoolbags to her customary place and settled herself next to her best friend, Bela Shah.

'Hey.'

'Hey.'

Tara slipped into what she believed was street-speak used by all American schoolgirls on the high-school TV soaps that came on late-night TV. 'What's happenin' dude.'

Bela, rising to the challenge, replied, 'Christ, jus' don' ask, dude.'

This promising conversation was interrupted by Mr Samuel knocking his duster on his table and demanding silence. Soon, Tara was in a semi-comatose state, only half hearing her history teacher's bewilderingly enthusiastic description of the state of British-Indian relations at the time of Lord Dalhousie's Doctrine of Lapse. She wondered if Horrible Histories had covered the subject, which would sure be handy, especially as it was bound to be available on Pia's crowded bookshelf.

After half an hour of Samuel's monotone, Tara sat up and widened her eyes, redoubling her efforts to concentrate. She had resorted to scratching her leg with a ruler every time she found herself nodding off but, to keep from sleeping during a lecture as dull as this, she'd need to carve a deep wound on her thigh and then rub salt in it. History was her least favourite subject but she was getting desperate now as she needed at least 70 per cent to get into one of the more decent Delhi University colleges. Who in their right mind would want to go to colleges that had names like Kirori Mal and Shri Venkateshwara? St Stephen's would be best but Tara was realistic enough to know that she was very unlikely to get the requisite grades. Wherever she eventually landed, however, she was greatly looking forward to university life, one of the biggest pluses being independence. *Independence* – she savoured the thought in her head like a guilty pleasure. Leaving Delhi and staying in a hostel would be even better, although, at the moment, Tara couldn't even imagine what it would be like to be able to eat when she wanted and sleep when she wanted and have sex ... well, that was Bela's area, really, as Tara had only had a couple of fumbling experiences so far that she hadn't really enjoyed.

By lunchtime, Tara's head was swimming from having had to concentrate so unusually hard. She knew it was her fault really as she'd spent most of the eleventh standard slacking and had only woken up last month with a jolt to the fact that the final exams were now barely three months away. Thinking all sorts of dire thoughts about the 50 per cent she had got in the eleventh standard exams, Tara left the school building for some fresh air, closely followed by her best friend. Bela was rambling on about something Ricky, her boyfriend, had said but Tara, nursing a slight headache, was only half listening when she noticed a Maruti van parked by the wire fence surrounding the basketball court. An unusual grey colour, it looked oddly similar to the one that had been blocking their driveway back at home this morning. Strange, she thought, before stowing away a passing uneasy feeling.

The two girls made their way to the canteen on the far side of the school but Tara felt completely unenthused by the usual offerings – insipid-looking samosas and a veg roll that was glistening with fat. Finally settling on the veg roll, she picked up a bag of Masala Munch and a bottle of Sprite before making her way to the cashier to pay. Slipping onto the bench next to Bela and Rick, Tara found to her dismay that she had descended right into the midst of a lover's quarrel.

'I did not!' a red-faced Rick was saying.

'You did!' Bela replied.

'Who told you anyways?' he demanded.

'Nobody needs to *tell* me anything, I saw for *myself*, Rickie!' Bela replied, raising her voice to just-about-to-cry levels. Fully aware of Bela's propensity for histrionics, Tara wondered how soon she could gulp her roll down and make a getaway. Not that she didn't want to support her friend but, of late, these Bela–Rick rows were coming around just a bit too often for her to handle. Her chance came when she spotted Neel come strolling through the refectory doors, flanked by a couple of friends.

'Sorry, just remembered, I gotta give Neel his lunch money,' Tara lied, in an unconvincing act of sisterly concern. Even if the weirdness of this had occurred to Bela and Rick, they were still too engrossed in their tiff to look up as Tara picked up her plastic tray and drifted away.

She wafted up to Neel and smiled at his two friends. She could never remember their names but gave them the benefit of her huskiest 'Hi' nevertheless, knowing it was likely to bring them close to fainting point. Fourteen-year-old boys pumping with hormones were no higher up the evolutionary chain than vermin in Tara's view but occasionally they were fun to practise her not inconsiderable, albeit still growing, feminine charms on. Picking up the remnants of her food and drink with one hand, she gave the tray to Neel with a loving, 'Here, Chhota Sibling, you can have *my* tray.' Then, twirling one strand of hair on a finger, she strutted away, watched, she knew, by at least two pairs of admiring – nah, adoring eyes.

Leaving the canteen, Tara shivered as a gust of wind caught her hair, cutting through her woollen leggings to pierce her skin. Perhaps Dad had been right about the shortness of her skirt. This was more a flannel trousers sort of day, if she was to be quite honest. It was nearing the end of January and ought to be lightening up a bit by now, Tara thought, hurling the balled-up butter paper wrapping of her veg roll into a bin. She shoved the last of it into her mouth and took a swig of her Sprite to help it down her throat. Perhaps a jog around the basketball court would warm her up, she thought, noticing that the grey van was still parked next to the fence. Had there been a sudden influx of grey vans into south Delhi today for some curious reason? Tara couldn't put her finger on it but the bloody thing was giving her the jitters – especially as the front windows were smoked glass and the back was all closed up, making it difficult to tell from this distance if there was anyone in the van or not. It was giving her the weirdest feeling of being followed and, rather than repeatedly run past it while jogging, Tara decided to go back into the building again where it was all warmth and noise and light.

After her maths extra class later that evening, Tara left the school gates with Bela and Neel who, she couldn't help observing, stayed back and accompanied her home only when Bela was around. He should really be ashamed at fancying a girl so much older than himself. And his elder sister's best friend too. Tara vowed to have a word with him once they were home.

The school buses had all left for the day and so the three made their way to the bus stop down Geetanjali Road, all swaddled in their jackets and mufflers to guard against the freezing evening. The grey van was *still* outside the school and Tara cast a quick glance into it as they passed by. She was close enough now to see through the front windshield that it was empty and the vaguely troubled sensation she had experienced earlier dissipated away. Exam anxiety nightmares sure did have a crazy way of affecting the mind.

Margaret's Journal Entry 1: 2 September 1857, Peshawar

So much has happened, so much has changed, it would seem unnecessary, even churlish perhaps, to look back. But such self-governance would seem beyond my control, for, while I am usually surrounded by people – a loving husband and his all-embracing family – it only takes a few moments of solitude to become aware of those old wounds that refuse to heal. It is only here, to these pages, that I can confess this at all. And there is little point in committing this to paper, but for the feeling that a river rages within me and will likely break its banks if I did not.

So, where shall I start, dear diary?

If there had ever been a 'warning sign' of the mutiny, I could only point to one thing. And that was the manner in which Nizam had looked at me when we were all still back at the camp in Cawnpore. I now know, of course, that he had been attracted to me from the start but then, by the searching way in which he gazed at me with his piercing black eyes when we were church-bound that morning, I should have seen something unusual. Native men did not usually even glance at the face of an English person, man or woman. That was merely the accepted way.

If I had told Papa about my observation, what he would have done, I cannot help wonder. Papa loved his soldiers, he would almost certainly have never imagined what was to come. Which is exactly why we were caught in such an unsuspecting manner. So it would appear that neither my instincts nor my father's had been accurate at all.

Given that it happened, would I have wanted any of the horrible alternatives? ... The truth is that, if I could have saved my parents and my brothers from being so cruelly massacred, I would have done so. Without a doubt, I would have done so. But, on the other hand, it took the cruelties of the uprising for me to find Nizam's love. Would I have ever found a man so tender in disposition and so passionate among my own people? Most of the Englishmen I had seen back in the cantonment had been strutting, self-important prigs. Nizam, in contrast, is thoughtful and gentle and completely in love with me. Would I willingly have given this up if the choice came before me today to turn back the hands of the clock?

Tara, 1997

Tara looked out of the window to check if it was still misty and was greeted with the depressing sight of yet another leaden grey sky. Winter had come late this year – December had been positively balmy – but it was sure making up now for its earlier lack of enthusiasm, the chill just going on and bloody on, seeping into one's bones. It was definitely a thermal socks sort of day. Well, unlike Bela, Tara didn't have to worry at the moment about the exploring hot hands of a horny boyfriend and so could pull on as many thermal socks and woollen vests as she liked with no worries. She ought to be pleased at not needing to subject herself to all those scratchy lace stuff that she'd once looked at in Ansal Plaza with Bela. Not that she'd ever admit it but a part of her was faintly envious that her friend had been going steady for nearly a year now. Tara had lots of boys crazy about her but, for some reason she wasn't sure of, none of them seemed too keen to pursue her seriously. Bela said it was the scary frowny expression she sometimes wore that frightened all the boys off but Tara wasn't convinced by that.

She pulled on that frown now, looking out of the window. The creepy grey Maruti van was back, parked on the other side of the colony wall and nearly hidden from view unless you were looking out for it. It had not been there when she and Neel had walked back home from the bus stop yesterday so perhaps it was indeed the same one that had been outside the school. But now here it was, near where it had been parked yesterday morning when Mum had first spotted it. Tara peered at the vehicle more closely but could not tell if it was occupied. There was surely some really simple explanation for why she kept seeing the same van – maybe it wasn't even the same van! – but Tara resolved to get her mother to check out whose it was anyway.

By the time she was washed and ready for school, however, Tara found that her mother had already left home.

'Her appointment at the hospital,' their father reminded at the breakfast table.

'Why didn't she wait to go with you, Dad?' Pia asked.

'Because I don't need to be at my clinic till nine at least and she had to be at the hospital early for her fasting sugar test. Therefore, my dear children, I've drawn the short straw for the school run so I want no fuss and no delay and a prompt seven thirty departure. Okay?' Neville Fernandez rolled his eyes at the chorus of groans his order was greeted with.

'You're such a terrible driver, Dad, I'd really rather walk!' Tara said.

'Thus speaketh the only seventeen-year-old in Delhi who still hasn't got a learner's licence,' Neel reminded her, earning a high-five from his father.

'Only because Mum and Dad won't let me,' Tara objected hotly.

'Plenty of time to take classes once you've finished your final exams, darling,' her father said. Tara knew that her parents wanted as few distractions as possible before her board exams, given her appalling mock-exam scores, and she hadn't protested too much as it would clearly be much easier to learn to drive once the summer holidays started. Already she was picturing the little red Zen she would sweetly persuade Dad to buy for her eighteenth birthday in which she would drive to Delhi University. Aunty Vee had promised her one of those new-fangled mobile phones for her birthday, so, with car and phone, she'd be quite the swinging student!

As they left the house in their father's gleaming silver Baleno – his midlife crisis car, according to Tara and Neel – Tara looked at the grey Maruti van, this time startled to see a young man standing at the open back door. He appeared to be loading a large plastic box into the back of the van as their car approached. He looked up as they passed and Tara caught a dark-eyed gaze from under a baseball cap. Innocuous enough and – as she had said yesterday – quite probably a workman getting something done in one of their neighbour's houses. She should really quit worrying, she thought as they drove out of the colony in the direction of their school. Nevertheless, remembering a few minutes later that the house was empty, Tara wondered if she ought to have got the number of the van just in case grey-van-man was a burglar and breaking into their house this very minute. It was too late, she hadn't got the number, and she dismissed the thought as nonsense as they turned off Geetanjali Road and the school gates came into view.

'Bye!' Pia called out as her two siblings disembarked. Tara blew her a kiss. She was glad she hadn't mentioned the van as it probably would have freaked Pia out and poor old Dad would have done that typical overanxious thing and immediately turned around and headed back to the house to make sure no one was breaking in. Then everybody would have been late and all for nothing.

Once again, Tara's school day was traumatic to say the least. Even drama, the only subject she had actively enjoyed at school, had lost its gloss because the practical and performance stuff had been finished in January, leaving just tons and tons of written work. Tara had managed to bullshit less than 500 words so far of an essay that was meant to be 2000 words long and, far worse, she hadn't even started prep on the theoretical bits for the final exam. It was Tara's firm belief that she ought to be accepted as a great stage performer without having to think about all those boring technical and aesthetic aspects and certainly without having to interpret text. What was *that* all about? All she wanted was to get on stage or, better still, get into films – at a pinch, maybe TV – but her parents were insisting on her going to college as a first step in any of those careers.

Feeling utterly downcast, Tara left the school building by herself that evening. Bela had made up with Rick and was necking with him in some dark corner of the school. Neel was staying back for band practice which left Tara with only her own grim and cheerless thoughts for company. The short February days didn't help; only five o'clock and it was already getting dark but there was nothing to do and nowhere to go in dull old Malviya Nagar market except for Lazeez Coffee Shop & Ice Cream Parlour – which would only make her *fat*.

Picking her way through a large, stinking pile of garbage, Tara dodged past a rag-picker and her fly-infested baby who had temporarily suspended their pickings to beg for money from passers-by. A cyclist swerved to avoid her and a motorcycle to avoid him. The screech of horns was deafening and Tara decided it was best to head straight home. More time for revision, ha ha ha.

She started to trudge down the road, avoiding cycles and scooters, all of whom were jostling for space at the edge of the busy main road. It was still bitterly cold but at least it wasn't raining any more and there was a faint chance that, once she had got past this crowded stretch of road, the damp evening air would help sweep her mental cobwebs away. When Tara was smaller, she'd thought that the approach of an eighteenth birthday heralded possibly the most exciting phase of one's life but, in fact, all that seemed to lie ahead was the doom and gloom of exams and the likelihood of poor grades and the consequent wrath of her parents. Worst of all, she'd only make it to some crappy college with a crappy name like Kirori Mal. Proper adulthood – not just a date on a birth certificate, that is – seemed *miles* away just yet.

Tara passed the big, new hotel and then Goel's provision store, lost in her thoughts, but backtracked a short way as she suddenly decided to buy a bar of chocolate to keep her going till she got home. The shop was busy as a lot of kids tended to come here straight after school. Choosing a bar of Fruit 'n' Nut – a favourite from her childhood – she made her way to the counter and fished out the required change from her pocket. Peeling off the wrapper, Tara walked to the bus stop, still uncertain of whether to walk home or not. Like the shop, the bus stop too was crowded with thirteen-year-olds pushing and shoving each other and generally behaving hysterically. The noise would be unbearable once they were all aboard a bus. Besides, local buses had the most god-awful stinky air in the winter months, when all the windows were closed. Tara made a snap decision to walk. A twenty-minute brisk walk would help burn off some of the calories of the chocolate bar, which Tara was feeling guilty about even as she took the first delicious bite of it. There was every chance she'd now end up with acne on her chin for the pleasure too. It was stupid to succumb to this kind of ridiculous comfort-eating just because of exams. Having managed to lose all that gross flab around her tummy by virtually starving herself to death last year, it would be just the most tragic thing if she simply piled it all on again by snacking.

Tara turned off Malviya Nagar Road at the chikwallah's corner and approached the open stretch flanked by an abandoned construction site on one side and a high wall on the other. The noise of the traffic receded as she walked on, and everything started to become a lot more peaceful. On winter nights, Neel referred to this stretch of road as 'Poltergeist Passage', mostly to try and frighten her when they were walking back late together, and on a freezing evening like this, with mist swirling around, it did actually look rather spooky. Tara looked up the empty road, wishing she had stayed and taken the bus. Home was a long seven minutes down this road, before she took a left turn at the row of terracotta flower-pot vendors and reached Saket.

She heard a car coming up behind her and saw its lights illuminate the road in front, throwing up an enormous shadow of her own self in school skirt and blazer, bag slung around her neck. As it started to slow down, Tara hoped for one happy moment that one of her parents had decided to come and get her on their way back from somewhere. But, unexpectedly, as she turned her head to look back at it, the car lights dipped. Tara jumped as the vehicle revved up again and came way too close for comfort, lurching wildly past her. Just beyond where she was, it stopped. Through the murk, Tara recognized the grey Maruti van, although its driver was not visible from where she stood. Her heart started to race with some deep-seated instinct for impending trouble but, just as she was contemplating turning tail and running like crazy back into Malviya Nagar, the rear doors of the van opened and a man with a scarf tied over his face leapt out. Before she could scream or even put up a fight, he had thrown what felt like a sack across her head and dragged her into the back of the car. She heard a door slam shut and felt the car take off with a screech of tyres against the road.

By now, aware of what was happening, Tara started to struggle, kicking as hard as she could, but the man she was wrestling with was far stronger than she was, his arms like iron bands around her wrists. Besides, she couldn't see what was happening and the scream that was finally rising – too slowly – in her stomach was suddenly stilled by a sharp blow to her head. There was the most excruciating pain but Tara was only distantly aware of it as she felt herself get swallowed up by an inky black cloud. Her legs were giving way beneath her and she felt herself being thrown onto the hard metal floor of the van. Something prickled through the woollen fabric of her school leggings – possibly a blanket, rough of texture and with a mouldy smell. She was vaguely aware that her wrists and her legs were being spread-eagled and clamped in metallic vice-like bands and her clothes were being pulled at in a manner that, even in her half-conscious state, she knew she must fight. It was imperative to fight as she felt her skirt being pulled up and her leggings and knickers yanked down. A hand was scrabbling around her privates but, even though she writhed, there was little room to move as the weight of a body landed on top of her, flattening and suffocating her. She could smell his sweat and some sort of cheap deodorant even through the canvas sack over her head. And then Tara experienced a sharp burst of concentrated agony – a lightning flash – in her groin and the middle of her spine, causing a part of her to disembody itself and float somewhere way above where there was no pain at all.

~

When Tara awoke – she couldn't tell how long after the attack it was – the pain was so bad she wanted to retch. She couldn't get up because of the way her arms and legs were pinioned. Vomit choked her throat as she lay in the dark, her head still covered by the sack. If she wasn't allowed to sit up, she would die. Did he not know that, did he not care? Who was he, her attacker? Was he still nearby? And how long had the vehicle with her in it been moving? It was still moving, she could tell from the rocking motion. She was probably miles away from Saket already. Tara started to cry, tears rolling down the side of her face and getting into her ears. How long had she been in this van? Who were these people; there were at least two, given that someone had been driving the van while the other ... the other ... Tara could not bear to think of the word 'rape'. It was what happened in those horrible hard-hitting 'A' rated movies, not in real life, not to *her*. Even when the papers mentioned abductions and gang rapes, the horror she felt was always diluted by those events happening to someone else. Maybe she was being punished for not having empathized enough with all those other victims.

Were Mum and Dad looking for her? And the police? Where were *they*? Feeling the most terrible panic overwhelm her, Tara tried to yell but the voice that emerged was a croak and, with sudden shock, she realized that her mouth had been gagged. A thin skein of fabric or rope stretched tightly between her teeth, cutting painfully into the sides of her mouth. The man must have uncovered her head and tied it while she had been unconscious. Despite her cold and aching body, anger rose within Tara like a wave, dislodging her pain. The bastards! The bastards! Why were they doing this to her? If she could only free herself, she would kill them with her bare hands. That's what she would do. She just needed to get out of this car, free her hands and then she would kill them!

Tara froze as the van stopped and she heard voices. Right next to her, outside the van. She strained her ears in order to catch the words. She needed to try and figure out where she was and whether she could escape. But all she could hear were raised voices (How many? Two? Three?) and gobbledygook. She couldn't understand what they were saying.

The rear door opened with a loud clang and, instinctively, Tara made herself go limp, hoping desperately that it would make her less prone to attack again. Had she read somewhere – or was it one of those ghastly things that girls said to each other while talking about staying safe – that a man was far less likely to want to rape someone when she was unconscious? The struggle, the fight, which was what made it exciting for them. Despite trying her best to remain lifeless, Tara started to tremble with fear, her whole body shaking so hard she wondered if it would look like she was convulsing.

The rear door was slammed shut and Tara heard the engine start up as the van began to move again. They were taking her somewhere else. Further away from home. But she needed to stay really still and try to control her trembling as she could tell that one of them was in the back of the van again with her. She must not get raped again, she must not.

The man came nearer – she could smell him now and hear his laboured breathing. Was he the same man? Another? He was close, too close, it was going to happen again. Tara, frightened beyond words, forced the cry emerging from her throat down again, even though the gag would have prevented it from emerging anyway. Luckily, the man couldn't see her terrified expression because of the sack covering her face. She winced as she felt his hands on her but this time they were on her neck. Was he going to strangle her, she wondered, bracing herself for the worst. But he was searching around her neck for something. A necklace? Was he hoping to rob her? She wasn't wearing any jewellery, though ... another one of Mum's rules about school. Would that make the man angry? That she was wearing no jewellery and had no money on her at all, except for a bit of loose change from the chocolate bar she had purchased? Tara felt the man tugging at a bit of twine that seemed to be holding the canvas sack around her neck. He was trying to get the sack off, that's what he was doing ... In a few minutes, he had succeeded and, despite wanting to take in great gulps of unfettered air, Tara had the presence of mind to keep her eyes closed. He needed to believe she was still unconscious or he would rape her again. Maybe he wanted to do it this time while looking at her face. Was this the same animal as before? Would it be worse now that she was conscious?

The sack was discarded and the man started patting her face and her cheeks – not painfully but softly, as though trying to wake her up. It was getting difficult to pretend any more and so

Tara finally opened her eyes and looked straight up at the face of a young man wearing a baseball cap. Short hair, jeans and a green fleece jacket. The same one who had been outside her house this morning. Had it been just this morning, or had many days passed already? And was he the same man who had wrapped his face in a scarf before raping her?

The man spoke. Swiftly, his voice low. 'Look, he wants me to rape you. So you have to pretend. Shout, struggle. I will make noises also.'

Tara blinked at him, unable to understand. She recognized the Hindi word for rape from numerous Hindi films but what did this man mean to say? Was he deranged? She tried to speak but the words would not come. She'd forgotten that she was still gagged. Seeing her attempts to speak, the man started to untie the cloth that was cutting into her mouth. Then he stopped, an expression of fear coming over his face. Tara wanted to assure him that she would not holler and shook her head in desperation, trying to speak with her eyes. She sensed that this man could be her ally. The 'he' referred to was obviously the other man, the rapist. She didn't know what they wanted of her but, from the way this man was behaving, there was a small chance he would help her escape. Clearly it was the other one who had raped her earlier. But why did the rapist want this man to do the same to her if he did not want to? She tried to speak again and, this time, the man hurriedly untied the knot on the gag. He was so close, Tara could see beads of sweat above his eyebrows and smell cigarettes on his breath.

'Please don't shout,' he whispered urgently, clamping his hand very tightly over her mouth as the gag came off. 'He's very dangerous. He will kill you and me if he knows I am talking to you.'

Tara shoved his hand off her face and asked, 'Who are you?' She heard her voice emerge in a croak. 'What do you want of me? What does *he* want of me?'

The man hesitated. The metal wall between the front and back cabins and the sound of the car engine were probably enough to mask their voices but he was clearly frightened nonetheless. 'I will tell you later. But you must not let him know I have spoken with you. Now I have to tie your mouth and eyes again and pretend to beat you.'

'Please don't hurt me,' she said, her eyes brimming over with tears.

The man's eyes slid away but he nodded. 'I promise,' he whispered. 'I will help you. But not now. Later.'

Tara nodded and allowed the man to gag her again. With a sinking feeling, she felt the sack go over her head too. How did she know he was not dissembling? Maybe this was some kind of nefarious plot to entrap her even further? Perhaps the two men were playing 'good cop-bad cop', like they did in those American serials to soften people up before they were interrogated. But she felt marginally reassured as she felt the man pull her leggings up and straighten her skirt. Almost a paternal gesture, making her think of her Dad when she was a little girl. She felt herself start to well up again, sorrow rising up from her belly as she thought of her parents waiting for her, but was distracted by the man thumping on the floor of the van, probably making as though he was either beating or raping her. Tara knew she was supposed to play her part too but she could barely move her strapped arms and legs anyway. Nevertheless, she strained at her bonds, hearing the chains creak against their hinges, then she tossed her head from side to side, making groaning sounds as she thumped the heel of her shoes on the floor.

What was she doing? How had she ended up here on the floor of this van? And where was she being taken by these two men? For the first time since she had been abducted, the true horrors of what might befall her came to Tara. Dear God, what was going to come next?

Then the thumping stopped and Tara felt the sleeve of her blazer being shoved up her arm. A cold swab, a prick of a needle and, finally, from somewhere far away, peaceful, blissful sleep.

Margaret's Journal Entry 2: 12 September 1857, Peshawar

I had a nightmare again last night, perhaps due to what I have seen in the newspaper. I have not suffered nightmares for many days now and thought they had gone but, suddenly, I was in the confines of that hut in the forest outside Cawnpore and, instead of Nizam, there was someone dressed in the same clothes as him but had another face. A cruel face with no mercy. It was, I believe, the man who had taken poor Amy away that day in the forest. What became of her? Where was she taken? Like me, she too has no parents who would not rest till she was found. We are lost souls, girls like us.

I find now from the newspapers that they are searching for me. Amy has been returned to a British camp and has told them that she saw me being taken. They know I am alive and want to come and get me. But I suspect that it is not me they seek as much as vengeance. Vengeance would make for a sweet prize but of what use would I be to them? A despoiled, mute and silent trophy?

It was only a small piece in the newspaper that was brought yesterday - an old paper as it sometimes takes days for the dak to reach us here in the mountains. It mentions a reported 'sighting' of Margaret Wheeler - but it did not say when or where. Will they really come all the way here, to Peshawar, which clings to the side of these far mountains that border Hindustan? And, if they do come, would they ask me what I want them to do? I am not Margaret Wheeler any more. But Mehrunissa, wife of Nizam Ali Khan. A respectable Muslim wife in a small, peaceful, law-abiding place. Here, in this town, people smile at me and ask me to help their children learn to speak English. They have accepted me as one of their own and seem to like me well enough. In a British cantonment, would I not be an outcaste for having lived amongst the natives for so long. Would I not be pitied and gradually hated?

In my mind, it is no choice really. But will they listen to me? Will they seek my permission or will they drag me away to another kind of hell?

Tara, 1997

Tara opened her eyes, taking a few swirling and confused minutes to become aware of her surroundings. As she remembered her abduction and rape, she felt that now familiar sick feeling in her gut. She was still in the back of the van but someone had unhooked her legs and her left arm from their moorings to allow her to sleep on one side. The sack had gone too, although she was still gagged. The van was no longer moving and so she slowly dragged herself up, trying to make as little noise as possible in case her captors were nearby. Although it was dark inside the van – and now stinking of what may have been her own bodily emissions – Tara could tell that it was broad daylight outside as a couple of small holes in the body of the van were letting twin streams of bright sunshine through. One from either side of the cabin. Dragging herself along as far as the clamp on her right arm would allow, Tara put one eye to the nearer aperture and recoiled as she saw both her captors sitting only a few feet away from the van.

When she gradually plucked up the courage to put her eye to the hole again, she saw that the two men were drinking something from plastic glasses using the box that had been inside the van as their table. One she recognized as the man in the baseball cap who had been kind to her but the other was completely unfamiliar … the scarf with which he had covered his face was now wound around his neck and Tara could see pockmarked skin with a flat nose and narrow, close-set eyes. A pitiless face. She wondered if they were brothers as there was something vaguely similar about both of them, although the pockmarked one was older by at least ten years and somehow cut from different cloth, having an air of latent belligerence about him in the way he sat with his legs wide apart and the coarse way in which he chewed his food.

Quelling the revulsion she felt looking at the man who had raped her, Tara watched the pair exchange occasional utterances in low voices as they ate and drank, and realized, with sudden horror, that the hole through which she was observing them had very likely been drilled in order for them to watch *her* before she had been captured. That explained the van parked near her house and near her school, its front seat always seeming to be empty. So her abduction had all been carefully planned and executed! Why her, though? And why had they come all the way to Press Enclave when it would have been much easier for them to kidnap someone from one of the slums or jhuggi colonies? Was it for ransom? Surely not, for they would surely not take a dentist's daughter if that was the case. They'd be much better off with a big industrialist's child, or the daughter of some businessman. Also, they wouldn't start by raping her if they needed her to be returned unharmed at some point. Tara pulled her eye away from the hole, getting more and more panicky. She did after all read the papers sometimes, and watched late-night TV programmes that showed girls being picked up for prostitution rackets. Sex-trafficking, they called it – but the subject had been just a bit too heavy for her and so she had turned it over to something else.

Tara had no idea if more than one night had passed while she had been driven along in her drugged state but by now Mum and Dad would surely have contacted the police. They would stop at nothing in their search for her, Tara knew for sure. She missed them desperately, yearning for them from the deepest part of her being. She missed Pia and Neel and their arguments and her noisy, warm home too. The whole family must be devastated by her disappearance. The neighbours would all have come around. There'd be police all over the place, in their house, in the school. Bela and the others would be in floods of tears. Her face would be on TV, and in the papers. Everyone would be looking for her. Perhaps the shop man from whom she'd bought the chocolate bar would remember seeing her! Maybe there had even been an eyewitness to report on her kidnapping at Poltergeist Passage. In which case, the police would be giving chase right now, combing the roads leading out of Delhi for grey vans. How did these guys think they could get away with this? Yes, there was the occasional murder – some cook or driver knifing their employer to make off with money and jewellery but this, carting her away like this in the back of a van, it was brazen. They would *never* get away with it.

These two men sounded like Biharis or maybe Hariyanvis – Tara wouldn't even recognize any of the dialects of Hindi as her family always spoke English at home and in school most people spoke either English or Hinglish. She wished now that her Hindi was less shaky as that may have enabled her to negotiate her release. At the moment, all she could think of to save her were some 'ma-behen'-type dialogues used in Hindi films to appeal to a villain's humanity.

With her left hand, Tara fiddled with the metal bracket that was pinioning her right wrist to the wall of the van but the lock on it looked solid. She had to be careful not to make too much noise as the two men were so close. It was best to make a proper attempt later on. Tara cast her eyes around the cabin and saw her school bag lying in one corner, just out of reach. Not that there'd be anything in it that would help her escape. Not even a nail file. It was Neel who carried things like pen-knives in his bag and even that had been prohibited by the school after a recent knifing incident in the playground. If only her parents had brought forward the purchase of that mobile phone ... Tara remembered Dad saying that the biggest boon offered by those new-fangled devices would be to women travelling alone. It was going to be her next birthday present, so she could take it with her to university...

Tara lay her head down again, tearful and exhausted by her confused ruminations. She so desperately wanted to be back at home and with her parents. Of course, she needed to stay calm so she could keep her wits about her but that was so much easier said than done. She felt so lonely, despite the younger man having offered to help. How could she trust him, given that he had assisted in her kidnap? He wasn't as bad as the older one but he could obviously be persuaded into wickedness. Else why was he here, sitting and chatting so amicably with the other guy? And why was he administering injections to her? It was all so confusing and Tara was having difficulty focusing again. She mustn't keep drifting off like this ... maybe it was the shot she'd been given ... had she been given more than one? ... It was no use ... she could feel herself fading and falling away again...

Margaret's Journal Entry 3: Undated

Sometimes when I wake up after a deep sleep, a curious sensation overcomes me. For, at the very moment that my eyes open, I am back in the confines of that hut in the forest, awakening from the sleep I slept after hearing of the murder of my mother and little brothers. I wondered later if Nizam had given me something to aid rest in that terrible time – a potion or drug perhaps. I remember Ayah who helped Mamma with Charles used to make a draught from wild berries and the small black seeds at the heart of a sunflower to help put him to sleep when he was ill and fractious.

I am now learning such things myself. Yesterday, Ammi showed me how to make a poultice from mustard and fenugreek seeds to soothe the inflammation she sometimes suffers in her joints. I think she is starting to like me now, despite all her suspicions at first. I cannot hold that against her, for which mother would not be anxious when her son turned up with a woman in tow who was helpless and unable to speak Pashto and knew next to nothing about running a house? I do not know if Nizam has told her much about me but I would wager not, from the puzzled manner in which she sometimes regards me.

It is hard enough even for me to understand how I came to become the person I am now. What a strange journey I have made in five short months, dear diary. Margaret is now a mere memory and Mehrunissa has stepped into her place. Does such an ability to transform myself make me a weak person or strong? I wonder.

Tara, 1997

The next few hours … or perhaps days … passed for Tara in a haze of sleep, interspersed with further spells of violence. She came to dread feeling the van come to a halt because, very often, this would be followed by the man with the pockmarks flinging open the back door of the van to inflict further cruelty on her. He was either a sadist or simply trying to beat her into total submission. She tried to switch her mind off at these times, floating into some distant ether from where she was able to watch, almost dispassionately, as he thrust himself into her, grunting and groaning like a wild beast. Sometimes he even burst in through the door to kick her viciously for no apparent reason.

Through this torment, Tara thought she saw the younger man try to pass non-verbal messages to her whenever he was in her presence, usually when he was injecting her with drugs. These were diffident glances that indicated a strange combination of anguish and complicit guilt. He also continued the charade of seeming to rape her when the older man thrust him into the back of the van with her. Tara did not question it, gagged as she was and was only thankful that she was not being subjected to the bestiality of two men. But it was the younger man who was in charge of her injections, and he was often supervised by the older man who stood watching him carefully, as though wanting to learn how to perform this procedure himself. Tara did not know what was in the syringe, but it made her sleep and that was way,

way better than lying trapped and unable to escape from this circle of torture.

When she was drugged, Tara came to her senses gradually, only slowly able to make her pained way through the mists that swirled through her brain. Except on one occasion when she awoke with a start, sweat breaking out on her upper lip as she sensed danger. Had she been dreaming of some horror even worse than her own? Perhaps she was still emerging from some terrible nightmare that was vying to compete with the horror of her situation. As her addled brain comprehended that it was not a dream, Tara heard a raised voice and started to cower, half expecting the evil man to come bursting in on her in another one of his rages. But his anger was targeted at someone else, someone outside the van, it seemed, from the sounds of the shouting and hitting she could hear.

Tara gingerly raised herself up into a sitting position and, pulling at the manacles on her wrists, put one eye to the hole nearest her. As her sight gradually adjusted to the light outside, she saw leaves and trees and then the two men. Their backs were turned to her but one was lying on the ground while the other loomed over him. Tara nearly let out a frightened yelp as the bigger man shouted, again in a language she did not recognize, and kicked the man who was on the floor. The latter – she now saw the face of the younger man – curled his body up into a ball, covering his ears and head with his arms. His face was wet with tears and grime and he was blubbering something that only seemed to infuriate the older man further. But, instead of kicking him again, he strode out of sight, leaving his accomplice grovelling in the dust. Terrified that he may be about to come into the van and vent his spleen on her next, Tara slumped back on the blanket and closed her eyes, wondering if the older captor had realized that his assistant had been kind to her. In that case, would he not have turned on her too? For a few minutes, there was silence before – mercifully – she felt the van's engine start up again and begin to move. Had they left the younger man behind, Tara wondered in sudden panic. Surely one adversary was better than two but something told her she would be much worse off left to face the cruelties of the older man all by herself.

When the van stopped again, however, it was the younger man who came in through the back door. He was on his own and, although he had cleaned himself up, he wore a subdued expression. His left cheek carried a large red bruise but he tried to keep this part of his face studiously turned away from Tara. She wondered if he had guessed that she had witnessed the assault but, too exhausted to care, she merely watched him through half-closed eyes as he put his medical paraphernalia down near her and began swabbing her arm with cotton wool. To her surprise, when it was time to administer the shot, he looked quickly over his shoulder and then pretended to plunge the syringe into her arm, squirting the liquid onto the blanket on which she was lying instead. He cast another quick glance over his shoulder at the older man who could be seen through the crack in the van door, sitting on a tree trunk and cutting an apple with a knife. Very swiftly and softly, the young man spoke to Tara, startling her. His words were accompanied by a piercing and earnest look from under the brim of his baseball cap as though he was really keen to emphasize the importance of what he was saying. 'Be ready to run,' he whispered. 'Not now. When I come in with the key. Don't know when. Be alert. Don't sleep.'

Surging with new hope but very unsure of what to make of this new turn, Tara lay back on the blanket, blinking at the grey roof of the van. She heard herself being locked into the cabin and felt the vehicle start to move. Her mind was racing with the possibilities this new development had to offer. Something had changed with the beating the younger man had received. Perhaps he had often been subjected to the kind of cruelties she had witnessed and experienced and had finally reached the end of his tether. Tara hoped, desperately, that he would not make the escape without her.

By this stage of the journey, the sack over her head had been discarded, as well as the clamps on her legs, but her mouth was still gagged and both hands were cuffed to the inside of the van. She had to presume that the younger man would remember all that while plotting an escape for both of them. He had mentioned a key but had he meant the one that would open up these clamps around her hands, or the keys to the van? Was he merely planning to take over charge of her captivity from the older man? Maybe, even if they escaped, she would be no better off at all and remain stuck in the back of another horrible van. Since embarking on this hellish nightmare, she had not been released once, not even to go to the toilet, and had ended up wetting herself and worse. It did not bear thinking about – this degradation. People did not treat animals the way she was being treated. How had she become no more than a sack of meat being transported in the back of a van? Was it some kind of terrible punishment for having been mean to people like Rajan Mathai at school, or mouthy with Mum and Dad back at home? Tara bit down on her tongue and lips, trying to make them bleed, punishing herself for the many wrongs she imagined she had done in her life. She looked up at the metal roof of the van, moaning under her breath, promising fervently that she would never ever be nasty to anyone again, not even Pia and Neel. She only asked for this torture to end…

Was it really about to end? Was it possible that the younger man may actually release her once they had escaped? Tara's thoughts were flying everywhere, every bump they went over making her heart race with anticipation.

When the van finally did come to a halt, Tara's nerves were at screaming point, the hair on her arms and at the back of her neck prickling, her heart thudding loudly in her ears. She strained to listen for any sounds or conversation from the front seat or outside the van but there was none. Then, after what seemed like an interminable wait, the back door burst open and the younger man clambered in.

'Hurry, hurry, we don't have much time,' he said in Hindi, lunging for the hand clamps and fumbling at them with a small key. He managed to unlock the right side without too much difficulty but struggled, seeming to take forever while tackling the one on the left. Keeping a petrified lookout for the other man over his shoulder, Tara saw the hands of her potential rescuer tremble so hard, she wondered if he would even be able to get the tiny key into the padlock. Her own body was shaking and she doubted the ability of her legs to move under her.

Finally, her hands were free and the man was pulling her up onto her haunches. He took a quick look on either side of the van before jumping out. Tara yanked the gag from her mouth and it dangled around her neck as she dragged herself across the metal floor towards the door. Falling out of the van, she blinked in the harsh glare of unaccustomed sunlight. She stumbled in her panic to get up and nearly fell to the ground, her legs turning to water. Once again, the man held her forearm to drag her up before starting to run. Tara followed him, pell-mell, feeling herself almost dragged off her feet with the force of his pull. But he said nothing to her, just continuing to run and run, swerving around tree trunks and skipping over roots. He pulled Tara after him without looking back even once.

They weaved their way through a forest, endless trees rushing past them. Tara felt her legs pumping under her, getting stronger, pounding the ground, using the earth to throw her forward with each step. Her breath was so loud, she sounded like she was sobbing … her ears were bursting … despite the cold air rushing against her face, she was sweating, her nose dripping, her mouth dry as ash…

They must have run for at least half an hour before Tara finally gave up. Her chest was exploding from the effort, every sinew in her body throbbing with pain. She pulled her hand away from the man's and fell over with a small whimper. She heard herself wheezing in pain and panic and rolled herself into foetal position because of the jabbing pain in her heart. She wanted to tell the man to carry on without her, to save himself, but her struggling lungs would not allow her speech. He seemed to understand, though. Bending over her, hands over his hips, he too was trying to catch his breath. Then, looking around the silent forest, he said in Hindi, 'Enough. Far enough. We will hide somewhere here. Soon there will be no sunlight. When it is dark, we will make our way to a town.'

He was still breathing heavily but he scooped Tara up and carried her a few paces away into the safety of a more heavily wooded patch. There, she collapsed again, watching him collect leaves and twigs to throw over her. Luckily her school jacket was green, and so was the man's fleece jacket, which meant they were well camouflaged. After her rescuer had burrowed himself down next to her, she saw that he was nearly invisible. They stayed like that, for what felt like hours, listening for the rustle of footsteps among the leaves, but there was none. The older man was surely looking for them but perhaps he had gone in the wrong direction. How big was this forest? she wondered. At one point, Tara made as if to speak but the man – who was clearly still terrified of being followed – put his forefinger on his lips and so she lapsed back into silence.

At first, the forest around them was quiet but insistent noisy birdsong began as the branches above them filled with flocks of birds returning for the night. Soon the birds too gradually quietened as the patch of sky that was visible from where Tara lay started to turn violet and then purple before darkening into a velvet, black night.

When it could not get any darker, the man stood up, making as little noise as he possibly could, and, tapping Tara on the shoulder, beckoned her to get up. She followed his actions, carefully taking her cues from him. Then, one behind the other, they silently picked their way through the forest. The moon was only just rising, lying low and chalky white, criss-crossed by tree branches. The birds had grown silent but the forest seemed to have been taken over by the sounds of other small creatures, rabbits and squirrels scurrying and rustling through the undergrowth. Tara's heart stopped every time she heard a sound but the man she was with now seemed a little less tense, pulling out a pocket compass and using it to look for a certain direction. Tara prayed that he knew where to go, and that it was in the direction of civilization. Though still unsure of what was going on, it was clear to Tara that the man they had escaped was clearly the dangerous one and, for the time being, she had no choice but to meekly allow herself to be led by the other. They pressed on through the woods, tripping on tree roots and stumps as the moonlight trickling through the trees was faint but, every time they stumbled, they stopped to listen for anyone who might be pursuing. Even if they'd had a torch, they would not have been able to use it and it seemed to Tara that, despite the compass, they were going round and round in circles in this godforsaken forest.

Finally, however – at first Tara was not sure she had imagined it – the faint sound of music rose on the night breeze. It disappeared briefly and then rose again, this time more clearly audible. It was some kind of cheesy Hindi pop music and, as Tara quickened her footsteps, she soon spotted distant lights dipping in and out between the trees. They were both now almost running in the direction of those lights. Lights … music … it could only mean that they were back amongst other people and normal life. Tara was so overwhelmed as she broke into a frantic run that she was close to breaking down and collapsing at that very moment.

Ahead of them, a road rose. And beyond it, what looked like a small grubby motel with a bar attached. But the man held Tara back, still not daring to step out without carefully checking the road in both directions as well as the car park in front of the motel. He took his time before eventually tugging on Tara's hand and running across the road with her. There were only a few cars in the car park and no grey vans among them. Tara looked up at the sign above the motel and saw 'Hotel Star' in pink neon lettering. She gradually discerned that the song audible from the bar was a recent Bollywood hit. So it looked they were still in the Hindi-speaking belt.

'Where are we?' she asked as they approached the building.

The man, still throwing nervous glances over his shoulder to ensure they were not being followed, answered briefly, 'Near Moradabad.'

The tiny reception of the motel had one bored-looking man sitting behind a counter. The countertop was greasy and crowded with a stack of cardboard ledgers, an old-fashioned black telephone and a vase that was stuffed with dusty sprays of plastic flowers and ferns. The man at the reception did not appear at all bothered by the strange sight of a young man and woman covered in mud and leaves coming through the door. Luckily, Tara's rescuer appeared to have enough money on him and so, without very much delay, they managed to get themselves a room for the night. There were no questions about who they were or where they had come from, or even why Tara was so grubby and wearing a school uniform. Instead, the man at the counter took the money without any change in his facial expression and a barely discernible nod.

She wondered if she ought to feel more anxious at the thought of being alone with a man in a motel room but the thought was almost laughable after what she had been through. For now, it was important to duck into the safety of a room without further delay as the more dangerous person was prowling around outside somewhere. Her rescuer, evidently aware of this possibility, nervously looked over his shoulder a few times as he hustled Tara down the corridor to their room. Even once they were in the room, he proceeded to check the window locks and the bathroom before moving the table across the door. It was only a cheap thing, made of laminate and aluminium, but, as there was nothing else at hand, it would have to do. Only when all that was done, did he finally throw himself down on the bed and look at Tara with strange, hunted eyes.

She was still standing in the middle of the room, uncertain of what to do. He took in her dishevelled hair and clothes and said in rough Hindi, 'We will be safe here for tonight. I will get you some clothes in the morning so we can travel on. For now, have a bath and get some sleep.'

Tara went into the small attached bathroom and silently slid the bolt shut. She stood looking at herself in a small mirror with total shock. The ghostly apparition with sunken eyes and hollow cheeks could not be her. Her school uniform, from what seemed like another life, was completely unrecognizable, brown with mud and filth, and her hair, usually long and glossy, was a matted clump of dreadlocks. Tara's chin crumpled and a couple of tears rolled down her cheeks as she mourned the pretty schoolgirl she had last seen in her mirrored wardrobe back at home. Had that girl gone forever? But Tara pulled herself together and started to undress. She should consider herself lucky to have got out of the vehicle as what would have awaited her at the end of that journey would surely have been far, far worse than this.

Nothing was wearable again – even her undergarments were soiled with blood and faeces – and Tara wondered what she would wear once she had had her bath. But she would worry about all that later as, for now, it was with the greatest relief she had ever known that she stood under a thin shower of lukewarm water, relishing the feeling of washing away the grime and the shame she had endured. A plastic holder against the wall had only the tiniest piece of soap but, after removing the cardboard packaging, Tara rubbed the hard white cake over and over again on her arms and chest and stomach and face, scrubbing and scouring until her skin felt raw. Finally, when she could take it no more, she stopped and rested her head on the shower taps, feeling clean water drip off her hair and body and swirl around her toes.

After she had wrapped herself in one of two greying towels hanging behind the door, Tara stepped out of the bathroom, conscious that she had occupied it for too long. Her rescuer would probably be desperate for a bath too, so it had been inconsiderate of her to take so much time. But Tara heard snores as she emerged and saw that the man was stretched out on one side of the bed, still fully clothed and now fast asleep. The thought of escaping him and trying to make a run for it on her own passed through Tara's mind but this would be impossible unless she wore the same clothes as before. Looking and smelling as filthy as that, she doubted whether anyone would want to help her. Certainly not that man at the desk. Besides, she had no money and what if the other man, the rapist, was waiting outside?

She cast a glance around the room, looking for a telephone but there was none. To call her parents she would have to go back down the corridor and it was too terrifying to think that she may then be spotted by the rapist. It was best to bide her time for now and hope that an opportunity to contact home would soon present itself.

Tara sat gingerly on the edge of his bed and examined the face of the man who had helped her escape. In sleep, he looked young and defenceless, a small frown creasing his forehead between his eyes. Given the risks he had taken, Tara was fairly certain that he was now as vulnerable as she was. His accomplice would surely fly into the most violent fury to find that they had both escaped. And she had already seen how neither of them could hope to be spared his rage. It would be to their benefit to stick together and Tara had no choice but to trust this man for now. Cautiously moving the blanket aside, she slipped into the bed, still wrapped in her towel. She covered herself with the sheets and the blanket and lay there, tortured thoughts running through her head before she finally fell into a disturbed sleep.

Margaret's Journal Entry 4: 15 October 1857, Peshawar

Sometimes, on nights like these, when the moon hangs like a heavy silver pendant on the breast of the mountains, I lie next to my husband and think of where I came from. So far away, so removed in every way from this life.

One day, when I have less to concern myself with, I will write the story of our flight from Cawnpore, my beautiful childhood home, to this far highland of Nizam's where we are making our new life. No Englishwoman could have ever undertaken such a dramatic transformation, nor embarked on such an expedition, of that I am sure.

We made that journey across miles and miles of dust and scrub and then the green of the wheat fields before veering off to head for the saw-toothed frontiers of this land. Halfway through our passage, Nizam showed me Hindustan on a map, and warned me of the great rivers that still lay ahead, perilous crossings on which many travellers lost their lives. But, when we came upon them, those riverine sisters were a thrill to behold – the Sutlej and Ravi and Jhelum – icy cold from the melting snows and travelling in roiling white-crested currents as they rushed back down to the plains from where we had come.

And then, after many more miles on horseback, came the mighty Indus, as stately as an empress, wide and slow. There is a massive fortification that overlooks it, built by the great Mughal emperor, Akbar. Nizam has promised to take me back to it one day when there is more time for leisure. But, hurrying as we were to reach Peshawar before the arrival of the winter cold, we could not stop, taking a long bridge of boats for the crossing.

Looking down at the waters as we crossed made me think of my beloved Ganges, of course, and the blood that was churning in its waters when last I saw her. My poor father's drowned body ... did a kind soul pull him out and give him a decent burial? Or did the currents of the river take him down to the riverbed to be preyed on by crocodiles and fish...

Memories like that are too painful to be held on to and, in the course of my journey, I taught my heart to let them go.

Tara, 1997

Tara awoke with a jolt, to sunshine streaming into the motel room. A quick look around showed that the man, her rescuer whose name she still did not know, was now up and looking out of the windows. If anyone did look in from the outside, he had made sure he was masked from sight by the nylon curtains. Hearing Tara stir, he turned around and gave her a small smile. 'I think now we are safe,' he said, speaking in accented English this time. 'No one is following.'

Tara sat up and pulled the sheets around herself, conscious of her state of undress. Picking up on that awkwardness, the man said, 'I think there is a town with some shops nearby, so I can get you some clothes. But it is a little bit too early now. Only nine o'clock. I will go in about an hour or so.'

'Thank you, you've been very kind to me,' Tara said slowly. Then, plucking up her courage, she asked, 'What is your name?'

He hesitated for a second before saying, 'Himal. I am Himal.'

'And the other man? Who is he? Are you brothers?'

Himal wavered again but he shook his head. 'We are not full brothers. But we are cousin brothers. He is Dinesh Thapa, my elder uncle's son.'

'Thapa. You're Nepali then,' Tara said, stating the fact with a frisson of disbelief that such evil as she had experienced could come from that beautiful country her father had taken them all to a few summers ago when Mum had wanted to see the Himalayas. Tara recalled Pia letting out a delighted shriek when they disembarked from their plane, pointing to a distant snow peak that was catching the last rays of the setting sun and yelling, 'Look, Tara, golden mountains!'

'I've been to Nepal once,' Tara said. 'I liked it a lot actually.'

Himal smiled in half-hearted acknowledgement, looking down at the foot of the bed rather than at her.

Still persisting, Tara said, 'I'm not actually pure Delhi myself. I'm a half Goan and half English. My mother's English.'

Himal nodded and finally spoke up in a low voice. 'I know. We had been watching you for some time so I know quite a lot about you. He – Dinesh – he saw you first. He was working at a dhaba near your house and had seen you walking past many times. He noticed that you were often alone, not always with your brother or with friends. By the time I saw you, it was too late.'

'What do you mean ... "too late"?'

The man hesitated before replying. 'Dinesh had already made his plan, then he called me to Delhi and told me about it. When I saw you, I thought you were too beautiful but...' he trailed off.

'What was the plan?' Tara asked but Himal had fallen silent and so she repeated her question, rewording it to make it easier for him. 'What was Dinesh planning for me, Himal?'

After a long while, Himal replied, unable to look Tara in the eye. 'He knows someone who takes girls ... they take beautiful girls from Delhi and other places to Mumbai and make money.'

'Sex-trafficking,' Tara said flatly, 'I know. I've seen it on TV. But they usually pick up uneducated girls from the villages, don't they? It's easier, isn't it, tempting them with offers of jobs in the city... '

'This was different. Dinesh ... Dinesh liked you. I think he wanted to keep you for himself for some time. His friend sells girls but then somebody said that more money can be made by keeping those girls, not selling them...'

Tara was shocked. 'He was going to *pimp* me? … *Where?*'

Himal looked ashamed and spoke hesitantly. 'His plan was to take you to Nepal first because he knows people there. They train girls to dance in bars and entertain customers in five-star hotels. Lot of rich Indian businessmen go to Nepal for fun. But he was also saying he might take you to Mumbai.'

'Mumbai? But in Mumbai it would have been easy for me to escape.'

Himal shook his head. 'You don't know,' he said. 'You don't know how they control these girls … rape, violence, drugs, sleeping tablets. After some time, it is too late. They don't even want to escape.'

Tara remembered her own doped state, when she had felt about a hundred years old, both in mind and body. And that had been the effect of just two sets of injections, as far as she was aware. She owed this man a lot. 'Thank you for not using that syringe to inject me yesterday,' she said softly.

Himal looked down at his feet. 'I am sorry I had to before … but Dinesh was always watching…'

'I understand. It's very brave of you to do this for me, Himal. I'll make sure you don't get arrested for any of this when we get out.'

But Himal shook his head. 'You will not be able to save me,' he said. 'The police are looking for me anyway.'

'Why?' Tara asked, cold fingers of fear squeezing her heart again.

'I am an illegal…'

Tara felt relieved. 'That's hardly the worst crime. There must be thousands of Nepalis working illegally in Delhi.'

'There are, yes. But they once caught me at the border when we were transporting wood and I escaped their clutches. So they have my details and my photo. Dinesh was going to help me get a new pehchaan patra, you know, Indian ID.'

'*Help* you? Is that what you call it! You should have run a million miles away from that man.'

But Himal seemed to want to explain, so Tara fell silent. He spoke hesitantly, weighing each sentence carefully. 'Please understand me. Two years ago, Dinesh came to our village in Nepal. He was like a VIP. He had been to Saudi so was foreign-returned, with watches and gifts for everyone. I was doing third-year medicine in Kathmandu – but my mother did not have the money to keep sending me to college after my father died. First Dinesh said he would send the money. Then he said, "Why should he do it here, in this small college? There will be no jobs in Nepal when he finishes. The Maoists will finish this place." My mother was so happy when he said he would take me to India and look after me there. I am her only son and she thought that our whole family would be lifted out from poverty. My sisters...' He stopped as though aware he had said too much.

But Tara wanted to encourage him to talk about himself. 'You have sisters?' she asked.

He nodded and flashed another small smile. 'Two. Sirjana and Siroopa.'

'Younger than you?' she persisted.

'Older. I am the youngest of three. They are both in their late twenties and my mother gets worried that no one will marry them because we have no money and hardly any property.' After a pause he gave a bitter laugh and said, 'She thinks I am soon going to be a doctor in India and start sending lots of money.'

'Did you start on a medical course at all? In Delhi, I mean?'

Himal laughed again, making the same hollow, mirthless sound. 'Never. Dinesh never meant anything he said. He arranged for a bus ticket one year ago and I landed up in Delhi. But for the medical course, he kept making excuses. Then he started to beat me and kick me every time I asked. After that he started using me to do his crimes. But this time ... this time what he did, it was too much…' Himal trailed off and Tara saw bitterness twist his face. When he said 'too much' she wondered if he was referring to her kidnap and rape or his own beating.

She thought for a minute and said rapidly, 'My father's a dentist, you know, and his father was a journalist. He has lots of influential friends. We might be able to help you.'

Himal flashed Tara a look, half hopeful and half despairing. 'How will you help me? I am illegal in India. With Dinesh, I have done so many crimes. They will definitely jail me if they catch me. If I even apply to a college, I will be arrested.'

'Perhaps we could appeal for some kind of amnesty, seeing how you've risked your life to help me? I know! You could offer to be an informant and help get Dinesh caught. The authorities would do anything to track down those sex-trafficking gangs. Maybe some NGO will help us.'

But Himal shrugged. 'Maybe,' he said, turning away and signalling a close to the conversation.

Perhaps it seemed totally futile to him, Tara thought, especially if he had already considered the various ways in which he could try to escape Dinesh's clutches. Perhaps he had discarded all such plans out of fear for what such an evil man could do to him, or his mother and sisters back in Nepal. She lapsed into silence.

A few moments later, Himal got up and said, 'I will go and get something to eat.' He avoided looking at her body swathed in sheets, but he added, 'I will also get some clothes for you.' At the door, he turned back to ask, 'What is your size?'

'Well, small to medium, I guess. You have money?'

For the first time since she had first laid eyes on him, Tara saw Himal smile. He had even white teeth and his face became that of a cheeky little boy as the grin reached his eyes. 'I stole Dinesh's wallet before we ran,' he said, tapping his chest pocket. 'So I have plenty money!'

Tara smiled back at him but her feelings turned to apprehension again as Himal left the room. She watched him looking carefully down the corridor, this way and that, before slipping out. Once he was gone, she got up and fastened the towel firmly around her body before bolting the door. Then she sat on the bed for a few minutes, shoving aside the possibility of escape once again as that would be impossible when she did not even have clothes to wear. She considered Himal's story, feeling instinctively that he was not lying to gain her sympathy. There was something genuinely sad and broken about him. Surely he could not be such a good actor. In fact, she felt strangely worried on his behalf. Escaping with her in tow and stealing Dinesh's wallet, there were many reasons for Dinesh to make it his mission to hunt them down. Who knew, he might even be following Himal right now and slowly closing in on them...

Shivering, Tara got up and made sure that the door was firmly latched. Then she pulled the table back to where it had been, shoving it against the door to barricade it rather ineffectively. Still not feeling safe, she went to the bathroom and locked herself into that as well. There was only one small window through which no one could possibly enter. Now, feeling marginally safer, Tara dropped the towel and stood on tiptoe to see what she could of her body. That was when she noticed the bruises Dinesh had left with his beating and kicking. A large blue one on the left of her waist was turning yellow at the edges. She touched it gently, feeling the flesh beneath that was still tender. A cold rage slowly gripped her from within as she remembered Dinesh's face and thought of the things he had done to her. And the horrors that would have lain ahead had Himal not rescued her – drug addiction and prostitution – they did not bear thinking about.

Tara wound the towel around herself tightly as she started to shake violently, both from the cold and from sudden remembered terrors. She sank to the floor of the bathroom, wrapping her arms around her trembling body, trying to calm herself. But her thoughts were running away from her again. She had forgotten to ask Himal if there had been other girls like her before they had taken her. How much had Himal been involved in those kidnaps and rapes? After all, Dinesh had virtually ordered him to rape her as well and, rather than stand up to him, he had merely dissembled. And, if the Delhi police were indeed looking for him, what were the implications for her if she went back there with him? Tara was confused and frightened again. She was filled with gratitude to Himal for having got her away from that van but she was still not sure she trusted him entirely. There was only one thing she was dead certain about and that was there was no punishment severe enough for a man like Dinesh. He ought to be castrated and killed. That's what she wanted to do. Rather than cower away in fear, huddled in this bathroom, she should have asked Himal to buy a gun so that they could hunt Dinesh down and ensure a death he deserved. She sat there on the floor for a long time before getting up and hobbling with a stiff, wounded gait to the tap.

Himal returned to the motel in less than an hour and knocked lightly to be allowed in. After calling softly through the door to check it was him, Tara opened the door and let him through. He had not only bought her a set of fresh clothes – a long-sleeved salwaar kameez, socks and a colourful woollen shawl – he had also brought with him a large pair of scissors. 'You should cut your hair,' he said. 'Try to look a bit different from before.'

Carrying all her things, Tara went back into the bathroom. She looked at her long hair, still damp from the shower she had taken at night. Except for the odd trimming session with her mother in the kitchen back at home, it hadn't been cut in a long time. It was, in fact, not just her pride and joy but her mother's too. Eleanor Fernandez certainly wouldn't be happy to see her daughter's crowning glory all shorn away but Tara smiled at the ridiculous direction her thoughts were taking. Her mum was hardly likely to be expressing annoyance over her hair when she would surely be overjoyed to simply have Tara back again. Were they assuming by now that she was dead? She ought to call them soon, to let them know she was fine but that would have to be with Himal's agreement. Having earned his trust and his support somehow, it was important to hang on to it until she could work out a way to get safely back to Delhi.

Tara turned her attention back to her hair. Given the state it was in now, all knotted up and matted, it was just as well she needed to cut it all off. It would soon grow back. Refusing to be negative about it, Tara started to hack away, first removing all the length and then using the scissors to snip away more lightly, trying to follow the shape of her head. When she was done, she stepped back and cocked her head. It didn't look bad, actually. Elfin, was that the word? Himal had asked her to look as different as possible, which this had certainly achieved. No more a Bollywood film star, though.

Tara gathered her shorn locks and filthy clothes together before shoving them into the large plastic bag in which Himal had brought her new outfit. It was strangely like some kind of purification ritual, the last stage of which was a second shower to wash the remaining bits of hair still clinging to her neck and shoulders. There was no underwear and so she got straight into the salwaar kameez. She didn't often wear Indian clothes, unless attending a wedding, and the thick cotton fabric felt strange against her skin. She wrapped the shawl over her head and around her neck and looked at herself again. Dark eyes stared out at her – they looked frightened and as though they belonged to someone else, not her. She picked up the scissors and stuck it into the waistband of her salwaar. It would make a useful weapon if she needed one.

Himal had sliced up some bread and fruit and was eating them at the table. He looked up as Tara came in and gave her an approving nod. 'Good,' he said, 'you look much different from before. Though I forgot to give you this.' He pushed a small black dabba across the table in her direction. Tara picked it up and saw it was a small pot of kaajal. 'It will make you a real desi girl. That's what we need.'

Tara went back into the bathroom to line her eyes generously with kaajal, something she was familiar with from her Goth make-up phase. She returned to the room to ask, 'If we're hiding from Dinesh, shouldn't you be changing your appearance too?'

Himal cast a rueful glance down at himself. 'I can't really make myself look too different, can I?'

'No, I suppose not. Although you could get a kurta pyjama?'

'I thought about that but buying new clothes for me also would have taken up more of our cash. We have to be careful not to finish it all off now.'

Tara nodded. Money was important to their survival. Even she, cosseted and pocket-moneyed as she had always been, knew that. Himal was rummaging in his pocket now, still speaking, 'But look what I have got for my disguise.' His hand emerged with a small crocheted skull cap which he unfolded and pulled onto the top of his head. 'One moment, Hindu, next moment, Muslim,' he said, grinning.

'Doesn't exactly hide your face,' Tara said lightly, not wanting to sound too discouraging.

'Still, at one glance, we are not the same pair that Dinesh last saw. This gives us a better chance, I feel.' Tara nodded and Himal pushed the plate of bread across the table to her, speaking now in a sober voice. 'What we should do is aim to leave Moradabad area as soon as we can. Dinesh must be already searching around all the towns near the forest.'

Despite her terror at those words, Tara kept her voice calm.

'How big is Moradabad district? And where is it exactly?' She was embarrassed. 'I know the name of the place but don't really know where it is.'

'It is in western Uttar Pradesh, on the way, as you travel east out of Delhi, towards Nepal.'

Tara cast about in her mind for what she might know about Uttar Pradesh. 'Is Moradabad not big enough to lose him? Where would be crowded enough? Are we anywhere near Lucknow or Kanpur?' she asked. She had travelled to the former on a school excursion many years ago and remembered an elegant but pulsing city full of beautiful old monuments.

'Moradabad is big enough but we are right now in a much smaller town called Rampur. I saw the sign when I went out. I think we are not that far from the Nepal border so maybe we should just keep heading there. At least there I have friends and family who will help us.' Tara felt a flutter of fear in her stomach but Himal seemed to be thinking hard so she remained silent. 'You must be wanting to go back to Delhi,' he said, suddenly looking directly at Tara. 'The thing is that it is the most dangerous place to go right now. Dinesh will go straight there when he knows he has lost us and, somehow or the other, he will catch us before we even get to your house. He is not only dangerous but also very, very clever. We have to think ahead of him somehow.'

Himal seemed to be waiting for Tara's assent, his eyes pleading for her to understand. Tara hesitated for a moment, feeling her heart pound in fear at the thought of Dinesh tracking them down before she got back home to Delhi. Besides, it was important to say the right thing so that she did not lose Himal's goodwill. She summoned all her courage with a deep breath. 'I trust you, Himal,' she said. 'You helped me escape. Or I would still be stuck in the back of that van with Dinesh drugging and raping me. I will go wherever you consider is safest for us right now.'

Himal smiled in relief before his expression turned serious again. He cast a glance at the glittering morning sunshine that was playing on the curtain next to him. 'We can't go anywhere until is dark. Rampur is small and we will be spotted by many people as we are clearly not locals. If Dinesh asks around, we will surely be remembered.'

The room was so quiet, Tara wondered if Himal could hear the thudding of her heart. The thought of Dinesh skulking around outside this town, looking for them, was plain terrifying. Equally, much as she knew she must trust Himal, she did not particularly like the idea of going to Nepal either. It seemed worth making a bid to stay on in India. Tara swallowed the saliva gathering in her throat before she spoke. 'I realize going back to Delhi right now isn't advisable, Himal, but wouldn't it also be dangerous to go to Nepal? After all, Dinesh was on his way there and might decide to carry on when he doesn't find us here.'

Luckily, Himal did not seem angered by her suggestion but appeared to be considering her words carefully instead. 'Kathmandu could be a dangerous place,' he conceded. 'Dinesh has too many friends there. But, in Nepal, Pokhara is a really safe place. He avoids going to Pokhara as he's wanted there for assaulting and raping a woman. His ex-fiancée. Maybe we can get a bus from here that connects us to Pokhara.'

Pokhara ... Tara had heard that name before. They had nearly gone there on that family holiday in Nepal and she remembered looking at pictures of forested mountains and ski slopes in a brochure she had found in their hotel lobby. It was with a sudden jolt that those memories returned to Tara. Of her family and the comfortable, unquestioning part she had played in it. Her confidence and mouthiness. It was almost like watching a play or imagining someone else's life. Yes, as though she was looking back at a different person who had lived in the past; another Tara altogether.

The sun was now high in a shell-blue sky and sounds of traffic from a distant road were filtering into the silence of the room. Seeing Tara gazing out of the window, Himal repeated, 'We can't leave now, you must understand that. We will stand out too much and Dinesh himself might see us if he is hiding out somewhere here. We will have to wait till night.'

Tara nodded. That did make sense. The last thing she wanted was to fall right back into Dinesh's clutches but she could tell from Himal's panicky tone of voice that he needed reassurance too. 'Don't worry.' She smiled. 'I'm not considering making a run for it. I agree completely that we ought to lie low right here and bide our time until it's safer.'

'I have given the man at the desk some money so he does not say anything just in case Dinesh comes to this hotel making enquiries.'

Tara nodded. This conversation was making her feel strangely robbed of breath. He ears were blocking up and all she could hear was a whooshing sound emanating from somewhere deep inside her head every time she spoke. She felt cold too, her fingers and toes stiff and frozen as though blood wasn't getting to them at all. But she tried to keep her voice cheerful as she said, 'But what shall we do, stuck in here all day, Himal?' She thought quickly. 'I could teach you some word games that my mother plays with us when we go on long car journeys. Would you like that?'

Himal smiled, his face flooding again with that look of relief and pleasure that Tara was now getting familiar with. Then he looked troubled. 'But your English is much better than mine, I will never win against you.'

'My English might be better but my general knowledge is useless. Whenever we play countries and capitals, I'm always last. Even my little sister is better than me.'

'And my GK is actually very good. Okay, so we will have one

round of word games and one of countries and capitals. Then we both stand a chance of winning.'

Himal got up from his chair to sit closer to her on the bed and Tara moved over to make room. 'Okay, here goes,' she said, 'we always start with a word that begins with A. Shall I go first?'

They played game after game, the awkwardness between them slowly melting away. Then Himal said they ought to take a break so he could go out and buy some lunch. 'There is a man standing just outside this hotel on the road making kulchas. Would you like some of those with chholey?'

Tara nodded and watched Himal leave the room again. Once more, she went through the ritual of locking up and shoving the table against the door, even though Himal would probably be back very soon. Again, she recognized that it would not be a good time to make a run for it and call her parents. She would just have to wait for a better time, she thought, feeling the comfort of the scissors pressed against her waist. Patience had never been Tara's best virtue but she had learnt a lot about survival in the past few days. She had to be clever and thinking all the time, not behaving like a flighty schoolgirl.

Himal returned within fifteen minutes, still wearing his skullcap and carrying a parcel with four kulchas wrapped around a polythene bag of chholey and two bottles of Limca. Tara finally felt able to eat and, after she had filled her stomach on this strangely sustaining meal, she fell asleep, sitting up against the pillows, comfortable with the idea that Himal was keeping a vigil on the window and door to their room.

Many hours later, when dusk had deepened, they finally decided that it was as safe as it would ever be to leave the sanctuary of their room. Tara's heart was thumping in her chest as they crept down the corridor and then hurried out of the well-lit motel reception. As quickly as possible, they tried to meld into the evening crowds. Every man she spotted from a distance was a potential Dinesh. But, as they made their way towards the centre of the small town and ordinary life unwound on the street ahead of them, Tara slowly started to feel herself relax. They had chosen their departure time well as dozens of people were out and about, all of them either on foot or on cycles and nobody seemed to pay them any heed. Some couples had little children with them, all bundled up against the cold, and the shops were busy with customers. When they reached a big intersection of roads, Himal told Tara that it was now safe to get rid of the bag containing her old clothes and lopped-off hair. Tara guessed that he had not wanted her to leave anything as incriminating as that in the motel in case Dinesh found his way there. With a sense of immense relief, almost as though she were letting go of some of the horrors of the past few days, Tara hoisted the bag into a large rubbish dump and let its contents drop onto the far side. Surely nobody would go poking about in there.

'I'll go into that shop and ask about buses,' Himal said. 'You wait here.' He gestured to a bullock cart. 'Stand behind that ... you will not be seen there.'

Tara took up position behind the rickety wooden wagon full of aluminium milk cans, still keeping her head tightly covered, her face half-masked by the thick cotton shawl, her kaajal-filled eyes darting anxiously around the street. The single bullock tethered to the cart continued to chew meditatively, ignoring her completely. Warily, Tara watched Himal going into a shop selling groceries and condiments. He bought a small pack of biscuits and waited for his turn to pay before engaging the shopkeeper in conversation. Again, an image popped into her head of making a break for it, running down that crowded road before her and losing herself in the throng. Then she saw Dinesh's face, imagining herself barrelling straight into him. No, she was better off with this strange young boy who seemed to have made it his genuine mission to help her escape Dinesh. He hadn't even tried to take advantage of her in the motel room the previous night; Tara was quite sure she was not wrong in trusting him.

When Himal returned to where Tara stood, the expression on his face was pleased. 'We are lucky. There is a railway station here in this town. Not far, just down that road there. Trains will go to Bareilly and Pilibhit and all kinds of other places from here.' His excitement was infectious and Tara felt a surge of relief. If the railway station was a junction, surely Dinesh would find it difficult to know in which direction they had fled.

'I've never even heard of Pilibhit before,' she confessed.

Himal looked around carefully before signalling that it was safe to start walking again. 'It is in India but very near the Nepal border,' he replied but Tara could tell that his mind was on other things. She too looked over her shoulder before following him, feeling a renewed frisson of fear at how close to danger they still were.

'Do they not ask to see passports and stuff at the border?' Tara asked.

'Not between India and Nepal.' The shortness of Himal's responses as he strode along was probably because of fear rather than irritation but Tara made the rest of the journey in silence, half-trotting in order to keep up with her companion. When they got to the railway station, she found it reassuringly busy and noisy. Big family groups were gathered everywhere, sitting amidst mountains of luggage, while droves of men were emerging from a train that was probably bringing them back from one of the bigger cities where cheap labour was a constant requirement.

On making enquiries at the station ticket desk, Himal found to his dismay that Rampur station wasn't as large as he had hoped and that the next train to Bareilly, from where they could get a connection to Pilibhit, was not for another day. Tara heard the distress in his voice as he asked the man behind the booth to check once again that there wasn't another train he had not thought of but the man shook his head, looking sympathetic but continuing to chew contentedly on his supari.

'We have missed the intercity,' Himal said to Tara, a worried expression on his face. 'We cannot spend another night here. It is too dangerous. We have to get away from this place quickly in case we have already been spotted by someone who could tell Dinesh. He may even have paid some local people to look out for us.'

'What do we do?' Tara cast another frightened look around. If Dinesh had paid local gangs to look out for a pair like them, it would be dead easy for them to be spotted in a sleepy little station like this.

The same thought was probably haunting Himal who seemed to be continually scanning the crowds over Tara's head. 'All I know is that we should leave this place as fast as possible,' he muttered. 'You go and stand there.' He gestured at an alcove in the wall. 'We are more conspicuous when we are standing together. I'll just buy a ticket on the first train that's leaving Rampur. Once we are on it, we can plan our next step.'

Tara, who was starting to tremble again, could not summon up the words and merely nodded in acquiescence. Quickly walking away from Himal, Tara shrank against a pillar, willing herself to be swallowed up by it. She leapt in fright as she felt someone shove against her but it was only an old man with a tin trunk on his head struggling to hoist a bag over his shoulder. When Himal returned with a pair of tickets, he gestured that she was to follow him and, without a word, Tara scurried down the platform behind him. Keeping a few feet between them so that they did not look like a couple, Tara followed Himal who was half-running and half-walking in the direction of an overbridge that led to the far platform. They must have taken a mere five minutes to get down the steps of the overbridge and onto a train but Tara was struggling for breath as she hoisted herself onto the rusty steps and clambered into a dusty compartment that was crowded with people and babies and even a pair of scrawny goats. Oddly, she did not mind being squashed among humanity in this way, finding strange comfort in proximity to such ordinary, everyday life. Squeezing herself into the bit of space that their fellow passengers made for them, Tara slowly let out her breath. She looked out of the nearest window, keeping her face hidden in the shadows as much as possible. Watching people milling about on the platform, she tried to quell the lurking fear that Dinesh's face might suddenly – terrifyingly – appear amongst them, right outside her window.

After what felt like an interminable time – even though it was only a few minutes – the train finally juddered and shook as though waking up from a long sleep. There was yet another long pause, however, before they heard a screeching toot and the train slowly started to move. Tara willed it to move faster as it began pulling out of the station while people continued to jump on board. Finally, as it picked up speed, vendors and travellers went past them as in a dizzying speeded-up home-video recording. There was no Dinesh amongst them. Tara could have wept in sheer relief.

The shops and houses thinned out as the train left Rampur and, in the distance, Tara could see a deep, dark forest. She looked at the gnarled, old trees and the darkness beyond. Was this the forest in which Dinesh had parked the van two nights ago? Tara imagined him returning to the vehicle and finding them both gone. When she had earlier asked Himal, on their way into town, how he had chosen their moment of escape, he had hinted that Dinesh was fanatical about finding an isolated place to 'do toilet', as he said. Himal had known that would give them at least fifteen minutes to get away which was, admittedly, not a lot so it had been a huge risk. It sounded as though Dinesh had never completely trusted Himal anyway for Himal had also mentioned that Dinesh always kept the van keys and his wallet in the pocket of his jacket. 'But he had forgotten his jacket in the van that day, which I saw,' Himal had said, grinning. Although Tara had smiled as he recounted the story while walking to the station, she now started to tremble again as she thought of how enraged Dinesh would have been to find them gone. Was he searching for them now? Could someone have spotted them at the station? Was the grey van following their train at this minute? Could it be awaiting them at the next stop? Tara did not even dare look at a thin road she could see in the distance on which occasional pairs of headlights were visible, shining intermittently through the trees.

Feeling her body tremble, Himal put his arm around Tara's shoulders and held her close. Tara did not shrink from this unexpected embrace because she felt oddly comforted by the gesture and by this strange man who had turned so unexpectedly from abductor to saviour. With mixed emotions churning inside her stomach, she continued to keep her gaze fixed on the dark of the passing countryside outside, seeing dimly lit huts and dark fields become a wide open land full of small scrubby shadows.

Here was another journey unfolding, taking her further away from everything she had known so far. Far away from all who loved her, from all that she loved. What could she imagine of this now except to hope that her trust in the man sitting next to her was not misplaced, and that she would not suffer any more.

Margaret's Journal Entry 5: Undated

We went this morning to the Quissa Khawani Bazaar where Nizam bought me a shawl as the weather is now turning slightly. It is a beautiful wrap, covered in fine, colourful embroidery and made from baby soft wool that will keep me snug as winter deepens. The cold will be far more severe here than in Cawnpore, of course.

We walked back from the bazaar, Nizam, Tabassum and I, stopping to buy kaajal for our eyes and then at a roadside barbeque to share a platter of fried and curried liver with giant, steamed kulchas. I have never tasted anything like it before, although it was clearly an old favourite of both Nizam and Tabassum. I watched them jostle with each other and laughed when Tabassum 'won' the last bit of liver off her brother, swiftly mopping it up with a remnant of kulcha and stuffing it into her mouth. 'We won't tell Ammi we've eaten,' Nizam said to me. I must have looked anxious, thinking of the trouble his mother would be taking to ensure a piping-hot meal awaited us on our return.

She has made it her business to fatten me up, insisting I am too thin! It is true that the turbulent events of my life this year have all taken their toll – the siege, the massacre at the river, my kidnap and confinement in the hut and then our long journey to Peshawar ... but my health – both mental and physical – is returning to me slowly but surely.

Do I remember all those hardships now? The honest truth would be that I often do, in my sleep. And sometimes when I am half-awake as well. But I try not to think of them because, when all is said and done, I have been fortunate. I could so easily have been killed in the massacres, or raped and mutilated. Should it be so odd, then, that I consider myself fortunate to be with a man like Nizam instead. In these months, yes, in these months I have learnt to love him well.

Tara, 1997

A clear, yellow dawn was breaking when the train pulled into Kathgodam station. After boarding at Rampur, Himal warned Tara against talking to any of the other passengers, lest she give away her urban accent and invite curiosity. Instead, he had found out in subtle ways from the other passengers which train they were on, and where it was headed. In a further whispered conversation with Tara, he informed her that they were on a slow, overnight train that went all the way to a railhead called Kathgodam. From here travellers usually went further afield to the tourist destinations of Nainital and Bhimtaal. 'But we can decide once we're there what we should do and where we should go,' he muttered in her ear.

Tara now looked around Kathgodam station, as passengers streamed out of a side exit. They joined the throng and found themselves immediately assailed by touts on leaving the building.

One persuasive man had attached himself to Tara's side and was insisting that she go to a place called Mukteshwar. She shook her head at him, unwilling to expose her Delhi accent, but Himal engaged him in conversation, asking him where Mukteshwar was and how long the journey would take.

'There is shared taxi waiting,' the man replied. 'Ten passengers. Last two waiting now. Two hundred rupees only. Off-season rate.'

'How far?' Himal asked again.

'Mukteshwar? Not far. High up in Kumaon mountain. Very

beautiful. No crowd like Nainital.' He waved at a string of dusty mountains that appeared to lie just beyond the town to indicate where Mukteshwar was.

Himal looked at Tara and then nodded. Perhaps it was the sound of the word 'mountains' that had decided it, Tara thought, or perhaps 'no crowd', but he seemed to have made up his mind. Tara obediently followed Himal as he hurried across the busy car park following the tout. Casting a glance at the mountains that surrounded the station, Tara saw that they were green and did not look very high, although, in the distance, a few snow-clad peaks were just visible through the early-morning mist. They reached a jeep which already looked full to capacity but, as Tara was wondering where on earth she was to sit, the other passengers moved over to make room and they squeezed themselves in. As there was clearly not an inch of space left for any more people, not even a very small child, the tout – who also turned out to be the taxi driver – climbed into his seat. After a few unsuccessful attempts, the creaky old engine finally coughed to life and they were off.

Within ten minutes, they had left the dusty little railhead of Kathgodam behind them and were climbing into the hills. As the road wound precariously around, going higher and higher with each bend, Tara looked down at the receding town with an overwhelming and growing sense of liberation. Surely Dinesh would not think of looking for them up here in the Kumaon mountains. It seemed so far from everything. Hopefully, they were finally safe.

The first stop was at a place called Bhimtaal, a small tourist town that clung around the edges of a large green lake on which a few boats were plying lazily. Tara took a deep breath and looked about in pleasure, enjoying not having to scour the faces in the crowd for Dinesh any more. To the left was a row of colourful shops selling sweaters and socks and trinkets and, nearby, a dhaba was getting ready with breakfast offerings of omelettes and parathas. By the side of the lake, a group of chattering children were lining up for rides on an ancient mare and Tara remembered a school excursion to Lucknow when she and her friends had similarly crowded onto horse carriages for a riotous ride down Hazratganj.

'Oh, let's stop off here in Bhimtaal, Himal,' she said. 'It's a lovely little town and look at this lake, so pretty!'

Himal hesitated for a moment before replying. 'It is pretty, yes, but it's also a very popular tourist place so it may be quite dangerous for us when the crowds come out from Delhi in a few weeks' time, you know, when the season starts. We need to go further up, I think, to hide properly. Somewhere really quiet.' He took in Tara's disappointed face and asked more gently, 'Do you want anything to eat?'

'Something to drink, maybe,' Tara replied.

'Tea? Or a soft drink?'

'Tea would be great.'

While they were buying their drinks, the taxi tooted its horn impatiently and they ran, giggling, balancing their paper cups so as not to spill hot tea on themselves. The euphoria of being free from Dinesh appeared to have infected Himal too. His features were considerably less pinched than before as he talked more animatedly, laughing at many of Tara's utterances. As they continued on their journey, the road took them further and further up, almost as though aiming for the bright blue sky above their heads. Tara felt a sudden sense of getting sucked in and lost among these hills and never being able to get out again. It wasn't an entirely displeasing prospect as they were now in the kind of place that seemed to have leapt out of the pages of a children's storybook, with its mountain slopes covered in tall fir trees, revealing glimpses of tiny houses with red tiled roofs nestling behind. The roadside was lined with fragrant brown pine needles and cones. The air was cold and felt cleaner and fresher than Tara had ever known before and, down below in the valley, clouds threw gentle scudding shadows over terraced fields. It was all so far removed from Delhi and Tara felt oddly energized by her freedom.

When they finally reached Mukteshwar, they found that it was no more than a hamlet with a tiny collection of shops and a makeshift restaurant called 'Maggi Point'. While getting out of the taxi, Tara spotted a cardboard sign propped outside a shop front that carried the words 'Public Call Office'. She glanced at it, and the small Bakelite phone that was sitting on a table by an empty chair, before looking away. Her overwhelming emotions at the moment were still relief and excitement at having successfully escaped Dinesh but she now experienced a searing flash of guilt deep in her stomach. She should not be putting off calling her parents any more. They would be desperately worried about her, and must surely have contacted the police by now. But Tara had still not found the right moment to ask Himal about calling them and was not sure at all of how he would react to the idea. For one, her parents would almost certainly order her to return to Delhi without delay. They were not to know of how dangerous it would be for her to go back right now. And, if she did tell them about Dinesh and all that had happened, they would instantly start a police case and then what would happen to Himal? Surely, he would invite terrible punishment for aiding Dinesh in his crimes.

But that wasn't all; Tara could tell that Himal was in love with her already. She had caught him looking at her almost with wonderment, as though unable to believe that she was by his side at all. Why else would he risk so much to help her escape Dinesh if it wasn't love? In truth, Tara was very confused by this situation. On the one hand, she was tortured by guilt when she thought about her parents but, on the other, she could not deny that she was relishing being catapulted into this strangely grown-up kind of scenario where a man had fallen in love with her, and they were on the run, escaping a villain. It was almost like being in a film. That old world of hers which encompassed parents and school and board exams and college admissions seemed remote and suddenly strangely alien. Of course, there were things to worry about over here – Dinesh, money, the police – but all those were so far removed from the mundane tedium of her teenage life that they were ... well ... exciting, if she was to be honest. Besides, Tara found Himal's careful attentions towards her both flattering and endearing. He had so far been unfailingly sweet and kind. Why, all she had done yesterday was mention a fondness for guavas and there he was running down a station platform to buy them for her with minutes to spare for the train to start moving again! Tara was conscious too that poor Himal hadn't had much of a life so far. Was it not only fair to allow him a bit of freedom before his fortunes turned again? Especially given how much he too had risked to help her escape. There was no tearing hurry to call home just yet.

They wandered down Mukteshwar's main road to look at a series of small shops all selling more or less the same things – potato wafers and Maggi noodles and boiled sweets. There were a couple more cafes and restaurants around the corner, all of them just opening their shutters and getting ready for the day's business. Tara felt a sudden stirring of hunger as the smell of parathas wafted in their direction.

'If we go down a side street, we might find something cheaper,' Himal suggested. 'Always these places on the highway are the most expensive as they are the ones who get the tourists.'

They walked up a steep street and, as Himal had predicted, found themselves in what looked like a less salubrious part of town, where clothes were drying on rickety wooden balconies and women and children gathered around a small water tanker, noisily filling their buckets and pots.

Tara saw a sign saying 'Uttara Taxi Service', and right next door was a dhaba with huge, steel vessels lined up and gleaming on a counter. Himal too had spotted the dhaba and was already crossing the road to walk towards it. The overweight and rather bluff man behind the counter could speak a smattering of English which he instantly wanted to practice, assuming, Tara guessed, that they were tourists from the city. They settled themselves on one of the three tiny laminated tables crammed into the back of the shop and Himal ordered for both of them as Tara confessed to being unfamiliar with dhaba offerings. Back in Delhi, meals out and takeaways had been restricted to Dominos and McDonald's or the fancy Italian restaurant in Crescent Mall that her mother adored going to whenever there was a family occasion.

Tara inhaled the smell of meat bubbling in a tomato puree, remembering the chicken curry they had had on her last Sunday at home. Every so often, her father liked to roll up his sleeves and enter the kitchen as though gearing up for a fight. This was generally cue for the rest of the family to roll their eyes and groan very loudly but Dad was adept at ignoring this. His efforts were, what Mum drily called, 'Hit and Miss' and that day's effort had definitely fallen under the latter category. So intent had Dad been on getting the chicken to cook right through that he had produced a bowl full of shredded chicken with a few bare bones sticking out here and there that everyone, even Pia, refused to touch.

Was that really just last Sunday? Tara, who had lost all track of time in her head, was sure it was an entire lifetime ago. She felt remorseful again, imagining how anxious her family would be at her disappearance but, until she was quite sure she had Himal's complete trust, she could not do very much. It was definitely too risky to ruin things between them right now. The last thing she needed was for him to turn back into her captor, rather than the co-conspirator and friend he was becoming right now.

'Smells good, na?' Himal asked.

'I can't imagine eating meat curry so early in the morning but, you're right, it does smell delicious!'

Within ten minutes, an enormous platter of greasy gravy with two bony pieces of mutton floating in it was placed before them along with a pair of spider-webbed enamel plates, a few roughly chopped onions and a basket of freshly made chapatis. Despite the early hour, Tara found herself falling upon the food with relish, realizing that it had been days since she had eaten properly, sitting at a table with proper plates and cutlery. They ate swiftly and without much conversation. Tara suddenly recalled the humiliation of Dinesh opening the back of the van to shove some fruit or a couple of slices of bread towards her which she would then have to eat with one hand. Bananas were particularly difficult as she needed to use her teeth to peel them but what had that evil bastard cared? It was so hard to imagine, sitting in this warm dhaba swirling with comforting aromas, that she was being treated like a caged animal just two days ago...

When it was time to pay, she saw Himal take out a small bundle of notes. He carefully pulled a few out and smiled as he saw Tara watching him. 'Don't worry. There is enough for us now.'

'How much do we have left exactly?' Tara asked after the boy had cleared their plates away. 'We'll need to find somewhere to sleep tonight ... a hotel will cost...'

'There is enough for another day or two,' Himal said, trying to make light of their predicament. 'But I should try to find some work soon.'

Tara nodded seriously. She'd never had to worry about money before but, rather than be overwhelmed by such a problem, she felt flattered to have Himal take her into confidence in this way. 'Do you think we'll be able to find work here in such a small place?' she asked.

Himal looked surprised but also pleased. 'I'll easily find work. In a dhaba like this, maybe. But you? Would you want to work?'

'I'd like to help.'

Himal paused for a long time before he asked his next question. 'Don't you want to go back home?'

Tara looked at him levelly. 'I don't see how we can. You said you were wanted by the police, didn't you?'

'I am. But you are free to go. After a few days, when it is safer, I can take you down to New Delhi railway station, if you like, and, once you are there, all you have to do is go to a police station and tell them who you are. They will make the necessary phone calls and take you home.'

Tara did not move her eyes away from Himal's face; she thought he looked very sad and very lonely suddenly. She tried to imagine what it would be like for him to take her to Delhi and watch her disappear inside a police station before turning around to face his new life alone. A life of being constantly on the run and forever having to look over his shoulder to ensure Dinesh or the police were not following him. Himal had no passport, no papers and, worst of all, he was a wanted man. She had no idea what his other 'crimes' had been but, by far, one of the worst crimes that Dinesh would have coerced him into was her own kidnap and rape. The sentence he would be served for that would not be insubstantial, even if she attempted defending him. All that was a terrible punishment when he had risked so much to help her escape the torture she had suffered.

Tara looked around – at the dhaba they were sitting in and the colourful street scenes she could see outside. For the time being, they could make some sort of life here in the hills, she felt sure of that. With her to help him, Himal could be back on his feet, and perhaps even make enough money to get back to Nepal someday. Didn't she owe him at least that much?

In order to emphasize her point, she took his hand in hers before replying. 'Yes, I do want to go back and see my parents someday, Himal. But not now. Now, I want to help you as you have helped me. Together we will be able to work and earn and save some money. I want to do at least that much for you. Then we can both go back to our homes. Me to Delhi and you to Nepal.' Tara's heart swelled with an unfamiliar sense of goodness. Then, because she felt embarrassed by it, she tried attempting a joke. 'Besides, if I went back to Delhi now, I'd have to sit for my board exams! This is my best chance to escape them, you know.'

They found a cheap hotel right next to the main bus stop, in a squat greying building flanked by shops. The first-floor room they were offered looked grotty and poorly lit, dank curtains masking the bit of natural light coming through greasy windows. There was the luxury of an attached bathroom but the sink was cracked and drippy and the tiles edged with grime. Tara was relieved, however, to see that the large double bed had sheets that, though threadbare, at least looked like they had been laundered many times over. She certainly wasn't going to fuss after all that she had been through. More than anything else, Tara needed to catch up on the sleep she had not had since her kidnapping. She still did not know exactly how many days she had spent in that hellish grey van and had stopped herself from asking Himal, having grown aware of how awkward he found the subject. Perhaps he felt genuinely guilty for the part he had played in her suffering but so far he had answered all questions relating to that episode in monosyllables and so Tara did not pursue the matter. All she knew, from her scanty knowledge of the topography of India, was that she was now miles away from Delhi, up here in the Kumaon hills, and she had decided to make a go of it.

After more precious money had changed hands, they took the room. While Himal talked to the hotel owner in the corridor,

Tara went into the windowless, airless toilet and locked herself in, using the rusty key. She felt another small frisson of unease at the thought of spending a night on the same bed with a man who – nice as he had been since they had escaped Dinesh's clutches – had so recently been one of her abductors. Despite some of the slightly forced banter of the day, Tara could not completely forget the part that Himal too had played in the kidnapping. Dinesh couldn't have done everything without Himal's assistance; all that stalking and following and watching, outside her house and outside her school, which had culminated in them grabbing her unexpectedly in Poltergeist Passage. And after that too, Himal had known that Dinesh was raping her in the back of the van and had done nothing at first. Of course Tara was enormously grateful that he had not joined in and done the same to her but the fact remained that he had – what was the term that newspapers used? – aided and abetted, that was it. Yes, he had aided and abetted Dinesh in the most horrible crime it was possible to inflict on a girl. Was she being really stupid in forgiving him so easily? Enough to sleep trustingly next to him on a double bed. On the other hand, she was relatively safe now; in a pretty little tourist spot where they were surrounded by shops and cafes. If Himal did anything bad, she only had to holler and someone or the other would hear her. There was always the option of making an escape when Himal wasn't looking, hop on a bus to Kathgodam and give him the slip.

Tara looked at her face in the mirror. She no longer did this admiringly as before, practising different expressions and pouts, now only seeing eyes that were dark and bewildered. She did not know what to think. There were many good reasons to make a run for it and go back home to Delhi. But there were also many reasons not to do so. She reminded herself again – it was Himal who had brought her here, helping her escape the most appalling fate. By doing so, he had exposed himself to danger and even death. And now he relied on her to not let him down, didn't he? It was all so muddling because, on the one hand, Tara wanted very much to place all her trust in Himal but a part of her was still that frightened girl cowering in the back of that grey van, desperate to get back home to her parents. But she was tired now and desperate for one decent night's sleep on a proper bed. The night on the train had been spent sitting squashed between an old man and a young woman who was trying to keep a squalling baby from falling off her lap. And in the shared taxi, she had been squeezed among a bunch of college students who were out on a pleasure trip from Ghaziabad. Perhaps she would feel stronger tomorrow, after having slept, and then she would be in a position to make an intelligent decision about what to do next.

Tara emerged from the toilet and saw that Himal had made up a small bed for himself on the floor, using one of the pillows and a sheet that he must have found in the cupboard. She stopped short. 'You don't have to do that,' she said, looking Himal in the eye and taking a deep breath. 'I trust you not to do what Dinesh did to me.'

Himal shrugged, his face reddening. He looked deeply embarrassed but did not say anything and so Tara spoke up again, now sitting on the edge of the bed. 'If you were that sort, you had your chances while I was trapped in the van and also yesterday in that motel in Rampur. Really. You can sleep on that side of the bed, Himal. It's big enough for both of us. You must be tired too.'

Himal continued to remain silent but he picked up the pillow and sheet and chucked them on the far side of the bed. Then he made his way across to the toilet but, before he went in, he looked back at Tara and said in Hindi, 'Thank you for trusting me.'

Tara took a few minutes, listening to the sounds of the town now alive and thriving as it woke up fully to the day. Then she got up and took off her salwaar and dupatta, folding and placing them on the end of the bed before getting in wearing only the kurta that came almost to her knees. Covering herself with the spare blanket, she closed her eyes and, possibly because she had both been too anxious to sleep properly during their one night in Rampur and too uncomfortable to sleep on the train, Tara felt a comforting darkness envelope her. Within minutes, she was fast asleep.

When she awoke, she could see pale light filtering through the single window but could not tell if it was evening or dawn. For a few minutes, she lay on her bed, listening to the unfamiliar sounds of a small town. Unlike Delhi, where vegetable hawkers' and kabaadiwallahs' cries penetrated the shriek of traffic, she could hear birdsong and the thin sound of a radio playing Hindi songs from somewhere downstairs. Without warning, Tara felt a sudden tremor of anticipation at what lay ahead. It would certainly be unlike those dreary and uneventful days of home–school–home back in Delhi. Bela and all the others would be slaving away, getting stressed out and preparing for the exams while here she was, far away from all the craziness, about to start living an independent life with this new friend she had made so unexpectedly. Was she being stupid? Was it stupid to start thinking of Himal as a kind of *boyfriend?*

Tara turned her head to look at the sleeping form next to her and felt a renewed and rather worthy sense of having done right by Himal in making her earlier decision. It wasn't that she didn't love her parents and didn't want them to stop agonizing over her – Dad in particular, she knew, would be beside himself with worry – but, at this point in time, she literally owed her life to the man who was sleeping next to her. He had been kind and brave and it would be nothing less than heartless and, in fact, deeply selfish to walk away from him right now. Perhaps she could call her parents, without telling them where she was, just to put them out of their misery. Hopefully, they would not send a search party out for her, or order her to return, but she would think of some way to avoid that. And then, once the fuss had died down, Tara vowed to go back home, where she would make enquiries about helping Himal to do some kind of legal bargaining to get a reduced sentence. As she had promised, her father would then assist him in getting admission to a medical college and perhaps he could still achieve his ambition of becoming a doctor and helping his mother and sisters back in Nepal ... that was definitely the best and most honourable course of action.

Himal came awake while she was still looking at him, and caught her gaze before she could glance away. He smiled drowsily and ran his hand through his hair as he stretched. 'What time is it?' he asked, his voice still thick with sleep.

'Oh, I dunno, maybe six or seven...'

'Morning or evening?'

'Evening, I think! Looks like we've slept through the day.'

'That's good,' Himal said, stretching. 'We can now step out and look for work in the dhabas. Have you been awake for some time?'

'Just ten minutes. I came awake with a start ... not in a bad way,' she said hastily, lest he think she was still having nightmares over Dinesh. 'In fact, having slept properly, it's all feeling quite nice.'

'Nice?'

'Oh, y'know, having escaped Dinesh, being here in this pretty little place, having you here for company ... it's worked out nicely, I think. Who would've thought just a day or two ago...'

Himal nodded, looking pleased. Then he pulled himself up to peer out of the window. Soft, wintry sunshine was just parting the clouds and a shaft of flecked light slanted across the room. 'Do you want me to go get some tea or coffee? There's that cafe just down the road from here.'

'I'd love a cup of tea, actually. Not too keen on coffee,' Tara replied, before adding, 'I'm wide awake, though, so why don't I come with you? No point lying around like this when there's a whole mountain waiting to be explored!'

They got out of bed, both self-conscious of the other's presence in the tiny room. Himal turned to face the wall as he pulled his jeans over his shorts and Tara used the chance to grab her clothes and dive straight from the bed into the bathroom. She opened the paper bag of things they had bought earlier in the day from a chemist, and pulled one of two toothbrushes out of its wrapping. After brushing her teeth, she got dressed and went back into the room.

Together they walked out onto the street that was now busy with people. Most seemed to have no particular business to attend to and were wandering up and down the main road, eyeing each other with interest. The cafe was a hive of activity, a group of hikers having stopped by for a drink. The man behind the counter was frantically filling paper cup after paper cup from a grimy, old coffee machine. There was much clatter and noise and the most delicious smell swirling through the air.

'I do love the smell of coffee,' Tara said, 'all grown-up and sophisticated. Just don't much like the taste, that's all.'

They collected their drinks, adding a couple of small fruitcakes to their purchase, before wandering outdoors again. Cold evening air was slowly replacing the warmth of the day as they made for a large rocky outcrop they could see across the road. Perched on boulders that were still warm from the day's sun, Tara looked around as she sipped her tea and warmed her fingers. In a small town, everyone seems to know everyone else and small clutches of people were sitting by the roadside, chatting and laughing. It was all very different from Delhi, peaceful and friendly, and Tara felt filled with a sense of well-being. If she and Himal worked hard and kept their heads down, she was sure that soon they too could become part of this tranquil place that did not seem to have heard the words 'board exams' at all. There was still the matter of calling her parents, of course – Tara could even see another PCO from where she sat – but she felt a clutch of apprehension, imagining how they would command her to return to Delhi straightaway. Dad would definitely jump on a train to fetch her. Yes, she did want to speak to them and see them but not right away. Not before she'd had a chance to experience this adult life that lay so temptingly before her.

They finished their drinks, watching the pale orange blob of sun dip slowly behind the mountains, turning the sky and the surrounding mountains into a shade of what Tara thought of as 'sari pink'.

'We should start our search for work,' Himal said presently.

'Now, or in the morning?'

'Well, everything will be open for another few hours so let's go now. Why wait?'

He was right. They would probably soon run out of money if they didn't find work. Tara got up and straightened her shawl around her shoulders. A light snow was now falling, sprinkling the trees and shop awnings like sugar on a cake and turning the little town into a little fairyland. Tara suppressed another small quiver of an emotion she could not name. Walking down this enchanted, sparkling street in the company of a man with whom she was setting out to explore job prospects made her feel not just grown-up but somehow *complete*. It was hard enough to rationalize this exhilaration to herself so there was no question of even beginning to try and explain it to Mum and Dad. It really was simpler to refrain from calling home for a while. Just another day or two.

At first they cut back through town to return to the dhaba where they had eaten their first meal. When Himal put his proposal of work to the owner, the latter looked mildly surprised that his tourist-client had so quickly turned into a potential employee. But he asked no further questions other than, 'You can chop and cook?' before offering Himal five hours of work every evening at hundred rupees a day, two days off in a month.

Tara's luck was even better. On the far side of town was a small shop selling sweaters and other woollen garments for women and children. Himal had spotted it on their way into Mukteshwar while travelling in the shared taxi but they had to ask a couple of passers-by and walk a mile down the main road before they found it, nestled in a grove of deodar trees just off the main road.

'I think you should go in and speak this time,' Himal said.

'But won't I sound too Delhi?"

'That's what they want in shops like this. These NGO-type places are full of English-speaking tourists. I might put them off with my tooti-phooti English.'

'It's not tooti-phooti,' Tara was swift to comfort, 'it's really quite good.'

Himal smiled. 'Well, it is getting better all the time when I talk to you and I will soon be sounding like an Angrez sahib, I think. But right now I think I'll stand here while you go in.'

'I'm not going alone, Himal!'

'You'll be fine, you'll be just great. Now go.'

He gave her an encouraging shove and Tara walked up two mossy stone steps to push at the wooden door. It opened with a clanging sound that brought a lady out of a room at the back. She was elderly and had a lined, kindly face but Tara's tongue seized up with sudden nervousness. Imagining Himal watching her through the window, however, she launched into the opening line she had practised as they'd walked up the road. She heard her voice emerging in an unnaturally high tone that made her sound like a seven-year-old which was annoying as she really did want to come across as grown-up and mature.

'Hello, good evening. We ... I'm new here in town and I'm looking for work. I wondered if I could be of any help to you here in your shop...'

The lady squinted at Tara as though trying to look right through her face to the truth that lay beneath. Tara felt herself squirm under such close scrutiny.

'Do you know exactly what it is we do here?' the lady asked finally.

'Er ... you sell sweaters and stuff?'

'Well, yes, we do sell sweaters but it's not as straightforward as that.' The lady was now smiling, so Tara started to relax as she listened. 'Let me explain to you, my dear. I'm a retired teacher and I now live in Bhowali, you know the village down the road? Well, with my retirement money, many years ago, I bought a few knitting and sewing machines and have got a small workshop in Bhowali where I train local women. It's so they learn a useful skill, you see. Then, as we started looking for a retail outlet for our products, one of the local rural NGOs came forward to offer us this shop. I don't know if you would be interested in that kind of social work ... you look very young.'

'I'll do anything, I mean any job, really,' Tara said before adding hastily, 'As long as it's paid, of course. I can't do social work ... I mean, I *like* the idea and all that but I'm not in a position to work for free right now.'

'We don't offer very high salaries,' the lady warned.

'How much would you be able to...?' Tara trailed off. This was completely unfamiliar territory to her. If she was asked how much she wanted, she wouldn't have a clue.

But it was the lady who looked uncertain now. 'Oh, I don't know. We've never thought about having someone here, manning the store. I've always done this myself so I'm not sure...' She hesitated a moment and then spoke again. 'I must say that I prefer to spend more and more of my time down in Bhowali, teaching my girls there and designing the sweaters. This bit...' She looked around the shop and waved vaguely in the direction of the street. '... this bit I am less excited about – all this selling and advertising and marketing. Yet, I know my women need customers if they are to make money. So I come here two times a week and try to keep this shop going but it isn't enough because I think we put customers off by being closed most of the time.' She looked searchingly at Tara again, assessing her more closely. 'I think you would be perfect, actually, with your pretty face and your nice English and nice manners. The foreigners and tourists who come here to this town in the summer months will love you. But you understand I can't pay you much. Would you be okay with two thousand a month? I can pay you on a weekly basis, if you prefer, while you try it out?'

'Two thousand rupees?' Tara had to hold herself from grabbing the woman and kissing her. A job, just like that! And for a salary of two thousand rupees! True, she had no financial sense and could never remember the price of milk or eggs if she was ever sent out to the shops to get them. Mum, in fact, had called her 'my little spendthrift' from the time she had been a child and for some time Tara had thought it was a compliment because of the word 'thrift'. Now she tried to work out exactly how much two thousand rupees was in terms of buying power but it was hard to know if it would cover the cost of things simply because she didn't know what the cost of things were. But it sounded ... well, if not quite a fortune, at least a generous amount. Her first salary! How proud her parents would be if they could only see what she was capable of...

'Yes, I'm happy to try out the job for that salary,' Tara replied, trying not to grin too much. 'And weekly payment would be fine, if you don't mind. I mean, I *can* take it on a monthly basis if you want. But you did ask my preference. Which is weekly, really, at least in the beginning...'

The lady was smiling broadly now. Then she rearranged her face into a faux-suspicious expression, casting a glance at Himal who was kicking his heels in the dust outside. 'I assume you're old enough to be out here on your own? Working and all that?'

Tara tried not to gulp and raised herself up to full height. 'I'm twenty this year,' she lied. Fortunately, the lady seemed to believe her but she had not quite finished her inquisition. 'Is that your boyfriend outside?' Tara hesitated and then nodded. 'You're here because your parents disapprove of him, I take it?' Tara nodded again, waiting with her breath held for fear that she would lose her first job within five minutes of getting it. A look of irritation clouded her potential employer's face. 'What *is* it with these parents,' she exploded. 'Sometimes I fail to understand the way in which they get all agitated about the wrong things – caste, religion, social strata, all this nonsense. Total nonsense! I should know ... I've been through all this myself many years ago. But obviously things will never change in this great country of ours. The only thing of importance should be that he loves you and respects you.' She dropped her voice and asked in a conspiratorial manner, 'He is nice to you, I hope?' Tara nodded again and the lady thumped her desk in relief. 'Good! And, if he ever gives you trouble, you know where to come, yes?' She said this with an accompanying tap of a forefinger on her ample chest. As Tara was agreeing to everything she said, there was not much more for the lady to say than, 'Okay, you can start tomorrow if you like. Ten o'clock?'

On leaving the shop, Tara let out a loud whoop and threw her arms around Himal's neck. He was startled but understanding dawned as Tara babbled excitedly about NGOs and salaries and lovely employers. He broke into a wide grin and then, seeing that the lady was watching them through the shop window, he extricated himself from Tara's arms and bowed in the direction of the older woman with a small salaam to indicate his gratitude.

Then they turned to walk back to their part of town, talking animatedly about how – now that they both had jobs – they should next try to find a proper house.

That night, Tara could not sleep for her excitement. Was she really about to start a new job when the sun rose in the morning. A *job*! Not go to school, that is? Not have to listen to Sammy's boring lectures? And not have to explain her every action to Mum and Dad. It was just incredible! Then, sobering slightly, she felt her thoughts meander back to her home in Delhi … her parents and siblings … except that it was now without the feeling of something inside her being torn up. Tara turned around and faced the window which was filled with enormous white stars hanging low over dark peaks. She felt much more at peace about things, much more in charge and very much more mature. She would call her parents, yes she definitely would. She just wished she could be surer of their reaction, less frightened of what they would order her to do…

The sound of Himal's breathing from the other side of the bed was soft and rhythmic. He was fast asleep. Tara turned again and studied his face. He looked like a worried little boy, lips clenched together and a small crease puckering up his forehead. Despite everything – or perhaps because of it – Tara felt a rush of protectiveness towards him. It was definitely her responsibility now to stand by Himal and help him through his own problems. She closed her eyes and told herself to get some rest too. She was going to need all her wits about her for the new life that lay ahead.

Margaret's Journal Entry 6: Undated

It is incredible, and so very gratifying, to be gainfully employed! Word has got out in our town that I can speak and read English. Perhaps the townsfolk have even worked out that I am English but no one has directly enquired yet about who exactly I am. Even if they know, I suspect that a web of protectiveness and secrecy would by now have grown around me in the town and I am thankful for this.

It started with some of the neighbours bringing their letters to have them read and now people come from quite far – a man from distant Nowshera, the other day! Government notifications, legal information, job offers, they all come first to me now. And it is my good fortune to be the one to disseminate happiness when it is good news.

They squat obediently before me, even grand old men resplendent in their turbans and shawls and sporting great big moustaches across craggy faces. They call me 'daughter' and look up at me with such awe and love in their eyes that I am sometimes moved to tears. Even though I protest, often they bring me gifts – a bag of walnuts, a dozen juicy yellow peaches filling a basket, large round pats of jaggery with which to sweeten my tea.

And now, when I go to the bazaar with Ammi or Tabassum, passers-by bow and say aadaab and shopkeepers will sometimes give us a small discount on our purchases.

I know Ammi is very pleased, perhaps her last doubts about me are now dispelled. Yesterday she talked again about starting a school for little ones, to teach them to read and write English. I would enjoy that very much, I think, and so we will ask Nizam whether we can do that when he comes back from the mountains.

Despite his absence, dare I say that my life here is growing happier by the day?

Tara, 1997

A month after starting her job, Tara looked up from the shop counter as the doorbell clanged. She put away the pile of mufflers she had been folding and smiled at the pair of women who were coming in, their faces pink from the cold. One of them took off her gloves and vigorously rubbed her hands together, looking around at the sweaters and ponchos Tara had spent all morning hanging up on bamboo hooks she had bought from the bazaar for this purpose. She listened to their conversation, hearing Delhi accents.

'Hey these are nice, yaar, these embroidered sweaters.'

'Ya, if you like that rough look. Maybe a bit prickly…'

'At least these are unusual, not the usual machine-made maal.'

'Hanh, that's true, but kinda home-made looking, na?'

Her tone was a bit disparaging so Tara was swift to say, 'All our knitwear is hand-knitted and hand-embroidered by local women. Here are some leaflets to explain how our cooperative works. You'll see that there are no middlemen so the women keep all their profits.' She pushed the stack of leaflets across the counter and the first woman picked up one to read it. These were the only customers who had come in all day so Tara hoped they would buy something before leaving. She left the counter to join them on the shop floor and moved aside the hanging sweaters so they could see the ones on the shelves behind better. 'Are you looking for anything specific?'

'No, not really. We just saw the shop when we came for a walk out of our resort so we thought we'll come in and see. So it's an NGO outlet?'

'Well, sort of.' Tara smiled before explaining the concept in some detail. Four weeks into the job, she had rehearsed Mallika's sales patter till she could now do it backwards. The women seemed interested enough and so Tara warmed to her theme. 'So, you see, if you look at this sweater here – it was made by a young girl called Shabnum who suffered from polio when she was a child. She needs crutches to walk around but, luckily, her hands were not affected so she turns out the most beautiful cardigans. This blue one is also one of hers.'

'Hey, this one is really pretty, yaar,' one of the women said, picking up a pale blue mohair sweater with tiny pearl buttons sewn along the edges. The woman held it against herself and looked into the mirror that Tara swiftly wheeled out from the corner if the shop.

'I like this one,' the other woman said, picking up a black angora with lacy cuffs. 'Can I try it on?'

'Of course you can,' Tara replied, watching the two women peel off their jackets to start trying on one sweater after another. She busied herself, folding away the cardigans that were being discarded, adding the rest to a small growing pile on the counter that she hoped desperately would all be purchased. The sales figures, since she had started, had not been great, although Mallika had assured her that things would pick up in the season.

'Are you tourists here?' Tara asked the woman standing near her, hoping she sounded pleasant, rather than nosy.

'Ya, we came up from Delhi for a small break.'

'At the White Cedar resort?'

'Yes, across the main road.'

'Never thought it would be so damn cold,' the other said, giggling.

Tara smiled. 'Actually things had started warming up here nicely but, last week, this crazy cold spell started. It'll last another week or so, they're saying.'

'Trust our luck to catch the coldest week here!'

'Ya, but we also wanted to escape the Delhi dust and heat, remember?'

'Is it hot already in Delhi?' Tara asked.

'Crazy heat, yaar! The day after Holi the mercury started climbing and climbing and I think it's already hitting thirty-four, thirty-five.'

'That's hot for early April.'

'You're telling me! Anyway, I think I'll take these two sweaters. The black and this green-and-white one. Have you decided?' She turned to her friend.

The other woman was looking more doubtful. 'We won't really get the chance to wear sweaters and all for some months now, will we? Till next winter even?'

'Hanh, not in Delhi of course. But I'm going to the States to see my sister, I think I told you na? Colorado. And it's always cold where she lives so these will come in useful. In fact, I think I'll take one more, as a gift for her. Do you have things for men too? I should take something for her husband also. They love all these NGO-type products over there in the States.'

Tara pulled out a stack of unisex scarves and mufflers and then yanked open a plastic box full of knitted caps. 'These are the products we have for men,' she said. 'The caps are very popular – especially the ones with flaps that cover the ears.'

Half an hour later, parcelling up six sweaters and an assortment of mufflers, caps and gloves, Tara could hardly contain her excitement. Mallika would be dead pleased with her sales efforts this afternoon. Using the shop's giant old calculator, she carefully wrote out the bill, going slowly so as not to get anything wrong. This was the bit where she still needed to pick up some confidence, maths having never been a strong point. Luckily the two women seemed in no hurry to leave the warmth of the shop, chatting with each other and warming their fingers on the bar heater near the door. When it was all done, Tara handed over their bags and said, 'Thank you for your generous purchases. The women who knit for us will be so pleased to know how much you appreciated their work.'

After the customers had taken a couple of leaflets and left, Tara sat down, feeling the adrenaline slowly seep out of her. It had been an exciting hour's work and she felt she had earned her whole month's salary in this one afternoon. She couldn't wait to tell Mallika. And Himal too. Sometimes he was more pleased than her at her little successes, or whenever anything happened to brighten her day – be it a compliment from a customer or praise from Mallika. 'You must be the best shop girl in all of Kumaon,' he had commented the other day, making her laugh, even though he seemed to have said it in seriousness.

Tara looked around her at the little shop that had so quickly become her domain. It was bright and cheery, especially with all the sweaters hanging from the hooks, their buttons and sequins catching the last bit of sunlight that was coming in from the window. From where she sat, Tara could see the banks of dirty snow piled up high on either side of the road. She cast a glance upwards – the sky was darkening again so it looked like there could be fresh snowfall. Himal had said he would come to get her during his evening break so that she wouldn't be sliding about on the icy road by herself.

When the bell next rang half an hour later, Tara saw that it was Himal coming in through the door. She had just finished stacking all the sweaters and hanging up fresh stock on the bamboo hangers, ready for the next day.

'Good timing!' she said, greeting him with a big smile. 'I'd just this minute put the last piece away. Getting very good at this folding lark. Back in Delhi, I was a bit of a shove-into-the cupboard-and-squeeze-the-door-shut type, can you believe it?' She surveyed the neat shop with proprietorial pride. 'Okay, I'm ready to leave now, I think.'

Himal looked at his watch. 'I thought I was early. But it was looking like it would maybe start snowing again, so I didn't want to delay.'

'Well, I doubt any more shoppers will come in now, especially as it's getting so dark. But you won't believe what a day I've had, Himal. Sold enough to keep the Bhowali girls going for three whole weeks. All bought by two women who came from Delhi.'

'Really? How many pieces?'

Tara pushed the invoice pad across the counter, opening it to the last page. 'Just look at that,' she said proudly. 'Six sweaters, four mufflers, two stoles and three caps! Fantastic, isn't it?'

As Tara had predicted, Himal's grin was wide enough to split his face. 'You are too good,' he said, pulling the pad towards him to peer at Tara's neat handwriting in disbelief. 'Your boss should give you five thousand rupees, not two thousand.'

'Well, if I hang around long enough, she just might, you know! A double-promotion when I complete a full month tomorrow.'

Himal did not say anything in response but leaned over the counter and gave Tara a kiss on her left cheek. She glowed with pleasure and, faintly embarrassed, busied herself with closing the last of the plastic boxes in which the caps and gloves were stored before shoving it away under the counter. Like best friends, she and Himal had grown comfortable around each other but there had been nothing more than the occasional peck on the cheek or handholding when walking on icy roads.

'Shall we go then?' she asked briskly, straightening up and pulling her jacket off the coat rack behind the back door. Mallika had procured inexpensive jackets for both Himal and Tara from the wool supplier who made a monthly trip from Ludhiana, and it had made them laugh to see that they were identical in colour and design, with only the size (medium for Tara and large for Himal) to set them apart. There had been an occasion when Tara, running late for work, had not noticed that she had worn Himal's jacket, leaving him with hers, which he was unable to zip up past his chest. Now, looking like a pair of identical twins, they left the shop, Himal waiting while Tara locked the door and put the keys safely into her handbag.

Back at their small barsaati an hour later, Himal let Tara in before leaving for the dhaba. It usually got busy again around this time and he did not want to be late. The snowstorm had set in, sending sparkling white flurries lighting up the evening gloom. Making sure Tara was safely indoors, Himal pulled the hood of his jacket over his head and stepped out onto the street again. Tara latched the door and sniffed the air. It smelt like Himal had been doing some cooking. Or perhaps he had brought something back for her from the dhaba. Feeling ravenous, she wandered across to the stove and peered into the covered dish on it. Rajma! And there was a pot of freshly cooked rice right there on the table. Tara pulled out a plate and helped herself to a generous portion before taking it across to the bed so she could sit comfortably cross-legged while leafing through a magazine someone had left behind at the dhaba, swiftly purloined for Tara by Himal.

It was two hours later when Tara woke up with a start. Her dinner plate, with remnants of her rajma-chaawal meal drying on it, was lying next to her on the bed. She must have fallen asleep minutes after finishing her meal. She had not realized how tired she was and the walk back from the shop, with both of them keeping their heads down to fight against freezing winds, couldn't have helped. Tara heard a small sound at the door and froze. She held her breath, all sorts of fearful thoughts coursing through her brain. Was someone trying to get in? Perhaps it was the noise that had woken her up. Himal had given her stern instructions not to open the door to anyone until she heard his distinctive three-taps and two-knocks. This was definitely not his usual signal but a small continuous tapping sound behind the door. Tempting as it was to dive under the bed, or pull a blanket over herself as she used to when small, Tara slowly uncoiled her stiff legs and slipped out of bed. Creeping along towards the kitchen, she picked up the knife Himal used to cut meat and then stood with her back to the wall, not taking her eyes off the door handle. The tapping continued, soft and insistent, and Tara wondered if the person on the other side of the door could hear the sound of her hammering heart. Her legs were trembling and, despite the freezing temperature in the room, she had broken out into a sweat. Beads of fear formed on her upper lip. Tara did not know how long she stood there, but by the time the tapping stopped, her neck was stiff as wood and her fingers carried deep, red marks where the handle of the knife had been cutting into her skin. Just as she was wondering if it was safe to put the weapon down, she nearly screamed out loud in terror as a mouse scuttled into the room from the crack under the door. A mouse! Tara did not know whether to laugh or cry at her paranoia but she took the knife with her to bed and slipped it under her pillow as she tried to go back to sleep. She lay there for a long time, looking into the darkness and fighting back those same old, dreadful memories that refused to leave on certain days. Finally, from sheer exhaustion, she sank into an uneasy slumber at midnight, when she knew it would not be long before Himal returned to their room.

The following morning, Tara told Himal about her encounter with the mouse while toasting bread over the gas hob. Although she was laughing as she recounted the tale, adding some comic exaggeration for effect, Himal looked worried. 'You must have been really scared if you stood there for so long with a knife,' he said, looking searchingly into her face.

Tara got up to retrieve the knife that was still stashed under her pillow. 'Just realized I forgot to put my weapon back! Now that would have given you a fright if it'd fallen out when you made the bed.'

Himal glanced at the rickety old door with its rusting hinges. 'Actually, that door will just fall down if someone pushes hard at it.'

'Well, I could shout really loudly if that happened. Someone would hear me. Nosy old Ramdevji from downstairs or his prying wife.'

'They're okay,' Himal said, adding, 'they've been quite helpful, actually, especially allowing us to cook here, even though it's supposed to be a hotel. But, I've been thinking, maybe we should find a better place to live?'

Tara considered it and nodded. 'I don't mind it here but, now that we're both earning, we could probably afford some place better than this.'

'We may have to move a little far out of Mukteshwar but that would be a good thing. When the tourist season starts, they say a lot of people come up here from Delhi.'

Tara knew he was thinking, not just about Dinesh and his network, but also about the possibility of someone who knew her parents spotting her and dragging her back to Delhi. They had talked about contacting her parents a few times and, even though Himal had told her that she should, Tara had grown more and more convinced that it would bring a swift end their to life here in the mountains. She had finally agreed that she would make that call when she turned eighteen in a few days' time, on the second of May. 'I'll call them on my birthday, Himal. Be a bit like a birthday present for them and for me, I guess. Also, maybe they won't be able to order me about so much once I'm eighteen, although I'm not sure about that. My mum's really bossy.'

That was that and, whenever they could get time away from work, Himal and Tara started looking for a proper house. Soon they found such a place without much trouble – a one-bedroom dwelling tucked away between flats and shops on a steep road parallel to the highway. It was far from luxurious but Tara loved the view they had from the back balcony which jutted out above a tree-covered slope. On breezy days, the sound of the wind in the trees was like a rushing river and, at night, with no habitation to puncture the darkness, it was like a carpet of black velvet.

This became their home and, one night, very late, they returned to their room, huddled together to stay warm against the intermittent snow flurries and hurried into what now felt like the cosiest place in the world, small and warm and snug. With only enough energy to fling off their coats and kick off their shoes, they fell into bed still fully clothed, sleeping the rich, deep sleep enjoyed only by the very young and very thoughtless.

When morning broke that day, it was Himal who woke first. His eyes were on Tara as she drifted awake and she became slowly aware of not just his gaze but also his intense longing. He reached out an arm with a tentative expression on his face. Tara hesitated a split second before rolling her head onto his shoulder and pulling her body closer to his. For a while, they lay like this, enjoying the quiet camaraderie that had grown between them in the past couple of months. With a surge of gratitude for many different things, Tara reached up to brush Himal's face with her lips but before she knew it they were facing each other in bed and kissing each other deeply on the mouth. When he reached down to pull her top and tee-shirt off, she did not demur and, as he started to massage her bare arms and breasts and stomach with firm, gentle strokes, her body – wound so tightly from its recent ravages – finally started to relax. They kissed and undressed and then made love in that dingy little room.

It was late afternoon when they finally drew themselves away from each other and tumbled out of bed. They dressed in one of their two sets of clothes and put on their identical navy blue jackets in order to set out for their jobs. Burning by now with the confidence of being able to conquer the world together, it wasn't surprising that they were simply unable to see the pain caused to others by their happiness.

Pia, 1997

The day my elder sister disappeared was the worst day of my life. The kind of day Mum called 'the pits'. We didn't know there would be many more pits to come but, at that point, it was totally and definitely the worst pits. Or it would, at least, be correct to say that it was the start of the worst period of all our lives. My whole family's, I mean. It marked the point when we stopped being happy. It might sound weird but it was really as simple as that. Even when *good* things happened to any of us later on, we could never quite feel the sort of happiness which we felt in that period that I refer to as 'BT' – 'Before Tara'.

Before Tara, we were a noisy family, not really that respectful or anything and sort of always getting at each other with the kind of tongue-in-cheek jokes we'd picked up from Mum. Even though I was just eleven, I knew it was only tomfoolery; it would have been silly to take any of the teasing seriously and I'm sure Tara knew that too. She was, like Neel and me, loved by Mum and Dad in their own rather vague, strict way and it would have been really, really stupid if she had taken any of their scolding and things to heart. Not that I ever thought that was why she had disappeared but I know Mum did.

Anyway, when Tara did not come in with Neel from school *that day* because of his band practice, and he said that she had already left school hours before him, I saw a scared look pass over Mum's face although she thought she had hidden it from me. She wasn't worried enough to call Dad and tell him straightaway but she sat on the sofa which faced the living-room window while we watched the 7 o'clock news and kept darting looks into the darkness outside for no other reason than to be the first to spot Tara through the flowers in the window-box when she finally showed up.

By the time Dad came home, Mum had given up trying to hide her anxiety, calling Bela's house and also calling Anahita Saxena and Malvika Pillai, even though Tara had not been friends with them for ages. Mum flew at Dad as he came through the front door, gabbling about Tara not being traceable while he was taking off his coat. Typical Dad, he did not react immediately, saying, 'Slow down, slow down, Ellie, there might be a simple explanation for her not having got back from school yet. Maybe she's got play-practice or something? No? Well then, let's go in and sit down and start at the very beginning, shall we?'

That only made Mum madder as she thought she was being 'patronized', especially as she had considered *everything* before she had started to worry. She had already called the school and checked Tara's room for any possible clues and had found none. But she did calm down a bit after we went into the living room and began to cry while trying to remember if she, or anyone else, had been more than usually sarky to Tara in any way.

'I think she's run away, Nev,' she said finally, blowing her nose.

'Nonsense,' Dad replied, which was not how he usually spoke to Mum.

This time she did not get cross with him, though, now sounding just really tired. 'Well, we've pretty much exhausted all of Saket's and Malviya Nagar's meagre possibilities. Where on earth can she *be?*'

'But, run away? Tara? Why on earth would she do that?' Dad tried to sound confident and forceful, like he did rather lamely when one of the neighbours parked in our slot, but there was a flicker of anxiety in his eyes too.

'Exams?' Mum offered. 'She was starting to get a bit stressed. Kids do extreme things at times like that. You should know. Remember Seb's daughter?'

Dad didn't pooh-pooh Mum's theory. His cousin Seb's daughter had not run away but suffered what everyone called 'a nervous breakdown'. It happened two years ago, just before she took her IIT entrance exams which everyone said was 'the tipping point' although, to me, she merely appeared to be the grumpy type, sitting by herself in her room a lot and writing terrible poetry that she stuck all over the walls of her room. Honestly, exam stress sounded like the silliest reason for anyone – even Tara – to run away in the middle of a cold winter night. Exams were a chance to show off hard work and knowledge, not run away. Although, if I'd said this in front of Tara, she'd have accused me of being a little swot as she often did.

'But we never stressed her out too much over the exams, did we?' Dad asked, looking even more puzzled. 'I mean, we're generally perfectly happy if Tara even *passes*, aren't we?'

'But this board exam was different, Nev. It was getting to her because she knew she needed the marks to get into a decent college. And ... and maybe the straw that broke the camel's back was all that stuff we said yesterday about her clothes and her make-up.' Mum's voice was getting wobbly.

'Don't be daft, Ellie, that was just usual teenage parenting talk!'

'Not when you're already a stressed-out teenager! We shouldn't have, Nev. It's not the worst crime in the world to wear a bit of make-up to school, for heaven's sake...' Mum trailed off, tearfully, but swerved back to being cross the next second. 'I only criticized her to support *you,*' she barked at Dad.

Dad's face was getting red now, which took some doing under his dark skin. 'What? *Me*? So I suppose I shouldn't have told her she was not to go to school looking like a bloody prost...'

'Shh,' Mum hissed, gesturing angrily at Neel and me, slumped at either end of the sofa.

'Okay, let's call the police then and see what they say,' Dad said, not looking too confident but getting up from the armchair to pick up the phone with a false air of being in charge that all of us could see right through.

He found the number in the big directory and then spoke to someone who asked for Tara's description, which Dad gave in a hesitant mix of Hindi and English, looking at Mum for confirmation every few seconds. 'Her eyes? Er ... brown. (Is there a Hindi word for 'brown', Neel? Pia? No?) Yes, it's dark brown. Hair? Long and sort of dark brown again, a bit curly around the ends ... identifying marks ... I don't know if there are any ... oh, sorry, her mother says she has a mole – a small mole near her upper lip ... on the left ... No, no, mole, *mole,* M-O-L-E ... you don't know what that is? Hang on ... how do you say mole in Hindi?' he asked the room in general again.

We looked at each other blankly. Hindi wasn't anyone's forte in the Fernandez family. In fact, it was always bringing my marks down, thanks to the curse of having an English mum and a Goan dad. But Dad couldn't keep his questioner at the police station waiting. 'It's a dot,' he explained apologetically in his anglicized Hindi. 'Mole, a ... *nishaan,* yes (thanks, Neel, old chap). That's it, a nishaan on her lip. Small, brown nishaan. She was wearing what? ... A miniskirt, I think ... What? ... I don't think so. Oh, no, no, sorry, correct that. Her mother says the skirt was yesterday. It was a usual uniform day today so she was in her school uniform. That's right, she was in her school uniform. Grey skirt, white shirt, dark green blazer.'

Dad was standing stiffly as he described Tara and her school uniform but, after he'd finished, he put the receiver back on its cradle and sat down heavily. He looked as though all the air had left his body but, because we were all waiting, he took a breath and said, 'Well, they'll put her details down on their computer and it'll be sent to all police stations nationwide after forty-eight hours. We have to call them again tomorrow, of course. And inform them soon as she's back.'

'Is that *all?*' Mum asked, aghast. 'Did they have nothing more to say? Surely they're not just going to *leave* it like that all night?' By now she was almost yelling but her voice turned tearful again. 'Forty-eight hours is a bloody long time to wait when our child could be in danger, Neville. She's only a teenager. Forty-eight hours! I don't believe it! Why didn't you argue? *Ask* them to do a bit better than that?'

'It's simply standard policy, Ellie. We can't expect them to flout that without good reason,' Dad replied before admitting, 'They were remarkably casual, I have to say.' This was the first time I'd heard my father say anything even remotely negative about the police but that was probably only because he didn't really have very much to do with them in the first place. No breaking of laws, no traffic offences even, despite his really inept driving. Today, however, he clearly felt let down, his strict rules that we should always 'obey authority figures' and 'be law-abiding citizens' sort of slapping him back in the face. Frustration and shock were mixed into his baffled expression when he added, 'The policeman on the phone was even trying to joke actually.'

'*Joke?* What did he say?' Mum demanded.

'Well, he was probably only trying to keep it light for my sake but, when I said she was in a miniskirt, he suggested that Tara must have gone off to meet a boyfriend whom we were unaware of…' He trailed off before asking, genuinely perplexed, '*Does* she have a boyfriend?'

He had put the question out generally but Mum shook her head saying, 'I'm pretty sure she doesn't'. Even though her tone had been quite vehement, they both paused before turning to look enquiringly at Neel.

Neel got all heated at first, saying, 'Don't look at *me*! How the hell would I know what Tara's been up to?' But he soon relented, realizing the gravity of the situation, and adjusted his tone. In an odd sort of wise and deep voice which didn't suit him one bit, Neel said, 'Well, some of the boys at school like her but I don't think she likes any of them very much.' He sounded like a teacher. Normally, my brother would have used that voice of his which came through his nose – the one that often had Mum snap, 'For God's sake, Neel, stop being so *sardonic*!' Then he would have broken up his remark with some little dig at Tara like – 'Some of the boys at school really like her ... can't think *why*!' Obviously he didn't say that but, for me, it was the fact that Neel wasn't trying at all to be funny and the fact that we were all talking without taking 'harmless little pot-shots' (Mum's words) at each other that was so weird. What I didn't know then was that, as a family, we would never return to doing that kind of thing again. Was it just *us* who behaved like that? Well, anyway I think it was gone forever that night.

The sudden peal of the phone made us all jump and I've never seen Mum dart for the instrument as fast as she did at that moment. 'TARA?' she shouted into the mouthpiece, her voice loud with hope. But her shoulders slumped and her face fell immediately as she said, 'No nothing yet, Bela dear ... I guess it's the same with you? ... Yes, I was sure you'd call us soon as you heard anything ... Well, we've called the police ... Yes, police. Didn't think there was any point waiting ... They wanted to know if she had a boyfriend ... Yes, that's what I said and Neel confirmed that too. But, just to reaffirm things, Bela dear, *was* there anyone at all she may have been interested in? Or who was interested in *her* maybe?' Mum paused briefly to agree with a hollow laugh, 'Yes, I know she thought everyone found her beautiful but my question was whether anyone seriously fancied her ... really *liked* her, you know, following her around, that kind of thing. Someone from outside school, particularly? ... No, I didn't think so ... It's not like her to hide her light under a bushel, is it? ... What's that? Oh sorry, I mean it's not like her to hide away any admirers ... Yes, what you see is what you get with our Tara, always way out there with her feelings! ... Of *course*, I'll let you know when she turns up ... thanks for calling, Bela. Bye. Bye.'

Mum hung up and started to cry again, this time going across to Dad and putting her head against his chest. I went to my room to see if being surrounded by my books and things would quell the horrible, fluttery feeling in my stomach. It was curious that, even though Tara and I didn't exactly hang out in each other's rooms much, I really wanted very much for her to be in her room down the corridor. Not doing anything sisterly necessarily – she didn't really *do* sisterly a lot – but I just wanted her there.

I jumped in excitement as I heard sudden sounds emerge from her room, the familiar clunk of drawers and cupboard doors slamming shut. Dashing madly down the corridor, I stuck my head through her door, which was ajar, hoping that maybe she had been in there all along and no one had noticed that she'd come in and the whole disappearance thing would then seem like a big joke. But it was only Mum and Dad looking through Tara's things. I guessed they were hoping once again to find some clues of her whereabouts. They turned as they saw me standing at the door and Dad said, 'Don't worry, sweetheart, you can go back to your room. Mum and I are just checking to see if Tara might have left a note or something for us.'

'Have you found anything yet?' I asked, a wave of hope surging in my chest again because Mum was holding a bunch of papers.

But Mum turned around and leaned her back on Tara's white chest of drawers, shoulders slumped and voice shaking as the pages slipped to the floor. 'Not - a - bloomin' - sausage,' she whispered.

I don't know if my parents slept at all that night because, when I got up to go to the loo at one point, I saw a crack of light under their door. Startled by my face brushing against something, I realized it was Tara's nightshirt hanging behind the bathroom door. On turning on the light, I looked at it from my perch on the pot. Mum called my imagination 'fervid' so maybe that was why the blue nightie looked sad, like a deflated balloon, unoccupied by its rather stroppy, larger-than-life owner. It scared me for some reason and so I bolted back to bed and then lay there for a long time, rubbing my frozen toes together, hoping Tara was warm and comfortable wherever she was, as there was a terribly strong wind howling outside.

~

Mum got her wish – and probably regretted it – when Tara hadn't show up the next day, and we suddenly had the police all over the place. Two constables, one male and one female, poked around in her room, even opening her wardrobe and examining her clothes, which made me think of warning them of how angry she would be by such behaviour. *Nobody* poked around among Tara's clothes, however messy her cupboard. Besides, I couldn't see the point in their hunting around our house for her with such fervour seeing that she was definitely not *here*. It was outside, somewhere *else*, that they should have been looking without wasting more time! No wonder all those Bollywood films and newspaper cartoons made the police look like such buffoons. Usha Aunty once said they were all 'chors' when the fruit shopwallah down the road told her that he had to supply his best mangoes free to the local beat cop but even at that time my dad had only smiled indulgently and said they didn't get paid enough for what they did. *Now* what was he thinking as these chors ransacked our house, I wondered, although it would have been mean to ask.

Later that morning, a more senior police officer turned up to show us CCTV pictures taken from outside that big five-star hotel near Tara and Neel's school. It was on a small portable TV-cum-video that was carried into the kitchen and we gathered around the breakfast table to watch Tara coming out of the school gates before going into a shop and emerging with a bar of chocolate. I watched my sister in grainy black-and-white, peeling the chocolate wrapper before turning left on leaving the shop. Her hair was blowing behind her as the wind caught at it and then, with a little flick back of a strand that had got into her mouth, she turned a corner and disappeared. The police knew that she had gone to the bus stop after that as plenty of people had reported seeing her standing there. But the police were quite sure Tara had not boarded any buses as they had already interviewed the bus drivers on that route and checked all their whereabouts. My sister had probably decided to walk home but, whatever it was, it was at that point that the trail simply went cold.

Mum howled a lot that day but was furious all over again when the police came a second time, this time to ask us a load of questions about Tara's affairs and boyfriends. But she stopped ranting and went all quiet and sober when they also took away Tara's toothbrush. ('DNA sample lene ke liye,' the police lady said matter-of-factly, slipping my sister's purple Colgate brush into a plastic bag.) My legs started trembling like crazy at that point because I knew DNA sampling was done in murder cases and my chest felt like a hammer was banging inside it. But I didn't say anything to Mum and Dad who didn't seem to be coping too well themselves at that point.

The next day, the police rounded up a whole lot of people and even a couple of sniffer dogs to start combing Jahanpanah and the deer forest and golf course near our house. Neel and Dad joined the search on the first morning but both came back silent and grey-faced and did not venture out again. I overheard Dad say to Mum that night that he was also bracing himself to become the chief suspect as that was the course police questioning almost always took in cases where young girls had disappeared or been found dead. But he got no sympathy there as Mum responded with a curt, 'Don't be so *ghoulish,* Neville, there'll be at least a hundred people to testify that you were at the clinic on the day she disappeared.'

As it happened, it was Mr Stanley, Tara's drama teacher at school, who became their first suspect and Ramlal, the old caretaker who had been at the school for years. But both were released after a few hours of questioning, I heard them say. Mum and Dad went for a press conference two days later, which I was told about when Usha Aunty came to get Neel and me from our schools. They said nothing about it when they got back, even to Usha Aunty, although I noticed Mum's nose had gone tomato red like it always did when she'd been bawling or had a really bad cold.

Then things went quiet on the police front for the next few days but we hadn't expected the media to gather around us in the meantime. A supposedly scary black-and-white comic book Neel had given me for my eighth birthday had a page in which huge, shaggy vultures sat waiting near the site of a train accident. They weren't doing anything gory, just waiting patiently for their turn to come, and that was exactly how I saw those satellite vans that seemed to have taken up permanent residence outside our colony that week. Journalists were sometimes seen talking into cameras, with our house as their backdrop, and sometimes eating samosas and sandwiches from paper boxes. Some of them came to the door and rang our bell but, after the first few times when all they did was ask silly questions like 'Did you fight with your daughter?' and 'Did you dislike her boyfriend', we learnt to ignore the screech of the bell.

Even though my parents tried to avoid having Neel and me watch the news in those days, we caught passing reports on Tara having gone missing a couple of times and I thought of how pleased she would be, if she was watching, to hear herself referred to as 'pretty teenager, Tara Fernandez'. She featured in a television crime programme too – where they got a long-haired actress to wear Tara's spare uniform. I didn't think the actress looked like Tara in the slightest. She was at least five years older and had a long nose, but, from a distance and when I squeezed my eyes together to make the TV image blurry, there was a tiny resemblance. They showed her coming out of the Delhi High School gates, going into the shop and then walking down the road to the bus stop in a kind of flouncy, hip-swingy way.

'Whoever told them Tara has that minxish sort of walk?' Mum asked, appalled, as we watched the programme.

Neel replied, 'Well, they've been all over the school interviewing people. You should have seen everyone queuing up to say how well they knew Tara.'

Dad shook his head and said in a mournful voice, 'That's what TV's done, make everyone crave their two seconds of fame.'

When they arrested Ramlal for the second time, I started to have sleepless nights even though I had never seen Ramlal at all. Neel said he was old and decrepit, at least fifty, and a bit creepy with paan-stained teeth and a musty smell that hung about his clothes. After two days, however, the man was released again and, even though Neel said it had been a 'wrongful arrest', I didn't feel any better knowing that he was out there rather than in jail.

The television programme came to nothing too. Except for a few false leads and fake sightings, it led to the same brick wall.

Tara had seemingly disappeared into thin air, just like that, leaving a great big hole right there in the middle of my family. I don't think anyone else was affected in quite the same way, even though some of Tara's classmates and teachers did sort of go through a whole grieving thing, creating a small shrine for her in a nearby church and setting up a 'Find Tara' fund.

Almost exactly one month after Tara disappeared, there was a mass murder in a Scottish town that even made it to the Indian papers because it was so horrible. Aunty Vee told Mum all the details during one of the daily phone calls she was making from Manchester in those days. Apparently, a man had walked into a primary school and fired his gun at a bunch of five- and six-year-olds who were using the gymnasium. The *Times of India* report said that fifteen little children had been chased around the school gym before being killed. Mum, who had always tried not to focus too much on reports from her home country, had a bizarre reaction to this awful piece of news. Till then she had been slumping lower and lower into a kind of silent despair over Tara's disappearance but she revived herself on hearing about the Dunblane massacre, becoming weirdly cheery on certain days, almost as though it pleased her to know that it wasn't just us and that other people suffered bad things too. Then she also said scary stuff like: 'Oh villain, villain, villain, smiling damned villain,' when she was looking at a picture in the papers of the Dunblane killer, who was not smiling at all.

At the end of March, a whole lot of people held a candlelight vigil for my sister at Jantar Mantar. Even though Mum thought it was the worst idea and didn't want to go, we kind of had to. It was uncanny seeing photocopied images of one of Tara's pictures converted into posters and held by people who did not even know her. But everyone seemed to want to be a part of the grieving thing and, perhaps because it was such a pleasant spring night, many came with thermos flasks full of coffee and packets of biscuits as though it was a kind of jolly midnight picnic. I'm not sure why, but for days afterwards I had nightmares in which I saw a sea of posters showing Tara's face; thousands and thousands of Taras smiling really happily at me.

Gradually, however, as the days passed and there was still no news of Tara, most people seemed to lose interest and drift out of our lives again. It was the journos who decamped first, then the few missing persons organizations that had popped up in their wake, offering to make flyers to drop through people's letterboxes and pin them up on trees. One NGO woman, wearing a very colourful sari and lots of blue eye make-up, even wanted to know what Tara's favourite colour was so that they could buy ribbons in that colour and tie them on every gatepost in our colony. I didn't think black, which was definitely Tara's favourite colour, would look correct under the circumstances but, in any event, Dad requested the NGO lady very politely not to pursue their plan so it never happened anyway. Maybe it was because we weren't exactly stepping up to the mark but, after a few weeks, we stopped hearing from all those people. In fact, we were barely hearing anything from the police too – unless we called them for an update or they'd had another one of those reported sightings which lent so much hope and always ended in disappointment. I know Mum and Dad had found it hard to share our anguish with folks we barely knew but, I think, they found it even worse when interest in Tara started visibly dwindling. I heard Mum call it a 'terrible loneliness' as, one by one, everyone started giving up the search and going away. Pretty soon it was just us.

Mum had refused to let Aunty Vee come down to India, due to Uncle Jeff's Parkinson's having taken a turn for the worse. His medicines were even making him hallucinate, apparently. And so it fell mostly upon Usha Aunty to 'keep body and soul together', as Mum said. Thank God for Usha Aunty. The best neighbour in the world who had even taught me swimming when I was nine years old after all others had failed, dragging me night after night to the DDA swimming pool down the road until my limbs finally got the coordination that was required of them. I adored her, even though she was bad tempered and sometimes even dirty mouthed, clapping her hand over her mouth and rolling her eyes whenever she let a bad word slip out in front of me, though Mum called it 'mock repentance'.

'Look, El,' Usha Aunty said one evening, planting her large self in front of Mum who seemed glued, huddled and weeping, to her armchair, 'you have to keep your chin up for the sake of these two.' She gestured in my direction while I pretended to be busy reading my book. 'And for Neville too.'

'Neville!' Mum exploded. 'Neville's got his work to escape to. Or haven't you noticed him escaping?' Her mouth twisted like it did whenever she ate karela.

'Escape?' Usha Aunty's voice rose in an indignant bellow too. Fluffed up with anger, they looked like a pair of hens in battle, except one was red-nosed and sitting in an armchair. 'You call that *escape*, Ellie? The poor man needs to endure visits from half of Saket every day, sitting there in his clinic. And, believe me, the good citizens of Saket are not above pretending to be needing bloody root canal treatment just so they can go back and tell everyone how wretched that poor dentist looked – you know, the one whose daughter's gone missing.'

'Oh I can't bear this any more, Usha,' Mum wailed. 'The not knowing – that's the worst. And I keep thinking the worst too, obviously. When I imagine some of the possibilities, I can't help thinking I'd rather she was *dead*!'

'Hush, El,' Usha Aunty said, rushing to scoop Mum's head into one of her chest hugs. From over Mum's head, she waggled her head at me, indicating that I was to scoot. I left the sofa obediently and went to sit in my room, gazing blankly out of the window. Normally, I only needed a book if I wanted to lose myself for a few hours but, these days, I couldn't even concentrate on *Watership Down*, my favourite book of all time, because of the way in which my mind kept zipping around all over the place. Neel was going the same way too, from what I could see. Not being himself, I mean. Which means that, instead of being his usual mouthy self, Neel had turned all proper and polite, even with me. It might have made for a nice change except that it was somehow sad to see him all transformed into someone he wasn't.

~

We lurched on in that manner, the rest of March and all of April; Dad dragging himself to the clinic and Neel and me to school because we had to. I liked going to school usually but, when I was there, I now spent a lot of time worrying about Mum. You see, she was still behaving like a part-time zombie, lapsing in and out of crazy behaviour and quoting her beloved Shakespeare whenever anyone would listen, though usually it was just mutterings to herself. Apart from Usha Aunty, a few other friends and neighbours had rallied around too and so Mum was not left alone for long periods, just in case. Tara's name was generally being mentioned less and less; people seeming to think it kinder to suggest by their silence that she'd probably gone for good, that is, she was dead. But this was impossible for us to accept and the only way we knew to keep alive our hopes was by badgering the police and demanding they *do* something to find her. Mum took to doing this on a weekly basis and even had reminders scrawled across the kitchen noticeboard – Monday: Call Police! Sometimes she wrote just 'ANGRY!!' on that board, or 'BAAAAD!!!', if it was not a Monday and it was too early to call the police again for a rant.

Even weirder was the media going all silent. Now, far from

making a jhamela outside our door or writing gossipy sort of non-news things about us (like a short feature on Dad's liking for bowties that made the *Daily News* describe him as 'a propah brown sahib'), they had gone off us completely. This was maybe the most clear sign that Tara's story was now finished, or as Mum said with her bitter-karela mouth, 'passé...', followed by '... those bastards', though no one really knew who she was talking about.

All we knew was that Tara had disappeared and, unlike everyone else, we were too chicken to accept she may be dead.

Tara, 1997

Tara stepped outside her shop and smiled as she spotted Himal waiting in his usual spot under the lamppost across the road. Mallika, locking up, chucked her head in his direction. 'Your fellow's waiting as usual, I see. He's such a sweet guy. Reminds me actually of my own Parvez. I used to think Parvez was the kindest husband in the world but your fellow might just be of the same mould.'

Mallika waved in Himal's direction and he returned the friendly gesture. Tara knew that he would be too shy to come across and talk to her boss and so, after bidding a hasty goodbye to Mallika, she darted across the road in his direction. Himal enfolded her in his arms for a moment before taking her hand in his, so they could walk back up the road together, the way he had come. Usually, he walked Tara to work in the mornings but it was only on his weekly day off, or if he got a long enough evening break, that he was able to pick her up at night too. He preferred to accompany her home if he could, stating the infamous leopard of Mukteshwar as the reason, even though none of the townsfolk had seen it for years and everyone was sure that it was by now elderly and toothless.

Tara's shop was tucked into a little alcove just off the main road, which was free of traffic at this time of night. She walked hand-in-hand with Himal, who was never very chatty even at the best of times, going past all the familiar hotels and houses that lay on this road, insignificant tiled buildings with yellow squares of light gleaming in the dark. Most people would have reached home by now and would be either preparing or eating their evening meals at their dining tables or in front of their TVs. She and Himal had not acquired a TV yet but she could not say that she had missed such things at all in the three months she had spent in Mukteshwar. Both of them had been busy, working all possible hours and earning as much as they could, which she had enjoyed far more than she had ever thought possible. She looked forward to his company on their weekly holiday and liked to take long walks with him, now that the weather was clearing up. Mukteshwar was to Tara, what her Dad would've termed in that moderate way of his, 'a most reasonable place to be'. The people of the town seemed to have accepted them too, probably imagining they had eloped from somewhere seeing that they kept mostly to themselves. As a precaution, they had taken false names too; Tara had become Nisha (the name of the first friend she had made in kindergarten) and Himal was Rajesh (a Nepalese film star), both relatively easy on the local tongue, as Himal – more familiar with the ways of hill people – informed her.

They walked together now, 'Nisha' and 'Rajesh', fingers entwined, as contented with their new life as they could be. Soon they had reached the central chowk, where the road widened and became busier. A small trickle of people was emerging from the gates of the veterinary institute up the hill. Tara had discovered that most local men had to go down to the plains in search of work, so the town largely comprised women and children and the elderly. By and large, Tara had found the folk who lived around here to be simple and warm but also very hardworking. Something about that spirit must have infected her too for who would have thought, just three months ago, that she would be capable of working the hours she did with no complaint at all. The two had even saved up enough money to pay the deposit on a small barsaati flat they had found in the next town two kilometres up the mountain. Already they had started furnishing it with odds and ends of furniture that they came across or pieces that one of their acquaintances was kind enough to offer them at a pittance. Mum and Dad would have been proud to see how hard she was working, Tara felt sure of that. But, of course, she couldn't let them into her life just yet because she was convinced that they would simply march her back to Delhi if they knew where she was and, much worse than that, poor Himal would end up in jail.

'Do you want to take a bus or walk?' Himal asked.

'Is it looking like rain?' Tara glanced up at an overcast sky. 'What do you think? Bus?' She gestured towards the chowk where a small local bus was idling, its engine spewing a thin curl of smoke into the night.

Himal, of course, never denied her anything she wanted and, in acknowledgement of that, Tara squeezed his hand as he turned immediately and made for the bus. As though it had been waiting for them, the engine revved up as soon as they boarded and took their seats. Tara sat at the window and it was as they pulled away from the junction that she saw something that suddenly made her blood run cold. Her insides turned to water as a shadowy figure disengaged itself from the shadows of the large peepul tree that stood at the road that led up to the Shiva temple. He was tall and thin. An icy hand pumped at Tara's heart, robbing her of breath. In the glimpse she got, she saw a figure wearing a shawl around his shoulders and a baseball cap on his head and, for as much as she could see in the dark, Tara was sure she had seen Dinesh's flat nose and a pockmarked face. A figure from hell. She instantly shrank back, pressing herself against the seat, willing the bus to swallow her up before she was spotted by him. Was it Dinesh? Had she imagined him? This, just when she had stopped feeling the need to keep a constant watch over her shoulder...

The bus picked up speed and Tara looked out at the swirling darkness, her heart still thumping hard in her chest. She was so breathless, she could not speak. As they left the edges of the town, she could see small pinpricks of light on the hillsides and the valley below that Himal had once said were stars fallen down from the sky. She was still trembling and so she edged away from Himal so that he would not feel it. There was no point in distressing him just yet. In the beginning, there had been more nights than not when Tara had woken up, bathed in sweat and trembling from the memory of what Dinesh had done to her. But, very gradually, she had started recovering with gentle encouragement from Himal. She shot a look at him now, sitting next to her on the torn rexine seat of the bus, oblivious to her terror and perusing the page of a magazine the person in front was reading. In a few moments, Tara regained her breath, very grateful that the shadow she had thought was Dinesh was not on this bus but back in the town somewhere. Besides, she could hope that he had not seen her. She tried to chide herself with a reminder that she wasn't even sure it was Dinesh at all but this brought little comfort.

When they got out of the bus at their stop, Tara decided she would not tell Himal about her possible sighting of Dinesh. After all, it had probably been an apparition, arisen from her worst nightmares, and there was little point traumatizing Himal with news that was so uncertain. He would be even more distressed than she was.

After leaving the main road, they walked down the uneven hill road that led to their small conurbation. Everything was very quiet; the few traders who operated in this area had shut shop and the only light on the damp streets came from the stray weak streetlights above. It had apparently rained here earlier in the evening but, although it was dry now, dark clouds were still rolling in the sky above, obliterating the stars and the moon and growling softly with thunder. Tara cast a quick, nervous glance behind them as they walked and thought she saw a shadow slip away behind a fir. She hastened her footsteps and Himal, sensing from her silence that something was wrong, hurried alongside her until they reached their small block and ran up the stairs without a backward glance.

Once they were locked into their little barsaati at the top of the building, Tara started to feel less tense, telling herself that her physical exhaustion from the day's work had probably made her a bit edgy. Nevertheless, she drew the thick curtain that hung on the single window of their flat, making sure there were no cracks at all, before turning on the lights. In the brightness of the naked bulb that hung from the ceiling, everything looked normal and homely again – the flowered razai cover that Mallika had given them, the leftover pot of chicken curry they had made yesterday that was going to be tonight's dinner, the aluminium clothes stand that had come with the flat and was now heaped high with an assortment of clothes and towels.

Himal came in from the bathroom down the hallway and made straight for the kerosene stove, as he always did, while Tara locked up again behind him. The division of labour they had devised seemed to work very well for both of them as Tara did not know how to cook but had found herself rather good at washing up, thanks to her mother's insistence that she take turns with Neel with the dishes. It was one of the few jobs Himal hated too, not least because he had to do it at the dhaba, and so it had all worked out rather well. With thoughts of Dinesh gradually receding from her mind, Tara went across to where Himal was stirring the pot and put her arms around him. He smiled over his shoulder as he felt her press her face into the back of his shirt.

'Hey ... hungry?' he asked.

'Mmm,' she replied vaguely. She had eaten one of Mallika's

stuffed parathas as a late lunch so was not as hungry tonight as usual but it would upset Himal if she did not eat his curry. She released him so he could carry on with all that vigorous mixing of salt and mysterious spices that he did with his customary flourishes.

They settled down to eat with their plates on their laps. Tara, determined not to let the thought of Dinesh spoil the evening, told Himal about a conversation she had overheard in the shop. 'There's going to be a big mela, organized by a new NGO who are trying to revive Kumaoni culture to boost tourism. They're apparently hoping to make it an annual affair and are inviting all the local towns to participate.'

'Where will it be held?'

'Just down in Kathgodam, imagine that!'

'Mela, meaning like dancing and music?'

'Dancers and performers from all over the Kumaon hills, I think. Dancing all the way down the street, in all sorts of gorgeous costumes. Oh, I'd love to be a part of it,' Tara said. 'Do you think we could join a local group, Himal? I'd happily learn dance moves if I could take part. Be quite good at it too, I should imagine.'

Himal looked thoughtful, rather than enthusiastic, which Tara couldn't help feeling a stab of annoyance at. '*What?*' she asked, upset that he was not sharing her enthusiasm.

He put his plate down. 'You know that I worry about anything that exposes us to a lot of people, Tara,' he said, his tone apologetic but firm.

'But, Himal, it'll be such *fun* and it's such a shame that we can't participate fully in things here. Isn't it about time we joined in properly with all the stuff life here has to offer?'

He shook his head. 'Right now, we do not have that choice, Tara. Just think what if…'

But Tara cut him short by getting up from her perch on the

bed with a flounce. She knew her expression was sulky and she was behaving badly, like she used to back at home, but she didn't care. It may have been the possible glimpse of Dinesh she had had that was stressing her out but now she didn't want to talk to Himal any more. Instead, she noisily scraped her leftover food into the bin before turning her back on Himal to start washing up. Unusually, though, Himal did not try to cajole or get around her, ignoring her instead by clattering his own plate at the sink and going off to change without saying anything further. Eyes now smarting with tears, Tara realized that this was the first time they were having a proper difference of opinion. She had sensed that Himal was capable of holding his own against her but had simply not needed to test this yet. And, even though she was still annoyed at his being such a stick-in-the-mud about taking part in the mela, she knew that he was probably right. It was silly of her to be so stubborn when she knew that Dinesh might be lurking in the hills.

Wiping her hands, she looked around to try and make up but Himal was already in bed, covered up by his end of the razai, his back turned firmly to her. She could not tell if he was asleep when she had got into her nightshirt and crawled in next to him. His body was still and his breathing even. For a little while, Tara lay in the dark, looking at the light leaking in from the edges of their undersized curtain.

Was Dinesh out there, searching for them? It was unlikely he'd have given up the pursuit, seeing how much information they had on him. Enough to put him away for the rest of his life. Of course, he would still be hunting high and low. And why not Kathgodam and then Mukteshwar, if he had worked out from the railway timetable that these could be the places they had escaped to from Rampur that night. Himal was absolutely right in insisting that they keep a low profile for the time being. He was only being sensible, not boring. Tara felt a wave of remorse at her behaviour. She obviously still had lots of growing up to do and who better to help her deal with it than this man with his quiet manner and patient ways. Tara shuffled up in bed to get closer to Himal and, like before, she put her arms around him. Whether it was in slumber, she could not tell, but she felt his body slowly relax and soften into hers until they lay comfortably together again, and only then was she able to fall asleep.

Pia, 1997

The second of May, Tara's eighteenth birthday, the day everything changed again. We had been dreading that date as it loomed, unsure of how to mark it when we did not even know for sure whether she was alive. I had made cards in secret, and written long poems in each of them – a couple copied from somewhere and one that I spent a long time over to get the rhyme and tune just right. But, as the day dawned and the bright summer light turned the windows of my room into a blinding blaze, the peal of the telephone rang through the house.

Later, Mum said that if all the best moments of her life had been taken together and rolled into one, the feeling lay in that one second when she heard Tara's voice on the line say, 'Hello, Mum, it's me.'

I heard a loud shriek from the living room and, by the time I'd tumbled out of my room in my pyjamas, Neel right behind me, I saw that Mum was sitting on the floor, slumped against the doorjamb with the phone clamped to her ear. She was red-faced and crying and jabbering totally senselessly, saying 'Tara, my baby' and 'Tara darling' in between great, big sobs. From the way she said it, we could tell it was actually Tara she was talking to and not someone who had called up with bad news about her. Dad was already there and quickly turned on the speaker phone so we could all hear Tara's voice. She sounded tinny and far away and, though it was hard to be sure, it sounded like she was crying too. With one arm held tight around my shoulders, Dad leaned down to ask, 'First of all, Tara darling, are you okay, are you *safe?*'

'Daddy…' We heard Tara breathe in relief at hearing his voice. Then her voice perked up again. 'Yes, Dad, I'm fine, thanks.'

'Where are you?'

After a moment's hesitation, although it could have been the fuzziness of the line, we heard her say, 'I'm in Nepal.' She said it in that Hindi way, 'Neypaal', rather than 'Ne-paul' like my parents did.

'*Nepal*! How on earth did you get there, Tara? Your passport's here in my desk drawer.'

'Oh Dad, it's such a long story … shouldn't it be enough to know that I'm okay?'

'When are you coming home, darling?' Mum cut in, being brisk now, taking charge. 'Do you need help? Dad and I can fly up there with your passport…'

'No, no, Mum, I'm fine, honestly. I just wanted you to know that I'm busy and happy here because I knew you'd be worrying. In fact, you won't believe it but I'm working!'

'What does that mean, *working*? What sort of work are you doing? You surely don't mean you're not coming back here?' In seconds, Mum's joy had turned to consternation. She looked up at Dad, her expression confused and shocked.

'Not now, Mum, I can't.'

'Why can't you, Tara?' Dad asked. I could tell he was trying to keep his voice really soft and calm. 'Is there someone with you? Are you being coerced in some way?'

'No, no, I mean it *was* … but not any more. I'm not being coerced to stay here at all, I promise you that.'

'But what sort of work can you possibly get without your passport?' Dad persisted. Now he couldn't keep the worry out of his voice either. 'You wouldn't do anything risky, would you?'

Tara laughed. She clearly wasn't talking with a gun pointed to her head or anything like that, although my heart was bumping around like crazy in my chest. "Course I wouldn't be doing anything risky, Dad. I *promise* you I'm safe. I just need to be away for a little while and all will be explained soon enough. Promise, promise. Please don't start looking for me. I'll come back to Delhi soon as I can to see you all.' Then she shifted her tone to a chatty one, 'How are Neel and Pia?'

But Mum cut in again, starting to sound angry now. 'What's going on, Tara? You can't just call up like this out of the blue and not say anything. Not explain what happened, I mean, to have you disappear on us like that. Three months and sixteen days, to be precise! Did you know that you've had the entire police force out looking for you? And *us*! Your brother and sister have...'

But the line went dead at this point. Tara had hung up! Well, she'd either hung up or run out of money but, knowing her, I'd put my money on the former.

Dad was furious with Mum after that, shouting at her for getting agitated and frightening Tara off. I'd never seen Dad in such a state ever. Mum was howling really badly. It hadn't taken long for our happiness at knowing Tara was alive to turn into something else entirely. My own head was spinning like a top and I started to cry too. Really quite loudly, I think, because everyone was shushing me at one point and Neel was holding me tightly.

Once we'd all calmed down, Dad called the police.

'Yes. Nepal, she definitely said Nepal, sir. But she wouldn't say any more ... Oh yes, it was certainly our daughter, I'm in no doubt about that ... I did ask her that and she confirmed that she hadn't been forced into anything. No, no ... I understand. Of course ... yes ... thank you for asking ... Yes, I will. Bye.'

Dad put the phone back on its cradle and turned to us, his face grey. 'They're closing the case,' he said.

'*What?*' said Mum, uttering the word as though all the breath were leaving her body alongside it.

'Tara's alive, Ellie. And she's not a missing person any more. They're right about that.'

Now it was Mum's turn to rant. 'How could you just roll over and agree to them closing Tara's case, Neville! That's ridiculous. The child has no idea what's good for her. Someone's obviously orchestrating this. An exploitative older man, I reckon. Such an old story. Oh God, will girls never learn? She has to be brought back. Forthwith! They can't just give up on us like that, the police, it's their *duty* to bring runaways back, isn't it?'

Dad ran a hand through his hair. When we were smaller, he used to do that deliberately to make his hair stand on end so he could do his Stan Laurel act but today, with his shoulders all hunched up in his dressing gown, he looked like a very old and sad version of Stan Laurel and not funny at all. He tried to reason with Mum. 'You surely don't expect we can waste police time any more, Ellie? Tara can't be forced to come back and she did say quite clearly that she didn't want to come back. She's eighteen now, don't forget, legally an adult.'

'But she doesn't know what she's *doing*! She's just a silly little girl!' Mum wailed. Then she turned angry. 'I can't believe Tara's done this to us. How could she? Missing for over three months and not a word. *Nepal*! Cavorting about in Nepal! And what's she doing for money? That's what makes me so certain some predatory old man's got her in his clutches. I know! Maybe we ought to call the *Nepalese* police? What do you think, Nev, shall we try calling the Nepalese police? I mean, she is in their territory after all ... they ought to at least check that all is well with her.'

Dad's patience was wearing thin again. 'Are you *joking*, Ellie? We'll be laughed all the way out of Nepalese territory if we showed up there asking them to locate an eighteen-year-old who has run away and doesn't want to come back to her boring old parents.'

Neel, who like me had been silent mostly, presented his theory. Or maybe it was his way of comforting Mum and Dad. 'I think it's the exams,' he said. 'Tara really was dreading them so she probably just wanted to lie low until they're over and done with. She'll waltz back in soon, you wait and see.'

My parents were silent for a moment, mulling over this possibility, before Mum exploded again. 'For Chrissake, she only had to *say* if she didn't want to sit the board exams. Hundreds of kids drop out, don't they? Isn't it a bit bloody *extreme* to run away and go all the way to fucking Nepal ... setting off a *police* case, no less, and all this ... this *anguish* that we've endured just ... just to avoid a fucking exam!'

We all jumped at the F-word but I could see that Dad had finally had enough. 'Eleanor,' he said, 'I think I'm going to give you a sedative. No, don't argue. You've been ... well, we've all been to hell and back and it's only natural to be feeling so agitated. But you need to calm your nerves to absorb this new twist. We need to move on. Let's take joy in the knowledge that Tara's alive and safe ... well, safe enough to call and tell us that she's okay. There's so many people to inform of this development – Vee, Usha, Robbie and Anita, the neighbours, bloody hell ... my sisters in Goa ... that's one helluva lot of explaining to do and we'll need all our strength in the coming few days while we try to find out more.' He turned to me. 'Pia, darling, would you go and put the kettle on, please? Neel, help her make a round of tea for all of us, will you? Good lad.'

I felt much better seeing Dad take charge, not looking as anxious and hangdog as he had now for many days. He pulled Mum off the floor and propelled her to their bedroom. She didn't protest, surprisingly, but went looking meek and tearful and kind of defeated. Neel and I trooped off to the kitchen and I yanked out the footstool to root around in the back of the cupboard where we kept the imported biscuits to prevent the cleaner from pinching them. Poor Mum needed cheering up and those special chocolate-ginger biscuits usually did the trick. Neel got the kettle going but, when I turned to pass him the mugs, I saw that his hands were clinging white-knuckled to the kitchen counter and his shoulders were hunched and shaking. I couldn't see his face, which was turned away, but he was emitting the most ghastly coughing gasps that were somewhere between sobs and low moans. Neel *crying*? I hadn't seen him cry since he was eleven or twelve at least, not since he had developed his smart-alecky teenage personality anyway. It was one of the scariest things and I did not know what to do to stop him. So I grabbed him around the waist and buried my face in the back of his pyjama top and said, 'Don't cry, Neel, don't cry, please.' Hoping it would comfort him, I added, 'After all she's not dead, is she?'

He did stop crying for a minute but only to pull away and shout at me with the most ugly grimace on his face. 'It would have been fucking better if she had died!' He took a deep tearful breath but had not finished yelling yet. 'Can't you see that would have been better, Pia. Less fucking *selfish*. How could she do this? How could she fucking *do* this to us?'

I hadn't heard so much bad language being used in my home ever and was very tempted to use some myself to see if it would make me feel better too. Honestly, I could not accept what Neel said though. How could it have been better to discover that Tara was dead rather than find that she was alive? But it did make me feel a bit sick too to think that she had been hoodwinking us all the time that we had been crying and grieving these past few months. And what about all those people and NGOs who had come to her candlelight vigil and stuff – wouldn't *they* get really, really angry to know that she had been working and having fun in Nepal all the time that they had been grieving along with us?

I blinked really hard and turned back to the mugs. Taking a deep breath to make my tummy feel less shivery, I put a teabag into each mug and, although I was still not allowed near hot kettles, I carefully poured the boiling water over them, quite certain that I would do a better job of it than Neel, given the terrible state he was in. I poured the milk from the pan as well and then waited while Neel washed his face and blew his nose into the kitchen sink – something not normally allowed – and wiped his face on the kitchen towel. He took the tray and I followed him into our parents' room. Mum was already tucked under her bedcover and Dad was pulling the bamboo chiks down. There wasn't anything more to do there because Mum looked like she was nearly asleep already and so I took a mug of tea and went back to my room. I hadn't asked Dad if it was okay to go to school but I started to get ready as usual because I couldn't think of what else to do. Once I was in my uniform and had brushed my hair back into a ponytail as neat as I could manage without help, I collected all the books I needed for the day and stuffed them into my knapsack. When I went back out, I saw Dad standing at the kitchen window as he often did. He was in his usual jacket and brown tie so I guessed he was going to the clinic too. He turned when he heard me coming in and said, 'Neel's asked if he can stay home today. Might be an idea for Mum to have company anyway so I've said yes. You can stay home as well if you like, Pia?'

I shook my head. 'I'd rather go to school, if that's okay, Dad,' I replied.

He gave me a long and careful look, like he was trying to look right inside me. I wondered whether he wanted to be sure that I too was not keeping secrets from him like Tara had done. 'Sure, it's okay for you to go to school, Pia darling. I'll run you down. Breakfast?'

We had a silent breakfast of toast with honey because the marmalade had finished many days ago and no one was going out for shopping much these days, not even Usha Aunty. Dad and I didn't even bother sitting down but stood at the kitchen counter as we were both already late. There wasn't much conversation in the car either – and nothing at all about Tara – but that was to be expected, I suppose. Dad was in a state of total distraction, driving even worse than he usually did and earning an angry toot at the Geetanjali Road lights but, when we got to the gate of my school, he stopped the car and then leaned over to my seat and, rather than the usual peck on my forehead, he gave me a hug instead. It was one that seemed never-ending and his body was shaking so I wondered if he was going to start crying too. Embarrassed beyond words to think that we may be spotted clinching like that, I wriggled out of his arms, opened the car door and then scampered into the school building without once looking back.

At school, I told no one of the phone call we'd had in the morning. They had all stopped asking about Tara weeks ago anyway, assuming she was dead, and, in a strange way, that seemed preferable than telling everyone of this new development and then having to deal with all their questions. I wouldn't have had answers to most of them anyway.

So that was how Tara's eighteenth birthday was spent. The cards I'd made remained unsent although I kept them under my mattress for a long time afterwards. I wondered how Tara was spending her special day. In Nepal. With an older man.

'Predatory', Mum had said. I looked it up, of course, in the dictionary Miss Aiyyer kept in class. It said: *a: of, relating to, or practising plunder, pillage, or rapine b: inclined or intended to injure or exploit others for personal gain or profit.*

None of that made much sense to me except that I could tell it was all pretty bad stuff. How weird then that Tara sounded happy. She really had sounded truly happy.

Tara, 1997

Tara stood in that PCO, jiggling the lever to try to reconnect but there was now only the sound of the dial tone blaring in her ear. She felt in her pockets for more change but, apart from a hair clip and a box of matches, came up with no money at all. She felt bad at having hung up on her mother like that – who could blame poor ol' Mum for getting so worked up. She also hadn't meant to leave it till so late to call and tell her parents that she was fine but there had been so many new things to take on board here in Mukteshwar and it had seemed safest to lie low for a bit longer, mostly for Himal's sake of course.

Leaving the phone booth, her mood all of a sudden deflated, Tara walked past the fruit and vegetable shop, wishing she'd taken enough cash to buy one of those delicious-looking watermelons stacked on the shelf outside. They were brought up from the plains on small lorries once a week and were terribly expensive but it might have cheered her up. It had been another difficult week, with the money she and Himal were managing to make by working all hours of the day and night, slipping through their fingers before they could take stock. The barsaati they had rented was tiny but it took up a major part of their earnings and that was before the electricity and water bills were paid. Then there was food to buy and clothes to replace. Tara especially had to look neat in her job and, even though Mallika had very generously allowed her to choose three sweaters from last year's stock, there remained so many other things on her 'must buy' list. Very rarely did they treat themselves to a meal out and that only when they were completely sick of Maggi noodles cooked on the electric hot plate that had come with the room. Himal was, in fact, getting to be an extremely imaginative and skilled cook, sometimes smuggling out bits of leftover meat from the dhaba when Manzoor wasn't looking and turning them into the most delicious dinners.

Luckily, Manzoor too had turned out to be a reasonably kind-hearted employer, paying Himal on time and allowing him to go home early on a quiet night. Like Mallika, Manzoor too seemed soft on the idea of troubled young love. Both employers had happily assumed that Tara and Himal were on the run from disapproving parents. From the way they spoke and comported themselves, it was clear that Tara had run away from home because her parents disliked the 'unsophisticated, Nepali, working-class boyfriend', as Mallika had said, her eyes flashing in indignation at such city snobbery. She had already told Tara of the battles she and her husband had had to wage when they had made their own Hindu–Muslim marriage so it was clear whose side she was on. It was a convenient story and it had been easiest for Tara to simply play along.

There were times when Tara had worried that her disappearance would make it to news channels or newspapers. She'd initially braced herself for being recognized by one of the many tourists who frequented this town, if not one of the locals, but the anticipated question had never come. Either the news of her disappearance had never made it on TV or the pictures they were using looked nothing like the short-haired girl these people saw behind the shop counter. She had, after all, been much pudgier when her last photographs back in Delhi had been taken. Her hair had grown out slightly by now, curling lightly around her shoulders, but Himal said that he couldn't wait for it to grow to the length it was when he first laid eyes on her.

'Like a beautiful Nepali girl, wearing your hair long, with kaajal in your eyes and glass bangles on your wrists.'

Tara had laughed at that. 'Don't know about Nepali because, when I dress like that, I'm told I look very Punjabi. "A real Punjab di kudi" one of our neighbours used to say. While my poor little sis is English through and through. Dad's Goan genes had long given up the fight against Mum's robust Brit ones by the time Pia was born!'

She had reached their building now and stood for a minute on the pavement, looking at its grimy stairwell. The concrete steps were littered with cigarette butts and plastic bags, the corners smeared with paan stains. Somewhere nearby, from one of the flats, came the sound of a child howling and a woman yelling. It was a world away from Press Enclave in Delhi but, with all kinds of new wisdoms learnt in these past weeks, Tara knew that this was, at least in part, its attraction. A bit like Bela had once said about a movie – 'If my mom likes it, I know it must be crap'. Or Swapna, the Bangladeshi girl who'd joined their school last year, who tried to explain why she wore a headscarf even though her mother never had. This life, though thrust on Tara by circumstance rather than design, was so different from the one she had always had, or that her parents would want her to have, it offered that same thrill of rebellion.

On the other hand, having just heard her parents' voices after so long, the thrill was admittedly dimmed as Tara walked up the four flights of stairs that led to their tiny little flat at the top of the building. Her strength had gradually built up again, after the ordeal she had suffered four months ago, and she no longer needed to pause on the third floor landing to take her breath, but today she took the steps more slowly than usual, her legs feeling like lead. Opening the door, she walked in to find that Himal was up and pottering at their 'dining table', which was only a couple of cardboard cartons covered with an old curtain they had salvaged from a construction site. He turned around when he heard her, wearing a guilty expression on his face. 'Ooof, I'm not ready yet,' he said, darting for his jacket that was hanging behind the door.

Tara walked up to the table and saw one of those bright yellow cream cakes that the local bakery specialized in, sitting on a plate with a tiny candle stuck in the middle of a pink sugar rose. Himal, who had been rummaging in his jacket pocket, returned to the table and said, 'I wanted to be waiting with your birthday cake lit up but I can't find the matches.'

Tara fished the box out of her jacket. 'I think I put them into my pocket when I was trying to get you off smoking. Here they are,' she said, tossing the box in his direction. She peered at the plate, 'I *love* my birthday cake,' she said.

'Wait, I have a birthday gift too,' Himal said, ducking under the bed. He emerged with a round package wrapped in pink tissue paper with a small bow stuck one side.

'What is it? A football?'

'Open it and see!'

When the paper fell away to reveal a large watermelon, Tara burst into shouts of laughter. 'Oh, you're sweet, Himal! I can't even remember telling you that I adore this fruit. Did I tell you?'

'You did, once,' he said.

Tara threw her arms around his neck and kissed him full on the lips. What *were* her feelings for this man? He was unfailingly generous and sweet-tempered and so unlike the cocky, mouthy lads she had known back in Delhi. Perhaps that was the reason she had never felt so tenderly disposed to anyone in the way she did for Himal. Was this really love? Who would tell her if it was? Mum might have, if she wasn't so angry with her, that is…

Himal dark eyes looked into Tara's, his face turning serious. 'So you spoke to your family?' She nodded. 'And what happened?'

Tara took a deep breath and stepped away from Himal. The

small kitchen table that had come with the flat was crowded with the assortment of crockery and cutlery they had gathered, leaving barely any room for much else, so she sat the fruit down on top of the rusty toffee tin in which they kept the biscuits. Finally, she turned back to answer Himal's question and heaved a big sigh. 'Well, they were over-the-moon delighted to hear from me, but also rather angry.'

'You can understand why. Maybe you should have called them earlier.'

'I know. But I just didn't want to risk anything before turning eighteen. Who knows what the laws are on these things. They might have ordered me back forthwith ... forthwith ... that's such a Mum word...' Tara paused, waiting for the sudden shaky moment to pass. 'I told them I was in Nepal.'

'Nepal!'

'Just didn't want any clues to lead them here. You never know.'

'Do you not feel like going back to Delhi?' Himal asked. He looked around their grubby little barsaati with a rueful expression on his face. 'This is not what you're used to, Tara. Your house in Delhi is modern and nice, you must have everything there.'

'I do ... I did have everything, yes, but somehow that wasn't enough. I was never totally happy. In fact, I was quite horrible to my folks sometimes...' Tara broke off, unable to explain.

'And you are happy here? With me?'

'Couldn't be happier,' she said, grabbing him again and propelling him backwards until he fell onto the bed with her on top of him.

'Careful! Mathur-ji will be angry if we break his bed.'

But that wasn't reason enough to stop themselves from staying in bed and making love. Besides, it was a Monday, which both of them had arranged to have as their day off and of course it was Tara's eighteenth birthday.

When they woke up it was almost noon and the sun was glittering in a jewel-blue sky. They cut the pastry with a tuneless birthday song, sung in a hammed-up Kumaoni accent, and then shared it with mug after mug of hot, black coffee before deciding to climb to their favourite part of the mountain called Chauli ki Jaali where – on a fine May day like this – one could climb up to its very crest and sit in the sunshine on a pair of rocks that jutted right out into the sky. From here, the mountain fell away steeply to the valley that lay miles below and, looking down with a giddy sensation, Tara felt like she was a bird riding the wind currents, flying high and free forever.

Pia, 2013

So that was how Stockholm Syndrome became such a source of fascination for me later on, when my family was finally able to start talking about what Tara had or hadn't done. Sometimes we grieved, sometimes we argued and shouted. And Margaret Wheeler's story was tied into all that. Therein lay my path to understanding what my sister had done, you see. What she did to us of course but, even more tragically, what she did to herself two months later.

We did have more phone calls but they were silent ones, just the odd bit of crackling at the other end to indicate someone was there. We used to get them before Tara's birthday call too – after she'd gone missing – but at the time we'd assumed they were journalists and simply hung up on them. Now, of course, we knew it was Tara and, although we tried to talk to her, she wouldn't say anything in reply. Once, Mum even apologized to this silent Tara-on-the-phone for having spoken to her in such an agitated way on her birthday, saying in an appeasing, ingratiating sort of manner that didn't suit Mum at all: 'Tara, darling, I'm not asking you to come back for good. I understand if you love Nepal and want to carry on living there – I really do. I'll even accept your friends or whoever you're with. Just come here once so we can see you, and see for ourselves that you're well.'

But Tara didn't say anything in reply even on that occasion. I have to say it got me madder and madder. Her silence was making the atmosphere in the house just horrible with Mum and Dad yelling at each other all the time and sometimes even snapping at Neel and me. And so I took it on myself to give her a piece of my mind when she called one day. Our parents were not around and, when I picked up the phone and got the silent treatment, I shouted really loudly: 'Mum's not *well*, Tara!' I so badly wanted to stay calm but found myself completely unable to control the tears from starting to fall, making my voice all wobbly. 'She and Dad barely talk to each other any more because each one blames the other for your disappearance. Stop behaving so selfishly and *come back*!' Neel had to wrench the phone from me and then he too gave Tara a piece of his mind, using all the swear words he knew in both English and Hindi, which was quite a lot.

Dad took matters into his own hands after that and, without even consulting the police, got a private investigation company to trace the phone calls. The information we got back from them was puzzling. Out of a total of ten calls, three were from different public phones somewhere in western Uttar Pradesh and three, also from public call booths, from towns scattered across Punjab – Chandigarh, Ludhiana, Jullundur. The others were from right here in Delhi, in fact from the call box outside the PVR cinema near our colony. None, oddly enough, were from Nepal.

As the investigator said to Dad, 'Begging your pardon, Dr Fernandez, but, unless your daughter is leading a most busy life, going from hither to thither all the time, it is different people making all these phone calls to your house.'

And that was the first clue we had of something very dangerous going on in which Tara had maybe got caught up. Mum was still convinced that she'd run off with someone, although she sometimes replaced 'predatory man' with 'bad crowd'. Dad's worries, though unspoken, clearly lay some place far more chilling, given the distraught air he could not always hide. As for me, I spent a lot of time veering between angry and sad. Angry because, if Tara was able to freely make phone calls, she was surely free to come home too. And sad because on most days I just wanted my sister back, even if it had to be with all her bossiness and hoity-toityness still intact. That would be so much better than this horrible hole she had left behind that I would spend the rest of my own life unable to fill.

Tara, 1997

Tara was not dissembling when she continually assured Himal of her general contentment but the truth was that a small speck of unhappiness had taken hold of her ever since she had made that phone call to her family on her birthday. Like a drop of ink in water, it swirled and spread slowly through her, darkening certain days in a manner that she could neither control nor explain. There were lots of things about her old life that she did not miss at all; school, for one, and the exams. But she missed her parents for many small things and twice she had succumbed to calling home again, simply to hear their voices. Both times it was her siblings she got on the phone. The first time it was Neel, whose voice seemed to be breaking, getting to that funny squeaky-gruff stage that boys went through. But he only barked hello a couple of times before saying, 'Bloody hell, I don't have the time for this,' and hanging up. It had made Tara grin. Typical Neel – no time for anything when there was so much hanging around to do!

But the second call was alarming. Pia had answered it and, guessing it was her, got all frantic, gabbling on about Mum being ill and Dad and Mum not speaking to each other any more. Could it be true? Or was Pia telling lies to alarm her into coming back? It wasn't like prim little Pia to play Drama Queen, though. That was much more Tara's own territory. Before she had been able to ask her sister anything further, however, Neel had taken the phone and let off a stream of angry invective. That level of fury had startled and distressed Tara and caused her to hang up. Were her siblings really that upset with her? Was her family suffering because of what she had done? She would call again and, this time, try to speak to Dad. Even if he knew she had been lying consistently, he would never be anything but gentle and understanding with her. That much she knew for sure.

For the first time since coming to Mukteshwar, she was terribly tempted to return home. Not for good, of course, oh no, she loved her life here in the hills too much for that. But a little visit would be nice. It had been ages since she'd eaten Mum's fish-macaroni pie and joshed around with Neel and Pia at the table. Of course, they'd all be angry about her disappearing on them and she'd have to take some real shit from both Mum and Dad. Dad's censure was always worse, being so quiet and sort of *pained,* unlike Mum's more noisy and dramatic displeasure...

But then she'd have to tell them about the circumstances of her disappearance ... Dinesh and the kidnap ... those ghastly memories that she had slowly tried to work out of her system. Tara had gradually convinced herself that that sighting of Dinesh at the chowk had thankfully been false. But, just two nights ago, she had woken up in a cold sweat and Himal had to hold her close until she was able to fall asleep again. Could she really tell her parents all that and expect them to let her return to Mukteshwar again? Did she want to rake it all up now and embark on a police case too ... just when she had started to overcome her terrors and move on in this new life?

Tara told Himal about it that night. He had brought back a mutton roll from the dhaba and was halving it while listening to her. She paused before concluding her narration in a rush with the suggestion that she return to Delhi to make sure her family was well.

'I don't want you to go to Delhi alone,' Himal said, bringing both plates to the bed where Tara was sitting cross-legged in her night-shirt.

'I don't want to go alone, Himal, but would it not be more unsafe if we went together?' Tara took the plate off Himal but, not having the appetite to eat, she placed it on the bed next to her.

'Don't be crazy. It would not be safe at all for you to go alone, Tara. Dinesh could be there in Delhi. What if he turned up at Press Enclave again? I will go mad if something happened to you…'

'Of course I thought about Dinesh too. But you know what? By skulking around here, we aren't doing anything to help get him caught. The more I think about it, the more sure I feel that we really ought to be telling the police everything so that they can catch him and give him the worst punishment. Imagine, Himal, he could be kidnapping other girls right now to cart them off to brothels! And, while I feel so relieved to have escaped him, I really do think we should make sure he doesn't ruin someone else's life. Don't you think so too?'

Himal looked as though he was deep in thought. He then turned to her, conceding in his usual reasonable way, 'Maybe it is time to do something about him. You're right, we can't keep running and hiding like this. And why should you have to struggle like I do, living like a servant when you don't have to?'

'That's not the problem, Himal, you know that. I'm enjoying myself much more here than I did back in Delhi … I like my life here with you. Really.'

'But?'

'But I don't think we can carry on like this forever,' Tara said in a sober voice. 'I need to see my family and reassure them that all is well. Then we need to get the police on to Dinesh. And, if you give them all the information you have, they will hopefully allow you to go without charges. We've got to risk that, Himal. My Dad will help you find a decent lawyer. Perhaps you could even get to medical college with my dad's help.'

'Your father will hate me, Tara, for keeping you away from your family all these days,' Himal said, looking worried.

'No, he won't hate you at all! I only have to explain the circumstances to him, for God's sake. You rescued me from the worst nightmare, risking your own life, Himal!'

Himal smiled. 'Maybe, maybe not.' He shrugged, using a favourite phrase that had stopped maddening Tara so much now that she knew him better. 'Okay, now eat,' he said. 'This is Manzoor's speciality. We'll eat and sleep and a plan will form when we're less tired in the morning. I promise.'

They finished dinner without mentioning Delhi again but, as they were turning in, Tara wanted to reassure Himal once again. 'Don't let's worry about going to Delhi, Himal,' Tara said as she got into bed next to him. 'Once we reach there my parents will help us deal with everything. I'm sure of that.'

Himal did not look wholly convinced but he was silent. Tara knew it was a gamble he would take only because he thought she was getting restless in her desire to see her parents. Was she putting them both at risk, she wondered as she lay back, watching Himal get up to turn out the light. As their little rooftop bedsit was plunged in darkness, Tara looked out of the window where a single tall fir tree cut right across the moon like a sword against a pearly shield. How strange to think that this was the same moon that shone over Delhi and every other place in the world. Tara had always felt that it cast some kind of special light on Mukteshwar, glassy and pure, as though showering benediction on this tiny town that had rescued her and hidden her from Dinesh and taught her to grow up and be an adult.

When Himal got back into bed, Tara lifted her head to accommodate his arm and tucked herself into his familiar shape. She swung one leg over his, as usual, and wound her arms around his slender body while he kissed her face a couple of times; small feathery, sleepy kisses. Lying comfortably, and tired from his more gruelling day, Himal drifted asleep before she did. Tara listened to his breath slowly fall into a steady deep rhythm while she returned his kisses, once on his lips and then once on each eyelid. She could see over his shoulder that the moon had now shifted away from the fir tree and was free-floating just above the deep blue silhouette of the distant Himalayan peaks. The night was completely hushed and silent except for the sounds of their combined breaths. Even the breezes in the valley seemed to have settled down for the night. Tara had not been taught to pray as a little girl, even though her Grandma Regina had once made a half-baked effort, but it occurred to her that, if there was a God watching from behind the moon, this was perhaps the right kind of moment in which to make a heartfelt request. And so she did, a little hesitantly, keeping her gaze fixed on the moon. 'Please bring us back,' she whispered. 'Back to this mountain home of ours. *Properly,* this time, okay? Not running away, but with our parents' blessings and all. Maybe even married to each other so we can have children and all that too. Please.'

Pia, 2013

The day was a usual sort of Friday. I hope it doesn't sound heartless but, it had been almost four months since Tara had gone and we didn't talk (or even think) about her that much any more. Especially since we now knew she was alive and cavorting happily somewhere in Nepal with her 'predatory man' and 'bad crowd' and not bothering about us *at all*.

For some reason, Mum had woken up in a foul mood that morning, muttering something about uncaring daughters, which made me feel really cross even though I knew she was referring to Tara and not me. As English Literature had been Mum's subject, she sometimes quoted Shakespeare when she was either really happy or really stressed. But she said something to Usha Aunty, when she came to pick Mum up for their weekly shopping trip that morning, about a serpent's tooth, which I could see Usha Aunty was a bit baffled by too. She knew, however, how to totally ignore these crazy rantings of Mum's. According to Usha Aunty, my mother's anger with Tara was healthy as it gave her lots of opportunities to vent, which Usha Aunty had told me was a good thing.

Dad, on the other hand, looked haggard and worried, coming back from the clinic on certain days with a sort of shrunken look about him, like he had suddenly become two or three inches shorter in height. He would then go straight into his den from where we would later hear opera music, lots of mournful trumpet sounds and clashing cymbals. Maybe it reflected his mood, all that wailing and clanging, but what I do know is that Mum and he barely spoke now. Each blamed the other for what Tara had done, which seemed not just weird but really stupid to me because what Tara had done, Tara had done by herself. Nobody had told her to do any of it, not even Bela at whom Mum flew in a really scary rage once when we bumped into her and her boyfriend in the PVR market sharing an ice-cream cone. Venting was all very well but it was a bit crazy to start off on people who really had nothing to do with Tara's disappearance. Maybe it seemed a bit unfair to Mum that Bela was able to have ice-cream in the middle of Saket while Tara was in Nepal or some other planet as far as we were concerned. But it seemed to me that Mum might quite simply have gone a bit mad after Tara disappeared. I kept hoping she'd snap out of it at some point but she was sure taking her time about it.

And then … yes, and then finally came *that day*…

I was at school, just starting my last period which was Art, when Mrs Menon, our school principal, poked her head through the door and asked Miss Gupta to come out into the corridor for a moment. I thought nothing of it, of course, continuing to help Gayatri Vasudeva get all the craft material that we needed for our competition entry out of the cupboard. We'd been selected by the school to take part in an art gallery scheme for schools and had loads to do in the week we had left before the hols started. So we got busy, even though we needed to check a couple of important things with Miss Gupta who was taking a long time to get back into the classroom. We didn't need to call for her when she did come back in because she walked straight to where Gayatri and I were sitting. Not in her usual jolly, cheery way but looking all red in the face and with her lips trembling strangely.

'Pia … I'm sorry but I'm going to have to ask you to come with me for a minute. Gayatri, would you mind carrying on with that for now … yes, green's fine there…' She looked around distractedly, trying to catch the eye of Miss Savitri, our classroom assistant, over the hubbub. I was puzzled but got up and waited patiently by her side while she signalled to Miss Savitri that she would be gone for a few minutes. Then, as I prepared to go with her into the corridor, Miss Gupta surprised me further by pointing to the back of the classroom and saying, 'No dear, you need to fetch your bag first. Sorry, I should have said...'

I trotted off obediently but by now I was seriously curious about what was happening, feeling the first stirrings of something like a tummy upset beginning deep in my stomach. Once I was ready with my things, Miss Gupta took me outside where – very oddly – Mrs Menon was still standing! She was the world's busiest lady but here she was waiting for me and, together, they took me down to her office. I knew I wasn't in trouble, because I was never in trouble at school. Plus, Miss Menon kept her arm around me while we walked to her office which, though an unusual thing, was her way of telling me that whatever trouble I was in, it wasn't my fault.

When we reached her office, she sat me down on a chair and Miss Gupta knelt next to me, her face now close to tears.

'Is something wrong, Miss?' I asked, my own voice starting to wobble as I was by now quite sure that something bad had happened to either Mum or Dad.

Miss Gupta placed her hand on my arm but it was Mrs Menon who spoke. 'Pia, darling, there's been some bad news. Very bad news. Someone's coming from home to get you but I promised I would explain things to you first.'

'It's not something bad happening to Mum or Dad, is it?' I asked hurriedly, my heart starting to pump really painfully in my chest. I could feel my breath coming in short sharp bursts.

'Oh no, no, not at all, Pia. Your mother and father are fine, don't worry. It's ... it's ... well, there's been some news of your sister,' she said finally. I felt a small wave of relief wash over my heart and instantly felt ashamed for not minding that the bad news was only about Tara. By then my sister had pretty much disappeared from my life anyway.

'Have they found her then?' I asked.

'Yes, yes, they have, Pia,' Mrs Menon said.

'Where is she?'

'Oh Pia, darling. How can I break such terrible news to you? Tara's been found, yes, but not in the way we had all hoped. She's…' Mrs Menon's voice dropped till I could barely hear it. 'Tara's been found dead. Oh my dear, I'm so, so sorry to have to be the one to tell you this but your father wanted us to prepare you because the police are around at your house…'

If she was still talking, I wouldn't know because everything stopped for a few seconds – that clock on Mrs Menon's wall, the cries of the basketball team practising outside, the traffic on the road, everything was silent, drowned out by a strange rushing sound like a whole ocean inside my head. Even the faces of the two teachers before me were shimmying about and, when Miss Gupta started speaking again, she may as well have been miming because I could not hear a word. Maybe I fainted or something because the next thing I knew was that I was on a sofa, lying down. I didn't want to lie down because I had a whole lot of questions to ask but my mouth didn't seem to be working properly. From somewhere far off, I could hear the phone on Mrs Menon's desk ring. She answered it and in a distant, hollow voice I heard her say, 'Yes, yes, please send her in.'

It was Usha Aunty who came rushing in a few minutes later. She made straight for the sofa to gather me up in that big comfy way she had. Maybe it was the familiarity of her smell (Chanel N°5, she once told me, a gift from an old admirer) or that massive hug I got less of now that I was growing up but, without really knowing it, I was sobbing. Great, big teardrops rolling off my cheeks and down the end of my nose to fall on to the front of my school uniform. 'They've found her, Usha Aunty,' I blubbed. 'She went to Ne-Ne-Nepal but now she's dead!' I mostly hadn't cried in all the time Tara had been away because I had been too angry with her to cry. But now, with that anger turning into all kinds of sorrow and pain and guilt, I wanted to weep without ever stopping again.

Even though I was now quite tall, Usha Aunty virtually picked me up off the sofa in order to bundle me out of the school and into her car. I half lay and half sat in a huddle on the passenger seat while she drove like a maniac through Malviya Nagar and Saket to get me home. She put her entire weight on the car horn to clear the traffic and muttered bad words under her breath but every so often she reached out an arm and patted me. Maybe because I asked her no questions, she did not tell me what exactly had happened. Not that I really wanted to know because something told me it would be really, really horrible. Didn't Mum always say, sometimes with a laugh and sometimes proudly and sometimes also a bit exasperated, 'Oh our Tara, she never does things by halves, does she?'

When we reached Press Enclave, we drove in through the wrong gate and took a really weird route to the house. Usha Aunty led me in through the back door that went into the kitchen and we found Mum and Dad in the living room. Neel was there too, although I don't know how he had got back from school. Everyone was, of course, red-faced and looked like they'd been through their own storms of weeping but Dad came straight to me and sat me down on the sofa next to him, keeping his arm held tight on my shoulder. That was when I saw the policewoman, sitting on the three-seater next to Mum. She had taken her khaki peaked cap off and was holding Mum's hand – not something I'd seen the police do on their previous visits to the house. She was also much nicer than those hatchet-faced men who had visited before and I couldn't help wondering if the police force kept one or two sweet-faced female officers ready for this sort of thing, you know tending to grieving families and victims of crime and making sure they didn't sue the police force for getting them into that situation, I guess.

The policewoman looked questioningly at Dad, checking with him, I think, to see if she could speak freely in front of me. I heard him say over my head, 'Yes, it's fine. She's a very mature child.' I didn't feel very mature at the moment, actually, wanting only to crawl into Dad's lap like a baby so I could hide from the horror of it all. I must have known what was coming.

The policewoman spoke, picking up from where she'd left off. She used a kind of soft and singsong Hindi, breaking into English every so often for Mum's benefit. 'As I was saying, Delhi Police have reopened the case and we will definitely find out as much as we can about what happened to your daughter.'

'She was trying to come home ... I know she was...' Mum said, before trailing off. She sounded exhausted and I wondered if the news had been broken to them long before I had got in.

'You are right, madam. That must be the explanation for her being found so near her home. There were bus tickets in their bag from Kumaon.'

Home. Kumaon ... not Nepal.

'In the old days, we used to take the children to Jahanpanah for summer picnics,' Mum said. I thought this was totally irrelevant but the policewoman nodded. She still looked sympathetic but there was something about her now – a sort of weariness – which said she had been in this position many times before. I was clearly missing something, though. What was all this about Jahanpanah? Was that where they had found Tara then? But why would she be wandering around in a forest if she was trying to come home? That would sure be ironic as Dad used to have such difficulty getting Tara to come along when he and I went to Jahanpanah for our morning walks.

It was Dad who spoke now, in a voice so quiet, I could barely hear him. 'By when do you think we'll have information on the man she was with?'

'Predatory man'? Was she with him? Was it he who had killed her? I simply couldn't bear the thought and felt a kind of murderous rage build inside me as thoughts of revenge floated into my still numb brain. I would find him and *kill* him! *Stab* him in his stomach, that's what I would do. My feelings were so strong that I could feel my hands shake.

The policewoman turned to us, making me jump. 'His identity is being checked right now, Doctor Saab.' She hesitated momentarily, flashing a discomfited look at me before saying, 'We may need to wait for DNA or dental records to be released...' She trailed off before gathering herself up again and trying to sound less downbeat. 'However, my senior officers will have further information for you by the end of today, I think. I'm so sorry not to be able to say any more.'

Dad sighed deeply. He was trying to speak in Hindi but kept having to dive back into the safety of English. '*Hummey pata tha ki* ... yes, we sort of knew there was a ... an element of coercion in Tara's disappearance, you know. It just wasn't like her to disappear on us like that. *Bilkul nahin karti aisey*. I would be very interested to know the identity of this man.' Despite his struggle with the languages, he sounded weirdly calm, my poor dad. He seemed to be done with all the timid suffering of the past few weeks which had washed away in the face of this much bigger crisis. Maybe death was easier to cope with than disappearance.

'Haanji, yes, that is what we are also trying to find out, Doctor Saab. Well, I have given you my number if you want to ask something. But I will leave you to rest for now. I'm your family liaison officer but Constable Sanghvi will provide back-up.' The policewoman got up as she said this and bent over to place a hand on Mum's shoulder as she said goodbye to her. She stopped at the living room door to address Dad again while Usha Aunty waited to see her out. 'Please also let me know if you wish us to prepare a statement for the paperwallahs, Doctor Saab. They find out these things very quickly usually, despite all our efforts to protect people.'

It was Dad who told Neel and me the rest, after the policewoman had gone and Usha Aunty had taken Mum to her room. We sat at the kitchen table with glasses of juice while Dad poured himself a whisky (he'd recently been going through our drinks cabinet at a rapid rate). He didn't drink today, though, merely picking up the glass, swilling the golden liquid round and round until the kitchen smelt like it did at Christmas. His voice was grim but he sounded calmer now, the fumes of the whisky probably having some sort of steadying effect. 'It's best I tell you two about all this before you hear of it from somewhere else.' He took a long pause and then, finally taking a big slug of his whisky, said, 'There were gunshots in Jahanpanah forest this morning. A sweeper who was cycling to work heard them and called the police straightaway. He thought it was someone going for the birds but was too nervous to investigate for himself. The police say they were there within fifteen minutes but it was too late by then. They found ... they found Tara's body in the woods ... she'd been shot straight through the heart so probably didn't even know what had happened. Nearby, they found another body. A man, unidentified till now. Nepali or north-eastern by appearance ... we know nothing else just yet.'

Dad, who had been doing really well as he opened up, started wobbling like crazy when he said the bit about Tara being shot through the heart. Which is probably why he wound up his explanation so rapidly too, his last few words coming out in a rush. Luckily, Neel thought up a question to help focus his attention again. 'Was Tara in the captivity of this man, do you think, Dad?'

Dad took such a long time to answer Neel's question, I wondered if there was something he didn't want us to know. Something really gross like rape and paedophiles and all those other things we had been warned about in one of our special moral science classes. But, just when I was about to reassure Dad of my general knowledge of such things, he spoke. 'That's the curious thing, Neel. Tara looked like she was there of her own accord, going by what the policewoman said. There was nothing to indicate that she'd been brought there by force.'

It was my turn now. 'How do we know that for sure, Dad?'

'That she wasn't being forced in some way?' He pondered my question before saying, 'Well, that would be hard to establish, of course, but there were some indications. For one, the policewoman who came was saying that Tara and the man had the same tattoo on their upper right arms – not a real tattoo but one of those transfers, you know. Nevertheless, it's the kind of thing that would indicate they were probably friends ... or of the same persuasion, shall we say.'

'D'you mean she'd joined some kind of *cult*, Dad?' Neel asked, his voice cracking on the word 'cult'. Not that his voice cracking meant anything as it was funny all the time these days, going from squeaky to guttural in a nanosecond.

Dad took another gulp of his whisky. After he'd swallowed and grimaced, he said merely, 'It could be, son. Who knows? They'll investigate all possible leads, I expect.'

Even though I really wanted to give Dad a break, I suddenly thought of something else. 'Dad, if they have been found dead in the woods, does that mean that there could have been a third person who did it?'

Poor Dad didn't seem to be coping at all well with our joint Q&As. I saw his hand shaking as he put his glass to his lips again. 'There may well have been more people involved, Pia. It's all those things that the police will be looking at now, I suspect.'

'Are the police there right now? And do they really know what they're doing, Dad?' The way Neel asked, I wondered if he planned to nip down there on his cycle to make sure they did things properly.

Dad ran a hand over his eyes and I could tell he was really tired now. But he may have made the same guess that I did regarding Neel's question. 'They've got the entire forest cordoned off, Neel,' he warned quietly. 'There will be policemen crawling all over Chiragh Delhi. We can expect more questioning too. Police and media. So be careful who you talk to. Pia, yes? Neel?'

Once we'd both nodded, he slumped back into the whisky-drinking, looking like he was hunkering down to it for the night. We got up and Neel disappeared into the garage. I knew he'd gone to repair his cycle, he always did that when he was upset. I didn't think he'd want me hanging around him and so I went to my room. The evening was warm and muggy and so I pushed open my window to let some air in. That's when I saw them: The Media. Three TV vans were lined up outside the colony wall. So that was why Usha Aunty had brought me back from school the wrong way. When had they all crept in and quietly lined up, stretching all the way down the main road? I knew that they needed some shots for the evening bulletin. Any photo or image that was even vaguely related to the case would be enough and they would keep showing the same thing in a boring, endless loop on the news. And soon the three vans would become five and then seven. Like those vultures in my comic book. And also a bit like the frogspawn we had once cultivated in our science lab, they would be growing and spreading overnight, becoming a mad frenzy at our doorstep by morning, leaving plastic cups and oily food cartons littering the street and gutter outside. But, for now, they were content to wait, as they had done before, for the really gory stuff to come out. They had left disappointed the last time, but it looked like things were going to be different now, both for us and them. Worse for us and I think better for them. Worse for us because my poor sister was dead in Jahanpanah forest and better for them because her being dead meant they now had a proper big story. Maybe it was the thought of my poor sister in the middle of the forest but it was then, all by myself in my room, that I finally cried and cried for Tara.

~

I was now nearly done with transcribing Margaret's diary entries and looked at the very last one that was left. Her handwriting was round, rolling and generous in size, covering more pages than I would have used up but here, about halfway through the notebook, the writing stopped abruptly. I leafed through the dozen or so yellowing pages that had been left blank, feeling frustrated by their sudden silence. What had happened to Margaret at this point? Why had she left off baring her heart at such a moment? It should have been a joyous period of her life but perhaps diary confessions were meant for unhappy times … that made sense … after all, my own writing stalled completely during busy and happy phases. But maybe this was wishful thinking on my part for Margaret.

Margaret's Journal Entry 7: 12 December 1857, Peshawar

Finally! A letter from Emma! How pleased I am to read that my dear friend, my heart's sister, is well and happy. That was all I needed to know. And much satisfaction lies in the knowledge that she too has the comfort of knowing I am well. The exact circumstances of my life can wait for another time, for none of this is easy to explain and I do not wish to grieve or confuse her.

She tells me, however, that the British authorities are determined to find me. I know, with as much certainty as there will ever be in my mind that I do not wish to be found. Perhaps I should write and tell them that. My life is now here, with my husband and his family, all of whom love me dearly.

Besides, I am with child, although my husband does not know of this development yet. He is travelling in the deserts of Kandahar, trying to make a decent living for us. He will be back in a week or two and then I will give him these glad tidings. For now, it is my secret!

Pia, 2013

I put the diary down and opened up my laptop again. Waiting for it to sputter back to life, I tried to transport myself to distant Peshawar, nestled against mountains, willing myself to forget the pressing heat of the Kanpur night beyond my window.

The night was almost gone and dawn would break any time now. Kanpur seemed to wrap itself around me, suffocating me with its silence and its heat while I sat in that little room at the top of Father Kuriakose's house. My laptop had gone into hibernation mode and was starting to show the slideshow of all my photographs ... my cousin Laila and me at Tarang's twenty-first birthday party ... Neel on his mountain bike, tanned and sporty, posing against the Grand Canyon ... Dad and Daadu on that last trip we'd made to Goa as a family ... Tara, about fifteen, smiling into the camera as the sun glinted off her braces ... I tapped the space bar and watched the words of my manuscript materialize before me...

The Story of Margaret Wheeler

Chapter Ten

Margaret thought she would never forget that moment when she caught the first glimpse of mountains. She had been a girl born and raised on the central plains of India and she now gazed in awe as the first of the Himalayan crags rose on the western horizon. They were at first no more than a faint, hazy, brown smudge where land met sky but, as the afternoon sun cleared the mists, the mountains grew in stature and magnificence, turning a bruised purple in colour, the colour of winter plums in the bazaars of Cawnpore. Some of the taller peaks were tipped with silver snow and Margaret thought of how cold and windy it would be up there. But Nizam had told her that his home town of Peshawar never got too wintry as it was situated on plateau lands near the Khyber Pass. Growing up in a valley was partly why he loved the mountains so much, he said, because they allowed him to escape to the quiet cool of the ranges whenever he tired of the city. Shrouded now, in a light haze that was neither mist nor cloud, those mountains looked otherworldly to Margaret, as though they may provide not just escape but a pathway to heaven itself.

Sitting behind her on their horse, Nizam seemed to sense her thoughts. He took one hand off the tether to wind it around her shoulders and put his mouth close to her ear. 'My home,' he said. 'That is my home over there. Beyond those mountains. And soon it will be yours too, my Mehrunissa.'

They had taken over three weeks to traverse the Punjab plains, having decided that it was safer to use the shorter route, rather than travel up to Nepal and take the mountain roads as Nizam had first intended. From local villagers, they found that the uprising had affected many of these British-controlled areas too but, by now, everything was back to where it had been before, the only difference being that the British masters had become far stricter and more suspicious of their troops than before the Mutiny.

On that journey, they had crossed great rivers too – the Sutlej and Ravi and Jhelum – icy cold from the melting snows and travelling in roiling white-crested currents as they rushed down to the plains. While Nizam refreshed the horse, Margaret stood on the banks of the Sutlej, remembering another river – the wide open Ganges that brought so much prosperity to Cawnpore but which had been the scene of such carnage when she had last seen it. Were those waters still flowing red with the blood of her father and his brave fellow officers, she wondered, her heart squeezing itself in sorrow as she remembered and prayed for their souls.

They rode on, Nizam telling her that the greatest of rivers was yet to come; the mighty Indus that they would have to cross on a bridge of boats at Attock. 'There is a fort there that rises on a hill. Built by the great Mughal Akbar. If the day is nice, we will ride up there so you can see the surrounding countryside. On clear days, you can sometimes even see Peshawar from there.'

But, when they arrived at Attock, Margaret could see that Nizam was keen to press on for Rawalpindi. They were now coming close to the end of their journey and Nizam's excitement was clearly building in anticipation of finally reaching his home. Margaret could not help feeling some apprehension about how she would be received by Nizam's family. But she looked at her husband, already visibly relaxing as he shared a language and laughter with the village folk he was talking to, and felt a small surge of confidence when he caught her eye and smiled at her.

She looked at the river that now lay in the valley below. It was already evening – that silver hour when everything seemed touched by a special light. Soon it would be dark. They had decided to spend the night in a riverside rest house and cross the bridge-of-boats at dawn. Once they—

Pia, 2013

I stopped typing on hearing a knock at my door. Grabbing a towel, I threw it over my thin nightshirt for modesty's sake but it turned out to be the girl who assisted Elsie in the kitchen. She was carrying a small tray holding a steaming mug of tea and a platter of biscuits. I took the tray gratefully, realizing how parched I was from the night's work, but that interruption was all I needed to break my concentration. Damn. Suddenly I was no more in the mountainous North-West Frontier but back with my feet firmly planted in hot, dusty Kanpur. Perhaps I wasn't meant to be a writer, given how easily I allowed myself to get distracted!

After the girl had cleared the empty water jug and glass and disappeared down the stairs, I stepped onto the small terrace outside my room to savour the first few rays of sun on my face. Early mornings were the only time of day when one could do that in the summertime and one of Mum's favourite exhortations in our childhood days still rang in my ears. 'Line up, line up, get yer free quota of Vitamin D, me hearties. Look at this, my pale-faced Indian clan!' This had been her standard yell from the garden when we were growing up, followed by its inevitable corollary – 'Madness, that Indians should live in a hot country and yet be deficient in Vitamin D. Would people really prefer to get rickets than a nice healthy tan?' Of course, Dad and Tara always greeted that little speech of Mum's with their counter-chant of 'Mad dogs and English*women*, out in the midday, out in the midday, *out* in the midday *sun*!'

A strange-looking sun that looked like a white-hot globe was rising above Kanpur's trees; it was going to be another scorcher. I hadn't yet decided what I was going to do with the rest of my day but, sipping on my mug of very sweet tea, I wondered if the local library was likely to have a few old maps of the region. Not only did I want to get a clearer picture of the layout of this city as it was in the 1850s, I needed a better sense of the marathon journey Margaret had made with Nizam as they cut across the heart of northern India that summer. Their path would have been fraught with dangers in the aftermath of the mutiny but she had only made passing references to these in her diary entries which she had started writing only once she had settled down in Peshawar. Some of her memories would surely have been blunted by the passage of time but I had worked late into the night, assiduously jotting down every entry in which Margaret had noted a personal reflection or memory.

I went back indoors and put my cup down in order to take another peek into Margaret's folder. It was almost as though I had to reassure myself again and again that I had not dreamt the whole thing up. I picked up the leather binder, using both hands with the gentle reverence people usually reserved for newborn babies, and leafed through the collection again. Margaret's clippings and letters were probably merely her way of staying in touch with her English side once she had become a traditional Muslim wife. Why, even my mother had once told me of how, as a new bride in Delhi, she had devoured every single copy of *Woman & Home* that the local lending library had a curiously large archive of. It was a magazine she had never bothered with when she had lived in England, she said, but there she had been, sitting in the dark of a Jorbagh library, reading issues of *Woman & Home* over ten years old as though they carried some special coded messages from home! Just like Mum, Margaret too had clearly taken immense comfort from these bits and pieces of news and I hoped that their gradual tailing off signified that she had needed less and less of that solace as she had gone along. Little would she have imagined the excitement with which a researcher like me would fall upon her papers a hundred and fifty years on!

I stroked a page with the palm of my hand and ran my forefinger over one particular line. Margaret's diary entries that recorded a kind of happiness held a curious value for me too. Because when Margaret said something like, '*We went this morning to the Quissa Khawani Bazaar where Nizam bought me a shawl as the weather is turning slightly,*' I found overwhelming consolation in remembering another eighteen-year-old who may have made a similar journey with a man she barely knew. My sister, like Margaret, had traversed what was almost certainly very dangerous terrain before finding refuge in a distant mountain town. According to the police, Tara had been living somewhere in the Kumaon hills for a while, although they were not sure of what had taken her there or why she had not called home for so long. Had she been forced? Had she gone willingly? The police had their preferred theories, while we had clung on to ours. After all, Tara had sounded genuinely happy when she made that first phone call to us. All these years later, it ought to suffice to know that my sister too had created a certain sort of happiness for herself, just like Margaret seemed to have done. Both had learnt at an early age that life was hardly ever perfect.

The Story of Margaret Wheeler

Chapter Eleven

That winter, the winter of her eighteenth birthday, Margaret was as contented as she had thought it possible to ever be again. At first, Nizam's mother was suspicious when he had turned up in Peshawar with her in tow. But his two sisters took an immediate liking to her – they were all about the same age, after all – and they set about with great enthusiasm teaching their new sister-in-law to speak Pashto and showing her the various deft ways of chopping vegetables and making rotis and washing their clothes, all those domestic tasks that Margaret had never done before.

'She is from some rich Angrez family, is she not?' Margaret heard Nizam's mother ask him, her whispered voice betraying her fear. Margaret knew enough Hindi and Urdu to get by, fortunately, and was trying as hard as possible to fit in. But she knew that she gave away her privileged background in many small ways, not least by having no skills around the kitchen at all. Even back in the British camp during the siege, her duties had lain in the sickroom rather than the storehouse and kitchen that her mother had taken charge of with surprising efficiency...

Yes, she still missed her mother, along with the rest

of her family. And there were days when she could not help standing at the windows of her room and, rather than seeing the misty mountains, felt her eyes pooling with tears for the cantonment and all the gaiety of its life that she had left somewhere far off. Then she reminded herself that the old life was gone forevermore anyway. Her parents, her siblings, her home. What was the point in mourning something that wasn't there any more? Besides, Nizam was doing everything in his power to compensate for her loss and the terrors she had gone through, bringing back little trinkets and baubles whenever he went out on work and being a tender and considerate lover at night.

Although horsemen were being recruited for a new army of irregulars, Nizam had decided that his soldiering days were over. Instead, he took up work in a British-owned company that traded in dried fruit for which he made regular trips into Afghanistan. From those travels, he brought back sacks full of almonds and apricots and skeins of wool and silk, always bringing some home for his womenfolk too. Once he had given his mother enough money to meet all the household needs, he gave the rest to Margaret, asking her to keep it somewhere safe. 'For you, to buy some pretty clothes. And for our children when they come.' Margaret kept the money safe under a loose brick in their bedroom, covered up with a prayer mat. She did not buy many things for herself, mostly because she could not think of many things she wanted, but she did get herself a small notebook to use as a diary and a leather-bound folder along with a stack of paper and pens. In halting Pashto, she also told the small boy next door to bring her English newspapers once a week and some stamps and envelopes from the post office in town. It was not that she was desperate to stay in touch with anyone from her old life but she knew she owed an explanation to those few who were still alive and would be concerned about her welfare. She kept those papers hidden only because she thought Nizam would be saddened if he thought she was missing her old life. And – because of all he did for her, small everyday kindnesses that added up to much more than any single grand act of heroism – she could not bear the thought of making him unhappy at all.

By November, as the weather turned cooler, Nizam's mother had yielded, finding less and less to object to in the quiet grey-eyed beauty her son had brought home so unexpectedly. The air of sadness the girl wore around her was also strangely beguiling and once, when Margaret had cut her thumb trying unsuccessfully to help in the kitchen, the old lady took her to the washing well to help bathe and dress the wound, scolding and chivvying her all the while. But, when she had fully finished telling Margaret off, she took the girl's chin between her fingers and, looking into her eyes, said, in Urdu rather than Pashto to ensure Margaret would understand, 'You are too good for kitchen work, an educated girl, meant for better things. Rather than wasting your time sitting with my two useless, giggling girls, you should read and you should study. I will help you to become a teacher. We will start a school here and, before you know, the local people will all want to send their children to be taught by someone who speaks English like you.'

Margaret looked into the old woman's eyes, and saw not the tenderness of her own dear mother's gaze but a kind of concern and admiration nonetheless. As some nameless emotion passed between the two women, Margaret lifted her hand to the rough-skinned fingers that were still holding her chin and stroked them with her palm. 'Shukriya, Ammi-jaan,' she said softly, with heartfelt gratitude for this unexpected gift of friendship.

Pia, 2013

I woke up to another hot Kanpur morning with a curiously positive feeling but it was only when I turned around in bed and saw Margaret's folder lying open on my bedside table that I remembered why. I lay back for a few moments, reliving that heady moment at Faisal and Fatima's house when I had stumbled so fortuitously upon Margaret's little bundle of papers, and relished the thought that I finally had all I needed to finish telling her story. Some of her diary entries had been the stuff of dreams and, to ensure once again that they were real and present, I sat up and reached out for my notes.

An indescribable pulsing excitement washed through me. My manuscript, languishing for so long in the depths of my hard drive, could finally be completed and be given that ring of truth which was oddly so essential to fiction. I felt I understood Margaret now and decided I liked very much the thoughtful and forgiving woman I had come to know.

Swinging my legs onto the floor, I made a quick trip to the bathroom before sitting down at the desk to open my laptop. While it came to life, I sprang up again to open the windows and let in a bit of fresh air. It was early and the surrounds of the cantonment were mercifully free of traffic and noise. Only the birds on the trees flanking the church were awake at this hour, cawing and chirping up a storm. It would have been a good time to go for a long walk and gather my thoughts but I reminded myself that I had a book to write. Such time-consuming pleasures were not for wannabe authors! Taking a slug of water from my bottle, I returned to the desk. Vowing to let nothing or no one distract me from my writing, I read the last few paragraphs of my growing manuscript. Then I placed my fingers on the keyboard and started to type...

The Story of Margaret Wheeler

Chapter Twelve

When, one day, Margaret came in with her sisters-in-law from the bazaar, all of them pink in the face from the cold and laughing at one of Tabassum's jokes, she realized from the horse tethered outside that Nizam was already home. After depositing the bags of fruit and provisions they had bought on the kitchen table, Margaret went indoors, calling out to her husband.

She found him in their bedroom, sitting on the prayer mat that covered her little hidey-hole. In his hands were the letters she had received from Emma and Amy, along with her clutch of newspaper clippings and her diary. He was pale and wore a stricken expression on his face as he looked up at her. Margaret stopped at the door, with the sudden awful realization that her decision to keep her papers hidden, an act borne from kindness, had in fact caused her husband to feel betrayed.

'My jaan, my dear husband,' she said, her voice full of remorse, as she flew to kneel by him on the floor. 'I only hid these because I did not want you to feel hurt by them. They do not mean anything…'

But Nizam's silent anguish said everything. He had taken her away from her people in the most cruel of circumstances, he had converted her to Islam, made her speak a new language and, in trying to help her forget where she had come from, he had robbed her entirely of her name and identity and sense of self. Was there anything that spelt it out as much as this wistful little clutch of letters and newspaper cuttings she had kept hidden from him? He could not read the English in it, only pick out a few words here and there, but that was enough…

Softly he said, 'I made you this offer once, a long time ago, and I will now make it again – let me help you get back to your people.'

Frantic to explain, Margaret started to cry. 'But I don't want to go back to my people now,' she said. 'My people are here. You … your family … you are my people now…'

Nizam's reply to that was to thrust her papers back into her hand. 'These letters are telling me something else,' he said, his handsome features steeped in sorrow rather than anger.

'I had to tell them I was alive, these were people who cared for my welfare…' She stopped, aware that her explanations were falling on deaf ears.

'And they will no doubt care enough to take you back in again,' Nizam replied, his voice now growing terse.

'Jaan, my beloved, please…'

But her husband had got up and left the room, and soon Margaret heard the sound of his horse leaving the gates of their haveli to gallop down the road.

He did not return that night, nor the night after and, finally, Nizam's mother could not hold her silence any more.

'Where has my son gone, beti?' she asked.

Margaret looked at her with grief in her red-rimmed eyes. 'I have hurt him, Ammi-jaan,' she whispered. 'I did not mean to, but I have hurt my husband grievously.'

'But marriage is nothing but a sequence of hurt and forgiveness,' the old lady replied calmly. 'When people love each other, they are bound to cause each other pain and, when one causes pain, the other is bound to forgive…' Despite dismissing it as a lover's tiff, however, the old woman seemed to know something about her son's strong-willed nature and looked anxious.

When Nizam finally returned to the house a week later, it was almost midnight. He came into the bedroom and saw Margaret sitting up in bed, having heard him come in.

'Where have you been? How we have all been worrying…' Margaret could hear the complaint in her voice.

'I had to go to Kandahar to make a delivery.' His tone was brisk, unwilling to apologize or explain. Margaret knew he was still smarting.

Pia, 2013

I snapped shut my laptop abruptly, feeling irritated and disturbed. This was not how I had intended Margaret's story to progress at all and I cursed the mischievous daemon that had infiltrated my mind to make it take this unexpected turn. Getting up, I stretched my arms upwards, feeling that old twinge in my spine, familiar from those exam months back in my college days. The writer's life ... how mistaken the assumption that it was one of leisure and ease! In writerly fashion, I had stayed in all day, spending much of it reading two books by Indian writers on 1857 that the local librarian had unearthed for me – one a turgid work of non-fiction and the other a historical romance based on the life of one of the uprising's later heroes, Lakshmibai of Jhansi, who had been a childhood friend of Kanpur's hero, Nana Sahib, and had carried on the fight against the British well into the summer of 1858. Reading that book had led me to ponder if Margaret might have followed the progress of the 1857 uprising from faraway Peshawar. Given her obvious interest in English newspapers, it was probably safe to assume that she knew quite a lot. And that meant I would have to insert the odd reference to those events while developing her story. I bent over to scribble a reminder to myself on a yellow post-it note and stuck it on my laptop.

It had been a long day. I had returned to my manuscript after lunch, hoping that the act of writing would help ease the flow of my rather scattered thoughts. No such luck as Mischievous

Daemon had seemingly snuck in, intent on turning my grand love story into an exposition of a marriage turned sour! Instead of having my protagonists retire to a life of wedded bliss among their beloved mountains – which, admittedly, would make for a boring and predictable romantic novel – I was cheerfully disrupting a comfortable narrative to have Nizam suddenly pack Margaret off to a British town a mere six months after their dramatic escape! Was it possible that my thoughts were flowing in that direction because it was exactly what *had* happened and I was being directed to it in some mystical, and not mischievous, way? From the marriages I'd seen, it would certainly be true to life if Nizam and Margaret had grown gradually disappointed with each other and drifted apart! But, rather than go back to a British cantonment to become an object of pity, I was sure Margaret would prefer to return to the Indian quarter in Kanpur and start a new life for herself. That last diary entry of hers had mentioned a pregnancy but there had been nothing after that to describe how she had broken the news to Nizam. Or whether she even had at all. Why she had stopped confiding in her diary at that particular point was such a puzzle and I had to assume that it was because she had got caught up with her pregnancy and, later, her baby. But maybe the reverse was true – she had never got the chance to tell Nizam that she was pregnant and, before she could, he had found her papers and they had parted ways. Which could explain how she had gone on to have a child and then grandchildren after returning to Kanpur. That she had become a mother was clear from my visit to Fatima and Faisal's house. And what of the possibility that she did not go to Kanpur alone? Perhaps Nizam's mother had gone with her to help care for her and the baby. Together, they may have started the school that the old lady had dreamt of ... now *that* would make for a truly lovely ending for my story.

But then, what would I make of Nizam? Having lost the love

of his life, I could imagine him continuing to live on the edge of his beloved mountains, with only a portrait of his lost English girl to remind him of the happiness he could have had ... and – of course! – *that* was the portrait Fatima had mentioned the day I was at their house.

I couldn't resist laughing out loud at my own propensity for churning out one fervid romantic possibility after another. I clamped my hand over my mouth lest Elsie hear the sound of my hoots and think she had a bloody lunatic living up in her barsaati! Flopping back on the bed, I looked at the ceiling fan swirling away, and my own little image spinning around in the central metal cap. Well, I had never thought it was going to be easy telling Margaret's story but I had always assumed that the difficulty would lie in not being able to find any proper sources on what had really happened to her after Satichaura. Now, despite having found her diaries and grown rather fond of the woman who had written those thoughtful entries, I was feeling inexplicably compelled to enforce an unhappy ending on her! Should I not fight that in order to help make something of her life? Was I still casting about in the half-dark, unable to bear that, given a similar set of circumstances, Margaret had lived on and found a kind of happiness while my poor sister had not.

To take my mind off this unexpected crossroad in my narrative, I finally clicked open my mailbox. The weight of memories threatened to engulf me as I first read Mum's mail. Ominously, its subject title was 'Tara's anniversary'.

'*Darling...*' it was like hearing her voice, that lovely seamless way in which Mum always wrote. '*Darling Pia. Oh how I miss you, my love. You can imagine how much I've been thinking of you, what with Tara's fifteenth anniversary coming up and the possibility of attention focusing on us all over again. Your rather sturdy emotional presence (forgive me, darling, I know how corny that must sound to you!) would have been a rock during this period. I think it's just your unflappable nature I'm talking about, you know, so don't mind my strange expressions.*

Your father's been talking about going away somewhere but I can't for the life of me imagine being on 'holiday' at such a time. He suggests going to spend a month or so with Neel in the States but, with Neel's new girlfriend having so recently moved in with him, I'm not sure this will go down very well with them! Aunty Vee's calling us over to Manchester too, which may on the face of it offer a better solution if I could only drag Dad out there. But I do worry that it would all be rather a strain for Vee, given the state of her knees. Did I tell you, btw, that Vee's refurbished Gran's old house in Mellor and now lets it out to Americans who apparently adore the views over the paddock and that marshy walk down to the river that you used to hate as a child.

But I should get to the point, lest I ramble on. Pia, I wanted to mark Tara's anniversary in some way and wondered what you thought of something like instituting a scholarship at her old school? Or perhaps we could pay for the MCD to get a wooden bench placed at Jahanpanah forest? I read a newspaper piece that showed some local neighbourhood groups campaigning for better facilities at Jahanpanah – toilets, benches, drinking water fountains, guards that kind of thing. No? Somehow I see you shaking your head at all those – especially the scholarship! Not very 'Tara', eh? Well, send me a couple of suggestions when you have the time. We only need to make a decision in a week or two. How are you faring out there in Kanpur? I do hope you're eating well and not gadding about in the sun too much. It's fiercely hot here and must be much worse there. Remember, sunhat, sunglasses, sunblock! With love, Mum.'

I couldn't help smiling at Mum's admonitions. Well, she sounded better than I'd expected. Not in as sombre a mood as she could have been and it was a good sign that she was thinking about positive things like organizing a memorial of some sort for Tara. I clicked on 'Reply' and started to write.

Hey Mum

Sorry I've taken so long to get to my mails. One thing after another over here. All good and exciting, you'd be pleased to know.

My most recent ramblings have led to a particularly thrilling find: a Muslim family directly descended from Margaret Wheeler who are ... wait for this ... in possession of a collection of her letters! Incredible stuff, and incredibly moving too. You can imagine what a treasure trove they are for my novel. The family was kind enough to hand over the entire collection to me, on the understanding that, when I was done with them, I would try selling them to a museum or archive back in Britain so they can use the money to educate their little girl. I saw the little girl – she would be Margaret's great-great-great-grandchild – and, despite the march of the generations, the Anglo-Saxon bloodline is unmistakable and truly astonishing. Which brings me actually to my suggestion regarding Tara's memorial. What would you and Dad think about educating this little girl (I don't even know her name yet actually), say, up to her college years? If she turns out to be clever, we could extend it, of course, or help her find a scholarship. The family did seem rather poor, I have to say, and, as far as scholarships go, this kid would be far more deserving that anyone at Tara's school, I think. Somehow the idea of a wooden bench and park facilities doesn't match up to the idea of the kind of fabulous 'living memorial' this would be.

Give it a think and ask Dad about it too. There's no tearing hurry to decide except that it would be nice for me to go and tell the little girl's family about it personally before I leave Kanpur. I plan to stay another couple of days, having been made really comfortable by Father Kuriakose (you know, the pastor I'd been corresponding with) and his wife, Elsie. But Delhi beckons, obviously, and perhaps I should plan the next stage of my Margaret Wheeler research in ... wait for this ... Peshawar in Pakistan. Wish I were sitting in front of you right now for I can picture the shock on your face as you read this!

And, yes Mum, I'm eating well. Well enough to have developed a little pot belly, believe it or not. Elsie feeds me far too much, you'll be pleased to find out! Yummy south Indian grub too, my favourite, as you know.

Anyway, I'd better end this here as I have about a zillion unread emails to get through. Oh, and a book to write too. Not much progress with that (bah!), travelling and researching are so much more fun!

Night, Mum, love and kisses,

Pia x

I wrote a similar mail to Dad, cutting and pasting bits from my message to Mum, knowing that they did not share each other's mails. Whenever I doubled up my mails to them like that, it was a stark reminder of the gulfs and silences that had grown between my parents over the years. I remembered Vikram, my ex-boyfriend, expressing surprise at how emotionally distant my parents were from each other. 'My mom and dad read each other's post all the time,' he had said. 'I don't think they even have separate email addresses, actually.' Then he added, 'Don't know which is worse, though, your folks or mine! My parents were such a tight unit, it was really hard to find a way in when I was a child.'

Mine are worse, Vikram, infinitely worse!

I signed off my mail to Dad before gazing balefully at the

long list of mails still left in my inbox. They'd take me at least a couple of hours to go through, mostly because I baulked at doing hasty one-line replies, a worthy habit at first carefully inculcated by my desire to be a writer but irksome whenever I hit busy spells like now. Luckily, nothing looked that crucial, going by my one glance at all the subject lines. Nothing but the mail from Max Dominic Darwin of the British Library, who, of course – being so dishy and so very helpful – was deserving of a really well-written reply crammed with my best witticisms ... I sighed. It was really far more important to get on with my manuscript, lest I lose the momentum of telling Margaret's story. The *Writer's Handbook,* which I had bought recently, had given me some terrific advice on maintaining the discipline of writing a little bit every day but I wasn't in the mood at all to open the damn document today. Perhaps I ought to just go out and do a little more research of some sort, I thought vaguely. A historical novel demanded research after all and what the past few days had uncovered of Margaret had been bloody useful.

With another huge sigh, I minimized gmail and clicked on the icon that had been named 'Margaret's Story'. As the full document materialized before me, I waited for the page numbers to form in the small corner on the left. I could barely remember where I'd left the story last and scrolled down to the last few pages...

It all seemed so far away at this moment, so *fake,* that made-up faux concern about characters I had never met, in a time and place that I could never hope to visit. Had it all been a total waste then? I had so much more on Margaret now; so much that explained her gradual conversion from captive to lover and documented her journey from life in an English cantonment to becoming a Muslim wife and mother. But something was distracting me terribly from sitting down and getting on with it. Some kind of emotional wall that I simply could not get past.

Perhaps it was the way I had left the manuscript, with those first ridiculous cracks appearing in Nizam and Margaret's relationship. I wondered if it would help to delete the entire last chapter and start all over again. Perhaps this was what writer's block was, I thought in sudden panic. I'd already invested so much time and money on my project, even passing up the chance of a paid assignment with *Travel Plus* in order to make this visit to Kanpur. It was really important to persist with it. I had to force myself to do so. For heaven's sake, I had nice people like Max Dominic Darwin diligently combing the BL filing system, searching for further records on Margaret Wheeler!

I walked over to the bathroom. Bringing a mug of water back into the bedroom, I refilled the cooler and switched it on again. Then, with renewed determination, I sat before my laptop and jiggled the mouse to stop it from hibernating. The words swam before my eyes ... Margaret ... mountains ... Nizam and Mehrunissa...

I could help Margaret find happiness in all kinds of clever and admirable ways. It was in my hands as a novelist to either take her back to Kanpur as a single woman determined to carve out a fulfilling future for herself, or I could repair her relationship with her husband so that they would one day return together to Kanpur and start a new life. It was entirely my choice, although the former storyline would offer an interesting feminist subtext that was rather appealing to me. Either way, I was sure I wanted Margaret's story to have a happy ending, not only because I had come to understand so many of the decisions she had made but because I, quite simply, *liked* her. However corny it sounded, the least I could do was gift her a bit of happiness, seeing how much she had lost.

I bent over and put my chin down on my arms, the wooden surface of the table feeling dry and cool on my forehead as a terrible wave of sadness washed over me. How swiftly my euphoria at finding Margaret's papers had dissipated. Of course, I was grateful for my discovery but how much more obvious could it be that it was the sad ending of my sister's story that was the real issue. Unlike Margaret, for whom narrative choices in my head lay scattered and various, Tara had been deprived of her whole story, of life itself. It had all gone at eighteen, that abundance of alternatives everyone else enjoyed without even thinking about them – college and jobs, relationships, love, marriage, children. All of that vanished with one snap of fate's fingers, with a mystery bullet that had lodged itself in her chest. And we didn't even know the reason. It was the ghastly unfairness of never having figured out why Tara had died that had left such a gaping wound in the very soul of my family, propelling Neel and me to escape to far corners of the world and driving Mum and Dad to live pained and separate lives even while they coexisted under one roof.

Never finding out exactly what happened to Tara had been like a double blow after her death. My sister's murder, alongside the unknown man she was found with, still remains one of Delhi Police's rare unsolved cases. The police officer in charge of the case seemed quite certain at the time that there was another man involved. According to him, the two men had fought over Tara, she had got killed, perhaps accidentally, and then one man had killed the other. The officer spoke in really old-fashioned language when he went over his theory, using words like 'suitor' and 'jilted', perhaps to make it all a little less sordid. What muddled his theory, though, was that Tara had been found lying dead in the arms of the dead man so, on the face of it, he had killed her and then taken his own life. But then it was always possible that their murderer had merely arranged their bodies to make it look like a double suicide. Who was the man who died alongside my sister? Were there other people involved? In which case, how unforgiveable that they had got away with it. More than anything else, though, the biggest question for us was how Tara had come to be in Jahanpanah forest at all, with someone we had never met. Would we ever know?

With pressure from a couple of NGOs and senior lawyers, the police finally set up something called a Major Crime Review Team to 'preserve evidentially' all the details of Tara's case in case a future reinvestigation was required. Which was also why the media maintained such a keen interest every time the date of Tara's murder rolled around again. If nothing else, it offered them an annual opportunity to bash our bumbling police over the head. That, or the possibility of filling in column space on a dull news day. Theories had abounded over the years, some pretty ridiculous – 'religious cult', 'gang warfare', 'jealous love rivals' and 'Stockholm Syndrome' being the most favoured from what I could see on the internet. We had accepted them all, working our way through each new theory over the years with an air of dazed, even hopeful, confusion. None of them had brought even the remotest shred of comfort. The story about Tara having run away from her 'British' home to seek her Indian roots and joining some religious cult was the one that depressed Mum the most, I recalled. 'And I tried so hard to be bloody *Indian* and not some kind of snobbish expat Brit,' she said sadly the day that feature appeared. She'd sat all morning in the living room, surrounded by the weekend supplements, nursing glass after glass of gin and quoting Berger with a hollow laugh to anyone who happened to wander into the room. The fourth time she said, 'Never again shall a single story be told as though it were the only one,' Dad had asked her to shut up, which, of course, led to the most frightful screaming row.

It came to me very slowly as I stared unseeingly at the mosaic floor beneath the table. Then I raised my head, random thoughts slowly coalescing in the unmoving, claustrophobic heat of that small Kanpur room. Perhaps there was something I could do after all.

Mum hadn't been that wrong when she said I had a talent that had never been put to its right use. A talent for 'making up nice sentences', as I sometimes called it when feeling self-deprecatory. That talent had its uses which, perhaps, weren't merely about telling stories. For what else did novelists do when they wrote? Did they not create alternative worlds in which to lure readers to lose themselves, however briefly? And, in doing so, did they not sometimes – in order to rouse the living – bring the dead to life? Sometimes they helped the voiceless speak and at other times they put tears into the eyes of those who had forgotten to cry. I knew, as an avid book lover from the time I was four, of the ability stories had to move and transform and heal ... so why had I not thought of it before? Why had I always blinded myself to the fact that my interest in Margaret was only because her story offered me a chance to recreate a similar one for Tara. Because Margaret's saga of loss and, I hoped, eventual love held out the smallest chance that Tara too may have found happiness before she had died. It was in the telling of that story – Tara's and not Margaret's – that there was the slightest chance I could salve my family's pain forever. What better use could there be for my gift of writing?

In all the years that I had been researching Margaret's history, I had never experienced what came to me now, as I saw, in some weird mind's eye, the entire structure of a novel materialize before me. It was certainly going to be far less effort than the book I had been writing so far. I would not need to spend long hours in libraries and archives because everything – every little detail, all those events that had brought such anguish – were within me, a part of my cellular structure almost. Tara's violent death was the most immovable part of the story; no amount of imaginative guff could erase the finality of that. But there was still the rest of my sister's story I could work on, the years we had and the months she had denied us knowledge of. Surely I could pull all that together to create a narrative that would reduce some of the torment my family had struggled with since her disappearance and subsequent death. In my story, Tara would be alive and exultant and in love, trying to make a decent life for herself in a little town that clung to the edge of a distant mountain. She would be with a boy with whom she would be dreaming up a happy life, with plans to get married and have children, my nieces and nephews ... I could ... *would* explain her sudden disappearance from our lives with a traumatic event – a brutal abduction perhaps. When the Nirbhaya gang-rape happened in December, my friends and I had all experienced the ghastliest feeling that it could so easily have been one of us ('There but for God's grace...' as Mum had intoned). Even now the papers still carried stories on a weekly basis of abductions in Delhi or Gurgaon of young girls, snatched as they walked home from college or work. Not that it would be easy to make such a terrible thing happen to Tara, even in fiction, but that story would in fact be oddly less heartbreaking than thinking, as we had always done, that Tara had run away from home, run away from us, a family that had loved her much more than she knew. Incredibly, it was in my gift to re-create that story for Tara and for us. Not only could I thereby give her the chance to live again but also offer my parents a version that would bring better comfort than anything they had got so far.

I knew instantly what I was going to do: I was going to cut short my stay in Kanpur, skip Peshawar, and go up to the Kumaon hills instead. A woman I had met recently – who worked with an NGO that helped hill women earn a living by knitting sweaters – had told me about an unspoilt hill town called Mukteshwar where they had a small outlet. Perhaps that was the kind of place I could take Tara to. Carve out a life for her somewhere really pretty and peaceful where the air was clean and the sky soft blue. In that small heaven, she would fall in love, get a job, make a home, plan on having children perhaps ... it wasn't the big glamorous world of films that she sometimes babbled about so excitedly but perhaps that was an alternative story I could reserve for another day.

Did I dare suggest to Mum and Dad that they come and explore Mukteshwar with me? So we could walk up winding hill roads together and smell the pine needles we crushed underfoot and wonder, laughing, if Tara had ever eaten in a quaint little café called Maggi Point that the NGO woman had said was right next door to her shop. Tara had gone to the Kumaon hills at some point, the police had found, so this construct of mine would not be beyond the bounds of possibility. She may have walked those very slopes, felt the same sun on her face and, as night fell over her home, she may have looked out of her window at a pearly moon rising over the mountains. Anyway, it was not too much to hope that Tara had been genuinely happy wherever she had last lived. We might even, if we were lucky, find a kind of happiness for ourselves in that thought, although, to be honest, solace would be good enough.

Acknowledgements

Having long left my teenage years behind, I found it hard on occasion to inhabit the heads of my young protagonists. Happily, however, my life is regularly criss-crossed by a handful of bright young people and, of course, I waylaid a couple of these innocents to saddle them with the task of reading my manuscript. Their suggested edits spanned mysterious information about Facebook to howls of, 'An eighteen-year-old would *never* talk like that!' I could not be more grateful, however, because being eighteen does mean one is usually very, *very* busy, and manuscripts are not the most exciting things. Reeva Misra, Valmik Kumar, Aranya Jain, thank you very much. A big hug too to Sneha Sunil, another busy (now nearly) twenty-year-old, for keeping me in touch with my younger self via long and amusing emails from America.

Gratitude is due also to Mr Russell Oppenheimer whose successful bid for a character's name at the Magic Bus charity auction resulted in a dishy librarian called Max Dominic Darwin. It was deliberate authorly decision on my part to prevent MDD from actually appearing on the page lest impressionistic readers should gatecrash the venerable British Library in hope of catching a glimpse.

Finally, a word about those young people who, like Margaret and Tara in the book, suffer terrible things at a time when life should in fact be starting to gently unfurl and bloom. This book was originally intended as a work of historical fiction, telling the story of what happened to Margaret Wheeler during the 1857 uprising. However, on witnessing the scenes of widespread anger in India following Nirbhaya's rape and murder, it felt unconscionable to pretend that young women do not continue to get snatched from our streets, raped, violated and killed. Tara's story grew out of that unbearable knowledge, and a desire to somehow make things better. Fiction feels like a weak instrument in such instances but this book is nevertheless dedicated to girls like Tara and Nirbhaya whose suffering can only make some sense if it ensures such things never happen again.